Praise for *The Little Bed & Breakfast by the Sea*

'A charming and delightful read!'

Pretty Little Book Reviews

'A really cute, uplifting read . . . perfect for summer!'

The Genre Reader

'[An] easy, warm summer read. Perfect for by the pool!'

Little Novelist

'An easy summer read which will have you smiling!'

The Reading Shed

'A sweet summer tale. Entertaining from beginning to end.'

Urban Book Reviews

'A lovely story, heartwarming and a perfect holiday read.'

Books4BookWorms

Jennifer Joyce is a writer of romantic comedies. She's been scribbling down bits of stories for as long as she can remember, graduating from a pen to a typewriter and then an electronic typewriter. And she felt like the bee's knees typing on *that*. She now writes her books on a laptop (which has a proper delete button and everything). Jennifer lives in Oldham, Greater Manchester, with her husband, Chris, and their two daughters, Rianne and Isobel, plus their bunnies, Cinnamon and Leah, and Jack Russell, Luna. When she isn't writing, Jennifer likes to make things – she'll use any excuse to get her craft box out! She spends far too much time on Twitter, Pinterest and Instagram.

You can find out more about Jennifer on her blog at jenniferjoycewrites.co.uk, on Twitter at @writer_jenn and on Facebook at facebook.com/jenniferjoycewrites

The Little Bed & Breakfast by the Sea

Jennifer Joyce

ONE PLACE. MANY STORIES

HQ
An imprint of HarperCollins*Publishers* Ltd
1 London Bridge Street
London SE1 9GF

This paperback edition 2017

1

First published in Great Britain by
HQ, an imprint of HarperCollins*Publishers* Ltd 2017

Copyright © Jennifer Joyce 2017

Jennifer Joyce asserts the moral right to be
identified as the author of this work.
A catalogue record for this book is
available from the British Library.

ISBN: 978-0-00-827447-4

MIX
Paper from
responsible sources
FSC™ C007454

This book is produced from independently certified FSC™ paper
to ensure responsible forest management.

For more information visit: www.harpercollins.co.uk/green

Printed and bound in Great Britain by
CPI Group, Croydon CRO 4YY

Also by Jennifer Joyce

The Mince Pie Mix-Up

The Wedding Date

The Little Teashop of Broken Hearts

For Chris, Rianne and Isobel

Chapter One

Mae

Mae was in a mad rush that morning as she flitted from room to room, eyes flicking to whichever clock happened to be nearest every thirty seconds. Right now, it was the digital display on the microwave that made her eyes widen in panic as she trundled into the kitchen, dumping the armful of goodies she'd collected onto the breakfast bar. Where had the morning gone? She could have sworn it was only five minutes since she'd dragged her weary body from beneath her sheets, forcing it in the direction of the coffee machine. And now it was almost time to go and she wasn't even ready. The caffeine hadn't had a chance to work its way into her system, even after her second giant mug, gulped down between bites of toast.

Taking a calming breath, Mae added the goodies to the baskets she'd set out on the breakfast bar with a practised hand, arranging the mini bottles of shampoo, conditioner and body lotion to the bed of scrunched-up tissue paper among the bottled water, individually wrapped teabags and sachets of coffee. The bar of chocolate, cellophane-wrapped biscuits and stick of rock added a sweet touch. Mae prided herself on attention to detail; it was the little

1

things that stuck with guests long after they'd packed their suitcases and returned home, the unexpected touches they gushed over with their friends and family or added to their TripAdvisor review. Although the welcome baskets she left in the rooms of her bed and breakfast took time, effort and extra cost, Mae knew they could tempt a guest to leave a sparkling, five-star review instead of a four-star, and entice them back next year – and the year after that. Mae had dreamed of running her own bed and breakfast since she was a little girl. Now her wish had come true, she would put her all into the venture and make it the best bed and breakfast she possibly could.

'Hannah!' she called as she popped the final item – a note for her guests written on a postcard with a photo of the seaside town on the front – into the basket. 'Have you got your shoes on yet?'

She grabbed the baskets – one each for the two rooms she had available in the house she'd inherited from her grandmother four years ago – and headed towards the stairs, stopping outside the family room where she spotted her four-year-old daughter still glued to the television. Shoeless.

'Excuse me, little lady, but aren't you supposed to be putting your shoes on?' Mae arched an eyebrow at her daughter. 'We need to set off for Nanny's in *two minutes.*'

'It only takes me one minute to put my shoes on,' Hannah said, eyes travelling back to the screen.

Mae's eyebrow arched further. 'And how long does it take you to walk up the stairs to grab them?'

Hannah scrunched up her nose, eyes still on the television, as she calculated. 'Ten seconds?'

'And do you know where your shoes are?'

Technically, Hannah's shoes should be lined up at the bottom of the wardrobe with her other shoes, but Mae knew her daughter too well. Mae might be a stickler for the little details, but her daughter was not. In Hannah's world, there was a place for everything, but nothing was in its place.

'One of them is under my bed,' Hannah said. 'I kicked it under there this morning when I tripped over it.'

Mae closed her eyes, briefly. 'And the other?'

Hannah shrugged. 'In my room?'

Mae *hoped* the shoe was in Hannah's bedroom. They had guests arriving later and Mae lived in fear of the day one of them would trip over an abandoned shoe or toy. She did her best to keep the house in pristine condition, but it wasn't always easy with a four-year-old tearing about the place.

'So, actually finding the other shoe could take you more than the fifty seconds you have left. Plus, we've been discussing this for...' Mae scrunched up her own nose as she calculated the wasted time. '...Twenty seconds? So, really, you only have thirty seconds to find your shoe. Probably twenty-five by now. So do you think you should turn the telly off and go and put them on?'

Hannah sighed, her little chest heaving dramatically. 'Fine.'

Mae watched as her daughter wriggled off the sofa and turned the television off before shuffling out of the family room and up the stairs. Hannah was four and already behaving like a teenager – how would Mae cope when hormones set up camp? But Mae didn't have time to ponder. She had welcome baskets to set out and less than two minutes to do so. She followed Hannah up the stairs, pushing open the guest room they had on that floor, and placed the basket on the end of the bed, smoothing the bedspread with the palm of her hand. The left curtain wasn't quite even so she moved across the room to open it a little more, smiling at the view as she did so. With the bed and breakfast on the seafront, Mae had the perfect view of the beach, with the pier in the distance, the Ferris wheel already turning slowly. The school summer holidays had started the previous week, so Clifton-on-Sea was jam-packed with holidaymakers hopeful of a warm and dry British summer. Growing up in Clifton-on-Sea, Mae hadn't always appreciated the beauty of her little town. Building sandcastles with her grandpa, the delicious scent of sweet candyfloss and hot doughnuts mingling with the sea air, eating fish and chips from the paper with her feet dangling over the harbour walls – these were ordinary occurrences for Mae as a little girl, and it wasn't until she left the town in her late teens, eager to see a bit more of the country, of the world, that she realised what a special place she'd left behind. Or how privileged she'd been to have such an idyllic childhood by the sea. She couldn't imagine a better place to raise her daughter.

'Mummy!'

Hannah's voice broke Mae's reverie and she backed away from the window, smoothing the bedspread one last time as she passed.

'I can't find my shoes,' Hannah said, poking her head out of her bedroom.

'What about the one under the bed?'

Hannah shrugged. 'It's not there any more.'

Mae pressed her lips together. She didn't have time to hunt for misplaced shoes. She still had to take the second basket of goodies up to the little room in the attic and drop the keys with Mrs Hornchurch next door (where she would no doubt get caught up in a ten-minute chat while she did her best to politely escape) before ferrying Hannah across town. They were already cutting it fine.

'You'll have to wear a different pair.' Mae was already shuffling backwards towards the narrow staircase that led to the fourth bedroom. 'Your sandals. Or your trainers if you really must.' Trainers wouldn't really go with the red gingham summer dress Hannah was wearing, but desperate times called for mismatched outfits.

Mae scurried up the stairs as Hannah's head disappeared back into her bedroom. Placing the basket on the end of the bed, she gave the pillows a fluff before heading back down to check on Hannah's shoe status.

'Wellies?'

Hannah looked down at the Doc McStuffins wellies and shrugged. 'They're all I could find.'

Mae could have made many arguments against the wellies – not least the ridiculous mismatching and the fact it was a glorious summer's day – but she really, *really* didn't have time to discuss the matter, nor locate more suitable footwear.

'They'll do.' With a decisive nod, Mae led the way down the stairs, heading for her desk to grab the keys for today's guests from the drawer. With her car keys, handbag and sunglasses in hand, she was ready to go.

'Hannah?' The girl had disappeared. 'Hannah! We need to go!'

Mae scurried through the rooms of the house, finding Hannah crouched in the kitchen, her outstretched palm full of Frosties.

'Hannah,' Mae groaned as the cat nibbled at the proffered cereal. 'I've told you not to feed him. And especially not Frosties. Come on, cat. Out!'

'But he's hungry,' Hannah said, hand still outstretched.

'And we'll be hungry if I'm late for work again and lose my job. *Come on.*' Mae swung the back door open and nudged the cat gently with her foot until it slunk away into the back garden. 'Please stop feeding him. It'll only encourage him to come back.'

'But I want him to come back,' Hannah said as Mae closed the door. 'I love him.'

'He isn't our cat.' Mae wasn't sure he was anybody's cat, judging by the state of his matted fur and lack of collar. The jagged ears from ancient fights gave him a definite alley cat vibe. 'Now, let's go, little lady. Nanny will be wondering where you are.'

As lovely as the Seafront Bed and Breakfast was, and as busy as it kept Mae, the profits generated from the small establishment weren't enough to pay the bills, so Mae topped up her income by working part time at one of Clifton-on-Sea's pubs. The Fisherman sat opposite the harbour, in the quieter part of town away from the beach, but it was popular with the locals and the holidaymakers who liked to venture a little further afield. Mae had known the owners – Frank and Corinne Navasky – for as long as she could remember, as Frank and her grandpa had been friends since childhood. Mae had fond memories of sitting by the open fire in the pub with a glass of lemonade and packet of crisps while Frank, her grandpa and their friends played dominoes on chilly Saturday afternoons.

'Ah, she's here. I was about to send out a search party.' Frank winked at Mae as she burst through the doors of the pub, breathless from the dash from the car. As predicted, she'd ended up chatting with Mrs Hornchurch for a good ten minutes when she'd dropped off the keys, plus she'd had to deal with a lady who wanted to book a room on her way out of the house, meaning she was even later for her shift. But she couldn't complain too much about Mrs Hornchurch as her neighbour was doing her a massive favour. As Mae needed to work, Mrs Hornchurch often stepped in to help, keeping watch for any guests and showing them to their rooms when they arrived.

Mrs Hornchurch was a godsend, so Mae could forgive her chatterbox nature.

'I'm so sorry.' Mae threw her handbag onto one of the shelves under the bar and rolled the sleeves of her cardigan up. 'I'll work through my break to make it up to you.'

'You will not,' Frank said. 'There's no harm done. It isn't like I'm rushed off my feet.'

It wasn't yet lunchtime so the pub was pretty much deserted, with only Tom Byrne, a permanent fixture in the Fisherman, sitting with his pint of bitter. Soon, however, the place would be filled with patrons wanting a pint to go with their fish and chips from the chip shop next door.

'Do you need me to do anything before we get busy?' Mae asked Frank. 'Any glasses need washing? Barrels need changing? Do the loos need cleaning?'

Frank raised his eyebrows at the last suggestion. 'You must be feeling guilty. But no, love, everything's in hand. Why don't we put the kettle on and have a quick game of dominoes before the rabble descends?'

Mae had learned to play dominoes by watching her grandpa play in the Fisherman, and the clatter as the pieces tumbled from the box onto the table always reminded her of him. Her dad hadn't been around much when she was growing up, so it had been her grandpa who'd been the father figure in Mae's life. She'd loved staying with her grandparents by the beach, going for a paddle with her grandpa, their skirts and trousers lifted or rolled up to their knees as the cold water washed over their feet, or sneaking off to the Fisherman with him when it was too cold to build sandcastles. Double trouble, that's what her granny had called them.

Mae missed her grandparents, but she cherished the memories she had of them and smiled now as she picked up a cool tile.

'So, how's that goddaughter of mine?' Frank asked as they set the dominoes out face down on the table. 'Enjoying the school holidays?'

'She's enjoying too much TV.' Mae had lost count of the number of hours Hannah had sat in front of the box over the past few days, but Mae had been so busy with the B&B – preparing rooms, looking after guests and taking bookings – and the television provided an easy distraction. Though Mae felt guilty, the school summer holidays were the busiest time of year for Clifton-on-Sea, and Mae couldn't afford to turn business away. She was fully booked from now until early September, with her largest booking due to arrive later that afternoon. Mae's B&B only had two rooms to let, but as well as a double bed, the attic room had a sofa bed, which her latest guests would be making use of. The Robertsons – made up of grandparents Shirley and Len, plus their daughter, son-in-law and two young grandchildren – had stayed at the Seafront B&B for two weeks every summer since Mae had opened for business three years ago, and although Mae was looking forward to their stay, she knew looking after six guests – plus Hannah and her part-time bar work – was going to be a tough juggling act.

'Why don't you bring her over in the morning?' Frank asked. 'Corinne and I are popping into Preston to do a bit of shopping. Hannah can come with us on the train and we'll take her for a burger for lunch. We might even throw in a trip to the cinema.'

Mae started to shuffle the tiles around the table to mix them up. 'You don't have to do that.'

Frank joined in the shuffling. 'I know that, but we love taking Hannah out. What are godparents for?' He gathered the tiles into the centre and, with a flick of his hand, invited Mae to choose a tile.

'She'd love that, thank you.' Mae plucked a tile and turned it over so they could both see it. 'One-Three.'

Frank chose his own tile and turned it over, giving a little whoop of victory when he saw the pips he'd uncovered. 'Five-Six. Me first.' They both returned their tiles to the collection on the table and gave them another quick shuffle.

'The vet was in here last night,' Frank said as they drew their tiles from the collection and placed them in front of themselves, balancing them on their edges so only they could see the value of their own tiles.

'Frank…' Mae said with a heavy sigh.

'What?' Frank's bushy eyebrows lifted and his mouth was agape. 'I was only saying.'

'Hmm.' Mae rearranged the tiles in front of her, mostly so she didn't have to make eye contact with her opponent.

'He's a fine young fella,' Tom Byrne piped up, his voice making Mae jump. He'd been so quiet in his little corner of the bar, she'd forgotten he was there. 'Our Tiddles had a tumour last winter. Thought she was a goner, but Alfie sorted her out. She's got a new lease of life. She's like a kitten again.'

'Maybe I should take a trip to see our vet,' Frank said as he placed his first tile face up on the table. 'I could do with a new lease of life with all these barrels needing to be lugged around the cellar. I feel like I'm ready for the knacker's yard some days.'

'Rubbish.' Mae selected a tile and joined it onto Frank's. 'You've got more energy than anybody I know, including Hannah. I hope I'm as fit and energetic as you when I'm in my seventies.'

'Ssh!' Frank's eyes roamed the near-empty pub. 'Will you keep it down? As far as everybody else is concerned, I'm not a day over fifty.'

'Tom won't spill the beans, will you?' Mae asked and he shook his head.

'What happens in the Fisherman stays in the Fisherman. Ain't that right, Frank?'

Frank chuckled. 'Sure is. The tales I could tell...' Frank chuckled again and shook his head. 'It's like being in a confessional some days.'

'I hardly think you can compare yourself to a holy man, Frank Navasky,' his wife said, appearing in the doorway that led to the living quarters of the pub. Corinne joined them at the table and dropped a kiss on Mae's cheek. 'And I don't think priests make a habit of mopping up vomit from their confessionals.' Corinne pulled a face and turned to Mae. 'Gary King, pissed as a newt, *again*. I've told him he's on his last warning. Once more and he's barred.'

'He's already barred from the Old Coach and the Lion,' Tom said.

'And no wonder. He'll be barred from here in no time, no doubt.' Corinne Navasky was short and slim with delicate features, but she was a no-nonsense kind of woman who had no qualms about chucking even the biggest, roughest blokes from her pub. She was so different from Mae's granny, who would weep over sentimental films and always, *always* gave somebody the benefit of the doubt, but they'd become as close as their husbands despite their differences. Corinne and Frank were like family to Mae, almost filling the gap her grandparents had left.

'That vet of yours was in here last night,' Corinne told Mae. Mae groaned and fought the urge to drop her head onto the tile-covered table.

Chapter Two

Willow

The morning hadn't started out as a usual Monday for Willow. Her husband usually caught the train from Clifton-on-Sea to Preston for his job and, as Willow worked a couple of streets away from the station, they'd walk together most mornings. But Willow had woken alone that morning and had to follow their routine by herself. She'd popped into the bakery opposite the pier as usual for a takeaway breakfast, munching on a cherry pinwheel and sipping a coffee as she walked to work, but it felt odd without Ethan there to chat to. With her mind free to roam, she found herself latching on to the memory of their argument the previous evening, the air thick with frustration and unspoken accusation and blame. Willow's hand reached for her phone, her finger hovering over the contact list, but she shoved it back into her handbag without making the call. Ethan would call her when he was ready.

There was nothing left of Willow's breakfast by the time she reached her shop, bar a few flaky crumbs she quickly brushed away before she unlocked the door. Willow's shop was a treasure trove of other people's junk: furniture and household items rescued from skips, junkyards, charity shops and the local tip, all lovingly restored or upcycled to breathe new life into the once-loved items. Willow's eye was immediately drawn to the dining table and chairs she'd finished the previous day. The piece had been commissioned by a local family who'd wanted a fun and quirky table for their playroom and Willow had risen to the challenge, decoupaging the tabletop with banknotes from old, unusable Monopoly sets and adding shallow drawers underneath that were perfect for storing board games and jigsaws without getting in the way of knees and legs while sitting down. The chairs had been painted in vibrant colours, with each of the children's names – plus Mum and Dad, of course – spelled out in old Scrabble tiles on the backs. Willow was proud of the effect and couldn't wait to see the reaction from the family when she dropped it off later that day.

Closing the door behind her, Willow switched on the lights and moved across to the shop's counter, which had been recrafted from an old oak sideboard. Her assistant would be there soon, allowing Willow to get creative in the workroom, but until then she would remain in the shop, catching up with admin and smaller jobs between customers.

The morning's second irregularity occurred when nine o'clock rolled around and there was no sign of her assistant. Gary didn't have Willow's eye for detail, but he was handy with a paintbrush and always willing to help her shift hefty items. Plus, he made a cracking cup of coffee, perfecting the milk-to-coffee ratio like an experienced barista. He'd been working with Willow since leaving college a few weeks ago and hadn't been late once in that time.

Another hour passed and there was still no sign of Gary. Willow had sold a pack of mini, spiral-bound notebooks she'd made using the property cards from the Monopoly sets as covers to a tourist looking for gifts for her grandchildren, and had arranged a house clearance for the following week, but her assistant hadn't arrived. She dragged the planters she'd made from wooden pallets, which were filled with a rainbow of fragrant blooms, out onto the pavement in front of the shop to attract passing trade and ran a duster over the furniture, but still there was no sign of Gary.

Her phone beeped with a new message mid morning as she was painting jam-jar lids at the counter. Wiping her hands on the apron she'd thrown over her dungarees, Willow grabbed her phone from her handbag, expecting it to be an explanation from Gary. But it was a message from Ethan. While Willow had been hoping for a phone call, desperate to hear her husband's voice, she was relieved he'd got in touch to let her know he was okay. She replied to the message, asking him to phone her as soon as he was able to.

While she had her phone in hand, she scrolled through her contacts and called Gary's number. The phone rang and rang until Willow was about to give up and return to her jam-jar lids.

'Hello?' Gary's muffled voice said as she moved the phone away from her ear.

'Gary? It's Willow. I was just wondering where you are as you haven't turned up for work.'

'What time is it?' Gary asked, his voice raspy and sluggish.

Willow glanced at the clock she'd created using driftwood and shells from the beach. 'It's after ten. Are you okay? You sound terrible.'

'I feel even worse,' Gary said. 'I must have slept through my alarm. Sorry.'

'Don't worry about it.' Willow pulled her diary from one of the counter's drawers and flicked through it until she found that day's page. 'You don't sound well at all. Go back to sleep – I can manage on my own for the day.' She was due to deliver the Monopoly table that evening, but it wouldn't be too much of a problem closing half an hour earlier just this once. Moving the table from the shop to the van solo would be a challenge, but she'd faced bigger obstacles before.

'Are you sure?' Gary asked.

'Of course. Rest up and I hope you feel better soon.'

Willow said goodbye and hung up the phone, but it beeped almost immediately, alerting her to a voicemail. She pounced, pressing to listen to the message and placing the phone against her ear, anticipating the sound of her husband's voice.

But it wasn't Ethan at all.

'We have a problem. A pretty major one. Call me back as soon as possible.'

Willow and Ethan had spent the first five years of their marriage renting a sweet but tiny cottage on the outskirts of town, but when the opportunity had come up to buy one of the Georgian, three-storey houses on the seafront, right in the heart of their seaside town, they'd jumped at the chance. From the outside, the house was beautifully grand with a dove-grey rendering and rows of tall windows either side of a porched front door. Yes, the rendering was starting to crumble, the windows needed a restorative touch and the front door looked as though it would fall off its hinges in a gentle breeze, but the asking price had been an unbelievable bargain and Willow was used to making neglected things shine again.

The inside of the house had been much worse, with rotting floorboards in every room, warped doorframes and damp throughout, but still Willow and Ethan had been undeterred. They'd gutted the house and started again with a clean slate. This way, at least, they could put their own stamp on the place and make it their own.

'What is it?' Willow asked now as she returned her builder's call, the jam-jar lids still abandoned on the counter. 'What's happened?'

Willow was thinking the worst: a burst pipe flooding the house, or the foot of one of the builders coming through a newly plastered ceiling, or, most heartbreaking of all, the bathroom tiles she'd sourced online from a reclamation yard being dropped from the van and shattering on the pavement.

Willow's worst wasn't even close.

'There's a problem with the foundations. I think you'd better come down here.'

'I can't,' Willow said. 'I'm in the shop on my own today so there's nobody to cover for me.'

'What about Ethan? Can he get over here?'

Willow scratched at a small, still-wet blob of pastel-pink paint that had splashed onto the counter. 'He's gone away for a few days. Working. I'm not sure for how long.' She wiped the paint from her thumb nail onto her apron. 'Can't it wait until this evening?'

'Willow…' The builder's tone was firm. 'You need to come down here. We can't carry on with the refurb until this is sorted.'

Willow straightened, the fingers on her free hand moving to rest on her chin. 'What exactly is the problem with the foundations?'

'We're not entirely sure yet. It needs investigating properly. But what I can tell you is that the whole structure of the house is unsafe.'

Willow's eyes widened and she had to put a hand down on the counter to steady herself. 'It's that serious?'

'It's that serious.'

Willow snapped her diary shut and shoved it roughly into the nearest drawer. 'I'm on my way.'

This was bad. Very bad. Willow and Ethan had sunk their savings into this house, had taken out a massive mortgage and loans for the refurbishment. If this went wrong, they'd be up to their eyeballs in debt. And worse – they'd be homeless. Although the house was nowhere near finished, Willow and Ethan had already moved in, living among the rubble as best as they could. Living on site while the work was being carried out wasn't ideal, but at least the money that would normally pay their rent could be redistributed towards the refurb. But there was no backup plan. If the house was unsafe, where would they live?

Her quarrel with Ethan the previous evening filtered into her head.

Maybe we shouldn't have bought this house. We should have thought about it more. Thought about us, our future.

But that's what we were doing. This house is part of our future.

Is it? At the moment, we don't even know *what's in the future for us.*

Willow pushed the memory away and scuttled out from behind the counter, throwing her apron in the general area of a chair and grabbing her keys from the pocket of her dungarees as she barrelled towards the door. The house was only a ten-minute walk away, so Willow usually walked to and from the shop, leaving her van parked on the side street next to the shop, but she jumped inside now, slamming the door shut, tugging on her seatbelt and starting the engine in quick succession. The van rumbled into life and she pulled out of the side street and headed down towards the seafront, her heart hammering above the hum of the engine. Within minutes, she was pulling up outside the house. You couldn't miss it, trussed up with scaffolding as it was, but Willow was glad it was still standing upright. Part of her was expecting to see the house in a heap, bricks tumbling out of the garden and towards the promenade, her hopes and dreams of her future with Ethan buried beneath the rubble.

'I'm here!' she called as she sprinted across the garden. The front door was open and she found the builders milling around the foyer, sipping cups of tea and working their way through a packet of custard creams. 'What's going on? I need to know everything.'

'Everything' turned out to be devastating. Willow didn't understand a lot of what the builder was telling her, but the gist of it wasn't promising. The foundations were no longer secure and the house might need underpinning. Willow wasn't entirely sure what underpinning a house involved, but the builder warned her it could take several weeks to do, eating severely into their budget and extending their timeframe.

'I'd strongly advise you to find somewhere else to live until we've made the foundations safe again,' he told Willow. 'I wouldn't stay and, if you were my daughter...' He shook his head. 'There's no way I'd let you either.'

The problem was, Willow didn't have anywhere else to stay in the meantime. They'd already given up their rented cottage when they'd moved into the new house, and both sets of parents lived over fifty miles away, which was impractical both for getting to and from work and overseeing the refurb.

But it would be okay. They would work something out. At least that's what Willow told herself as she walked away from the house and climbed back into her van. She sat in the immobile vehicle for a few minutes, staring out of the open window at the pier and the sea beyond, listening to the cacophony of seagulls, holidaymakers and crashing waves she'd been drawn to. Pulling out her phone, she dialled Ethan's number but it went straight to voicemail, as she suspected it would.

'What are you going to do?' Liam asked, wandering towards the van. Her builder's face was creased with concern, and Willow was pretty sure it mirrored her own.

'I don't know.' Willow shrugged and started the engine. 'But I'll figure something out.'

She had to. With Ethan's absence even more noticeable now, it was down to Willow to sort this mess out. It wasn't in her nature to crumble, no matter how tempting it was, and she wasn't about to let herself – and Ethan – down now. She set off in the van, eyes peeled for the nearest B&B. She knew there were several in the seaside town and she managed to locate one easily, further along the seafront. She parked the van, jumping out and rushing along the pavement when she saw a woman and her child leaving the property. She didn't know whether the woman was the proprietor of the B&B or a guest, but she didn't have time to pop inside first. If this woman *was* in charge, she couldn't miss her.

'Excuse me…' Willow was breathless from her dashes that morning. 'Is this your B&B?'

The woman was in her late twenties but looked as though she'd been plucked from the wrong decade. She wore a red-and-white polka-dot dress, cinched in at the waist, with matching heeled, peep-toe slingbacks, and her dark hair was pinned back in victory rolls. The style suited her, though, and Willow suddenly felt frumpy in her striped T-shirt and dungarees.

The woman slipped the quirky red, heart-shaped sunglasses from her eyes. 'It is, but I'm afraid we're fully booked for the next few weeks if you're looking for a room.'

Willow's shoulders slumped. 'Oh.' Maybe finding alternative accommodation at a B&B wasn't going to be as easy as she'd thought. 'It's just I'm refurbishing a house up the road.' Willow pointed further up the seafront towards the pier. 'But there's a problem with the foundations and it isn't safe to stay there.'

The woman's face softened and she patted Willow's arm briefly. 'I'm sorry. That sounds terrible.' She bit her lip, which was a glossy pillar-box red, and shook her head. 'But I'm afraid I can't fit you in. Have you tried any of the other B&Bs? There's a lovely little one in the harbour that's a little quieter, being away from the beach and everything, so you might have better luck there. Or there's the hotel up by the pier, but that's a little more expensive, or you could try the caravan site?'

'Nanny says we can stay in a caravan when Mummy isn't so busy,' the little girl standing with the woman piped up, squinting in the sun as she looked up at Willow. She was cute and had a rather more relaxed look than her mother with her sundress and wellies combo.

Willow crouched down to the little girl's level. 'That'd be nice, wouldn't it? I've never stayed in a caravan before but it sounds fun.'

The girl nodded. 'You get to sleep in a little room in a little bed and watch a little telly.'

Willow gasped and widened her eyes. 'That sounds amazing! I hope you get to stay in your caravan soon.' Willow stood up again. The woman had returned the heart-shaped sunglasses to her face. 'Thank you for your help.'

The woman nodded. 'Good luck.' She turned to her daughter and took her hand. 'We'd better get going. I need to drop the keys with Mrs Hornchurch and then get you to Nanny's.'

Willow watched as the woman and her daughter disappeared into the neighbouring house before climbing back into her van. She'd work her way through town and try the other B&Bs, the hotel and caravan site. There *had* to be a room available somewhere.

Chapter Three

Melody

The train was packed with bodies, heat and noise as Melody crab-walked down the aisle in search of a seat, battling with the hefty rucksack and laptop bag she held in her hands, tucked in tight to her body so she didn't bash anybody about the head with them. Melody was thankful she'd decided to travel light during her trip, packing only the essentials: a handful of outfits she could chuck into a washing machine at a laundrette every few days, her washbag with the necessities, a couple of pairs of pyjamas, her laptop, and her camera. Okay, the laptop was hardly light, and her rucksack was cumbersome, but it would have been much worse if she hadn't been so strict with her packing. She was hoping to find a seat so she wouldn't be forced to hold on to her bags for the duration of the journey, but it wasn't proving an easy task.

'Excuse me.' She flicked the corners of her mouth up into an apologetic smile as she attempted to squeeze past elbows and shoulders. 'Sorry. Can I just...' She managed to shuffle past without knocking anybody out cold with her rucksack and then she saw it, just ahead. An empty seat! Or rather a seat empty of a human bottom.

She waddled towards it sideways, resting against the headrest with a relieved sigh when she finally reached the seat without somebody else nabbing it first. She looked down at the laptop bag currently sitting there and then over to its owner in the neighbouring seat. The owner – a suited man in his mid-to-late twenties, currently tapping away at the laptop in front of him – glanced in her direction briefly before returning to his screen.

'Excuse me,' Melody said, using her most polite voice. 'Is this seat taken?'

By anything other than a bag? she silently added.

The man sighed heavily and turned away from his laptop, performing an elaborate eye-roll as he moved his face towards Melody.

'I need to keep my bag close by.'

Melody nodded. 'Fair enough.' The man shifted his gaze back to his screen. 'I assume you've bought an extra ticket for your bag, though.'

The man frowned, sighing again as he snapped his head back up to Melody. 'What?'

'I assumed you've purchased two tickets, since you're taking up two seats.'

'Obviously I haven't bought a ticket for my bloody bag.' The man rolled his eyes again and, shaking his head, resumed tapping at his keyboard.

'In that case...' Melody reached up to push her rucksack into the overhead storage rack. 'I'm taking this seat. You can move the bag if you want to, but I don't mind either way. I'm sitting whether it's there or not.'

Melody eyed the man. He eyed Melody. Melody pushed her own laptop bag under the table and lowered herself onto the seat, pressing her lips together so she didn't display a smug grin as the man's laptop bag was whipped away at the very last second. The bag was shoved under the table, wedged between the wall of the train and the man's feet. She could feel the glare from her neighbour as she unlooped her camera from around her neck and switched it on. She looked up, smiling sweetly at him.

'I'm Melody, by the way.' She thrust a hand out towards him, but he made no move to shake it.

'And I'm very busy.' With one last glare, he turned back to his laptop, tapping furiously.

And very rude, Melody thought, but she didn't dwell on her neighbour for too long. She'd met lots of different people on her recent travels – some lovely, some not so much – but she didn't hang around for long enough to let the negative ones impact her life. In fifteen minutes, she'd shuffle off the train and wouldn't see this dude again.

Melody clicked through the menu on her camera, loading up her latest photos to scrutinise. Some of the photos were good – she particularly liked the snap of Blackpool Tower at dawn – but some weren't so great. The composition was wrong, or the lighting didn't quite work, so she deleted those she definitely wouldn't be using. She'd take a closer look once she had her laptop set up, but for now she'd weed out the obvious duds – she'd taken hundreds of better photos over the past three weeks so they wouldn't be missed.

Melody's plan was to spend a chunk of the summer visiting as many seaside towns and villages in northern England as she could and was currently working her way along the Lancashire coast. Clifton-on-Sea was her next destination and she'd already looked the town up online beforehand. She knew there was a mile-long beach surrounded by cliffs, with a pier at one end and a harbour at the other, and she was hoping to capture some magical seaside moments there on camera over the next day or two.

The train came to a stop at a rather rustic-looking but quaint station. She'd visited many train stations lately, some large and filled with shops and kiosks, while others were more basic and little more than a platform with a ticket booth. Today, the train had pulled up alongside a single-storey stone building with a row of small, arched windows and an open, bottle-green door. The outside was decorated with wooden planters bursting with a rainbow of flowers, sitting either side of a couple of wrought-iron benches, and a sign welcomed those disembarking to Clifton-on-Sea. A ginger cat lay stretched out on one of the benches, basking in the sun.

Melody grabbed her bags and made her way to the nearest exit, hopping down onto the platform and following the crowd through the green door. Inside was as quaint as the outside, with a traditional tearoom staffed by two little old ladies, an information booth manned by a man in a smart uniform, and a little shop selling souvenirs. Melody hadn't eaten since early that morning and, as it was now almost lunchtime, she was tempted to sit down with a cup of tea and a slab of lemon drizzle cake. But she should be getting on. She'd had a laissez-faire attitude to her travels so far, hopping on trains and travelling to her next destination when she fancied, so she hadn't booked any accommodation in advance. So far, it had worked out, but she didn't want to leave her lodgings until the last minute and run into trouble.

Reaching into the back pocket of her cut-off shorts, she pulled out the photograph she'd carried throughout her travels, smoothing down its slightly crumpled corners. She studied the familiar image for a moment before returning the photo to her pocket. Hitching her rucksack onto her back, she headed out of the station to see what Clifton-on-Sea had to offer.

Chapter Four

Mae

As predicted, the Fisherman had burst into life around lunchtime. It was a tradition for those working nearby to buy their lunch from the fish and chip shop along the harbour and, as Frank didn't serve food himself, he didn't mind when they migrated into the pub with their parcels of hot, delicious-smelling food, unwrapping them after ordering drinks at the bar. No, Frank didn't mind at all – profits soared as soon as the chip shop opened its doors. The dominoes had been packed up in preparation (Frank had won, though he hadn't gloated *too* much) and it was all hands to the pumps as Mae, Frank and Corinne served the customers as quickly as they could before their food grew cold. Mae chatted as she worked, enquiring about husbands, wives and children as she filled glasses and took payment. She knew most of the customers well, though there was the odd less familiar face too.

Her latest customer, who technically should have been served by Corinne, was very familiar. The landlady had not-very-mysteriously vanished as soon as it was Alfie's turn to be served.

'What can I get you?' she asked, while secretly plotting ways to torture her boss.

'Would you judge me if I ordered an extremely large Jack Daniels and Coke?'

'That depends.' Mae leaned across the bar towards the local vet. 'Are you going to be operating on any unsuspecting creatures this afternoon?'

'Good point. I'll just have the Coke then, thanks.'

Mae grabbed a glass and started to fill it. 'Stressful morning?'

Alfie gave a long, loud sigh. 'Very. We're still without a vet nurse until tomorrow and the one the agency sent is...' Alfie tilted his head to one side, trying to conjure the right words. 'Incompetent seems like such a harsh word.'

'But she is,' Mae said and Alfie nodded.

'I'm afraid so.' He grinned as Mae placed the glass of Coke on the bar. 'But do you know what would cheer me up?'

Mae placed a finger into the corner of her mouth, her eyes wandering to the ceiling as though she were deep in thought. 'Hmm, let me think... A date with me?'

Alfie puffed his cheeks out before letting the air seep slowly from them as he shook his head. 'Blimey, Mae, that's one hell of an ego you've got there. I was going to say a bag of cheese and onion.' He looked past Mae, at the boxes of crisps stacked against the wall.

'Oh.' Mae could feel her brow furrowing into a frown, so she fought against it, keeping her features as neutral as possible. 'Right. Yes. Cheese and onion.' She turned to grab a packet of the desired crisps, but a hand pulled her back. Alfie was leaning across the bar, his hand on her arm.

'I'm kidding about the crisps. Of course I was going to ask you out. It's what we do, isn't it?' He let go of her arm and straightened, reaching into his pocket for some loose change. 'I ask you out, and you cruelly turn me down.' He shook his head as he grabbed a few coins from the palm of his hand. 'Every. Time.'

'I'm not being cruel,' Mae said as she took the money. 'We're mates. Good mates.'

'It's okay. I get it.' Alfie held his hands up, palms facing out. 'You don't fancy me.'

Mae felt her stomach tie itself in a knot, tightening as she looked at poor Alfie's downturned mouth. It wasn't that she didn't fancy Alfie. He was a very attractive man and a few years ago she'd have agreed to a date the first time he'd asked instead of dodging his requests time after time. But a lot had happened in that time. Dating men – even fun, caring and handsome men – wasn't an option.

'Are you fishing for compliments again?' she asked to lighten the mood, and Alfie's mouth curved into a smile that loosened the knot in her stomach.

'Am I that obvious?'

'You're about as subtle as Hannah when she's hinting for ice cream before dinner.'

Alfie's entire face seemed to crinkle as he smiled, the areas around his eyes and mouth most prominently. 'How are the summer holidays treating you? As stressful as you feared?'

Mae made a seesaw motion with her hand. 'At times. She's a good kid, but it's hard on my own.'

'I often wonder how Mum coped on her own with the four of us.' Alfie shook his head. 'We could be terrors. I should visit her more, make up for it.'

'Your dad wasn't around?' Mae asked and Alfie gave a humourless laugh.

'When he wanted to be, which wasn't that often, and only when he wasn't busy wooing his women. He was pretty useless, actually.'

Mae gave an understanding nod. 'Sounds familiar.'

'Hannah's dad?'

'Hannah's dad has never even met her. He wasn't interested beyond conception.' She wiped at an imaginary smear on the beer pump, just to avoid eye contact. 'My dad, however, stuck around for a while, just to make sure I was truly screwed up.'

'Some of us men *are* decent.' Alfie smiled weakly.

'I know you're one of the good ones,' Mae said, and Alfie's smile strengthened. He grabbed his drink and the bag of chips he'd brought into the pub with him and winked at Mae.

'You still won't join me for dinner, though?'

Mae rolled her eyes. 'Not a chance, mate.'

Alfie shrugged. 'Worth a shot, I suppose. I'd better get on with my lunch. I'm half expecting to go back to the surgery to find all the animals have escaped under Anna's supervision.'

'She can't be that bad,' Mae said and Alfie pulled a face.

'She really, really can.'

Mae laughed as Alfie backed away, still pulling the face.

'I don't know why you won't just put the guy out of his misery and agree to a date,' Corinne said, miraculously appearing as Alfie sat down at one of the tables and unwrapped his chips.

'We're just friends.' Mae busied herself with the till, sorting through Alfie's coins and placing them into the relevant tray. 'And he isn't my type.'

'Nah,' Corinne said, wrinkling her nose. 'Smart, caring, cute blokes aren't my type either.' She gave Mae a pointed look before heading for the customers still waiting to be served. Mae closed the till and plastered on a smile as she too returned to the small gathering at the bar.

'Any luck with the B&Bs?' she asked as she filled a glass with lemonade. She'd recognised the woman immediately as she'd shuffled into the pub, her hands stuffed deep into the pockets of her dungarees. Clearly the instant recognition wasn't mutual as the woman frowned at Mae. The confusion didn't last, however, as there weren't many twenty-somethings who dressed like they were from a bygone era in Clifton-on-Sea. It had been Mae's granny who'd taught her the vintage hairstyles she herself had worn as a young woman, curling, waving and rolling Mae's hair for fun as they waited for her mum to return home from work. Mae had adopted the look full time a few years ago, complete with vintage fashion choices, and she couldn't imagine looking in the mirror and not seeing the woman she chose to present to the world.

'No luck at all,' the woman said, shaking her head. 'I've tried every B&B I could find, plus the hotel, but there aren't any rooms available anywhere. I feel like a non-pregnant Mary in Bethlehem. You don't happen to know if there's a stable around here, do you?'

'If you're looking for a stable, you're better off talking to our local vet.' Mae nodded in the direction of Alfie, who smiled as he caught Mae's gaze and gave a little wave. 'Seriously, though…' Mae gave a sympathetic smile as she placed the glass of lemonade on the bar. 'Did you try the caravan site?'

The woman nodded and handed over a five-pound note. 'Fully booked too. There's room in the campsite, which I may have to take. The problem is, I don't have much in the way of camping gear. I have a little stove but no tent. I guess I'm going to have to buy one, which means more money from the budget.' She shook her head. 'Sorry for boring you with this. I haven't been able to get hold of my husband and I'm in a bit of a flap.'

'Don't worry.' Mae reached across the bar and gave the woman's arm a squeeze. 'I just wish there was more I could do to help. If I had a tent, I'd lend it to you. But I'm kinda too high-maintenance for camping.' She flicked her hands towards her face and hair. The woman laughed and Mae was pleased to see the harassed look melt away, if only for a moment.

'You look fabulous, though. Look at the state of me – I have paint under my nails!'

'Are you serving or what?' a gruff voice asked as a pair of elbows rested on the bar. 'Or are you going to start comparing beauty tips?'

Mae flashed the woman an apologetic smile before turning to the till, returning with the change before moving on to the next (impatient) customer in line. By the time she'd managed to clear the bar, the woman had wandered across the pub and nabbed a vacant seat. Mae was contemplating heading over, to see if there was anything else she could do to help, when her phone started to buzz from her handbag. Although she was working, she always kept her phone switched on in case Hannah or the B&B needed her.

'Do you mind if I take my break?' she asked Corinne after fishing the phone out of her handbag and seeing her mother's name on the display.

'Of course not,' Corinne said. 'We've got through the worst of it. Frank and I can manage now.'

'Thanks.' Mae accepted the call and pressed the phone against her ear as she moved through to the back of the pub. 'Hello?'

'Mummy!' It was Hannah, rather than Mae's mum, who answered, her voice happy and high. 'We went to the beach!'

'Wow. Did you build sandcastles?' Mae moved through to the small yard at the back of the pub, heading for an old crate to perch on in the shade of the tall walls.

'Yes! Mine was the biggest! Nanny bought me sandals!'

'Did she?'

'Yup. They're pink with yellow butterflies.' There was a whistle of air down the line as Hannah sighed. 'Nanny had to help me with the buckles.'

'It just takes practice, sweetie,' Mae told her. 'You'll get it. Do you think I could speak to Nanny for a minute?'

'Yup, yup!' Mae heard a faint giggle before the phone was switched and she heard her mother's voice.

'You didn't have to buy her new shoes, Mum. She has sandals at home but we were in a rush.' Mae needed her mum to know this, to know she didn't need help providing her daughter with clothing. Money could be a little tight at times, but they were coping.

'I know that, darling, but we were passing the shop and I saw the sweetest little sandals. I couldn't resist.'

Mae wasn't sure how true this was. She knew her mum worried about her; she'd brought Mae up pretty much without any help from Mae's father, so she knew how tough single parenthood could be. Eloise couldn't have coped without her own parents' help so she was always on hand for Mae and Hannah, whether that was for babysitting duties or buying footwear.

'Well, thank you,' Mae said, swallowing her pride painfully. 'I appreciate it. We both do.'

'I know, sweetie. Hannah certainly does – I think she'll try sleeping in them tonight.'

'Great.' Mae laughed softly. 'I know who I'll be ringing when I have a battle on my hands at bedtime.'

'You only have to say the word and I'll come round.'

Mae had only been joking, but her mum was serious. 'I'm sure we'll be fine. I should go now, though. I'm on my break and I'm gasping for a cup of tea before I go back behind the bar.'

'Okay, sweetie. Give my love to Frank and Corinne. I'll see you later.'

'Bye, Mum. Kisses and squishes for Hannah.'

Mae ended the call and heaved herself up from the crate. She really didn't know where she'd be without her mum. She'd been there from the start, when Mae had returned to Clifton-on-Sea with a badly bruised heart and a twelve-week scan photo. The father – Mae's boyfriend of eight months – had bailed upon the news of her pregnancy, and though Mae had been determined to stand on her own two feet, she'd soon realised she needed her family and had returned to the town she'd been desperate to escape since her teens. It was only upon her return that she'd realised how special Clifton-on-Sea was and just how lucky she was to have Eloise Wright as a mother.

Mae was halfway across the yard when her phone started to ring again. She paused and, answering the call, headed back towards the crate.

'Mae? It's Shirley. Shirley Robertson.'

Mae reached the crate, but didn't sit. 'Shirley? Is everything okay?' Shirley and her family were due to arrive for their stay later that afternoon, but had they arrived early? Mrs Hornchurch knew they were due, but Mae's neighbour couldn't be expected to wait in all day on the off-chance they'd show up a few hours sooner than anticipated, so perhaps the family were camped out on the B&B's doorstep, waiting to be let in.

'Oh, love, no,' Shirley wailed. 'It's my Len. He had a bit of a stumble lugging the suitcase downstairs this morning so we've been stuck in A&E ever since.'

Mae gasped. 'Is he okay?' She was fond of the Robertson family – they'd been among her first paying customers when she'd turned her grandparents' house into a bed and breakfast and she looked forward to their annual visit.

'Nothing a plaster cast and rest won't sort out,' Shirley said. 'He finally got an X-ray and he's broken his ankle. The rest is just superficial cuts and bruises.'

Mae sank onto the crate now and placed a hand on her chest. 'That's a relief.'

'Yes,' Shirley agreed. 'But the thing is, we're having to cancel our holiday. I'm so sorry to do this at the last minute. I feel so terrible. We all do.'

'Don't be daft,' Mae said. 'The important part is that Len gets better. You'll give him my love, won't you?'

'Of course. And we'll be back next year, for sure. I'll bring the cases down myself!'

'Take care of Len – and yourself, of course. I'll see you next summer, fit and well.'

Mae sat for a moment after she'd ended the call. She was glad Len was okay – broken bone and bruising aside – but she couldn't help worrying about the empty rooms she was now left with, which left her with an icky feeling of guilt that she could have such selfish thoughts when a lovely man like Len Robertson had taken a tumble down a flight of stairs. But those unoccupied rooms represented lost earnings. She'd had to turn people away because she was fully booked and now she wasn't.

Mae's eyes widened as she realised all was not lost. There was a woman sitting in the pub who was in desperate need of a room and Mae now had *two* going spare for a couple of weeks. Gasping, she shot up from the crate and scuttled back into the pub, scanning the room as she propelled herself behind the bar.

33

'Where is she?' she wailed, eyes darting around the room. The seat the woman had nabbed earlier was now vacated.

'Who?' Corinne asked as she popped behind the bar with an armful of empty glasses.

'The woman in the dungarees.' Mae pointed at the empty seat.

'Oh, her.' Corinne slipped the glasses onto the side and bent to open the dishwasher. 'She left a few minutes ago.'

'Do you know who she is?' Mae asked, already trying to work out how to track the woman down before she set up camp with a newly purchased tent.

Corinne shook her head. 'I'm pretty sure I've seen her around town but I don't know her name.'

Bollocks, Mae thought as she scurried towards the pub's door. *Big, sodding hairy bollocks!*

Chapter Five

Willow

Willow took her change from the bed and breakfast lady/ barmaid and wandered over to an empty seat, placing her glass down on the table and taking out her phone to check for any messages from either the builders or Ethan. There was an uncomfortable feeling in her gut, as though there was a small but hefty bowling ball in there, clogging and silently damaging her insides. She tried to ignore the feeling, knowing if she paid it too much attention it would take over completely and send her into a panic. So far, with the distraction of her mission to find accommodation, she was coping with the catastrophe, but she knew once she stopped and really thought about the situation she and her husband were now in, she would fall to pieces.

Falling to pieces wasn't usually Willow's style. She could be cool, calm and collected at the worst of times, thinking rationally about the bigger picture instead of giving in to dread. When her caterers had cancelled at the very last minute on her wedding day, phoning just minutes before she was due to have her hair and make-up done with news of a faulty fridge and ruined food, Willow hadn't flapped. She'd been momentarily disappointed she wouldn't get to enjoy the menu she'd planned weeks in advance, but she knew it was only food. Good food, but food all the same. Marrying Ethan was the important part, the part making her heart race and her hands jitter, so she'd let the lack of catered food slide as she slipped her phone into her pocket and sat on the hairdresser's chair. Later, once she was Mrs St Clair, Willow led her guests to the seafront, where she and Ethan bought them the most delicious fish and chips, which they ate on the beach. It had been a chilly evening, but everyone said it was the best fish and chips they'd ever eaten and Willow remembered the day with fondness. The smell of battered fish and salt and vinegar-drenched chips filling the pub now reminded her of that day. Everything will be okay, the aroma reminded her. She and Ethan would sort everything out. This was a tiny blip they'd maybe laugh about one day.

Or maybe not. Only time would tell.

She checked her phone again. Still no word from Ethan. She wasn't too surprised or worried about the lack of contact under the circumstances, but hearing from him would have offered a little bit of comfort and gone a long way in preventing her from teetering over the edge.

Placing the phone on the table, she took a sip of her drink, swallowing hard against the miniature bowling ball, which had crawled stealthily to sit in her throat.

'Fancy a chip?'

Willow placed her glass back down on the table and glanced first at the bag of chips being proffered and then its owner sitting at the neighbouring table. He was perhaps in his early thirties, with smooth, brown skin and closely cropped black hair, and when he smiled – as he did now, while pushing the bag of chips ever so slightly closer to Willow – he displayed an enviable row of neat, white teeth.

'No, but thank you.' Willow didn't think she could manage it. The lemonade had been battle enough.

'Are you okay?' he asked, removing the chips – and the strong vinegar scent that tickled Willow's nose – and placing the bag on his own table. 'You look... sort of stressed.'

Understatement! Willow was *this* close to weeping, right there with a pub full of witnesses.

But no. Deep breaths. Deep, calming breaths.

Everything will be okay.

'Are you a doctor or something?' Willow asked, and he smiled again.

'Not for humans.' He wiped his hand down the thigh of his jeans to rid it of any grease and held it out to Willow. 'I'm Alfie Michaels, the local vet.'

'Ah.' Willow shook the hand. 'You're the one I need to speak to about a stable.'

'Sorry?'

Willow laughed. 'Sorry, bit of an in-joke. There's no room at the inn – or the local B&Bs – so I was hoping a stable would be free. Oh, excuse me...' She pounced on her phone as it sprang into life, but it was neither Ethan nor the builder and she didn't recognise the number on the screen.

'Hello? Is that Re-Create?' a male voice asked once she answered.

Willow pushed the bowling ball to the very back of her mind as she switched to business gear. 'It is. This is Willow speaking. How may I help you?'

'It's Malcolm Kershaw?' The man on the other end of the line posed the name as a question, as though Willow might be familiar with it. 'We've been exchanging emails about the bed?'

Ah! Willow recognised the name now. She and Malcolm *had* been communicating about one of the old, disused rowing boats she'd rescued from the harbour, upcycling her treasure into a bed that hung from the ceiling, creating a gentle rocking motion for the sleeper. Malcolm had spotted the bed on her website and was keen to buy it.

'I've got a van,' Malcolm said now. 'I'm about ten minutes away from Clifton-on-Sea.'

'You're on your way?' Willow knew from their exchanges over the past couple of weeks that Malcolm lived in Huddersfield, which was around seventy miles away. This was not a quick trip and he'd be disappointed – to say the least – if he arrived to find an empty shop.

'Yep. Won't be long. You still have the bed?'

The bed was currently taking up a huge chunk of her workroom at the back of the shop, and the prospect of finally having that space back almost made her lightheaded with relief. The bed was quite a niche piece, and she'd been worried she wouldn't find a new owner for it. On the other hand, she was in the middle of a crisis here and – it had just occurred to her – she could use the rowing boat bed if she failed to come up with another solution.

But no. Malcolm had been so excited about the bed, which he'd told Willow he wanted for his son as part of a sea-themed bedroom makeover. She couldn't deny it him – especially when he'd travelled so far to pick it up.

'I do have it,' Willow confirmed. 'But I'm not at the shop right now. I can be there in...' She calculated the distance between the Fisherman and her shop. 'Twenty minutes?'

'Great. I don't mind hanging around for a few minutes. It might take me that long to find your shop. Where exactly is it? I've just got off the motorway and pulled over. I can see a sign for the train station.'

'Head that way.' Willow stood up and headed for the pub's door. 'My shop is just around the corner from the station. It's your first left. Thorpe Lane.' She reached the door and pushed her way through it, saying goodbye to Malcolm as she reached her van and hopped inside. A text message beeped through to her phone as she dragged her seatbelt across her chest.

Sorry, only just got your message about the house! Can't talk now – will phone in about an hour.

Slotting the key in the ignition, she left it to dangle for a moment while she tapped out a reply. Slipping her phone into the pocket of her dungarees, she started the van and pulled away from the Fisherman, heading back towards the station, her shop and the rowing-boat bed. Behind her, just as she turned away from the harbour, the doors of the pub flew open, a pair of red, peep-toe slingbacks clattering onto the pavement.

Chapter Six

Mae

She threw herself out of the pub, eyes darting left and right as they hunted the dungaree-clad woman, a hand held against her forehead to shield her eyes from the bright midday sun. She was greeted by the familiar line of wooden benches opposite the Fisherman, their backs against the seagull-lined harbour wall, but the only people around were a young couple wandering hand-in-hand, a bag of chips held between them, a mother holding her toddler son up to the harbour wall, pointing out the boats bobbing up and down on the water beyond, and the owner of the B&B a couple of doors down watering her hanging baskets. The woman had vanished.

'Everything okay?' Alfie asked as, shoulders slumped in defeat, Mae made her way back into the pub. She held in a sigh and headed back towards the bar, where Alfie followed.

'Yes. It's just...' She shook her head. 'I was looking for someone. She needs a room and I've just had a cancellation. It would have helped us both out.'

Mae could have kicked herself. Those rooms being empty for two weeks was a massive blow for her business.

She relied on the money the bed and breakfast took in over the summer as it made up the bulk of her earnings for the entire year. During off-peak times, she rented out her rooms to students from nearby colleges and universities, but that didn't bring in anywhere near the revenue the summer holidays did, so every booking was crucial. She needed to fill those rooms as quickly as possible, otherwise she'd be in trouble further down the line.

'Do you mean Willow?' Alfie asked. Mae's brow crinkled. She didn't actually know the woman's name. 'The woman in the dungarees?' Alfie turned to look at the now-empty seat at the table with the abandoned glass of lemonade.

'Yes!' Mae reached forward, grasping hold of Alfie's forearm. 'Do you know her?' Her grip relaxed as Alfie shook his head, her shoulders slumping once again.

'But I know where she was heading, if it helps?'

Mae's fingers curled around Alfie's forearms again. 'It does. It really, really does.'

Alfie dropped his gaze down to his arm and Mae snatched her fingers away. There was enough gossip about her and the vet around here without her fanning the flames.

'She was meeting someone at her shop. It's on Thorpe Lane, near the station. I didn't catch which shop it was, but it's a start.'

'Thank you!' Mae would have happily leapt across the bar and planted a kiss on Alfie's cheek in return for his help, but that really would have set tongues wagging in overdrive. Instead she gave his arm another quick squeeze. 'I owe you a pint!'

'Only if you'll join me,' Alfie said, flashing the grin most women found irresistible. 'How about tonight? After work? I could pick you up, or meet you back here?'

Mae was shaking her head before Alfie could finish his request. 'I'm sorry. I'm so busy right now, especially now it's the summer. I've got the B&B, Hannah...' Mae trailed off as Alfie nodded and started to back away. He'd heard it all before, many times. 'I still owe you that pint, though. I'll get it for you now.'

'It's okay. Another time.' Alfie grabbed his jacket from the back of his chair. 'I should be getting back, make sure Anna hasn't wrecked the joint in my absence. I hope you find Willow.'

Mae pushed her mouth into a brief smile as she lifted a hand. 'Thanks again. And sorry about... Well, you know.'

'No worries.' With a wave of his own, Alfie ducked out of the pub and, although Mae was relieved she'd sidestepped the messy date request, she couldn't help the feeling of dread worming its way into her stomach. Alfie was a good bloke and for most women he'd be perfect with his unquestionable good looks and caring profession, but dating him was out of the question for Mae. Dating *anyone* was out of the question for Mae. She hadn't been lying when she'd told Alfie she was incredibly busy – between the B&B, her bar work and Hannah, she simply didn't have any time left over for romance.

Or so she told herself on a regular basis. She was almost starting to believe it.

'Did you manage to catch up with her?' Corinne asked, nodding at Willow's vacated table.

'No, but I know where she's gone.' Mae looked up at the clock hanging on one of the pub's low beams. 'Hopefully she'll still be there when my shift's over.'

Corinne grabbed a pint glass and started to fill it with bitter from the pump. 'What did you need her for?'

Mae explained about Willow's situation and her own sudden vacancy.

'You'd better get off now then.' Corinne placed the filled glass on the bar and accepted the money from her customer, thanking him before turning back to Mae. 'Hurry, before you miss her. You don't know how long she'll be hanging around this shop for. If she leaves, you might not find her again and then you'll both be screwed.'

'I can't leave now.' Mae looked at the clock again. She still had a couple of hours left of her shift.

'You can.' Corinne tapped at the till and plonked the coins into the tray. 'I'm the boss and what I say goes. So go.'

'But…'

Corinne held up a silencing finger. 'We'll be fine, honestly. And think of that poor woman having to kip in a bloody tent on her own. Think of the cold, the spiders.' She shuddered. 'Plus, you'll be losing out on money if you leave that room empty. Think of Hannah – your granny would never forgive me if I let her great-grandchild starve.'

'I hardly think Hannah is going to starve,' Mae started to protest, but Corinne was already guiding her out of the pub and pressing her handbag into her hands.

'I'll see you tomorrow,' Corinne said as she nudged Mae towards her car. 'Frank says you're letting us have Hannah for the day. You're not down on the rota so we'll pick her up from yours in the morning, give you a bit of time to yourself.'

'You don't have to do that,' Mae said, but Corinne rolled her eyes.

'No, we don't *have* to, but we don't get the chance to spoil our goddaughter often enough.'

'You spoil us both too much,' Mae said, but Corinne gave a dismissive wave of her hand.

'Nonsense.' She reached up on her tiptoes to kiss Mae on the cheek. 'Now, go on, before it's too late.'

Mae knew Frank and Corinne didn't necessarily need her help in the bar as much as they claimed to, that the offer of the job at the Fisherman had been nothing less than a charitable act. They'd have simply handed over a sum of money every month to help her out if Mae hadn't been too proud to accept it, but at least with the bar work she could feel independent. She hadn't returned to Clifton-on-Sea to sponge off her loved ones, though she knew she was incredibly lucky to have the support of her mum, Frank and Corinne.

Climbing into her car, she blew a kiss through the window and headed towards the station, hoping it wasn't too late for either her or Willow.

Thorpe Lane was short and narrow, with a row of little cottages on one side of the cobbled road and a row of shops on the opposite side. Just six houses and six shops made up the lane, but even if the lane had stretched further across the town, Willow and her shop wouldn't have been too difficult to spot. You could hardly miss the rowing boat, which had been stripped and polished and now appeared to contain a custom-made mattress, being lugged from the shop to a waiting van squeezed between the two pavements. Willow was at one end, her head poking around the side to guide the boat towards the van, with a couple of blokes taking up the opposite end and the middle. Together, the trio staggered from the shop, with Willow calling out directions.

'Do you need a hand?' Mae asked as she climbed out of her car and scurried towards the rowing boat party.

'From you?' one of the blokes asked before snorting unattractively. 'No offence, love, but we wouldn't want you breaking a nail.'

Mae looked down at her hands, fingers splayed and nails facing upwards. The pillar-box red was stark against her pale skin, but she wasn't about to apologise for painting her nails. These nails never got in the way when she was changing barrels at the pub, and if one did happen to break or chip, it was no big deal. She liked to make an effort with her appearance, but she had no qualms about rolling up her sleeves and getting stuck into a task.

'Take no notice of this plonker,' Willow said between puffs and groans as she navigated the kerb. 'We'd love a hand, thank you.'

'Plonker?' the bloke spluttered, either through indignation or the fact he was manoeuvring a rowing boat through the street. 'That's the last time I offer to help you.'

'This is the first time you've offered to help me,' Willowed huffed. 'And, if I recall, you didn't actually offer to help out at all. Your mam threatened to whack you with her rolling pin if you didn't – and I quote – "get off your fat arse for one day in your life".'

'I could have said no,' he muttered as Mae reached the middle of the boat and took some of the weight.

'You bloody well try, lad,' a voice, which Mae presumed belonged to the bloke's mum, called out from one of the houses across the street. 'This is the most work I've seen you do in the last thirty-six years. And no, playing on that Playstation-Cube-whatsit doesn't count.'

'What is this, anyway?' Mae asked as they reached the van and jostled the tip of the boat inside.

'It used to be a boat.' Mae gave the boat a shove and it began to slide across the van's floor. 'But now it's a bed. I upcycled it and Malcolm's just bought it for his son.'

The other bloke, who had yet to speak, gave a nod.

'You made this into a bed?' Mae stepped aside as the boat was completely swallowed by the van. 'Wow.'

Willow wiped her hands down the sides of her dungarees. 'It's what I do. I have a shop.' She indicated the premises behind her. 'You can go in and have a look if you'd like, though I'm not technically open at the moment.'

Leaving Willow to talk business with Malcolm, Mae wandered into the shop, her eyes widening as she took in the assortment of products on offer. There were larger items of furniture, all given new and vibrant leases of life, smaller household objects transformed into beautiful, decorative items, and things that might have been thought useless given a new purpose. Old light bulbs had been filled with small, delicate flowers and hung from a chandelier, mismatched glass goblets and flutes had been turned into stylish candles with white, fragranced wax, and old jars had been scrubbed, their lids painted in pastel shades, ready to be filled with sweets, buttons, cotton buds – anything small that was looking for a new, chic home. Mae could picture the jars in her bathroom or the guest bedrooms, and the champagne-flute candles would look divine on top of the chests of drawers in the rooms.

'This is all amazing,' she told Willow when she returned a few minutes later. The van trundled past, its horn beeping, and Willow waved through the open door.

'Thank you. It all started off as a hobby, but it's really taken off.' She looked around her shop, a contented smile on her lips. 'I love it.'

'I feel the same about my bed and breakfast,' Mae said. 'Which is what I'm here about. I've had a cancellation, so if you're still looking for a room…'

Willow threw her hand up to her mouth to catch a gasp. 'Oh my God. Are you serious?'

Mae nodded. 'The call came through while I was on my break. By the time I came back through to the pub, you'd gone. The room's only available for two weeks, but it'll give you a bit of breathing space to find somewhere more permanent until the work on your house is done.'

'Thank you!' Willow launched herself at Mae, throwing her arms around the woman and squeezing hard before she got a grip of herself and let go. She giggled, her cheeks turning pink. 'Sorry. I'm just so relieved.'

Mae laughed. 'I bet you are. I hope you haven't bought a tent since I last saw you?'

'Thankfully not.' Willow giggled and did a little jig on the spot. 'I should let my husband know I've found somewhere. He isn't here at the moment. He's working away, but should be back in a few days. Will it be a problem if I'm still at the B&B when he returns?'

Mae shook her head. 'No problem at all. The room's a double.'

'Brilliant.' Willow heaved a huge sigh of relief. 'I could do with moving some things over to my room. Luckily most of our stuff is in storage, but I need clothes and my essentials. When would be okay to drop them off?'

'Whenever you're ready. If I'm not there, my neighbour can let you in and show you where everything is.'

'Thanks again.' Willow paused in thought before she shrugged and threw herself at Mae for another squeeze.

Chapter Seven

Melody

Melody took her time as she wandered towards the seafront, her rucksack on her back, her laptop bag looped across her chest and her camera dangling from its strap around her neck. She'd been dipping into little cobbled side streets, taking photos of anything that caught her eye: a seagull perched on a garden wall with a pretty cottage and flower-filled hanging baskets in the background, a family loaded with buckets and spades and folded deckchairs on their way down to the beach, a little shop with its window full of quirky seaside treasures: tealights made from shells, driftwood wreaths to hang on doors, and a mirror beautifully surrounded by smooth pebbles in shades of blue and grey. Melody had been particularly taken with the seashell tealights, but the door had been locked and there didn't appear to be anybody inside.

Melody had continued on her way, the tang of salt and seaweed growing stronger as she made her way through the town, until she found herself on the promenade. The noise was incredible: waves sloshing, children playing, music blaring from the pier and the nearby arcade, seagulls crying out as they swooped along the beach in search of food. Melody closed her eyes and allowed the music of the seaside to wash over her. This was what she was searching for. The heart of the British seaside beating loud and clear. It was everywhere; the joyous sounds of nature and humankind combined, the smell of the sea and fried food mingling to create the distinct scent that took Melody back to her carefree childhood, the crunch of sand underfoot, swept up onto the promenade. Melody made her way to the railing and looked down at the beach, at the happiness sand and sunshine created. Families, couples, dog-walkers, all enjoying this bright, hot day on the stretch of beach. To her right and stretching out into the water was the wooden pier and its fairground-style amusements, and to the left, about half a mile away, were the cliffs that cut off the beach. She'd like to climb to the top of the cliffs and take a photo of the beach from there, but first she needed to find somewhere to stay. The straps of her rucksack were digging into her shoulders, the movement as she walked causing them to rub at the flesh. She'd find somewhere to stay, freshen up, and head back out to discover Clifton-on-Sea's hidden delights.

Her stomach rumbled as she pushed away from the railing, reminding her she had yet to eat lunch. She'd been so caught up in her new surroundings that she hadn't thought about eating since she'd clapped eyes on the cakes at the train station's tearoom.

Food first, she decided, then accommodation.

Turning, she could already see several options before her: a pub – the Red Lion – with a chalkboard outside, claiming great food and a family atmosphere; a restaurant with black paintwork and matching awning stark against its creamy rendering; a bakery with its window crammed with tempting sweet treats; and a fish and chip shop that made Melody's stomach grumble even louder at the mere sight. That was settled then.

The delicious smell wafting from the fish and chip shop made her stomach growl again as she crossed the road but, hungry as she clearly was, she didn't step inside straight away and join the queue. There were a few things Melody couldn't resist, and adorable dogs were one of them.

'Hello, little guy.' Crouching, Melody held out a hand for the dog to sniff. His lead was tied around a lamppost, but he stood, his tail swishing from side to side like windscreen wipers in heavy rainfall, and gave Melody's palm a thorough investigation with his wet nose. Finding the hand disappointingly empty, he sat down again, his head on one side as he observed his new friend.

'Aren't you a cutie?' Melody cooed, stroking the dog's head. 'Yes, you are. You are lovely.'

The dog closed his eyes as Melody started to scratch his ears, enjoying the fuss. He was quite a small dog, with scraggly golden fur on his body, legs and head, with a darker, greyish shade on his muzzle and ears.

'And smartly dressed too.' The dog was wearing a red tartan bandana around his neck, which Melody reached out to touch. 'So handsome. Who's a handsome boy then?'

'The ladies often tell me I am.'

Melody twisted away from the dog, looking up as the owner of the voice swaggered out of the fish and chip shop. Perhaps 'swaggered' was too strong a word. Perhaps he'd simply exited the shop in a normal fashion, but Melody was annoyed and flustered he'd caught her baby-talking to a dog.

'Is that so?' She stood up, readjusting the rucksack on her back.

He grinned at her, which only infuriated her further. Smug bastard. 'Not as handsome as this fella, obviously.' He indicated the dog and Melody felt her cheeks burn.

'Obviously,' she said, trying to subtly swish her blonde hair so it would cover her hot cheeks. 'No contest.'

'I wouldn't dream of trying to compete against this little dude.' The door behind him opened as another customer was exiting, so he stepped out of the way. Before the door could swing closed again, Melody stepped forward and reached out a hand to stop it. 'See you around!' he called as Melody stepped into the shop, but she didn't turn around.

The fish and chips had been as delicious as the enticing aroma had promised. Melody ate her lunch on the beach, her rucksack and laptop bag wedged into the sand next to her, as she people-watched. She took a couple of photos between bites of food, but there'd be plenty of time for more later. For now, she was happy soaking up the blissful atmosphere of this particular beach, absorbing the happy vibes and feeling the sun on her skin. British summers didn't always deliver and she was usually stuck in a stuffy office even if they did, so she was determined to make the most of the sunshine.

She'd visited lots of beaches over the past few weeks; some had been large expanses of sand sweeping along the perimeter of bustling towns, others tiny strips and coves, but they'd all had one thing in common for Melody: they were idyllic spaces offering a sense of freedom, of possibility. Clifton-on-Sea was no different. The beach was smaller than that of nearby Blackpool, and the town wasn't as busy, but Melody felt a similar carefree atmosphere, the same sense of fun and adventure. She liked it here already, and she was sure she'd find exactly what she was looking for.

Scrunching up the greasy paper, now devoid of fish and chips, Melody picked up her bags, brushed down her shorts, and headed up the sand-brushed steps towards the promenade. There was a bed and breakfast across the road from the pier and she headed towards it, popping her rubbish in a bin on the way. Unfortunately, before she'd even reached it, she saw the 'No Vacancies' sign propped up in one of the windows.

Damn. It looked as though finding accommodation wasn't going to be as easy as Melody had thought, but she wasn't worried as there were no doubt several more B&Bs in town. Taking out her phone, she tapped on the Project: Planet app she'd been using during her travels, typing her location into the accommodation search bar and waiting for the results. As predicted, a list appeared, though it wasn't quite as extensive as she'd hoped. The app provided phone numbers for each establishment, but Melody decided to walk to the nearest on the list as it was a good opportunity to explore the town.

The nearest bed and breakfast was a couple of streets back from the beach, on a tree-lined street filled with a jumble of mismatched houses of varying sizes, colours and periods, which somehow gave it a charming feel. The bed and breakfast was a short walk away and was one of the larger properties, set back from the road with a sizeable drive. Melody couldn't see a 'No Vacancies' sign as she made her way to the stone steps leading up to the entrance, which was promising. A couple of minutes later, however, after a short conversation with a bored teenager behind the reception desk, Melody trudged back down the steps, the Project: Planet app open on her phone again.

There was a similar story at the next two B&Bs and Melody found herself back on the seafront, heading away from the pier in search of the next one on the app's list. Her hope of finding accommodation in Clifton-on-Sea was dwindling. If she couldn't find lodgings, she'd have to hop on a train and search elsewhere, which wasn't too much of a problem, but not ideal when she was so keen to explore the town. Still, she could always return if she had time to spare before she returned home.

Thinking of home, she took a quick selfie of herself in front of the red railings of the promenade, the gorgeous view of the beach and sea behind her, and sent it to her mum with a quick message to let her know she was safe and enjoying her trip.

See you soon, she ended the text. *Love to you, Dad and Brett xxx*

She slipped her phone back into her pocket and shrugged her rucksack off her shoulders for a minute's reprieve. Rummaging inside, she found a hairband and pulled her hair off her neck, securing it in a high ponytail. The afternoon was growing hotter and the walk through town was proving to be more arduous than she'd thought it would be, with unexpectedly steep streets and an even more unexpected scorcher of a day. There was a bottle of water in her rucksack, which she drank from gratefully before fastening the bag and hitching it onto her back. There was another bed and breakfast just up the road, but if that was also full, she'd have to reconsider her plan of action as she was quickly running out of options.

She set off again, sticking to the promenade so she could watch the action on the beach as she walked. There was a game of volleyball going on using an inflatable beachball, a couple of Frisbees were zipping through the air, and there were sandcastles galore. Melody stopped for a moment to take a couple of shots before moving on, but she hadn't got very far when she stopped again, gasping as she spotted a couple of donkeys, a child on each of their backs, plodding along the sand towards her. She froze for a moment, just watching, as the donkeys placed careful hooves on the sand, the giggling children – a boy and a girl – jostling gently as they clung tightly to bright red reins.

The donkeys had almost passed by the time she'd pulled herself together enough to grab her camera. Jogging back up the promenade, Melody leaned over the railing, lining up the perfect shot, clicking several times as the donkeys plodded on.

Lowering her camera and taking a small step back from the rail, Melody continued to watch as the donkeys continued up the beach, tails swishing lazily behind them, her mind wandering back to a different time, a different beach.

Finally, the spell broken, she set off again, adjusting the rucksack on her tired shoulders. Ahead, the promenade widened, but the space was currently being filled with little bodies and their parents as they sat in a haphazard semicircle in front of a vintage, red-and-white-striped Punch and Judy booth. Melody navigated the crowd but hesitated as she made it to the other side of the booth, glancing at the ice-cream van that had conveniently parked close to the show. The van was sky-blue and white, with a giant, plastic ice-cream cone – complete with Flake and dripping strawberry sauce – on the roof, while large lettering identified the van as belonging to the Marsland Brothers with their homemade ice cream. An ice cream in the hot weather did seem appealing, especially as she drew closer and saw the delicious flavours on offer. Toffee fudge, orange chocolate chip, bubble gum, passion fruit, banoffee pie, cappuccino, as well as the more traditional vanilla, strawberry and raspberry ripple. She'd already decided on a banoffee pie cone by the time she reached the van, but the serving hatch was empty. Never one to miss a photo opportunity, Melody grabbed her camera and aimed, taking a step back so she could line up the perfect shot. A figure suddenly appeared in the hatch, making her jump.

'I'm ready for my close-up,' he said and Melody groaned, seeing the bloke she'd encountered outside the fish and chip shop earlier. 'How do you want me?'

'You really don't want me to answer that one, pal.' Dropping her camera so it hung from its strap around her neck, she stepped forward. 'Can I get a banoffee pie ice cream?'

'Cone or pot?'

'Cone, please.' She shrugged her rucksack off her shoulders and rummaged inside for her purse. 'And can I get a Flake too?'

'Anything for you,' he replied with a wink before turning to prepare her ice cream. Melody fought the urge to gag. Was he this cheesy with all his customers?

'One scoop or two?' he called over his shoulder.

'Just one.' Melody located her purse and unzipped it, grabbing the appropriate coins. The ice-cream-van man reappeared at the hatch, the delicious-looking cone outstretched. Melody made the switch, unable to resist licking the toffee sauce that was already starting to drip down onto the cone.

'See you around!' he called as she wandered off, mentally in heaven as her tongue lapped at the ice cream. It was truly amazing and so refreshing in the heat. She raised a hand in lieu of a goodbye, already knowing she would re-enter the cheese zone tomorrow for another go at one of his ice creams.

Chapter Eight

Mae

'Mummy!'

Mae hadn't even swung the gate open at her mum's house and Hannah was already hurtling towards her, her new sandals slapping noisily against the garden path as she propelled her little body forward. Moments earlier, Hannah had been playing with her dolls on the small patch of grass in front of the house while her grandmother relaxed with a book in a deckchair.

'Hello, little lady.' Mae opened the gate quickly and scooped her daughter into her arms, planting a noisy kiss on her cheek and making her giggle. 'I hope you've been behaving for Nanny.'

'She's been an angel,' Eloise said from the deckchair. She twisted her wrist to check the time. 'You're early, aren't you?'

'There was a bit of a problem with the B&B, so Corinne sent me home early.'

'Typical Corinne,' Eloise said as she placed her book face down on the grass. 'Is everything okay with the B&B now?'

Mae shifted Hannah onto her hip and made her way across to her mum. 'It's all sorted. I've had a cancellation on both of my rooms, but I've managed to fill one of them already.' Mae placed Hannah back down on the grass in front of her dolls. 'Hopefully I'll be able to fill the other quickly and won't miss out on too many days.'

'It's high season, so I'm sure it won't be a problem.' Eloise slotted a bookmark between the pages of her book and closed it. 'So, this guest. Is it a female guest? Or male?' She'd adopted a casual tone as she enquired, but she was fooling no one. Though single herself, Eloise was desperate to see her daughter coupled with a man – any man, it sometimes seemed to Mae.

'It's a woman,' Mae said, trying not to smile when she saw the clear disappointment on her mother's face. 'She's married, but her husband's working away or something.'

'Working away, eh?' Eloise said. 'That's what I used to tell people whenever your father buggered off with one of his floozies.'

'I'm sure it's nothing like that,' Mae said, though her voice was filled with little conviction. In her experience, men and relationships usually came hand-in-hand with heartache.

Eloise shrugged. 'Maybe not. There are some decent fellas out there, if you look hard enough. Or look at all in your case.'

'Mum…' Mae groaned.

Eloise held her hands up in surrender. 'I'm just saying.'

'Well, don't just say anything.'

'Sorry. I just worry about you being on your own.' Eloise battled with the deckchair to get her feet on solid ground. 'Are you staying for a cup of tea?'

'I shouldn't, really. My new guest is picking some things up and I'd like to be there to settle her in. You know how grateful I am having Mrs Hornchurch on hand, but she does like to chew people's ears off.'

'She's lonely,' Eloise said. 'That house used to be full to the brim with people when I was growing up next door. There were Mr and Mrs Hornchurch, their three children, Mrs Hornchurch's parents and an aunt or cousin – I can't remember which now. It was bedlam! Now there's just poor Mrs Hornchurch rattling around the old place with only the dog for company.'

'I do try to stop and chat when I can.' Mae felt bad now. She knew how much loneliness could bite.

'I know you do.' Eloise, having freed herself from the deckchair, gave her daughter a kiss on the cheek. 'Now, are you sure I can't tempt you with a cuppa? I'm parched in this heat.'

'I really should be getting back. I'm not sure how long it'll take Willow to pack her things. She said she won't be bringing much.' Crouching on the grass, Mae started to gather the dolls and place them in the plastic box that housed them and their accessories.

'Okay, darling.' Eloise took the box of dolls and tucked it under one arm before leaning in to kiss Mae's cheek. 'Take care – and don't work too hard.' She stooped down to kiss her granddaughter. 'Bye, sweetheart. Be good!'

Taking Hannah's hand, Mae made her way to the car, strapping Hannah into her seat at the back before climbing in herself. She waved to her mum – who had returned to the deckchair and her book – before driving back to the bed and breakfast.

The house Mae had grown up in – and which Eloise still occupied – was only a few minutes' drive from the seafront, but it had always felt like a big adventure whenever Mae had visited her grandparents as a child. It felt different at Granny and Grandpa's, as though the town was more alive down by the seafront, and it was certainly more fun with the beach, pier and arcade within easy reach. She'd loved the house as a little girl, with its three floors of rooms to explore and the large garden at the back with a rope swing and slide. It hadn't been a bed and breakfast back then – it had simply been Granny and Grandpa's house, almost a second home for Mae growing up. It had been a happy place, away from the drama of her parents' often turbulent relationship, and she hoped she'd created an equally happy home for her daughter.

'Can I watch telly?' Hannah asked as soon as they arrived home, sliding her new sandals off her feet without unbuckling them and kicking them onto the hallway floor.

'Don't you think you should put these away first?' Mae scooped the sandals up from the floor and handed them to her daughter. 'Before our guest arrives and breaks her neck before she's even unpacked?'

'Who's coming to stay today?' Hannah asked as she and Mae climbed the stairs. Mae was about to tell her about Willow when the doorbell rang, the sudden and piercing sound making her jump.

'Make sure you put those in the bottom of the wardrobe,' she said, pointing at the sandals before scurrying back down the stairs again. She opened the door, expecting to see Willow on the doorstep, but it was a young woman, blonde rather than brunette like Willow, wearing cut-off denim shorts and a blue-and-white-striped T-shirt. She had a hefty-looking rucksack slung over her shoulders, the strap of a laptop-style bag crossing her chest, and a camera looped around her neck. How she was still standing under the weight of it all was a mystery to Mae.

'I don't suppose you have a room free?' she asked. She bit her lip as she waited for an answer, her eyebrows inching slowly up her weary-looking face.

'You're in luck,' Mae said, opening the door wider and stepping aside. 'I've had a cancellation this afternoon and the room's still free. Come in and I'll get you booked in.'

'Really?' She smiled now, her lips stretching wide across her face. She had such a pretty face, with rosy, defined cheeks and blue eyes that sparkled now she was no longer grimacing. 'Thank you so much. I've been wandering around for *ages*. I couldn't find a room anywhere! I thought I was going to have to move on, which is a shame as this seems like such a lovely town. I'm sorry, I'm babbling.'

Mae laughed as she led the way into the living room. 'Don't worry about it, and I'm glad you've found somewhere to stay. I'm Mae Wright, by the way.'

'Melody Rosewood.' The woman held her hand out and Mae shook it. 'This is a gorgeous house. I've stayed in some pretty grotty places over the past couple of weeks, but this is not one of them.'

'Thanks.' Mae looked around her living room, which, she had to admit, she loved. There was the original fireplace in the centre of the room, with bookcases built into the alcoves either side, and although she'd painted the whole room a warm cream shade, she'd brightened the space with splashes of colour, from the teal sofa and its lime-green and fuchsia scatter cushions, to the yellow tub chairs either side of the bay window and the vases and trinkets dispersed around the room. It was an inviting, comfortable space for Mae and she hoped her guests felt the same.

'Take a seat.' Mae indicated the sofa, which, she now noticed, had a light film of short, dark hairs in one corner. That bloody cat! 'I won't be a minute.'

As much as the cat hairs bugged Mae, their removal would have to wait a moment as whipping the cushion

61

away would only draw more attention to them. Instead, while Melody settled herself, Mae dashed into the family room to grab her laptop. The family room had once been her grandparents' dining room, but when Mae opened the bed and breakfast, she'd wanted a space for herself and Hannah, a place separate from the guests, for them to relax in without having to share with strangers. As the kitchen was large enough to dine in, this seemed like the perfect solution. This room was smaller than the living room (and seemed smaller still as Mae's desk was squeezed into an alcove), but she'd made it a cosy space for them both. An old but sigh-inducing sofa took up the bulk of the space, with hand-knitted patchwork blankets draped over the back for chilly nights curled up in front of the telly.

'Here we go,' Mae said as she returned to the living room with her laptop. Thankfully, Melody had chosen the side of the sofa that hadn't been abused by the feline intruder, and Mae sat there now, cringing inwardly about the state her dress was going to be in when she stood up. 'I'll just take a few details and tell you a little bit about our bed and breakfast, and then I'll give you a quick tour and show you to your room.' Mae opened her laptop, which she'd already turned on at her desk, and clicked on her bookings file, deleting the Robertsons' data so she could add Melody's details instead. 'We're a small bed and breakfast – there are just two rooms available – and I live here with my four-year-old daughter, Hannah. She's upstairs, but I'm sure she'll make her presence known soon.' Luckily, Melody laughed and didn't run for the hills (or cliffs) at the prospect of cohabiting with a small child. 'Breakfast is available from seven, and there'll be a selection of fresh pastries, cereal, toast and fruit to help yourself to. There's a kettle in your room, but feel free to make tea or coffee in the kitchen too. I'll take you through in a moment and show you where everything is.'

Mae continued with the bed and breakfast details, making sure to include vital information such as the price per night, before taking down Melody's details and booking her in.

'How many nights were you planning on staying in Clifton-on-Sea?' she asked. 'The room is available for the next two weeks.'

'I'll only need a couple of nights,' Melody said. 'I'm sort of flitting from one town to the next.'

'Oh? Sounds interesting.'

'It's for a photography project.' Melody held up the camera dangling from the strap around her neck. 'I'm visiting as many coastal towns in the north as I can and capturing moments of the great British seaside.'

'That sounds wonderful. I'd love to see your photos so far.'

Melody's gaze dropped to her camera, her hair falling in front of her pink-tinged cheeks as she fiddled with the buttons. 'Um, maybe. I'm not sure if they're any good. I'm not a professional photographer or anything.'

'I'm sure they're amazing.' Mae smiled at Melody before closing the laptop and shifting it onto the coffee table. 'Shall I give you the brief but grand tour?'

Mae led Melody through the house, starting with the kitchen, which Mae adored. The room was large, with a light and airy feel due to the high ceilings and French doors that led to the garden at the back of the house. A long breakfast bar separated the kitchen and dining area, with four tall stools lined up along it.

'The breakfast things will be set out here,' Mae said, indicating the breakfast bar. 'But, like I said, feel free to make yourself a drink in here whenever you want. Make yourself at home, in here and the living room. There's just one room that's private down here.' Mae led the way out of the kitchen and indicated the family room. 'There's a bathroom upstairs, but your room is up in the attic and has its own shower room. Come up and have a look.'

Mae led the way up the stairs, pointing out the main bathroom before continuing up to the attic room. The room was gorgeous and cosy, with dove-grey walls and soft-blue furnishings. She'd managed to fit a double bed in the middle of the room, with built-in storage on one side and an en-suite shower room on the other. There was a dormer window at the back, with a sofa pushed along the wall, invitingly dressed with fluffy scatter cushions in shades of blue, pink and grey.

'I'll leave you to get settled in,' Mae said after the tour. 'Give me a shout if you need anything.'

Climbing down the attic stairs, Mae checked on Hannah, who had forgotten about the telly and was busy playing with her Shopkins figures in her bedroom. Mae had just returned to the kitchen and was about to put the kettle on when the doorbell rang and the bed and breakfast tour started all over again.

Chapter Nine

Melody

Melody hadn't been kidding when she told the landlady of the bed and breakfast she'd stayed in some grotty places over the last couple of weeks; there had been gloomy rooms, questionable stains on sheets, clogged plugholes and drains, and a general air of ickiness. But the Seafront Bed and Breakfast was truly beautiful. The rooms looked like lifestyle-magazine spreads come to life, but they had a homely, lived-in feel too. She'd been a bit apprehensive to begin with, stepping into such a luxurious home when she was feeling dishevelled – and, let's be honest, a bit sweaty – after her train journey and trek through town in the heat. But then she'd spotted the cat hairs on the sofa and felt more at ease. Any home owner who allowed their cat to laze on their posh sofa couldn't be too precious, so she'd been able to relax and sink into the sofa herself.

Melody's room was just as beautiful as the rest of the property. The room was tastefully – and thoughtfully – kitted out and the welcoming basket of goodies she found on the bed was a nice touch, as was the private shower room, which Melody made use of as soon as she'd unpacked her rucksack. She felt much better as she emerged from her room in a clean pair of shorts and a T-shirt. Heading downstairs, she found the landlady sitting in the kitchen with another woman. Both were perched at the breakfast bar with cups of tea and coffee in front of them.

'Melody, come and meet Willow,' Mae said, twisting on her stool to face her. 'She's just arrived too.'

'Hello.' Melody stepped towards the pair, holding out a hand for the new arrival to shake. But, completely ignoring the proffered hand, the woman hopped off her stool and threw her arms around Melody for a quick hug.

'It's lovely to meet you! Where are you from? How long are you staying?' Willow hopped back up onto her stool and patted the empty seat next to her. 'Come and sit with us and tell us everything.'

Melody hesitated. She'd been planning on heading out into town again, perhaps heading up the cliffs to take some photos of the town from up there. There were so many towns to visit, so many views and moments to capture, that she didn't really have time to sit and chat. She'd be returning home – and to her day job – in less than a week, so she had to squeeze every precious moment out of the next few days.

'I'll pop the kettle back on,' Mae said, sliding off her stool. 'Tea? Coffee?'

The cliffs could wait a few more minutes, Melody decided as she climbed up onto the stool. She was suddenly gasping for a cup of tea now the offer had been made. She hadn't had a cup since early that morning, before she'd checked out of the last bed and breakfast and hopped onto the train to Clifton-on-Sea.

'Tea would be great, thanks. Milk, no sugar.'

'Did you find everything you needed in your room?' Mae asked as she flicked the kettle on.

'Yes, thanks. The room's great – much better than all the others I've stayed in.'

A cautious smile teased the corners of Mae's pillar-box-red lips. 'Really?'

'Absolutely. You wouldn't believe some of the dumps I've stayed in. This place is amazing.'

'It really is,' Willow agreed. 'And I'm not just saying that because I've been living in a work site.' She explained about the work-in-progress state of her new house and the disastrous turn of events that day. 'I hope my house is half as nice as this place once we've finished.'

'I've seen some of your creations,' Mae said, placing a cup of tea in front of Melody and joining the ladies at the breakfast bar. 'Your house is going to be beautiful.'

'Creations?' Melody asked.

'I upcycle,' Willow explained. 'I take old, unloved objects and breathe new life into them.'

'She made a boat into a bed,' Mae said. 'It was incredible!'

'Incredibly heavy,' Willow said. 'Thanks for your help at the shop earlier, by the way. I don't know how Malcolm's going to manage once he gets it home.' Willow drained her cup of coffee. 'Speaking of the shop, I really should be getting back. It's been closed all day and I've got a delivery later.'

'I think I passed your shop earlier,' Melody said as Willow hopped off her stool. 'Up by the station?'

'That's it,' Willow said with a nod. 'I usually have an assistant, but he's not well so I had to close when the builder phoned with the impending doom news.'

'I'll try and pop in before I move on,' Melody said. 'Buy a souvenir or two, though perhaps not a boat bed. It might be a bit of a squeeze on the train.'

'I'm not sure it'd fit in the overhead compartment,' Willow agreed as she looped her handbag over her shoulder. She checked the time on the kitchen clock and pulled a face. 'Really sorry. Must dash, but we'll have a proper chat later.'

Melody nodded as she picked up her cup of tea, though she didn't commit verbally. She didn't want to appear rude, but she really was pushed for time and had a lot of work to do. She drank her tea quickly and then she, too, was on her way, her camera around her neck at the ready. The sun wasn't quite as intense now the afternoon was pushing on, but it was still hot as she made her way towards the cliffs. She found the path easily and followed it to the top, gulping down water due to the heat and steepness, until she reached the top.

The clifftop was covered in a carpet of grass, thistles and wild flowers, with a path worn through to the cliff's edge. As predicted, the view was amazing as she looked down onto the beach and the sea, with its frothy waves lolling towards the sand. The stretch of sand wasn't as busy now, but there were still plenty of families making the most of the good weather. She couldn't see the donkeys from earlier, but took a few shots of the beach, capturing the pier in the distance, before turning her attention to the town, snapping the rooftops, clusters of trees and cobbled streets. Once she felt she'd caught the essence of Clifton-on-Sea on a sunny late afternoon, she wandered to a bench set a safe distance from the cliff's edge and flicked through the photos, deleting any obvious duds before moving on to the next. There were some pretty decent shots already, but Melody knew she'd have to return to the clifftop to see the view at nighttime or before dawn. A shot at sunrise would be incredible and might be just the moment she was hoping to catch.

She'd scrolled back through her photos of Fleetwood a few days earlier, scrutinising the shots as best she could on the small screen of her camera, when a dog's bark made her look up. The clifftop had been deserted since her arrival but it seemed she now had company.

The bark came again before a small body bounded into view, the small golden ball of fluff hurtling towards her. It barked when it saw her – twice, in quick succession – and picked up speed until it stopped suddenly, plonking itself at her feet and giving a quieter woof of greeting.

'Hello again.' Melody reached down to stroke the dog on the head, giggling as he twisted his head so he could lick her hand. She recognised the dog from outside the fish and chip shop earlier, though he'd swapped his red tartan bandana for a bright yellow one. 'Aren't you a friendly chap?'

'He loves the ladies, the old charmer,' a voice said and, when Melody looked up, she groaned inwardly. It was the bloke from the ice-cream van. The bloke she'd spoken to briefly outside the fish and chip shop. The one who'd caught her talking to a dog. *His* dog, it transpired, judging by the lead dangling from his fingers. His dirty blond hair had been tied back earlier, but now the longish curls were free and dancing around in the breeze.

'Don't fall for it, though. He looks all adorable and sweet now, but wait until you find him with your favourite, *expensive* trainers in his gob.' He gave the dog a reproachful look before sitting down on the opposite end of the bench to Melody. 'Taking photos again? How do you want me?' He flicked one long leg up onto the bench and leaned back, pouting at her and, though she tried hard not to, Melody heard a giggle escape.

'You're not quite what I'm looking for,' she said.

'No?' He righted himself and leaned down to scratch the dog's ear. 'What are you looking for?'

'Just this.' She swept a hand out to indicate the view. 'The town. The seaside. The Britishness, I guess.'

'Got anything good?' he asked, nodding towards the camera, and she shrugged. 'Can I see?'

Melody switched the camera off and pulled it closer towards her body. 'I'd rather you didn't.'

He gave a lazy, one-shouldered shrug and leaned back against the bench. 'Fair enough.'

'It's just...' She frowned, wondering why she was explaining herself to this stranger who was managing to get on her nerves despite doing very little to justify it. 'I don't really show my photos to people.'

'Blimey, what kind of photos do you have on there?' He grinned at her, still lounging against the back of the bench. 'Now I'm even more intrigued.'

'Get stuffed.'

'Hey, I was only kidding,' he said as Melody rose from the bench. 'Don't go. I'll shut up, I promise. I won't say another word.' He mimed zipping his lips and Melody was annoyed further as she felt her lips pull up into a hint of a smile.

'Sorry, I'm not usually this touchy. It's just...' Melody lowered herself back onto the bench, her fingers fiddling with the camera as she tried to find the right words to excuse her grouchiness. 'My photos are sort of private. Not in *that* way. I just find it difficult to show people. It's daft, I know, and I'm working on it, but...' She shrugged. 'It isn't easy.'

She dragged her gaze from her camera to look at her bench companion, but while he was watching her intently, he was true to his word and didn't open his mouth.

'Your dog's very cute,' she said, blatantly changing the subject. She reached down to stroke him again and he sneaked another doggy kiss onto her hand. 'What's his name?' She scratched behind his ear, but looked up when she received no reply. Her companion raised an eyebrow at her and pointed at his closed mouth.

Crossing her arms, Melody sighed. 'Are you telling me your lips are still zipped?' He nodded and Melody rolled her eyes. 'Fine. You can unzip them now.'

Giving a closed-mouth smile, he reached for the corner of his mouth with a pinched-together thumb and index finger, but instead of sliding the fingers across his mouth, he gave a couple of short tugs before widening his eyes at Melody. He gave a few more tugs before he gave up and threw his hands up into the air.

'The zip's stuck, isn't it?' Melody asked, suppressing a sigh. He nodded before pointing first at Melody's hand and then at his mouth. 'You want me to help?' He nodded again and so, giving another eye-roll, Melody reached towards the guy's mouth, feeling like the biggest fool as she made a pincer movement with her finger and thumb. Grabbing her hand, he helped 'tug' the zip back across his mouth.

'Thank you,' he gasped, slumping against the bench.

'You're an idiot,' Melody said, but she was smiling.

'You're not the first to make that observation,' he said with a grin. 'Luckily, I'm also thick-skinned.' He reached down to give the dog some fuss. 'His name's Scoop Dog, in case you're still wondering.'

The giggle erupted without warning and Melody pushed a hand to her mouth to muffle it. 'Scoop Dog?'

'Scoop to his friends. He seems to like you, so Scoop it is.'

'Scoop as in ice-cream scoop?' Melody asked.

'We've found ourselves a clever one here, boy,' he told the dog, giving his head a good scratch.

'Hey.' Melody folded her arms across her chest. 'I could always zip you back up, you know.'

'Sorry.' He picked the dog up and sat him on his lap, giving his head another scratch. 'Let's start again. Meet Scoop, the bravest dog in Clifton-on-Sea, perhaps even the world.'

'Pleased to meet you, Scoop.' Melody gave the dog a stroke and received a lick in return. 'What makes him so brave, other than being seen out in public with a madman?'

'I'll ignore that last comment,' Scoop's owner said. 'And launch straight into the story of how Hugo – that's me – met Scoop Dog.'

Scoop, Melody learned, was a rescue dog who'd been found cowering in a bush, bloody and collarless, five months ago. He'd been savaged so badly by another dog – perhaps more than one – the vet wasn't sure the poor fella would make it. But after lots and lots of TLC – plus surgery and numerous stitches – Scoop had surprised the vet by making a full recovery.

'He has a bit of scarring,' Hugo said, lifting Scoop to show his underside. 'And his fur is only just starting to grow back on his neck.' He popped the dog back down and lifted the yellow bandana to show the patchy fur underneath. 'But other than that, he's on top physical form.'

'So how did you come to own him?' Melody asked.

'The vet's a mate of mine from the pub,' Hugo said. 'Scoop wasn't tagged and nobody came forward to claim him, so once he was ready to be rehoused, I asked to meet the little guy and that's how we became buddies.'

'You *are* brave,' Melody told the dog, stroking his golden fur. 'And lucky to have found a good bloke to look after you.'

'I thought I was an idiot,' Hugo said.

Melody shrugged. 'Against all the odds, you seem to have redeemed yourself.'

Chapter Ten

Willow

Willow had been eighteen when she met Ethan in a bar close to the university where they were both studying. She was in her first year, Ethan in his second, and they'd hit it off immediately, though just as friends. Willow had a boyfriend back home and Ethan was seeing a girl on his course, but even when she split up with Alex, the boyfriend from back home, it was Ethan's housemate she started seeing, beginning a not-very-serious five-month relationship. Through the relationship and subsequent break-up, Willow and Ethan remained good friends, and the friendship lasted until they went their separate ways after university. It was four or five years later that they met up again after one of the guys from their group of uni mates set up a reunion on Facebook. Willow hadn't really thought about Ethan all that much, to be honest, but as soon as she saw him again in the arranged bar, she knew they were meant to be together.

It was supposed to be simple from that moment on. Both single this time round, they started dating, fell in love and got married. But fairy tales were for children's books, and real life didn't have a guaranteed happy ending.

Willow was painfully aware of this fact as she looked up at her poor, scaffold-clad house, its fate unknown. They'd had such high hopes when they'd bought the house, when they'd moved their essential possessions into the little room at the back, the one requiring the least work that would become their living and sleeping quarters during the renovation. The little room Willow couldn't wait to decorate and fill with furniture she'd lovingly upcycled.

But now?

Maybe we shouldn't have bought this house. We should have thought about it more. Thought about us, our future.

Willow didn't know what was in their future now. She'd been so sure, naive perhaps, but she'd assumed their wedding day was the start of the life they both wanted, this house the setting, the anchor, a place to fill with beautiful memories.

At the moment, we don't even know what's in the future for us.

Pushing Ethan's words from her mind, Willow pulled away from the house, moving away from the dream home that was turning into a nightmare, and drove towards the harbour, where the new owners of the Monopoly table lived.

The shop had been pretty quiet for the rest of the afternoon, so Willow had managed to finish off her repurposed jam jars, though she'd really wanted to get stuck into the chest of drawers she was planning to update, as sanding it down would have been a great stress reliever. However, she couldn't commit to any of the bigger jobs without Gary around to keep an eye on the shop. She'd also used the quiet time to scour the local newspaper for any houses – or even single rooms – up for a short-term lease in the next couple of weeks but hadn't had any luck. She'd keep looking – she had little choice as she couldn't stay at the bed and breakfast long term. She'd been lucky to secure the room for a couple of weeks in the first place.

Once she'd closed up at the end of the day, she'd loaded the Monopoly table and chairs into the van with the reluctant help of the bloke from across the road (who'd complained about missing his gaming time non-stop, right up until the moment Willow handed over a fiver for his help). She'd taken a massive detour to catch a glimpse of the house, desperate to cling on to a tiny shred of hope, to feel the same elation as when they'd bought the property. Instead, she'd been left feeling lost, confused and slightly sick.

The family were delighted with their new purchase and the children set up a game of Kerplunk as soon as the table was set down in the playroom. A smile twitched at Willow's mouth as she watched them thread the straws through the holes, little tongues poking out from their lips in concentration, the smile spreading slowly across her face until her cheeks started to ache.

'I think they approve,' the mum said, also smiling as she watched her children. 'Thank you so much.'

Willow cleared her throat and nodded, already backing out of the room. 'It was a pleasure. I hope you have lots of fun with it.'

Saying goodbye to the family, Willow hopped back into the van and headed to the bed and breakfast. She usually kept the van near the shop, preferring to walk to and from work, but she was tired after a day of running around, and the thought of trekking through town didn't fill her with any sort of enthusiasm. She'd go back to the B&B, enjoy a soak in the bath, phone Ethan and then have an early night. She yawned at the thought of crawling into the sumptuous bed at Mae's place, at snuggling beneath the smooth sheets and sinking into the soft pillows.

Mae was in the kitchen, singing quietly to the radio as she stirred a pan of something delicious-smelling on the stove, when Willow arrived back at the bed and breakfast. Willow's stomach growled at the hint of food and she suddenly realised she was ravenous. When was the last time she'd eaten? She'd had a pastry that morning during her walk to work, but had she eaten since? She thought back over the day and realised she hadn't, so it was no wonder her stomach was protesting.

'Oh, hello.' Mae stopped stirring and placed a hand on her chest. 'I didn't hear you come in.'

'Sorry, didn't mean to make you jump,' Willow said. 'I was just wondering if it was okay to commandeer the bathroom? I could do with a soak after the stressful day I've had. I won't hog it for too long, I promise.'

'Of course,' Mae said. 'Would you like to join us for dinner first? It'll be ready in a few minutes.'

'That's really kind, but I wouldn't want to put you to any trouble.' Willow ignored her stomach as it roared in protest.

'It's no trouble at all. It's only spaghetti Bolognese and I always end up making way too much. I don't know how it happens: I put the right amount of spaghetti in the pan, yet enough comes out to feed Italy.' She shrugged and picked up the spoon to give the sauce another stir. 'It'll be nice to have some adult company, actually. That's if you don't mind eating with me and Hannah. I must warn you – she can be a bit of a chatterbox at times.'

'I wouldn't mind at all. It sounds lovely.'

'Then sit down and relax.' Mae indicated the table. 'Shall I open a bottle?' She grabbed a bottle of wine from the rack integrated into the kitchen units and held it up.

Willow waved her hands in front of her. 'Not for me, thanks. Red wine always gives me a terrible headache.'

'I can open white instead,' Mae said, already slotting the red back into place.

'I'm fine with water, really.' Willow sat down at the table. 'You go ahead, though. Don't let me spoil your evening.'

'I'm probably better sticking to water too, actually.' Instead of reaching for the bottle of white, Mae moved across the kitchen and grabbed three plates from a cupboard. 'A hangover with a child who seems to think jumping on your bed before dawn is acceptable isn't such a good idea.'

'No, I'd imagine not.'

'She's great, though,' Mae said, opening a drawer and grabbing three sets of cutlery. 'Drives me up the wall sometimes, but I wouldn't be without her.' She placed the cutlery on top of the plates and carried them over to the table.

'Let me do that,' Willow said, rising from her seat. She took the plates and cutlery and set them out on the table while Mae grabbed glasses and filled them with water, still chatting away.

'I never really thought about having kids before Hannah came along. I was happy being free to go out there and do what I wanted, when I wanted. I suppose I thought I'd have a family one day, just so far into the future I didn't have to think about it. I never thought for one minute I'd end up having a baby, on my own, at twenty-six.'

'So Hannah's dad isn't around?' Willow asked and Mae shook her head.

'I haven't heard from him since I broke the news I was pregnant.'

'What a tosser,' Willow said. She didn't know the man, but she despised him immediately. How dare he leave Mae – or *any* woman for that matter – to shoulder sole responsibility for a child *he* helped to create. And what sort of scumbag abandons their child?

'I'm probably better off without him,' Mae said as she added the glasses of water to the table. 'But it isn't fair on Hannah. She doesn't really understand why some of her friends live with their dad and she doesn't.'

'You're doing a great job, though.' Willow didn't really know Mae, but she seemed to have her life sorted. Her house was immaculate, her little girl was delightful, judging from the brief encounter they'd had earlier, and Mae herself was so poised and polished.

'I have a great support network,' Mae said as she returned to the stove. 'My mum is fantastic. I don't know what I'd do without her, to be honest. She's a school librarian, so luckily she can look after Hannah for me during the school holidays and at weekends. And then there are Hannah's godparents, who are amazing, and Mrs Hornchurch from next door is happy to step in and help in an emergency. I'm so lucky to have them.'

Mae did sound lucky, despite her useless ex. For a moment, Willow imagined what it would be like switching places. Would she be happier in Mae's shoes? Her slingbacks didn't look particularly comfy, but then Willow was more used to ballet pumps and trainers. She wasn't glamorous like Mae – the lovely dress she was wearing now would be ruined after a day in Willow's workroom – but there were aspects of Mae's life that Willow was sure would be a perfect fit.

The doorbell ringing nudged her out of her musings. Mae headed for the door while Willow took a sip of her water. She didn't really want to switch lives with Mae, but sometimes the grass *did* seem lush and green on the other side, especially when you were feeling low.

'Hello again.'

Mae had returned to the kitchen with a man in tow. Willow frowned at him, wondering why he looked vaguely familiar. Had he been in the shop recently?

'Sorry, we met in the pub earlier. Local vet, bloke with a bag of chips?'

Ah, yes. Willow remembered now.

'This is Alfie,' Mae said. 'He helped me track you down this afternoon.'

Willow flashed a grateful smile. 'Thanks for that. I don't know what I would have done if Mae hadn't offered me the room. I'd probably be staring at a pile of canvas and poles, wondering why they didn't look like a tent.'

Alfie laughed. 'I have to admit, erecting tents isn't really my thing either. Camping in general has little appeal, actually.'

Willow shuddered. 'Just think of the bugs. Ugh.' She shuddered again before turning to Mae. 'I really can't thank you enough.'

Mae gave a wave of her hand. 'There's really no need. It's what I'm here for.'

There was a series of thumps from the hallway before Hannah bounded into the room, throwing herself at Alfie, who scooped her up and held her wriggling body in the air, the kitchen filling with the girl's happy squeals.

'Put me down, put me down!' she demanded, but as soon as Alfie returned her feet to solid ground, she demanded he do it again. Which he did, three times. Willow watched, amused by the game.

'No more now,' Mae said when Hannah insisted on another go. 'It's dinner time, little lady. Go and sit down, please.'

'Aww, no fair.' Hannah's whole body seemed to slump as she made her way to the table. She clambered onto one of the chairs and picked up a fork, twisting it this way and that so it shone in the light. 'Is Alfie having tea with us?'

'Oh. I'm not sure. That wasn't the plan, but there's plenty. If you'd like to?' Mae looked flustered as she spoke to Alfie, her cheeks taking on a reddish tinge, her hands taking on a life of their own as they flapped about.

'Thanks, but I should be getting back to the surgery,' Alfie said. 'I have a few late appointments. I just wanted to pop over and make sure everything was okay after this afternoon. We'll have dinner another time, though. When it's planned and not sprung on us by this very cheeky little monkey.' He tickled Hannah, making her giggle, before turning to Willow. 'It was nice to see you again. I'm glad it all worked out.'

Hannah leaned in towards Willow as Mae led Alfie out of the kitchen.

'That's Alfie,' she whispered. 'He wants to kiss my mummy.' She giggled while Willow sneaked a look towards the hallway, but Mae and Alfie were out of earshot. 'I heard Aunt Corinne tell Mummy that he's a good man, but Mummy said she doesn't need him. I think that's because Alfie's a vet and we don't—'

'What are you whispering about over there, little lady?' Mae asked, suddenly appearing back in the kitchen and making both Willow and Hannah jump.

Hannah threw herself back in her seat. 'Nothing.'

'Hmm.' Mae cocked an eyebrow at her daughter. 'I hope you weren't gossiping over there.'

'Nope,' Hannah said, smiling sweetly.

'Good, because I'd hate it if it slipped out who I saw you sharing a packet of sweets with in the school playground on the last day of term...'

'*Mu-um*.' Hannah covered her face with her hands while Mae giggled.

'You thought I hadn't seen, but mums know *everything*.'

'It was just a packet of sweets,' Hannah said. 'I don't want to be his *girlfriend*. Ugh!'

'Then why are you blushing?' Mae teased.

'I'm not,' Hannah said while covering her hot cheeks with her little hands. 'Can we shut up about Jack now?' Her eyes widened while Mae burst out laughing at Hannah's slip-up.

Willow sat back, surveying the scene between mother and daughter. She had no doubt life could be tough for a single mum, but Mae seemed to be doing a wonderful job and taking it all in her stride. Willow was terrified at the mere thought of a life without Ethan by her side, but here was Mae, getting on with her life, despite the setbacks.

She wasn't simply lucky, Willow thought. She was strong and determined and in control, and Willow only wished she had a tiny scrap of Mae's capabilities.

Chapter Eleven

Melody

Melody somehow found herself sitting in the pub with Hugo, two pints sitting on the table in front of them and Scoop curled up by their feet. One minute they'd been up on the clifftop, Hugo annoying the hell out of her, and the next they were strolling down to the harbour, though Melody had been in search of a photo opportunity rather than a cosy night in the pub with this strange man and his dog.

'You're not originally from round here,' Melody had guessed as they'd strolled along the main road into the harbour earlier. 'Your accent reminds me of… someone.'

Hugo had slid his gaze sideways towards Melody, but she didn't elaborate. 'I'm from Manchester, but I've been living here for the past five years.'

Melody nodded. Ollie had been from Manchester too. 'What brought you to Clifton-on-Sea?' Hugo glanced at her again with a smirk, and all became clear. 'Ah, a girl.'

Hugo sighed dreamily. 'Yup, a girl.'

'Are you still with her?'

Hugo laughed. 'She dumped me three weeks after I moved here to be with her.'

'Ouch.'

Hugo gave a gentle tug on the lead as Scoop started to scrabble towards the road. 'Ouch indeed.'

'But you stayed here anyway?'

'I'd fallen in love again.'

Melody turned to Hugo, an eyebrow quirked in either shock or admiration – she wasn't sure which.

'But not with another girl,' Hugo said. 'With Maisy.'

Maisy sounded like a girl to Melody. She frowned, trying to figure it out.

'Don't look so confused,' Hugo said. 'You've met Maisy.'

'I have?'

'Yup, and she's a beauty.'

'I thought Maisy wasn't a girl.'

'She isn't.' Hugo gave another gentle tug on the lead, steering Scoop away from the kerb. 'She's an ice-cream van.'

Oh God. Melody felt a little bit queasy. 'Are you *in a relationship* with Maisy?' She'd watched a documentary about these fetishes a couple of years ago, her face pressed into Ollie's shoulder to shield her eyes as blokes did unthinkable things to their cars. Ollie had found the whole programme hilarious while Melody had felt grubby and quite sick.

'You what?' Hugo threw back his head and roared with laughter. 'Jesus, woman, no. Yes, I like to enter her, but not like that.' Hugo laughed again and wiped tears of mirth from his eyes with his free hand. He looked at Melody and cracked up again, spluttering about ice-cream-van love.

'All right, all right, I get it.' Melody gave Hugo a nudge with her elbow, but she was laughing herself now. 'But you did say you fell in love with it.'

'*Her*,' Hugo corrected. 'Not it.'

Melody tutted. 'Shut up.'

'But yes, I did fall in love with her – *in a non-weirdo-sexual way*. I'd spotted her dumped up by the caravan site, wasting away and rotting. So I found out who owned her and bought her before restoring her to her original beauty. My brother's a mechanic, so he came over to help and ended up staying to set up the business with me.'

'So you make the ice cream yourself?' Melody asked, remembering the cold, creamy ice cream on her tongue. It was by far the most delicious ice cream she'd ever tasted.

'Ice-cream making is in my blood,' Hugo said. 'My grandparents on my mum's side are Italian. We spent every summer in Florence when I was a kid, helping out in their ice-cream parlour. It was only a tiny place, but really popular. I loved it.'

'So you went into the family business,' Melody said.

Hugo shrugged. 'Sort of, yeah.'

'But how do you make a living when it isn't summer?' Melody asked. 'I mean, it's pretty busy now, but I'm guessing there isn't much trade on the seafront during winter.'

'No, but then we're mobile. We go where people need us. We're pretty popular with wedding receptions and parties. The local church hired us for their Christmas fair last year. We made festive flavour ice creams – mince pie, Christmas pudding, gingerbread, that kind of thing – and they were such a hit, we were booked again for the following Christmas before we'd even finished for the day.' Hugo pointed ahead to the harbour wall and they crossed over, peering over into the water where the boats were bobbing gently on the current. Melody made an immediate grab for her camera, taking a step back to line up the perfect shot.

'So, what about you?' Hugo asked, once Melody had stopped clicking. 'If this isn't your job…' He indicated the camera. 'Then what do you do?'

'Who says this isn't my job?' Melody asked, jumping down from the harbour wall, where she'd perched to take a few photos from a different angle.

'You did.'

'Did I?' Melody didn't recall divulging any personal information.

'You said you don't show your photos to people,' Hugo reminded her. 'I'm no expert on photographers, but I'm pretty sure it's in their job description to show them off.'

Melody narrowed her eyes. 'Are you an ice-cream-van man or a detective?'

'I prefer to think of myself an ice-cream connoisseur.' Hugo had adopted a serious expression, but he couldn't hold it for too long and his face broke into a smile once again and he shrugged. 'I guess I'm a good listener. So, what is it? No, wait! I know what you are.' He nodded slowly. 'You're a nurse.'

'A nurse? You've met me. Do you think I really have the right temperament to be a nurse?'

'I didn't say you were good at your job.' Hugo grinned, already sidestepping to avoid a thwack. 'Besides, it's creating the most amazing mental picture.'

Melody folded her arms across her chest. 'I'm not a nurse.'

'Flight attendant?'

'I hate flying.'

'Police officer?'

'Nope.'

'Firefighter?'

'Stop naming jobs that require uniforms.'

'Lifeguard? Please tell me you're a lifeguard who wears a *Baywatch*-style red swimsuit.'

'Purlease.'

Hugo sucked in his breath and his eyes lit up. 'Lollipop lady?'

Melody screwed up her mouth to stop a giggle from escaping. 'You're a strange man.'

'I am, but we still haven't established what you do for a living.'

'I'm an admin assistant at a solicitors' firm. No uniform. No glamour.' Melody scrunched up her nose. 'No fun or creativity. I have a lovely boss, though, so I'm lucky.'

'But you're not doing a job you love.'

Melody shook her head. 'How many people get that luxury?' She rolled her eyes when Hugo thrust a thumb at his own chest. 'Smug git. You can buy me a pint to make up for reminding me how shitty my life is.' She pointed across the road to the Fisherman. Which is how she'd ended up sitting in the pub with Hugo.

He was actually good company, now she'd allowed herself to enjoy his presence rather than being irritated by it. He made her laugh with his weirdness and tales from the ice-cream van trade, and she started to relax and open up a bit more about her own life, though she steered away from Ollie and the reason she'd set off on her seaside adventure.

'Another?' Hugo asked once they'd finished their pints, and Melody was surprised to find she wasn't desperate to escape back to her room at the bed and breakfast. She realised she was actually having fun with Hugo, which brought a pang of guilt, jabbing her in the chest and settling uncomfortably in her stomach. There was something else there too, a faint twinge of longing for the life she'd once had. A life crammed with fun, with nights out in the pub, chatting and laughing and feeling alive. But she couldn't dwell on the past. Remembering was too painful.

'I'd better be getting back,' she said, already scraping back her chair. 'Early start in the morning and all that.'

'I'll walk back with you,' Hugo offered, and Melody found herself accepting gratefully. She wasn't confident she'd find her way back to the bed and breakfast easily, plus she wasn't quite ready to end their evening, though she felt selfish for it and the guilt gave her another stab as punishment.

Scoop, who'd been enjoying a snooze under the table, snapped to attention as Hugo stood, alert and ready for action instantly. Melody took the lead and guided the dog out of the pub, but paused as she stepped outside and looked across at the harbour. It was growing dark, the sea turning inky rather than its usual grey, with the lights from the pub and other nearby buildings shimmering on the surface.

'Would you mind if we stopped for a minute?' she asked, itching to reach for her camera and capture the moment.

'Go ahead.' Hugo, who had followed Melody's gaze and knew what she needed to do, reached for the dog's lead, following as she headed across the road to the harbour wall.

'It's gorgeous, isn't it?' Melody said as she climbed up onto a bench for a slightly higher viewpoint. 'I can see why you decided to stick around, Maisy aside. I bet there's loads I haven't even seen yet.'

'There's so much more,' Hugo said. 'You should go down to Chapel Cove. It's so quiet and peaceful. It's one of my favourite places. And Scoop's.'

'Chapel Cove,' Melody mused. 'Where is it?'

Hugo pointed further down the coast. 'About a mile and a half that way. I could take you, if you'd like. I'm not working until the afternoon tomorrow, so we could head up there in the morning with Scoop. He'd love it.'

Melody hopped down from the bench. She hadn't planned on befriending any locals on her travels, but Hugo could prove invaluable. What if she found the perfect spot at this cove? Plus, she was unable to prevent herself from thinking, she'd like to spend more time with Hugo. The stab of guilt made itself known in response, overriding any other feelings she might have.

'I'm not sure I have time,' she said, reaching for Scoop's lead and wandering away from the harbour wall. 'I'm only staying for a couple of nights and I was hoping to explore more of the main beach and the pier. But thanks for the offer. It's very kind of you.'

'No problem. Just give me a shout if you manage to find a bit of free time. You know where to find me.'

'In your *lurve* machine,' Melody said with a giggle.

'Hey.' Hugo adopted a mock-stern expression. 'Don't cheapen what Maisy and I have and make it sordid.'

Melody cleared her throat to kill the giggles. 'Sorry. Do you want me to zip my lips together?'

'Nah. You can make it up to me by telling me all about your job as a lifeguard.'

'I'm not a lifeguard,' Melody pointed out.

Hugo gave a one-shouldered shrug. 'Make it up. And be specific about the little red swimsuit.'

'You're a fucking pervert, do you know that?'

Hugo grinned. 'Yes.'

'I'm glad I decided not to go to that cove with you now,' Melody said. They'd moved past the Fisherman and were heading back along the main road back into town. 'You'd probably have pretended to drown so I'd give you the kiss of life.'

'Or I could have just done this,' Hugo said before stepping in front of Melody and kissing her on the lips. It was a brief kiss, no more than a peck and definitely without tongues, but Melody was stunned. Her feet froze on the ground, her eyes wide as their lips made fleeting contact. Hugo turned, striding off along the path again as though nothing had happened, leaving Melody to scuttle after him with the dog.

'Do you always go around planting uninvited kisses on women?' she asked, swiping a hand across her mouth, ignoring the butterflies swarming in her stomach.

Hugo narrowed his eyes and looked up at the darkening sky before shaking his head. 'No, you're the first. Unless you count Nicola Smart. We were six and she ratted on me to the dinner lady. I didn't kiss another girl until I was fifteen.'

'Fifteen? Really?' Melody had caught up to Hugo and was now walking alongside him. She flashed him a sceptical look.

'Yes, fifteen. I haven't always been the self-assured man you see before you now.'

'Self-assured is one word for it, I suppose,' Melody muttered. The butterflies were still fluttering in her stomach, though at a less frenzied rate now, but she still wouldn't acknowledge them. She felt guilty enough being with Hugo in the first place, and that was before he'd kissed her.

Chapter Twelve

Mae

Once they'd eaten, Willow insisted on washing the dishes while Mae took Hannah upstairs for a bath. The kitchen was gleaming by the time Mae and a fruity-smelling and pyjamaed Hannah returned.

'You didn't have to do all this,' Mae said. Not only had Willow washed the dishes, she'd dried them and put them away before giving the worktops and top of the stove a thorough clean, removing any hint of sauce splashes.

'Are you kidding me?' Willow said. 'I haven't had a kitchen of my own to clean for weeks. It was a treat.'

'So you don't have a kitchen at all at your new place?' Mae asked as she flicked on the kettle.

'Not much of one, no.' Willow climbed onto a stool at the breakfast bar with a weary sigh. 'We have an old sink still in there, but it's certainly seen better days and I can't wait to rip it out and put a nice new one in. But at least we have running water.'

Mae selected a couple of mugs from the cupboard and turned to frown at Willow. 'How do you cook?'

Willow pulled a face. 'We have a little portable hob and a microwave, so we have to be a bit creative with those.

It all seemed so romantic when we moved in, but living on a building site with all the dust isn't fun and you do miss the homely touches and comforts, like a hot bath. We only have a temperamental old shower we've nicknamed Groucho because of the racket it makes at the moment. Would you mind?' She flicked her gaze towards the ceiling. 'I've been dreaming of soaking in a bath for weeks now.'

'Go ahead,' Mae said. 'Enjoy.'

'Oh, I will,' Willow said, giving a happy little squeal and rubbing her hands together. She practically leapt off the stool and scurried out of the room and up the stairs.

'She's a strange lady,' Hannah whispered once the footsteps on the stairs had faded away.

'Is she?' Mae asked. She quite liked their new guest. She was down to earth and friendly and Mae had enjoyed having adult company that evening, having somebody to share a meal with whose conversations didn't revolve around animated TV characters, Shopkinsh figures, and their desperate need to adopt a scruffy cat. Of course she loved Hannah with every cell in her body, but she sometimes craved grown-up companionship and, although she usually had a house full of people, being a single mum could be lonely at times.

'I *hate* having a bath,' Hannah said as an explanation of Willow's weirdness. She wrinkled her nose to illustrate her distaste. 'It's all wet and you get wrinkly fingers and you make me wash my face.'

'Don't you want to be clean?' Mae asked and Hannah gave a firm shake of her head.

'I like being dirty and smelly.'

'But your friends at school wouldn't like sitting next to you if you were stinky.'

Hannah shrugged her shoulders. 'It's the summer holidays. I don't need a bath until I go back to school.'

Mae laughed and crossed the kitchen so she could pull her daughter in close, sniffing her raspberry-and-apple-scented hair. 'Not going to happen, little lady. Everybody has to have a bath.'

'Chilly doesn't have to,' Hannah said.

'Chilly?' Mae frowned. 'From *Doc McStuffins*? Well, no, he doesn't have to have a bath because he's a stuffed toy. He might sometimes have to go in the washing machine, though.'

Hannah dropped her little face into her hands and shook her head. 'Not *that* Chilly. *Our* Chilly.'

'Who?' Mae didn't know any other Chilly.

'The cat. I named him Chilly.'

'No, no, no.' Mae shook her head and folded her arms across her chest. 'No, Hannah, you are not naming that cat. He isn't *our* cat, and never will be. Get that idea out of your head right now.' She was about to explain the reasons behind her anti-cat stance, mainly that she was too busy looking after Hannah and working two jobs to take on another dependent, when the door opened and their second guest stepped into the room, her cheeks flushed from the cooler evening.

'Did you find what you were looking for?' Mae asked Melody, who'd explained earlier about the view she'd been hoping to capture from the clifftop. It had been Mae who'd pointed her in the direction of the right path.

Melody picked up her camera, which was, as ever, looped around her neck. 'I think so.'

'You don't sound too sure,' Mae said.

Melody ran her thumb over the power switch, but didn't switch the camera on. 'It's just…' She shook her head and flopped onto one of the chairs at the table. 'I'm sure I've taken some beautiful photos, but I don't think I've quite got *the one* yet. I thought I'd know. That I'd feel it.'

'And you haven't yet?'

Melody shook her head. 'I can't have.'

'Maybe you'll find it tomorrow,' Mae said. 'You'll have the whole day to explore. Clifton-on-Sea really is a wonderful place.' Despite being eager to escape in her teens, Mae had grown to appreciate the town's positive points and wouldn't have wanted to bring her daughter up anywhere else.

'Do you know anything about Chapel Cove?' Melody asked and Mae nodded.

'It's quite a bit off the usual tourist routes, but it's a lovely little place. There isn't much there – no arcades or pubs – but it's great if you want a bit of peace and quiet.' Mae smiled, her mind wandering away to memories of long ago. 'Or if you're a teenager wanting a bit of time away from your parents. I had my first kiss behind the tearoom that used to be there.'

Hannah screwed up her face and stuck her tongue out. 'Eww, *mu-um*. Kissing's yucky.'

'It is, isn't it?' Melody agreed. 'Boys should keep their lips to themselves.'

Hannah gave a solemn nod. 'Riley Watson-White tried to kiss me once. It. Was. *Horrible*.' She stuck out her tongue again. 'So I stamped on his foot and ran away.'

'You go, girl.' Melody raised the palm of her hand and Hannah giggled as their palms made contact in a high-five.

'Alfie wants to kiss Mummy, but she won't let him either,' Hannah said, which made Mae's eyes widen. 'I don't think she's stamped on his foot, though.' Hannah looked to her mum for confirmation, but Mae was too gobsmacked to speak.

'Ooh, I sense a bit of juicy gossip.' Melody leaned forward in her chair. 'Come on, spill.'

Mae shook her head. 'There's nothing to tell. There's certainly been no kissing.'

'But he does like you?'

Mae wasn't really comfortable discussing her love life – what little of it there was to discuss – in front of her daughter, so she decided to engineer a swift subject change.

'We're just friends.' She turned and pulled open a drawer, grabbing a couple of teaspoons. 'Cup of tea?'

'I'd love one,' Melody said, but, from her tone, Mae knew the subject of Alfie hadn't been swerved. She remained silent as she made the drinks, hoping Melody would have forgotten about it by the time she was finished. To make sure the topic moved on, she created a new one as soon as she placed the mugs down on the table.

'So, your photos...' She dropped into a neighbouring chair, avoiding eye contact with Melody. 'You said you wanted to capture British seaside moments for a photography project, but you didn't go into detail.'

'Didn't I?' Melody started to fiddle with her camera, turning it over in her fingers. 'I guess I've just always enjoyed the beach and want to show why.'

'But what's the project for?' Mae asked. 'Yourself? Or something professional?'

Melody removed the camera from around her neck, setting it down on her lap. 'I'm thinking of entering them into a festival. You get to display your work – possibly even sell it – and enter a couple of competitions.'

'Wow, that sounds exciting,' Mae said. 'Good luck!'

Melody returned the camera to its position around her neck. 'Thanks, but I don't think I've got much chance of winning.'

'Why not?'

She shrugged. 'I'm not a professional photographer or anything. It's just something I do for fun. The other people taking part will be really talented.'

'And who says you're not really talented too?'

Melody shrugged again. 'I don't really show my photos to people, so I haven't had much feedback.' Melody glanced up from her camera, her eyes flicking around the room. 'I really love this house. Have you always wanted to run a B&B?'

Mae spotted the blatant conversation swerve, but she let it pass as Melody was obviously as reluctant to discuss her photography as Mae was to chat about Alfie.

'It's been my dream ever since I was a little girl. My mum and I stayed in one when I was a bit older than Hannah. We didn't go far – only a short train ride away to Blackpool – but I loved it. The couple who ran the B&B were so nice and I got to share a big bed with Mum. Mum and Dad had been arguing a lot back then, so it was nice to get away, just the two of us. Not long after, Dad moved out and it was just the two of us all the time, but it wasn't the same. Mum was obviously sad and I was confused about why my dad wasn't there any more, so that time away at the bed and breakfast felt almost magical. The feeling stayed with me, and I dreamed of running my own, even though it never seemed possible. Then, when I inherited this house and moved in with Hannah, it seemed like the ideal solution. I needed to work around Hannah's needs, so it seemed like a good idea to let out the spare rooms. That was three years ago and I'm so glad I decided to go for it. I love it.' Mae felt a shiver of happiness. She didn't stop to appreciate the business she'd created enough, didn't congratulate herself on a job well done. 'I love meeting new people and feel like I'm making their holidays that bit more special. I can't imagine doing anything else.'

'I feel that way about photography,' Melody said. 'But I've never been brave enough.'

'It's tough to allow yourself to reach for your dreams sometimes,' Mae said. 'And I won't pretend I wasn't terrified of making a mess of everything, but sometimes you've just got to take that leap of faith, to believe in yourself and go for it. They say you only regret the things you *don't* do and I agree.'

Melody nodded, toying with her camera once more. 'I guess.'

'You're already taking the first steps towards your dream,' Mae said. 'By entering the photo festival, you're putting yourself – and your work – out there. So you're braver than you think.'

Mae felt like a bit of a fraud as she spoke those words. How could she encourage anyone to be brave when she lacked courage herself? Yes, she'd been brave with the bed and breakfast, but she shied away where it really mattered. Was she brave when she laughed and chatted with the strangers occupying her spare rooms before crawling into an empty bed, trying her best to ignore the vast space beside her? When she caught a glimpse of tenderness between Frank and Corinne – a hand on the small of a back, a hand held in the other's, a cheek resting on a shoulder – and yearned to share that closeness again? When she sat in the family room, on her own, with the whole evening stretching ahead of her, pretending she enjoyed her own company? She managed to hide behind the persona she'd created most of the time, but during those moments the mask slipped and the courage seeped away. Rather than feeling brave, she was afraid. But mostly, she was lonely.

Chapter Thirteen

Willow

The warm, bubbly water was glorious as Willow submerged herself up to her chin. She couldn't believe quite how much she'd missed a simple bath and how luxurious it now felt as she closed her eyes and allowed herself to relax. She pushed all thoughts of the house and the latest argument with Ethan from her mind and concentrated only on the slow breaths as her body unwound and unknotted itself.

Not wanting to hog the bathroom for too long, Willow dragged herself from the tub, wrapping herself in the towel she'd left warming on the radiator. Having a towel that wasn't covered in a thin layer of dust only added to the luxury.

Still wrapped in the towel, she scurried to her room to dry off and change into her pyjamas. She noticed a missed call from Ethan on her phone so, after securing her damp hair into loose plaits either side of her head, she settled herself on the bed and returned the call.

'Hey,' her husband said, his voice heavy and weary. 'Sorry it's taken me so long to get back to you. How is everything?'

Willow had updated Ethan about the housing situation through text messages over the course of the day, but this was the first time they'd spoken since Liam had dropped the bombshell that morning. She relayed everything she could remember, trying to keep the rising panic from her voice.

'So, it's bad,' Ethan concluded.

'Really bad.' Willow closed her eyes, imagining Ethan was sitting in the same room as her. She'd be able to deal with this whole situation a lot better if he were here with her. The argument last night – all of the arguments they'd had lately – didn't matter. 'Liam says we need to get a surveyor in to take a look before they get started. It's something to do with building regulations, but Liam said he'd sort it and get back to me.'

There was a sigh at the other end of the line, and Willow braced herself. 'This is going to cost thousands.'

'I know.'

'We don't have thousands,' Ethan said. 'Everything's already gone into the house. There's nothing left.'

Maybe we shouldn't have bought this house.

'We'll figure something out,' Willow said, but her voice lacked any sort of conviction because she didn't have a clue how they would ever claw their way out of this mess. How they'd get back on track. She lay back on the bed, her eyes squeezed shut. She missed Ethan and wished he was back home. Being apart didn't feel right. It was as though there was something missing; nothing as dramatic as a limb, but more like when you've gone out without your phone or a watch and you're slightly confused about what time it is. It was an odd feeling and not one Willow was familiar with.

'I'd better go,' Ethan said all too soon.

'I miss you.' Willow's grip tightened on the phone, as though she could keep hold of Ethan for longer that way. 'When will you be home?'

'I don't know,' Ethan said, and her heart sank. She wanted him to say he was on his way, right now, that he'd be back in a couple of hours. 'I'll phone you in the morning, okay?'

'Okay.' Willow sat up, the phone still pressed to her ear. 'I love you.'

'I love you too.' There was another sigh down the line. 'We'll get through this, Willow. We've faced worse.'

Hanging up, Willow grabbed her robe and threaded her arms through the sleeves, securing the belt around her waist. She'd heard voices downstairs when she emerged from the bathroom, laughter drifting up the stairs, so although she was sleepy after her bath, she thought she'd pop down for a few minutes before crawling into bed.

'Did you enjoy your bath?' Mae asked as Willow stepped into the kitchen. She and Melody were sitting at the table while Hannah watched from her position perched on a stool at the breakfast bar.

'I did, thanks.' Willow conjured a convincing smile. 'It was just what I needed after the day I've had. It was so relaxing, I almost fell asleep.'

'Speaking of sleep,' Mae said, standing and ruffling Hannah's hair. 'It's past your bedtime.'

'But it's the school holidays,' Hannah grumbled.

'I know, but you're going to Corinne and Frank's tomorrow. You don't want to be too sleepy for your day out, do you?'

The little girl shrugged, still not moving from the stool.

'Come on.' Mae held out a hand. 'Let's go and read a story.'

Hannah reached for the hand, but hesitated before making contact. 'Do I have to brush my teeth first?'

'What do you think, little lady?' Mae asked, which caused Hannah to emit a heavy sigh before she slipped down from the stool and trudged up the stairs. Willow watched them leave before turning to Melody with a wry smile.

'Do you remember when trying to get out of brushing your teeth was your biggest problem?'

Melody nodded, twisting the strap from her camera round and round her index finger. 'You think life is so unfair, but you have no idea.'

'None at all,' Willow agreed. 'Wouldn't it be nice to have that innocence back?'

'If only.' Melody unravelled the strap and wriggled the blood flow back into her finger. 'Things were much simpler back then. Easier. Being a grown-up actually sucks.'

Willow nodded and laughed. 'Why were we so desperate to grow up?'

'I don't know about you, but I was desperate to be grown-up so I could marry Freddie Prinze Jr.'

'It was Jordan Knight for me.' Willow smiled at the memory of her New Kids On The Block crush. 'We were going to get married and have five babies who would form a pop band when they were teenagers.' She sighed dramatically. 'Didn't happen.'

'You did get married, though,' Melody said. 'And there's still time to squeeze out your pop band.' Melody winced and crossed her legs. 'Five, though? Makes me want to swear off sex for ever.'

Willow sat down at the table and rested her chin on her hand. 'I don't know about that. I can't wait until Ethan comes back home. It's weird sleeping on my own.'

'Try being single for nearly a year,' Melody said with a sigh. 'I think I've forgotten how everything works.' She caught Willow's eye and they both giggled.

'You've seriously been single for nearly a year?' Willow asked. 'How? You're gorgeous.'

Melody batted away the compliment with a wave of her hand. 'I haven't really been interested in starting anything new after my last boyfriend.' Melody picked up her mug and drained the last of her tea. 'How long have you and Ethan been married?'

'We had our five-year anniversary last month.' Willow couldn't help smiling as she thought about the day they'd spent together. Gary had been relatively new at the shop, but he'd assured Willow he could cope on his own for the afternoon, so she and Ethan had spent a precious few hours together. With every spare bit of cash going towards the house, they hadn't been able to partake in anything too costly, so they'd simply enjoyed their local surroundings, taking on the role of tourists as they made their way along the promenade, stopping off at the pier and arcade before enjoying fish and chips on the beach, just as they had on their wedding day. They'd put aside their problems for the afternoon and had fun together for a change. It had been perfect.

'I've never even been in a relationship that lasted that long,' Melody said.

'You're still young. I didn't get together with Ethan until I was a little bit older than you. There's plenty of time.' Willow covered another yawn with the palm of her hand. The day was really taking its toll now.

Mae returned to the kitchen once Hannah was tucked up in bed, and washed and dried the mugs. The light through the French doors was starting to diminish as the sky darkened, so Melody suggested they move through to the cosy living room.

'Aren't you joining us?' Willow asked as they moved through the hallway. Mae had stopped at the family room and was about to push the door open.

'Me?' A smile flickered on Mae's face. 'Yes. Yes, of course. I'll be through in a minute.'

Willow followed Melody into the living room, holding in a dreamy sigh as she lowered herself down onto the sofa. At the new house, the airbed she and Ethan slept in also doubled up as a not-very-comfortable sofa, so the luxuries of the B&B kept adding up.

'Who fancies a drink?' Mae asked, stepping into the room and brandishing a bottle of wine.

'That'd be lovely,' Melody said, but Willow was already shaking her head, her mouth gaping into another yawn.

'Not for me, thanks. I really need my beauty sleep.' She forced herself from the sofa and stretched. 'Enjoy the rest of your evening.'

'Have a good sleep,' Mae said. 'See you in the morning.'

Willow felt weighed down as she climbed the stairs, so she was grateful to finally collapse into bed, barely having the energy to pull the covers over her body before she dropped off.

It took a moment for Willow to get her bearings when she woke just after seven the following morning, to work out why she was alone and why she appeared to be sleeping in a bed, with an actual mattress, rather than on the inflatable bed she'd become accustomed to over the past few weeks. As she stretched out, the events of the previous day seeped back into her brain. It was a pretty depressing chain of thoughts, but Willow wouldn't allow herself to succumb to the anxiety that was threatening to tie her stomach in knots. Ethan would be back soon and they would fix everything.

Peeling back the covers, Willow swung her legs out of bed and placed them on the floor, rather than carrying out the ungraceful roll from the inflatable mattress she was used to. The plush carpet, plus the lack of dust underfoot, was also a novelty as, back home, no matter how many times they swept the bare floorboards, there was always a layer of grit and grime wherever they went.

She wasn't the only occupant of the house awake as she could hear the faint sounds of a television downstairs as she padded her way to the bathroom with her washbag. She was so busy trying not to make too much noise as she tiptoed along the hallway, she almost didn't see a plastic dog slumped on its side in the middle of the floor. She sidestepped it just in time to stop herself from flying over it, the noise of which would no doubt have woken anybody who still happened to be sleeping. She righted the dog and moved it to one side, standing it against the skirting board where it would be less likely to cause an injury.

Once she was washed and dressed, Willow headed down to the kitchen where she found a selection of pastries and cereals laid out for her to choose from. She usually ate breakfast on the go, but she made herself a coffee and sat at the table with a buttery croissant smothered in strawberry jam. She'd just taken her first bite when she heard a scrabbling at the back door. Curious, she put her breakfast down, licking the sticky jam residue from her fingers as she made her way to the door. As soon as the door was open a crack, a black ball of fur catapulted itself into the kitchen, springing up onto the breakfast bar where it made a beeline for the pastries.

'No, no, no.' Willow quickly scooped up the cat, who gave a disgruntled mew at being thwarted. 'This isn't your breakfast. Shall we go and find Mae? See if she'll give you your breakfast? Because I have no idea where your things are.' She scanned the kitchen floor, but there wasn't a food or water bowl in sight. Willow, however, wasn't surprised. Mae's house was so immaculate, the cat's things were probably tidied away somewhere so they didn't clutter the kitchen.

With the cat tucked under her arm, purring as she stroked his head, Willow moved through to the living room, but Mae wasn't in there. She could hear the television sounds coming from the family room, but as that room was private, she didn't venture inside.

'I'm afraid you'll have to wait for your breakfast,' she told the cat as they returned to the kitchen. She set him on the floor and he wound around her legs as she made her way back to the table and her breakfast, making her giggle as his fur tickled her bare legs. He continued to rub himself against her as she sat at the table, constantly reminding her of his presence as she ate.

'Chilly!' Mae's daughter appeared in the kitchen doorway, her eyes lighting up when she spotted the cat pacing under the table. She scuttled into the kitchen, dropping to her knees so she could bundle his little furry body into her arms.

'I think he's hungry,' Willow said as Hannah planted kisses on the cat's head and neck. 'But I wasn't sure where you kept his bowl and food.'

'He has Frosties for breakfast,' Hannah said, marching over to the breakfast bar with the cat still dangling in her arms. His face was rather gloomy, but he didn't wriggle from Hannah's grasp. 'He sometimes has Coco Pops, but Frosties are his favourite.'

'Are you sure about that?' Willow didn't currently have a cat – she couldn't as the mere sight of a furry feline made Ethan's asthma flare up – but she'd had a couple at home growing up and they'd never fed them sugary cereal.

'Yup.' Hannah placed the cat on the floor and he started to wind his way round and round her little calves. 'He likes them.'

'Perhaps we should wait and see what your mum says,' Willow said as Hannah reached up on her tiptoes for the

106

box of cereal. Whether the cat liked cereal or not, it didn't seem like a good idea at all.

'Mum feeds them to him all the time.' Hannah reached into the box and pulled a handful out.

'I really think we should wait,' Willow said, but it was too late. Hannah tipped her hand over and the cereal rained down onto the floor. The cat wasted no time pouncing on them, wolfing down the flakes at an impressive rate.

'See?' Hannah pointed down at the cat as he attacked the final flake. 'He loves them.'

Willow's attention was drawn to her handbag under the table as it started to vibrate, her ringtone filling the kitchen with a cheery tune. The cat, having finished his unconventional breakfast, had slumped down on the floor, legs wide so he could lick himself, so Willow left him to it and went to answer the phone. Her stomach performed a happy little flip when she saw her husband's name on the screen.

'Good morning,' she sang, immediately forgetting about the kitty drama. She wriggled her fingers at Hannah in a wave before looping her handbag over her shoulder and grabbing her croissant. She'd have to eat on the go after all. 'It was so weird sleeping on my own last night, but I'd forgotten how comfortable a normal bed is.' She made her way along the hallway to the front door, shielding her eyes from the sudden sunshine as she opened it. She stepped outside and closed the door behind her. 'When the house is finished, we'll buy the biggest bed with the comfiest mattress. I'd forgotten how wonderful it is to wake up without a twisted spine from that stupid inflatable bed.' She headed down the path, well aware Ethan had yet to say a word, that she was waffling on and on. But she was afraid to stop, afraid of what Ethan would say when he finally did speak. 'We also need a bath. A big bath. In fact, that should be first thing on our list.'

'Willow…' Her body tensed at her husband's ominous tone. 'I've been doing a bit of research, and the work on the foundations is going to cost a small fortune, which you know we don't have.'

'But the work needs doing.' She'd reached the gate, which she swung open before stepping out onto the pavement and heading towards the van. 'The house won't be safe until it's done. We'll just have to cut back on other things.'

'Like a bed and a bath?' Ethan suggested. 'Or a new kitchen sink? Central heating? Any kind of flooring?'

'All right, all right, I get it.' Willow, having reached the van, yanked the door open.

'I don't think you do, Willow. We can't afford to do this work.'

'Then what do you suggest we do?' Willow threw herself into her seat and slammed the door shut. She waited for an answer, but none was forthcoming. She closed her eyes and took a deep breath, preparing herself for what was to come. 'You want us to sell, don't you?'

They'd argued about the house before – and not just the other night. Ethan had been as enthusiastic as she was about refurbishing the property to begin with, but lately he'd grown less passionate about the project, and it had nothing at all to do with the work involved.

'That would have been a solution a few months ago,' Ethan said. 'But at the moment, the house is in a far worse state than when we bought it. If we sell now, we'll make a loss.'

'So what else are we going to do?'

Ethan sighed. 'I honestly don't know. We're stuck.'

'There has to be a way,' Willow said, and Ethan sighed again, but the sound was angrier this time, more of a growl.

'Do you have to be so optimistic all the bloody time?'

Willow's eyes started to sting, tears threatening to spill at any moment. She wasn't usually prone to tears, but she hated fighting with Ethan.

'Would you rather I was negative and ready to give up?' she asked. 'Do you want me to cry and moan about our situation? To sink into depression because it isn't working out how we planned?'

'No, of course not.' Ethan's tone was softer now, but still the tears threatened to spill. 'I just wish you'd admit when we need help. We need to stop and think about the future instead of burying our heads in the sand.'

They were no longer talking about the house. Willow wasn't sure when the conversation had migrated from bricks and mortar to the problems in their relationship.

'My head isn't in the sand,' Willow said. 'I'm well aware things aren't working out. I'm simply not willing to give up as easily as you are.'

'I'm not giving up,' Ethan said. 'Far from it.'

'We need more time, that's all.'

'Maybe you're right,' Ethan said, but he didn't sound convinced. 'I have to go now. I'll call you later when I get the chance.'

After saying goodbye, Willow ended the call and slipped her phone into her handbag. She took a bite of her croissant, but found she'd completely lost her appetite. How had it all gone so wrong, so quickly?

Chapter Fourteen

Melody

With her camera looped around her neck, and a bottle of water and the tourist pamphlet she'd picked up at the train station yesterday in her rucksack, Melody set off in search of more British seaside moments. She was still curious about Chapel Cove, but as she couldn't find any information about it in the pamphlet and it didn't seem to be on any of the bus routes, she'd had to shelve the idea. Instead, she made her way along the promenade, the sun already warming her skin even though it was still quite early in the day. The shops on the front were starting to open, their shutters revealing windows full of the usual seaside fare: sticks of rock, buckets and spades, inflatable crocodiles, candyfloss, and cones of sweets tied with shiny, curling ribbon. Displays of postcards, magnets and keyrings were dragged onto the pavement, and you could already hear music blaring from the arcades and pier, with the occasional cry overhead from the seagulls as they searched for breakfast scraps, joining in the soundtrack of the seaside.

Melody raised her camera towards the pier, capturing the looming red-and-white-striped helter-skelter perched on top in the morning light. The town wasn't quite fully awake yet as the Ferris wheel had yet to commence its almost continuous turning, but the beach was already starting to collect families as they claimed early spots on the sand, setting out towels, books and sun cream, and baskets stuffed with picnic food. A couple of children were already braving the water, splashing and jumping over the sloshing waves as their skin took on a bluish hue. In the distance, strolling close to the shallows on a quiet part of the beach, Melody caught sight of a lone dog-walker. Though they were little more than blurred specks, she knew immediately it was Hugo and Scoop. Raising her camera again, she zoomed in to take a couple of shots as Hugo launched a ball into the water and Scoop bounded after it. She giggled as the dog trotted out of the water, dropping the ball by Hugo's feet before shaking himself dry. She clicked the shutter again, managing to catch the moment, smiling to herself as Hugo raised his hands in an attempt to protect himself from the spray.

Lowering the camera, she continued along the promenade, taking the odd photo whenever something caught her eye: a seagull snacking on an abandoned cone of chips, a display of shiny metallic pinwheels spinning in the breeze, a row of beach huts in a rainbow of colours. By the time she made it to the pier, the Ferris wheel was in motion, raising people up towards the sky before bringing them gently back down to earth. She purchased a ticket for herself, her camera at the ready as she climbed inside her designated compartment. From up high, she was able to snap a few decent photos of the beach and surrounding area.

Back on solid ground again, Melody explored the rest of the pier, documenting the other rides, fairground games and food stalls. It was still quite early, yet the smell of doughnuts frying in hot oil filled the air and, although Melody had eaten breakfast before she'd left that morning, her stomach rumbled. Resisting temptation, she moved away from the pier, crossing the street and heading into one of the arcades. The noise was almost overwhelming: the music, blasting so loudly it was on the brink of becoming uncomfortable, the chink, chink, chink of coins being spat from slot machines into the troughs beneath, and the general hum of numerous conversations and excited chatter. Melody allowed herself to be swept up by it all, stepping further into the darkened room illuminated by flashing screens and multicoloured lights. She snapped away, adding to the collection of childhood fun already stored on her camera. There were victories as two-pence pieces were shoved from their sliding trays, clattering into the troughs before being transferred into paper cups, their new owners grinning and cheering over their wins, which couldn't actually equate to more than twenty pence. And there were misfortunes as final coins were slotted into machines without payouts and tears as claws grabbed uselessly at stuffed toys with the promised prize failing to appear.

Melody moved on from the arcades, making her way along the parade of shops, picking out a postcard to add to the collection she had in her rucksack back at the bed and breakfast. She spotted Hugo's ice-cream van on the promenade and made her way over, but it wasn't Hugo's face she spotted in the hatch. He looked so similar with his dirty blond hair that Melody guessed it must be Hugo's brother, but the hair was closely cropped in place of the dishevelled curls Melody had seen the previous day on the cliffs. She bought an ice cream anyway, opting for a chocolate-orange cone and eating it as she made her way to the bed and breakfast. The memory card on her camera was filling up, so she'd transfer the images to her laptop before heading out again.

The bed and breakfast was empty, the house completely silent as she stepped into the hallway, and it felt strange as she made her way up the stairs of a stranger's home without any kind of supervision. She found herself creeping, as though she was about to burgle the place rather than heading up to a room she'd paid for. She made her way slowly and quietly up to her little attic room, easing the door open and wincing at the tiniest of sounds. As beautiful and homely as the house was, Melody didn't feel entirely at ease, but then she hadn't at any of the bed and breakfasts she'd stayed in during her travels. She hadn't felt at ease since she'd left her flat three weeks ago, closing the door on her possessions, her comforts, her life. Back home, everything had carried on as normal after Ollie: her mum and dad went out to work, her brother lounged around the house in his pants under the pretence of studying, her colleagues sat at their desks, her friends met up at the pub after a long day. The only place that had changed was her flat, which was sad and empty without Ollie, but at least it was reflecting Melody's own mood and she didn't have to try to pretend to be okay with what had happened. Pretending was exhausting, so Melody had plucked herself from the game, had taken herself off on this project, had escaped from it all, just for a little while.

She sat on the bed in her latest temporary room and pulled her laptop out of her rucksack, tearing into the cellophane-wrapped biscuits Mae had left in her welcome basket while she waited for it to load. She watched the screen, waiting for the punch in the gut as the desktop wallpaper appeared, unable to look away even though she knew it would ache. It would be easy to remove the photo, to select a different image to greet her every time she used her laptop, but she couldn't bring herself to remove any of the images of Ollie, no matter how much the reminders pained her. Removing the images would be like erasing Ollie from her everyday life, and she couldn't do that.

And then there they were: Melody and Ollie, arms thrown around one another as they grinned at the camera. They were at the top of the Empire State Building, but you couldn't really tell as their faces filled most of the screen for the selfie. It had been Ollie's dream to visit New York, to cram in the sights they saw regularly on TV and the big screen, and they'd done it together during a mad weekend filled with landmarks, subway rides, crazy cab drivers and stomach-clutching laughter. The days had passed in a blur. They hadn't been able to tick off everything on their list, and had never got the chance for a second go. But still, Melody would cherish the memories of that weekend. There was no way she could erase it.

Melody had transferred the photos and checked her emails when she heard the distant ringing of the doorbell downstairs. She froze, finger hovering over the trackpad, wondering what to do. Did she pop downstairs to answer a stranger's door? Or stay put until they went away? There was another ring, louder now she was listening out for it, and, decision made, she hurried down the two flights of stairs. She wasn't entirely comfortable with answering the door, but what if it was the postman with a parcel and she saved Mae from having to arrange redelivery or – worse – having to schlep over to the sorting office to pick it up?

Opening the door, slightly out of breath from the dash down from the attic, Melody was surprised to see Hugo on the doorstep and not a postman halfway through filling out a 'sorry you were out' card.

'Oh. Hello.' Melody hoped she didn't look flustered after the exertion of the stairs. She casually placed a hand on her cheek to check for any untoward heat or clamminess. 'Are you here for Mae or...?' She didn't want to presume he was here to see her, but Hugo hadn't mentioned he knew Mae when he'd walked her back to the bed and breakfast the previous evening.

'I was at a loose end so I thought I'd come and see if you needed a tour guide,' Hugo said. 'We could go down to the pier, or the beach. It's going to be a scorcher, so it'll be a good photo opportunity.'

'I've already been to the pier this morning,' Melody said. 'But I haven't seen the beach properly yet. I've only been as far as the railings.'

'You've already been to the pier today?'

Melody nodded. 'I went to the pier and the arcades and had a walk back down past the shops.'

Hugo's brow furrowed. 'But it isn't even ten o'clock. How did you do all that already?'

Melody shrugged. 'I just did.'

Hugo shook his head. 'You obviously didn't do it properly. Come on.' He cocked his head and started to back away from the doorstep. 'Let's go and do it right.'

Melody's mouth gaped open. The cheeky sod! 'I *did* do it right. I took some pretty decent shots, if you must know.' Melody wasn't one for blowing her own trumpet, but she was happy with her morning's work and there were a couple of strong contenders for the photo festival in there.

'I'm sure you did,' Hugo said. 'But that's not what I'm talking about. Why don't you leave your camera behind for an hour – two, tops – and experience the town through your actual eyes rather than a lens?'

Melody folded her arms, remembering how irritating she found this man. 'Because that's not what I'm here for.'

'You can't take a couple of hours off?'

Melody didn't have an answer. She'd never considered having an actual jolly. She was here to take photos. For Ollie. Enjoying a day at the beach rather than capturing other people's joy wasn't part of the plan.

'Come on,' Hugo coaxed, reaching a hand out towards her. 'Come and have some fun.'

Melody glanced at the hand before turning towards the staircase that led up towards her room and her camera. Fun. Could she do it? Could she leave her camera behind and forget about her promise? Forget about Ollie, even if it was only for an hour – two, tops? It had never occurred to her to experience the seaside towns for herself. It didn't feel right, not without Ollie there to enjoy it with her.

It suddenly seemed like a long, long time since she'd let go and allowed herself to have fun. Last night, at the harbour, she'd briefly felt a fluttering of her old self, the Melody she'd been before her safe, happy little bubble of life had burst. But that had crept up on her unexpectedly. Could she do it now, purposefully? Could she allow herself to be swept up by this man's enthusiasm? Would she be betraying Ollie if she stepped over the threshold with him now? It wasn't as though it would last; Melody was leaving in the morning, heading on to a new town, with new beaches and new moments to catch and savour. She could go with Hugo now, just for the tiniest amount of time, and see what Clifton-on-Sea had to offer. Ollie wouldn't object, wouldn't hold her back from clutching a little pocket of happiness, surely.

'Come on, Melody.' Hugo took a step closer, that hand just inches away from her now. 'Stop capturing moments with your camera and seize some for yourself.'

Melody pressed her lips together, her fingers clutching the doorframe, her head preparing to shake. She couldn't do this. It wasn't right.

But then, quite unexpectedly, her foot was on the doorstep, her hand was in Hugo's and the door was closing behind her.

Chapter Fifteen

Willow

Gary was waiting outside the shop when Willow turned onto Thorpe Lane, perched on the tiny doorstep, his long legs folded so his knees reached up to his chin. Despite his height and the fluff on his chin attempting to be facial hair, he looked like a lost little boy, waiting for someone to find him and take him home. Mind you, he sometimes had that look about him when he wasn't huddled on doorsteps. It had been his naive qualities that had endeared Willow to him when he'd answered the ad for the assistant's job. Fresh out of college and with no idea which direction to take now his education was over, Gary seemed to be floundering. He wasn't simply waiting to be nudged towards the next chapter of his life – he wanted a guided tour. And while Willow wasn't about to hold his hand and tell him what to do with his life, she did offer him the job. It was working out well so far: Gary was growing in confidence with the customers and his help was invaluable.

Willow eased the van into the lane beside the shop and headed round to let him inside.

'You're early,' she said when he jumped up from the doorstep so she could unlock the door. The shop wasn't due to open for another forty-five minutes and although Willow usually arrived early to set up and make an early start in the workroom, Gary wasn't expected to follow suit.

'I wanted to make up for yesterday,' he said as he followed Willow into the shop. She flicked on the lights, illuminating her collection of repurposed pieces.

'Don't worry about it. You can't help being ill.'

Gary scratched the back of his neck, turning to close the door as he mumbled, 'I suppose not.'

'I take it you're feeling better now?' Willow asked as she moved across the shop to the counter, taking her notebook out of the drawer to check when her next commission was due. She had a client who wanted some unique, stylish storage for her kitchen and she'd finally sourced the perfect dresser, which was screaming out for a makeover. It needed picking up ASAP, so with Gary back in action, she could arrange to pop over that morning.

'Yes, thanks.' Gary shuffled towards the back of the shop. 'Shall I put the kettle on?'

'Ooh, yes please.' Willow had already had a cup of coffee just before she set out, but she couldn't really get going until she'd gulped down her second cup of the day. She closed the notebook and headed into the workroom. There were three rooms beyond the shop: a tiny room Willow suspected had once been a cupboard but which now housed a loo and sink with minimal floor space to manoeuvre, a little kitchen, and the workroom, which was large enough for her to work on her more substantial pieces and store her supplies. She moved over to her paint supplies, running a finger along the tins as she searched for the shade she hoped to have in stock so she could start working on the dresser as soon as she had it in the workroom. She was thinking duck-egg blue for the dresser, with pretty vintage paper behind the shelving unit, and luckily, as she'd thought, there was a tin containing the perfect shade. Grabbing a screwdriver, she eased the tin open and was pleased to see it was almost full. She should have more than enough for a couple of coats on the dresser, saving her a trip to the big out-of-town DIY store.

'I might need your help with a dresser later,' she said as Gary brought her coffee into the workroom. He nodded before a frown creased his face.

'Where did the boat go?'

It was difficult not to miss its presence. It had taken up most of the available space, resulting in awkward shuffles and sidestepping whenever they needed to use the room.

'The guy I've been emailing about it came to pick it up yesterday.' Willow rolled her eyes. 'Completely out of the blue, but it's a sale – and quite a big one too – so I can't complain too much.'

Gary's frown deepened. 'I'm so sorry. How did you manage that on your own?'

Willow blew on her coffee before taking a tentative sip. Yep, still volcano-hot. She placed the cup on the side. 'Don't worry, one of the neighbours gave me a hand. And stop apologising – like I said, you can't help being ill.'

Gary nodded, scuffing his trainer on the floor, looking lost once more.

'Shall we get the planters outside?' Willow asked. Gary was a good worker, but he needed prodding into action at times. They hefted the planters out onto the pavement before Gary set to work getting the shop prepared for opening, sweeping and dusting and making sure the displays were looking their best, while Willow made a start on a chest of drawers waiting to be sanded. There was no commission for this piece, so Willow would be free to let her imagination run wild once it was primed. She loved this aspect of her job and couldn't imagine being satisfied doing anything else.

At just after nine o'clock, she rang the current owner of the dresser, who said the piece would be available for pick-up in an hour. In the meantime, she continued her sanding until Liam rang with news about the house.

'I've arranged for a surveyor to come out, but he can't get here until Friday,' Liam said, his tone cautious in case Willow took the delay badly.

'It's three days,' she said with a resigned sigh. 'It could be worse. Thanks for letting me know.'

'I'll be in touch as soon as I have any updates,' Liam said.

Not wanting to disturb Ethan with a phone call at work, she sent a quick text to update him. Three days didn't seem like a particularly long time, but it would be three days full of worry, doubt and stress, and if Ethan didn't come home before then, she'd have to deal with it all on her own.

'If we're quiet later on, you can help me with the painting if you like,' Willow said as they set off to pick up the dresser. She didn't like to close the shop during the day unless absolutely necessary, but she wasn't sure she'd have any help once she arrived at the house, and there was no way she'd be able to manage such a hefty piece of furniture on her own.

'Are you sure you trust me after last time?' Gary asked, and Willow had to press her lips together to stop herself from giggling at the memory of Gary tripping backwards over a tin of red paint, landing on his arse in the puddle he'd created when he'd upended the tin. Covered in the gloopy red paint, Gary looked like his rear had been on the receiving end of a savage attack.

'It could have happened to anyone,' Willow said, her voice cracking only slightly as she fought against the humour of the memory. 'And it's all practice. You'll be creating your own pieces soon.'

Before working in the shop, Gary hadn't had much creative or DIY experience, but he was learning new skills under Willow's guidance. He liked getting his hands dirty with the painting and varnishing, and he was getting pretty good at using the scroll saw to make intricate cuts. He'd been a little wary of using the power tool to begin with, but Willow was proud of the progress he was making, how much more confident he was working with his hands, and the artistic side she'd unleashed in him. Becoming a mentor to Gary had been unexpected, but it was a joy seeing him grow and she hoped he was getting as much out of their working relationship as she was.

'Okay,' Gary said with a shrug. 'But only because I'm wearing my scruffiest jeans. I learned my lesson last time.'

The house wasn't far and they were back at the shop within half an hour, manoeuvring the bulky piece around the back of the shop so it could go straight into the workroom. It was a beautiful dresser, with three small cupboards and drawers below a unit of four shelves. There were a few scratches and scuff marks, but Willow could easily fix those before she applied the duck-egg paint and decorative paper. She wasn't too keen on the brass handles on the cupboards, but after a rummage in her collection of salvaged handles, she found three heart-shaped wooden knobs that would be perfect once she'd painted them the same shade.

'Coffee?'

Gary stood in the doorway of the workroom, Willow's favourite mug held aloft. The mug was chipped on one side and there was a worrying crack along the top rim of the handle, but it was an old mug of Ethan's, one she'd somehow ended up keeping during their university days. He must have loaned her the mug, because it had ended up in her cupboard, moving with her when she returned home after graduation. She'd still had the mug when she and Ethan started dating years later and he'd recognised it as she was making coffee for them both in her flat.

'My Kenny mug!' She'd been pulling a couple of mugs out of the cupboard when Ethan appeared behind her, reaching to pluck the mug from the shelf. 'I forgot all about this. I can't believe you still have it.'

'It's yours?' Willow hadn't had a clue about the origin of the mug with the orange guy from *South Park* on it. She'd rarely used it, to be honest.

'Did you keep it as a memento of me?' Ethan asked, and Willow had rolled her eyes.

'As if.'

'You did.' Ethan folded his arms across his chest and leaned against the kitchen counter. 'You knew, even back then, that we'd end up falling in love.'

Willow had been about to scoff when the words hit her. They hadn't used that word before. Hadn't even hinted at it. They'd had a laugh. Had sex. Lots and lots of it. But they hadn't spoken of feelings.

'Have we? Fallen in love?' She waited for Ethan to retract his words, to get flustered and explain he *hadn't meant it like that*. He was messing around. Fallen in love? Pah! Was she making that brew or not?

'I have,' Ethan said, matter-of-fact. Willow expected his face to crack, for him to nudge her with his elbow and tell her to get a grip. But his brow furrowed, his eyes darting, trying to read hers.

He's nervous, she'd realised. *He isn't sure I feel the same way.*

But of course she did. She counted down the hours, the minutes, until she could see him again, dreaded the moment they parted, already counting down to the next time. She grinned like a loon whenever she thought about him, prompting questions from her colleagues about what she was thinking about – or *who* she was thinking about. She'd had constant butterflies, whether she was with him or waiting to be with him, since the night of the reunion.

She couldn't imagine her life without Ethan in it.

'I have too,' she said, and Ethan exhaled loudly, the creases disappearing from his brow and being replaced by the tiny crinkles around his eyes as he grinned at her.

'You can keep the mug then,' he said before taking her face in his hands and showering her with kisses.

Willow took hold of the mug now, wrapping her hands around the porcelain and feeling the warmth from both the drink inside and the memory. How easy life had been back then. How simple their relationship. Had she known back then how much heartache was on the cards, would she have continued along the path with Ethan? Or would she have got out relatively unscathed while she could?

Willow placed the mug on the side, keeping it in sight as she resumed her work on the dresser. Of course she knew the answer. She didn't even need to consider her options. Life with Ethan had become complicated, but she wouldn't throw away her marriage, the life they'd created, no matter how tough the road ahead might be. They'd stumble over this latest obstacle somehow and find their way again.

Chapter Sixteen

Melody

Melody's grip on the golden pole tightened instinctively as the ride started with a slight jerk, the horse rising slowly as the tinkly music grew louder, reaching its maximum height before dipping again and repeating the process. The rise and fall of the horse reached a rhythm as the carousel turned until Melody felt as though she was gliding through the air. Up and down, up and down, the salty breeze whipping at her hair as she whizzed past the helter-skelter, the dodgems, the Ferris wheel, the ticket booth, the fairground games and concession stands until she reached the helter-skelter again. She turned to Hugo on the neighbouring horse and held out her hand, giggling and whooping as they twirled hand-in-hand on the pier. She was a child again, giddy and joyous and living life in the moment instead of feeling the pain of the past and worrying about the future.

She was glad Hugo had managed to talk her into leaving her camera behind so she could concentrate on *feeling* this experience instead of simply seeing it. Her visit to the pier earlier couldn't compare to this. Earlier, she'd been too busy searching for moments to capture rather than creating any of her own. Too busy to let go and have fun. But now she felt free and foolish and cheered all at once, the mixture of emotions bubbling just below the surface, ready to burst, filling her with a jittery sense that *something* was about to happen; something good, something terrible, she didn't know, just *something*, and she was half afraid and half exhilarated to find out which it would be. Either way, she felt alive, and that she, Melody Rosewood, was still here, still going despite the pain of the past year.

'What next?' she asked once they emerged from the ride, somehow finding her hand still in Hugo's. She should remove it, gently, without causing offence. But she didn't. She held on, ignoring the guilt gnawing at her gut.

'What would you like to do?' Hugo asked.

Melody, wide-eyed, took in the pier. They'd already chased one another on the dodgems, roaring with laughter as their bodies were catapulted forwards, backwards and sideways in quick succession, they'd raced down the helter-skelter on scratchy rugs, and attempted to win prizes at the hoopla and coconut shy (but had walked away with nothing at all but a sense of fun).

'The Ferris wheel?' Melody had been on the Ferris wheel earlier, but she knew that without her camera – and with Hugo – it would be like experiencing it anew.

'Let's go.' Hugo led the way, purchasing tickets (and refusing absolutely when Melody attempted to pay) and joining the queue. They had to wait a few minutes as the wheel was mid ride, but the time passed quickly as they chatted and picked at a bag of candyfloss bought from one of the stands. The fuzzy pink clump melted on her tongue and she closed her eyes, savouring the sugary hit and the nostalgia it brought with it, opening them again as she was hit with a thousand memories, emotions and regrets.

'Are you okay?' Hugo, brow creased with concern, placed a gentle hand on her cheek, sweeping a tear away.

Melody swallowed hard before taking a deep breath, gathering strength and mentally sorting through the jumble of emotions bombarding her. She wanted to run, to escape the pier, Hugo, the fun-filled day. She didn't deserve this and the guilt that she was taking it all, greedily and readily, was making her chest ache. She reached behind her, grasping hold of the photo in the back pocket of her shorts. She didn't take it out – she didn't need to. Feeling its presence was reminder enough of why she'd come to Clifton-on-Sea.

'I shouldn't be here.' Her voice was low, hoarse. Hugo had to bend closer to hear it and his face, his lips, were tantalisingly close. She could kiss him if she wanted to, just as he'd kissed her the previous evening. She could close her eyes and forget all about Ollie, feel something new, something other than the absolute misery she'd been living through.

'Do you want me to walk you home?' he asked and Melody shook her head. Home wasn't the bed and breakfast. Home was the flat she'd shared with Ollie, a place she'd escaped from, if only for a little while.

'Can we just...' Melody shrugged. 'Go? Somewhere else? Somewhere quieter?' Somewhere she could clear her head of the mishmash of emotions clogging her thoughts.

Hugo nodded, the corners of his mouth stretching into the beginnings of a smile. 'Of course.'

She expected him to take her hand again, so she placed it in the pocket of her shorts, out of the way. She attempted a smile of her own but it wasn't forthcoming.

'I'm sorry,' she said once they'd battled their way through the queue that had grown behind them and made it back out onto the promenade. She wanted to explain, but couldn't, so an apology was all she had.

'It's okay.' Hugo shrugged and sneaked a sideways glance at her. 'I've been on that thing a million times already.'

'Have you?'

Hugo scrunched up his nose, his right eye closing as he thought about it. 'Actually, a million times may have been a slight exaggeration.'

'How many times have you been on it?' Melody asked. She was starting to feel a bit better with the sounds of the pier fading behind them.

'Once.'

Melody laughed. She couldn't help it, but she shoved a hand over her mouth to stop it in its tracks. 'Once? Just a *slight* exaggeration then.'

Hugo shrugged. 'Just a teeny one.'

'Then I'm sorry I ruined your chance for a second go.'

'The first time can't have been that great,' Hugo said. 'It isn't as though I've rushed back to repeat the experience.'

'That's true. Now I don't feel so bad for spoiling your morning.'

'Spoiling my morning?' Hugo paused, placing his hands on Melody's shoulders and solemnly turning her to face him. 'Do you realise the moment I did that sneaky turn, expertly zipped past that kid in the yellow car, and shunted into you as revenge for smashing me into the barrier was one of the best moments of my life?'

Melody giggled, remembering the dodgems and their momentary but fierce rivalry. 'What about the moment that sweet little girl with pigtails rammed into you?'

Hugo rubbed at his chest with one hand. The other remained on Melody's shoulder. 'That sweet little girl with pigtails winded me.'

Melody pressed her lips together. She wouldn't giggle again, no matter how hilariously shocked Hugo had looked at that moment. A smile flickered at her lips but she fought it. She wouldn't think of the sweet little girl turning to high-five her mum as Hugo's car performed a spectacular spin as that would send her over the edge.

'I wasn't expecting it,' Hugo said, his voice lower now, less confident. 'It took me by surprise.'

'Don't worry,' Melody said. 'It was just the dodgems. Your manly pride is still intact.'

Hugo grinned now. 'Glad to hear it.'

His hand was still on her shoulder, Melody realised. Just sitting there as they stood facing each other. She remembered the previous evening as Hugo had pressed his lips against hers. *She* hadn't been expecting that, and it had certainly taken her by surprise. A few minutes ago, waiting for the Ferris wheel, she'd been confused as she contemplated kissing Hugo, but her mind was clearer now and she wondered how she'd react if he kissed her again. Here. Right now.

He didn't.

'Why don't we go and grab Scoop and take him for a walk?' Hugo dropped his hand from Melody's shoulder and resumed their stroll along the promenade. 'I could show you some less touristy parts of town. The hidden gems.'

Melody nodded, striding after Hugo. 'Sounds good.'

Hugo lived a short walk from the seafront, in a Georgian, three-storey property now divided up into six flats. He lived in a two-bedroomed flat on the ground floor, overlooking the slightly dishevelled garden at the front of the house, with his brother and Scoop Dog, who barked in excited greeting as Hugo pushed his key into the lock.

'Hello, boy.' Dropping to his knees, Hugo rubbed at the dog's head, ears and belly – whichever part was available – as Scoop bounced around him like Tigger chomping on

E numbers. 'Did you miss me? Was I gone too long?' He scooped up the dog, who wriggled and lapped at his chin. 'Aren't you going to say hello to our new friend? She's come to see you and you've completely ignored her.'

Melody stepped towards the dog and gave him a scratch behind the ears. 'He clearly adores you.'

'The feeling's mutual.' Hugo kissed the dog on his little furry head and placed him back on the ground. 'I'll just grab his lead and we'll get going.'

Scoop's ears pricked at the word 'lead' and he trotted after Hugo as he headed into the kitchen. With the lead attached, they made their way out of the house and up the sloping street, moving further away from the beach.

'So, you're definitely moving on tomorrow?' Hugo asked as they strolled along the pavement. Scoop seemed to know where they were headed, trotting slightly ahead of the pair.

'Yes.' Melody would be checked out of the bed and breakfast and on a train heading towards her next destination in the morning. 'So many seaside towns, so little time.'

Hugo quirked an eyebrow at her and she realised she hadn't explained about the photo festival and her month-long sabbatical, which was coming to an end very soon.

'You must have a very understanding boss to let you have so much time off,' Hugo said and Melody nodded.

'Work have been fantastic.' She hadn't been sure what her employers would say when she'd requested the month of unpaid leave, but she'd been leaning heavily towards a no. But they'd granted her request and wished her well as she set off on her adventure. She'd hoped her work hadn't suffered over the past year, but perhaps it had and her employers were hoping the break would do her good and she'd return somewhat back to her old self.

'You're lucky,' Hugo said. 'I work with my brother and he's a slave driver.'

'I saw him earlier, at the ice-cream van. At least I think it was him. Looked a lot like you.'

'He's devastatingly handsome, huh?'

Melody rolled her eyes and nudged Hugo with her elbow. 'I see your pride wasn't dented *too* much by the little girl on the dodgems.'

'I have an ego the size of the whole of Britain. Or so I've been told.'

'Something tells me you're not quite as confident as you make out,' Melody said.

Hugo scoffed and pushed out his chest. 'What are you talking about, woman?'

'You're overcompensating for something. Were you an ugly child?'

Hugo barked out a laugh. 'Oh God. The *ugliest*. I had cheeks like this.' He puffed out his cheeks until they were straining. 'And teeth like this.' He did a good impression of Bugs Bunny. 'And, to add insult to injury, I was considerably shorter than every kid in my class until I shot up during the summer between years ten and eleven. Most of the kids – and some of the teachers – didn't even recognise me and thought I was new to the school. To be fair, the new height had stretched out the puppy fat and I'd had my train-track braces removed, so I *did* look like a different kid.'

Melody couldn't help feeling a tad smug she'd seen through Hugo's façade and spotted the cleverly hidden vulnerability beneath the surface. It made her warm to him more; he seemed more real, more like her, with his weaknesses.

'So, where are we going?' she asked as they rounded a corner and Scoop started to tug more insistently on his lead.

'We're going on one of our favourite walks,' Hugo said.

'Not the beach?' Melody didn't know the area, but she was sure they'd been walking away from the sea. The sounds of the waves and the raucous pier had faded so much you could only detect them if you strained.

Hugo shook his head. 'No, not the beach. Scoop doesn't like it when there are a lot of people about – there's a much higher chance of there being other dogs around when it's busy, and he's wary after the attack. That's why we prefer Chapel Cove. It's so secluded, we're pretty much guaranteed free rein of the beach.'

'I saw you on the beach this morning.' Melody hadn't meant to divulge that information, in case Hugo got the wrong idea and thought she'd been seeking him out. But there it was, out in the open.

'We have to time it right,' Hugo said. 'Too early and people are walking their dogs before work. Too late and families have migrated down there for the day, taking their furry friends along too. We got it right this morning.'

'You really love this dog, don't you?' Melody asked.

Hugo nodded. 'He's my best mate. Wouldn't know what to do without him. I do wish he wouldn't piss in my favourite shoes, though.' He grinned at Melody. 'I bet you don't have the same problem with your best friend, do you?'

Melody shook her head. 'Nope. Never had that problem.' She shoved her hands into the pockets of her shorts. 'You never actually said where we were going.'

'Here.' Hugo pointed just ahead, to a set of iron gates. With Scoop now tugging furiously, he led the way inside.

Chapter Seventeen

Mae

As Hannah was spending the day with Frank and Corinne, Mae had already taken a child-free trip to the supermarket (and was almost giddy with the novelty of the fuss-free tour of the aisles) and was now taking the opportunity to whizz through the communal living areas while the house was empty to make sure the place was clean and tidy for when her guests arrived back. With the dishwasher taking care of the breakfast dishes, she ran the hoover over the downstairs rooms, gathering stray books, toys and wellies along the way. Once she'd wiped down the kitchen surfaces and mopped the floor, she moved through to her desk in the family room, using this rare alone time to get on top of her admin. Her website was given a long-overdue update and she sent out a quick newsletter to her mailing list. The Robertsons had booked the attic room for two weeks, so once Melody left, the room would be unoccupied for eleven days, which was a huge chunk of time in the B&B world. Mae needed to send out a gentle reminder of her presence and hopefully find some new occupants.

The dishwasher had completed its cycle by the time she'd finished at her computer, so she wandered back into the kitchen to empty it.

'What are you doing here?' she asked with a sigh when she spotted the scruffy cat curled up on top of her freshly scrubbed table. 'You don't live here, so scram.' She headed to the back door, opening it wide and indicating the cat should hop it. She hadn't opened the door since arriving back, so the cat must have been lurking in the house since earlier that morning, no doubt let in by Hannah.

'Come on, out.' She wafted her hand towards the garden when the cat refused to budge, watching her through heavily lidded eyes from the table. When it still failed to budge, she crossed to the table and scooped it into her arms, noting it was pretty plump. Either it wasn't a stray, as she suspected, or it was pushing its luck and snacking elsewhere too.

'No,' she said firmly when the cat mewled. 'You're not staying.' She placed the cat on the grass before backing her way inside the kitchen and closing the door. She gave the table another scrub before locking up the house and heading to a café a couple of streets back from the seafront. It wasn't often Mae and her mum were both free, so they were making the most of it and meeting for lunch.

The café was smaller and quieter than those on the seafront, but it had a sun-trapped patio area outside, filled with parasol-covered tables. Mae was the first to arrive, so she chose one of the outdoor tables and ordered a coffee. With the sun warming her skin and the whole afternoon stretching ahead of her, Mae felt as though she were on holiday, pre-Hannah, in Italy, France or Spain. There were some fantastic memories of trips away stored in her brain, and she smiled as she remembered sitting outside a similar café in Barcelona, sipping coffee and trying her hardest to catch the eye of a neighbouring customer she thought was pretty cute. In the end, his girlfriend arrived, practically sitting in his lap, but it hadn't spoiled the memory. Back then, anything was possible (as long as it didn't have a girlfriend) and she sometimes ached for those times again. She would never wish Hannah away, would never regret her decisions, but she sometimes wished life was a little bit simpler. A little bit easier. And fun. Mae couldn't remember the last time she'd let her hair down and allowed herself to enjoy life outside of motherhood.

Not that she would ever admit this to anyone else. She was fine as she was, that was what she told people, because it was safer that way. Her fun and carefree life had led to heartbreak, and she wasn't ready to put herself through that again.

'I'm so sorry I'm late,' Eloise said as she scurried over to the table, dropping a kiss on Mae's cheek before plonking herself down in the opposite chair. 'I was watching *Jeremy Kyle* and must have dropped off. I never found out which one was the dad.' She tucked her handbag under the table and smiled across at her daughter. 'This is a nice treat, isn't it? I can't remember the last time we had lunch, just the two of us.'

Mae frowned, shaking her head. 'No, me neither. I've usually got Hannah or one of us is working.'

'Speaking of work,' Eloise said, raising her hand to catch the attention of a waitress. 'Did your guest get settled in?'

Mae nodded and took a sip of her coffee. 'I managed to fill the other room for a couple of days too. They both seem nice.'

Mae usually spent her evenings in the family room, her only company the television or a book once Hannah was tucked up in bed, the hours leading up to her own bedtime stretching ahead of her, but last night she and Melody had shared a bottle of wine, chatting as they curled up on the sofa until nearly midnight. She'd been great company, chatting without probing too deeply, and they'd had a giggle. Most of Mae's friends from Clifton-on-Sea had moved on by the time she returned to the town – either physically or having forged new lives that no longer included her – so it had been like starting afresh. With two jobs and the restraints of motherhood, Mae didn't have much free time for building friendships, so most of her interactions came from working in the Fisherman and rarely made it beyond the pub's walls. Only Alfie had breached the bar staff/customer connection and become an actual friend, but she'd never invite him to curl up on her sofa during the evenings. They had a good rapport and Alfie was a great support, but there was always the issue of his feelings for Mae in the background. Feelings Mae just couldn't return, no matter how kind and sweet – and, yes, attractive, *extremely* attractive – he was.

'So the bed and breakfast is doing well then?' Eloise asked as the waitress headed back into the café with their order.

Mae nodded. 'It's doing okay, especially now it's summer, and one of the rooms is already booked for the autumn term.'

'Your grandparents would be so proud of you, you know,' Eloise said. 'It's a lovely house and should be filled with people, but it was awfully quiet once your uncles and I moved out. I think that's why they liked having you to stay so often, even though we were only a short drive away. You kept the house alive, and you're certainly doing that now.'

'I sometimes worry they wouldn't approve of my turning their home into a business,' Mae admitted. It hadn't been the plan when she and Hannah first moved in, but with rising bills and nursery fees Mae just couldn't afford, she'd needed to find a way to bring more money in, and having Hannah at home while she brought in an income from the house seemed the perfect solution, especially as it had been Mae's childhood dream to run her own bed and breakfast.

'They wanted you to be happy,' Eloise said. 'That's all that mattered to them.' Eloise traced a pattern on the tabletop. 'And are you?'

'Am I what?'

Eloise tilted her head to one side as she observed her daughter. 'Are you happy?'

'Of course I'm happy.' Mae gave a little laugh, just to prove it. 'Why wouldn't I be?'

Eloise reached across the table to place her hand on Mae's. 'I sometimes worry you're lonely.'

'Lonely?' Mae scoffed. 'How could I be lonely? I've got Hannah and my guests. I barely get a moment to myself.'

'That isn't the same thing as not being lonely,' Eloise said. 'I've been there, remember? The single mum. Yes, you're kept busy enough, but what about fun? Companionship? When was the last time you had sex?'

Mae's eyes widened as they darted around the outdoor space, praying nobody had overheard. There wasn't so much as a flicker from the other customers, but still her cheeks turned a rosy pink.

'*Mum!*' she hissed, leaning across the table.

'Well?' Eloise asked. 'When was the last time you…?'

Mae held up a hand to silence her mum before the question was repeated and her cheeks burst into actual flames. 'Does it matter? I'm not interested in relationships right now, and I'm certainly not interested in one-night stands. Never have been, never will be.'

'I'm not suggesting you sleep around with just anyone,' Eloise said. 'But as far as I can recall, you haven't been on one date since you had Hannah.'

'So?'

'So, I think it's time you put yourself first for a change.' Now it was Eloise's turn to raise a hand. 'I know, I know. You've got the bed and breakfast and Hannah, but I can babysit. Frank and Corinne are always happy to look after Hannah. They *love* spending time with her. Go out. Have fun. Meet new people. I've heard about this app where you swipe at people or something. Why don't you give it a go? I'll sign up too. It'll be fun.'

Mae had been shaking her head during her mum's whole speech. 'I'm not interested in dating, Mum.'

'I know he hurt you, darling – and I'm not just talking about Shane.' Mae winced at the mention of her ex, the bloke who'd walked away from his responsibilities and had never been heard from again. 'Your dad didn't just let me down, he let you down too, but not all men are like him and Shane.'

Mae hadn't seen her father since she was fifteen. It had been an accidental sighting – her dad hadn't really been in contact for the past five or six years – but then there he was, out shopping in Preston. With his new family. A wife, a little girl clasping hold of his hand, a boy in a buggy. A family Mae had known nothing about until that moment. But the worst part was, he'd walked straight past her, not a hint of recognition on his face.

Mae hadn't seen or heard from him since. It had dented her confidence, made her reluctant to trust men as she started to date, but Shane had managed to worm his way in, earn her trust – and look where she'd ended up.

Mae stuck her chin in the air. 'I know that, but I'm still not interested. I'm happy as I am.'

Eloise cocked an eyebrow. 'Really?'

'Yes, Mum, really.'

Eloise's eyebrow remained at full attention, not convinced in the slightest. 'I just don't want you to end up like me.'

'What's wrong with you?' Mae smirked. 'Apart from the obvious?'

Eloise straightened the condiments on the table, even though they looked perfectly neat to Mae. 'I wanted more children. Not a great horde, but I wanted you to have at least a brother or sister.'

'Then why didn't you?' It wasn't as though Eloise had been short of admirers. She'd had plenty of boyfriends and flings since her divorce.

'I never let myself trust another man completely. It's why most of my relationships fizzled out. Yes, I liked to go out and have fun, but I'd never let my guard down enough to fall in love again. By the time I did, it was too late to be having babies.' Eloise finally looked up from the salt and pepper pots and caught her daughter's eye. 'Do you remember Martin?'

'Of course.' Martin had been Eloise's longest-lasting boyfriend after her divorce, the relationship spanning from shortly before Mae's eighth birthday until after her eleventh. Mae had liked Martin and been gutted when the relationship ended.

'He asked me to marry him, back when we were together.' Eloise rubbed at her finger, where her wedding band had once sat. 'He asked me four times but I turned him down every single time. In the end, he left.' She shrugged. 'He wanted more than I was willing to give, so he found it elsewhere. There's only so much rejection a man can take before he moves on. I heard he got married six months later.'

'I'm sorry, Mum. I had no idea.'

'It's my biggest regret,' Eloise said. 'That, and the frizzy perm I had in the eighties.'

She smiled, and Mae found herself returning the gesture. The perm *had* been horrendous. Mae had giggled over the photos many times.

'I saw him a couple of weeks ago,' Eloise said, serious again. 'Bumped into him at the supermarket. He's still married, with three teenage kids now. So he got everything he wanted from life.' Eloise reached across the table and took Mae's hand. 'I don't want you to get to my age and look back with regret. Or worse, get to Mrs Hornchurch's age and end up alone. Her children all moved out to start their own lives, poor Mr Hornchurch passed away, and now she's all by herself in that big house. We both know she's lonely.'

'But that's the thing,' Mae said. 'I'm not lonely.' Not always. 'And I'm not interested in starting a new relationship, or even going on a date or two. I'm happy as I am.'

'I suppose you don't have to go to the effort of shaving your legs.' Eloise shrugged. 'But I still don't believe you.'

'You don't have to believe me,' Mae said before lowering her voice. 'But can you promise me you'll never, *ever* speak about my sex life in public again?'

'Sex life?' Eloise said, raising her eyebrows and failing to lower her voice. 'What bloody sex life?'

And it was at that moment that two things happened: the waitress arrived with their order and Alfie passed their table, both no doubt overhearing Eloise's scornful enquiry.

Chapter Eighteen

Melody

The ground was soft underfoot, the spongy mud carpeted with twigs, leaves and patches of moss. The canopy of leaves above them, green and lush and celebrating the days until autumn sent them fluttering to the ground, provided a screen against the baking sun. With the sunlight largely blocked, the ground was prevented from drying out and the screen had the added bonus of providing relief from the intense midday sun as Melody, Hugo and Scoop Dog ambled along. As she stepped over an exposed tree root, the scattered twigs sinking into the dirt track worn through the copse they were trailing through, Melody was glad she'd slipped her trainers on that morning and not a pair of flip-flops.

'This is a popular spot for dog-walkers too,' Hugo had said as he'd led her through the iron gates of the park earlier. 'But we should be okay for a while.'

They'd headed straight for the wooded area of the park, with Scoop bounding as far ahead as his lead would allow, sniffing at the ground and trees (and relieving himself against a few). Melody trod carefully over nature's obstacles, but she still managed to stumble over a particularly well-hidden root, crying out as she lost her footing and headed for the ground. Luckily, a pair of arms caught her before she hit the deck, righting her and making sure she was steady again.

'Are you okay?' Hugo asked, checking her over with his eyes. 'Did you hurt yourself?'

'Only my pride.' Melody rotated her ankles in turn to make sure she hadn't injured herself. 'But I'm fine. Can we gloss over the fact I'm a clumsy idiot who nearly went down like a sack of spuds?'

Hugo made a show of puffing out his chest. 'And forget I just saved you from certain injury?'

'Yes, please.'

Hugo exhaled, relaxing his upper body. 'Fair enough. It's forgotten. Are you hungry?'

Melody placed a hand on her stomach. Had it growled without her realising?

'There's a café just through here.' Hugo pointed to the right, where the path forked to a clearing in the trees. 'I'm starving. Shall we get some lunch before I have to start my shift?'

'Only if you'll let me pay,' Melody said, though they'd already turned towards the clearing. Now food had been mentioned, she realised she was pretty hungry too. 'You paid for the rides and candyfloss this morning, so it's only fair.'

Hugo shrugged. 'That's fine by me. As long as I get some food, I'm happy.'

Melody held up a hand to shield her eyes from the glare of the sun as the trees petered out. They followed the path as it wound its way across a patch of grass until it reached a paved area of the park. An octagonal building lay ahead, an awning reaching out from one of the sides to provide shelter for the small cluster of tables and chairs beneath it.

Melody headed inside to order the food while Hugo and Scoop secured a table.

'I can see why you like this place so much,' Melody said when she joined Hugo at the table after placing their order. There was a large children's playground ahead, with sprawling fields either side. Currently, there was a game of rounders taking place, while others made the most of the sunshine as they stretched out on blankets to read or enjoy a picnic with friends and family. Melody stretched her legs out in front of her, enjoying the warmth on her skin. The awning was providing almost as good a shield as the trees had, so she didn't feel like she was being baked to a crisp.

'We love it.' Hugo reached down to rub Scoop's fur. The dog was panting under the shade of the table. 'Scoop and I come here most days, and when the weather's cooler, James and I park the van over there.' Hugo pointed towards the playground and winked. 'Pester power earns us a decent wage.'

'Do you drive along the streets with music playing to signal your arrival?' Melody asked.

'Of course, though at the moment we're sticking to the beach. We make more money down there while the sun's shining.'

'I thought you were all about the ice cream,' Melody said. 'But you're actually a ruthless businessman, aren't you?' She nudged Hugo to show she was only teasing.

'Yup, that's me. I show up, take the kiddies' money and drive away, laughing maniacally.'

'Do you swim through giant piles of money like Scrooge McDuck?'

Hugo leaned in towards Melody. 'You should see my backstroke.'

Melody giggled, but shut down her mirth as the waitress appeared with their drinks.

'Two Diet Cokes,' she said, lifting the glasses from the tray and placing them on the table. 'And a bowl of our finest tap water for Scoop.'

Melody hadn't asked for any water for the dog. She watched as the waitress placed the ceramic bowl in front of Scoop before straightening and flashing a bright – flirty? – smile at Hugo.

'Thanks, Carla,' Hugo said with a beam of his own.

Carla placed a hand on Hugo's shoulder. 'You're always welcome.' She removed her hand and started to back away. 'Your food should be ready in a few minutes. Give me a shout if you need anything.'

You're always welcome, Melody mocked in her head. *Give me a shout if you need anything*.

Melody wasn't sure why she was being a cow; the waitress seemed pleasant enough, and she was obviously kind-hearted enough to think of Scoop. The dog was lapping enthusiastically at the water, droplets of water splatting onto the hot concrete in his haste. The bowl was almost empty by the time the waitress returned with fat hotdogs smothered in fried onions.

'I brought the ketchup out ready,' Carla told Hugo, placing a hand between his shoulderblades. 'I know you can't eat a hotdog without it.'

Did she have to keep touching him? It was hardly professional, was it? Melody didn't paw at the clients who came into the solicitors' office.

'Can I get you anything else?' Carla was looking at Melody as she asked, though she still had the palm of her hand resting on Hugo's back.

'No, thank you. This is great.' Melody picked up her hotdog and sank her teeth into it, watching as Carla made her way back into the café. 'Oh my God,' she said after swallowing her first mouthful. 'This is *amazing*.'

146

'You didn't think we visited the park just for the trees and grass, did you?' Hugo broke off the end of his sausage and, blowing on it to cool it down, passed it down to Scoop. 'It's a shame they're closing down.'

'They are?'

Hugo nodded as he squirted a long, generous line of ketchup onto his hotdog. 'At the end of the summer. The owner's selling up and moving.'

'That's a shame.' Realising Carla might be out of a job in a matter of weeks, Melody wished she'd had kinder thoughts towards her. 'But hopefully the new owners will make hotdogs just as delicious as these.' She took another bite, sighing with pleasure. This was hands down the best hotdog she'd ever tasted. It was far superior to the hotdog she'd had from a street vendor in New York. She'd been bitterly disappointed by *that* experience.

'Mmm, maybe.' Hugo took his first bite, already reaching for a napkin to mop up any ketchup smears.

'You don't sound too optimistic,' Melody said. Hugo shrugged, still chewing. 'You never know, it might end up being an even better café.'

'Or maybe not even a café at all,' Hugo said.

'What else would it be?' They were sitting in the middle of a park – it was hardly likely to reopen as a bank or estate agency.

'An ice-cream parlour?' Hugo suggested. He took another huge bite of his hotdog, chewing slowly while Melody digested his words.

'You?' she asked. 'You're going to buy the café?' She had to wait until Hugo had swallowed before receiving the answer.

'We're thinking about it.' Hugo scratched the back of his neck while giving a one-shouldered shrug. For the first time since Melody had met him, his tone wasn't filled with the bravado she'd become accustomed to.

'You don't sound too sure,' Melody said and Hugo shrugged again.

'It's been a dream of mine to open an ice-cream parlour like my grandparents had for as long as I can remember. But dreams and reality are very different, aren't they?'

Melody nodded. She understood completely. 'It's like me and my photography. It's been a hobby of mine for years, but while other people have told me I'm good enough to turn it into a profession, I'm not so sure.' She held up a hand. 'But I've tasted your ice creams and they're absolutely delicious. I think you'd ace it as a…' She scrabbled around her brain for the correct term, but didn't find it. 'An ice cream-atier?'

Hugo laughed. 'You just made that up, didn't you?'

'Maybe,' Melody said, dragging out the word. 'It works for chocolate makers.' She shook her head. 'Anyway, the sentiment is still the same.'

'I'm keen to go ahead,' Hugo admitted. 'But James is more reserved. He's thinking more practically – like how much custom would we get during the colder months? – whereas I'm thinking more passionately, remembering our grandparents' place, packed and happy and fun. I've already planned the décor.'

'Have you?'

Hugo nodded and turned to the café's window. 'I'd want a curved counter with tall stools for customers to sit on, black-and-white-checked flooring, chrome tables and chairs with cream leatherette seating. And it'd be bright, with neon lights and one of those fifties-style jukeboxes.'

'It sounds wonderful,' Melody said. 'But is your brother right? How would you stay in business during winter?'

'Our van proves it's possible,' Hugo said. 'People *do* still want ice cream outside of summer. We could make the winter-themed ice creams we sold at the Christmas fair, but we could also offer hot chocolate, tea and coffee – I'm sure that'd entice the parents in when they bring their kids to the park to burn off some energy.'

Hugo's face was lit up, his free, non-hotdog-holding hand animated as he spoke. He was obviously passionate about this new venture and Melody found herself looking into the café, imagining it for herself.

'It does sound fabulous,' she said. 'And definitely the kind of place I'd call into regularly.'

'You'll have to come back and visit when we're up and running.' Hugo winked at her and shoved the last portion of his hotdog into his mouth.

It was a nice thought, but Melody doubted she'd be retracing her steps once she returned home and the project was over. She was doing this for Ollie, after all, and befriending an ice-cream-van man wasn't part of the plan.

They wandered back to Hugo's flat once they'd finished their lunch, dropping off Scoop before they made their way to the ice-cream van on the promenade in time for Hugo's shift.

'I've had fun today,' Melody said as they stopped outside the van. She pushed away the memory of the failed Ferris wheel ride that morning. 'Thank you.'

'I've had fun too,' Hugo said. 'It's been nice to see the town through fresh eyes again. You grow accustomed to it, so it's great to be reminded of how special this place is.'

There was an awkward moment as they stood facing each other, knowing now was the time to say goodbye. They probably wouldn't see each other after this.

'I should get going,' Melody eventually said. 'Let you get to work.'

Hugo nodded, stepping closer to the van. But he paused and turned back around. 'Or you could stay? Help out?'

Melody narrowed her eyes. 'Are you just wanting some free labour for the afternoon?'

Hugo grinned. 'Damn it! You know me too well.'

'It *does* sound fun,' Melody said. 'I've never worked in an ice-cream van before.' In fact, she'd never even stepped foot inside one.

'It's fun, trust me. *And* I'll let you sample the goods.'

'Okay.' Melody nodded. 'On one condition.'

'Name it.'

'I get to bring my camera.'

Chapter Nineteen

Mae

Mae wanted to slide slowly down her seat, lowering her body until she disappeared under the table where she could hide from Alfie, the waitress, and anyone else who might have overheard Eloise's questioning about her sex life.

'Hello, Mae.' Alfie, pausing by the table to increase her mortification, gave an awkward little wave.

He'd definitely heard.

Bollocks.

Mae forced her lips into what could be described as a smile – but only if you weren't quite sure of the definition. 'Hello, Alfie. Nice to see you.'

'Ah!' Eloise gasped and clapped her hands together. 'So *you're* Alfie!'

Mae's eyes widened. Her mouth gaped. What the hell was her mother playing at? *So* you're *Alfie!* Spoken as though Mae had been discussing the bloke with her mum, which she absolutely had not. She didn't think she'd ever mentioned him in front of Eloise before this very moment. She knew how her mum's mind worked: male friend = love interest.

'I've heard lots about you, young man,' Eloise said with a tinkly little laugh.

You have not! Mae wanted to yell, but she found she was mute from the shock.

'Don't worry, all of it's good.' Eloise reached out to pat Alfie's arm while Mae changed her plan of action. If Plan A was to hide under the table, Plan B involved running away from this café – and her mum's big gob – as fast as she could manage in her four-inch-heel Mary Janes.

'I'll, er, just pop these down here for you,' the waitress, who had been hovering awkwardly during the exchange, muttered as she placed their lunch order on the table. Mae would have to grab her bagel before she legged it as she wasn't only humiliated, but hungry too.

'Thank you.' Eloise beamed at the waitress before she turned back to Alfie. 'Why don't you join us?' She patted the seat next to her, prompting Mae into action.

'I don't think Alfie has time to stop.' Mae widened her eyes at her mother, conveying her extreme discomfort and imminent plans to disown her mother if Eloise continued in this manner.

'Don't you?' Eloise asked Alfie. Mae couldn't bring herself to look at him. She didn't think she'd be able to for at least a year. Perhaps five or six.

'I've just been on a house call,' she heard him say. She sensed some movement in her peripheral vision, as though Alfie were indicating the direction he'd just come from. 'I was about to head back to the surgery, but I suppose I could stop for a few minutes. It is my lunch break, though I've left my sandwiches back in my office.'

'Eat with us,' Eloise said. Mae wondered if she had it in her to kick her mother under the table, but found she couldn't. Damn. 'Come on, sit down.' Eloise patted the seat again before waving to the waitress and beckoning her over again.

Well, this isn't awkward at all, Mae thought as Alfie lowered himself slowly into the seat, stowing his leather medical bag under the table.

'I'll just have a coffee, thanks,' he said when the waitress – the same one who'd overheard the sex-life comment – stopped at the table. Mae was relieved he wouldn't be staying for a whole meal and hoped he could drink fast.

'So, Alfie…' Eloise said when the waitress popped back into the café. 'You're our local vet. What an amazing vocation! It must be a very interesting job.'

Mae started to relax as Alfie spoke about his profession. If he and her mum were discussing cats, dogs and hamsters, the conversation couldn't possibly return to her sex life – or severe lack of one. Besides, it was nice to hear Alfie speak about his job so passionately. He obviously cared about his furry patients, and that was never a bad thing.

'So, you always wanted to be a vet?' Eloise asked as the waitress brought Alfie's coffee over. Mae had relaxed enough to start picking at her lunch.

'From the age of about eight,' Alfie said after thanking the waitress. 'Before that I wanted to be a fireman or Winnie the Pooh's best friend.'

'You mean Christopher Robin?' Eloise asked but Alfie shook his head.

'No, no. I still wanted to be me, I just wanted to play with Pooh in the forest.' Alfie groaned and shook his head. 'That sounded bad. I didn't want to play with *poo* in the forest. *Winnie* the Pooh.'

'Mate…' Mae said, leaning forward and forgetting her own awkwardness. 'It sounds wrong either way.'

Alfie laughed and nodded. 'I suppose it does. I was a bit obsessed with him when I was little, though. My bedroom was plastered with him: wallpaper, curtains, bedspread, not to mention the toys.' Alfie cleared his throat. 'There goes my macho image.'

'Don't worry about it,' Mae said. 'It was never there in the first place.' Grinning at Alfie, she tucked into her lunch, enjoying every bite.

'What was that about earlier?' Mae asked once she and Eloise were alone again. Eloise had tried to coax Alfie into staying a little bit longer once he'd finished his coffee, but he'd insisted on getting back to the surgery. He was climbing into his car now, a few yards down the road.

'What do you mean?' Eloise's face was the picture of innocence: wide eyed, serene smile on her lips. But Mae wasn't fooled.

'All that "I've heard so much about you" crap.' Mae used air quotes and a suitably mocking tone.

'That wasn't crap, darling.' Eloise dabbed at her mouth with a napkin. 'I *have* heard lots about Alfie.'

'From who?'

Eloise checked the teapot, pouring a little more into her cup. 'Corinne. She speaks very highly of our vet and she thinks you'd make an excellent couple.' She added a splash of milk to her cup and gave it a stir. 'And after meeting him, I agree.'

'But you made it sound like *I'd* been talking about him,' Mae said, putting aside the last statement for now.

Eloise placed the spoon on her saucer and lifted the cup, stopping just short of her lips. 'Did I?'

Mae's foot tapped underneath the table. Did I? *Did I?* 'Yes, you did. And don't think I don't know you're well aware of how it sounded.'

'It didn't sound like *anything*. You're overreacting.' Eloise drained her cup and returned it to the saucer. She waved at the waitress again for the bill. 'Do you fancy a little walk before we head back?'

'I can't.' Mae grabbed her handbag and rummaged inside for her purse. 'I have things to do.'

'Things?' Eloise raised an eyebrow. 'Is that a codeword for sulking?'

'I'm not sulking,' Mae said sulkily. 'I just don't need you interfering like that.'

'Interfering?' Eloise tutted. 'Darling, I'm simply concerned.'

'Concerned? Why? Because I haven't had sex for nearly five years?'

Of course, the waitress appeared at that very moment, hearing everything.

Oh, for fuck's sake.

'Don't worry, Mum, it isn't going to seal itself up.' Mae grabbed a banknote – she didn't even know which one it was – and threw it down on the table. 'And I've got a vibrator that keeps me more than happy.'

With her head held high – if only physically – she stalked away from the café and yanked open the door of her car. Okay, so she'd humiliated *herself* that time, but she was hopping mad. How dare her mum and Corinne gossip about her behind her back? They were too underqualified and overdressed to be playing Cupid, and their services weren't required. Mae didn't plan on forming a relationship – with Alfie or anyone else – until *she* was ready. And if that meant she remained single for eternity, so what?

She could see Eloise now, tottering along the pavement towards her, with what looked like a twenty-pound note wafting between her fingers. Throwing herself into the car, Mae clicked her seatbelt in place and shoved the key into the ignition in record time, pulling away from the kerb before Eloise could even reach her.

She'd managed to calm down by the time she made it to the Fisherman to pick Hannah up. She'd spent the remainder of the afternoon giving the house an extra-thorough clean, working through her frustrations with the help of a cloth, a bucket of hot, soapy water, and the use of every attachment on the hoover. By the time she'd finished, the house resembled the after-shot in a cleaning product's advertisement.

The Fisherman was already starting to fill, despite it only being late afternoon. Tom Byrne was sitting at the end of the bar as usual, chatting to anyone who happened to hover close by, while small clusters of locals sat at tables or gathered in corners. Tobias, a student who usually worked evening and weekend shifts but was happy to take on more work during the summer, was behind the bar, currently having his ear chewed by Tom. He seemed relieved as Mae approached.

'Are Frank and Corinne back yet?'

'They're upstairs,' Tobias said, using the opportunity to break away from poor old Tom. Mae made her way through to the back of the pub, heading up to the living quarters. She found them in the living room, sitting on the sofa while Hannah played on the rug in front of the fireplace. She scrabbled up as soon as she saw Mae and threw her arms around her waist, hugging her tight. Any hint of irritation vanished as she hugged her little girl, her nostrils filling with the familiar scent of her fruity shampoo. She gave her one final squeeze and kissed the top of her head before releasing her.

'Have you been a good girl?' she asked and Hannah nodded.

'Good as gold,' Corinne said.

'We went on the train,' Hannah told her mum. 'And to the cinema. I had popcorn and juice and sweeties and

Uncle Frank bought me this.' Hannah dashed away, returning shortly with a plastic, rectangular box with two control sticks. Sticking her tongue out in concentration, Hannah fiddled with the sticks until a yellow figure, alternating jerky movements with pirouettes on the carpet, stumbled out from behind the sofa.

'It's a remote-control Minion,' Hannah said. 'Watch this!' She erupted into giggles as the Minion spun round and round on the carpet.

'Did you say thank you to Frank and Corinne?' Mae asked and Hannah nodded.

'I gave them a big hug too.'

'And it was the *best* hug ever,' Corinne said.

'Thanks for today.' Mae hadn't had the most pleasant of days, but she was glad Hannah had enjoyed herself.

'It was an absolute pleasure,' Frank said. 'You know we love having her.' He winked at Mae. 'Though I won't pretend I'm not exhausted.'

With goodbye hugs and kisses and the new Minion toy tucked under Hannah's arm, the pair left Frank and Corinne to recover from their day out, making their way back down to the pub, where Tobias was once again being subjected to the life and times of Tom Byrne. Mae was about to lift her hand to wave goodbye when she saw Alfie standing close behind them, chatting with a couple of women. She recognised the receptionist from the surgery, but the other woman wasn't familiar at all. She was younger than Mae, perhaps early twenties, with long, swishy, TV-commercial-blonde hair and a light sprinkling of pale freckles. She was laughing at something, and Mae guessed the punchline had come from Alfie, judging by the way she was clutching his arm as she giggled.

Mae snatched her hand back down, deciding she wouldn't draw attention to herself, and was about to turn and usher Hannah through the door when Alfie glanced over and spotted her, raising his own hand in greeting. Mae waved back in return, hoping that would be it, but Alfie was already threading his way over as she lowered her hand again.

'Hello again,' he said when he reached them.

'Hi.' The one simple word struggled to emerge, as though her mouth was filled with glue.

'Hey, you.' Alfie ruffled Hannah's hair and she giggled. 'Who's this?' He pointed at the Minion, and Hannah took delight in introducing it, even giving it a quick spin on the pub's floor.

'I'm sorry about Mum earlier,' Mae said as the Minion performed a figure of eight on the floor. 'She isn't usually so...' Pushy? Embarrassing? '...Forthright. And I hadn't been talking about you to her, by the way.' It was important for Mae to put that out there. 'I don't know what's got into her. Too much sun, maybe?'

Alfie laughed. 'That could be it.' He shrugged. 'But I thought she was fun.'

'You would. She isn't your mum and you weren't the one she was embarrassing.'

Alfie laughed again. It was a pleasant sound and Mae found she liked being the cause of it. 'That's very true. You should meet my mum, though. There isn't a word to describe that force of nature.'

Mae was distracted for a moment as the Minion trundled towards a customer's legs. 'Careful, sweetie. You're going to trip somebody up.' She scooped up the Minion and switched it off before turning back to Alfie. 'I hope we didn't keep you from your work.'

'Not at all,' Alfie assured her. 'I didn't have many appointments today anyway. That's why we've sneaked out early for a quick drink to celebrate Carrie's first day

158

working with us.' He nodded towards the two women, and Mae saw that the young blonde one – the new veterinary nurse, she presumed – was watching them.

'I'll leave you to celebrate,' Mae said. 'I need to get this one home for tea, though I'm not sure how hungry she'll be after being spoiled by Frank and Corinne.'

'See you later, Munchkin.' Alfie reached down to ruffle Hannah's hair. 'Be a good girl for your mum, okay?' Hannah gave a nod, though there was a mischievous glint in her eye.

Mae said goodbye to Alfie before leading Hannah out to the car. It had been an odd day – not always pleasant and definitely not as structured as she'd normally like – but there was something niggling at her. A warmth in the pit of her stomach, almost like the beginnings of butterflies.

Feeling foolish, she pushed the sensation to the back of her mind and headed home.

Chapter Twenty

Willow

Willow removed the dust mask and straightened, rubbing her back with one hand as she reached for the Kenny mug with the other. She'd been hunched over the dresser for most of the day, scraping off years worth of varnish and sanding the wood. There were a few more cracks in the woodwork than first anticipated, but she was sure it wouldn't be a problem to fix.

She moved through to the shop, where Gary was packing and labelling items that had been ordered from the website. She placed the mug down on the counter and stretched.

'Do you think you could lock up for me tonight?' She was suddenly weary and the thought of resuming the sanding of the dresser wasn't met with even a hint of enthusiasm. She'd worked hard on it all day; she deserved an early finish.

'Really?' Gary's eyebrows shot up his forehead before they relaxed again, his mouth stretching into a wide smile. 'Yeah. I can do that.' It was a responsibility he hadn't had before, but he was nodding, ready to take the step forward.

'Great.' Willow reached into the drawer under the counter and handed Gary the set of keys for the shop, firing off a set of instructions. She tidied her things away in the workroom and finished her coffee before leaving Gary to it. She was putting her trust in her assistant, but she was confident he'd prove her instincts right.

Climbing into the van again instead of walking, Willow drove to the supermarket, picking up the ingredients for a stir-fry. As a thank you for the food and company the previous evening, she'd decided to cook a meal for Mae and Hannah. The house was silent when she arrived back at the bed and breakfast and, guessing the others weren't home, she headed straight for the kitchen to make a start.

The chicken was browning in the pan as Willow sliced a red pepper into thin strips. She added the peppers and made up some chicken stock, pouring it into the pan, along with soy sauce and a handful of mangetout. She loved cooking and hadn't realised quite how much she'd missed creating dishes until she'd started to prep the stir-fry. Her makeshift kitchen at the house couldn't compare.

Her phone rang as she was adding sliced mushrooms and broccoli to the pan. Seeing her husband's name on the screen, she pressed to answer, tucking the phone between her shoulder and ear so she could chat and continue cooking at the same time.

'Hey, you.' She was unable to keep the smile from her face as the butterflies took flight in her tummy. Things had been a bit tough lately, but the Kenny mug had reminded her why they were together. She and Ethan were a strong team who could get through anything.

'I've just finished work,' Ethan told her. 'So I thought I'd ring and see how you were.'

'I'm okay.' Willow checked the noodles cooking in a pan next to the stir-fry. 'But I really miss you.'

'I miss you too.'

'Do you know when you'll be coming home?' Willow transferred the noodles to the frying pan and combined them with the other ingredients, silently praying the answer would be soon. She hated being apart.

'I really wish I could come home now,' Ethan said. 'But we're not ready yet. Things still aren't right, but we'll get there.'

Willow turned the heat off on both hobs and grabbed the frying pan. As though on cue, she heard the front door open, followed by the excited chatter of a child.

'I have to go now,' Willow said as Mae and Hannah bustled into the kitchen. 'I'll speak to you later. Love you.'

'Love you too,' Ethan said, causing the butterflies to take flight once again. Willow had learned it was especially important to hear that when times were tough.

'Something smells good,' Mae said once Willow had hung up.

'I thought I'd repay the favour and cook for you tonight,' Willow said. 'I hope you don't mind me using your pots and pans.'

'Are you kidding? You can use whatever you like if you're feeding me.' She laughed and made her way over to the stove, inhaling deeply. 'What are we having?'

'Chicken stir-fry, and you're just in time.' Willow grabbed some plates from the cupboard and started to serve the dish.

'Perfect. Thank you so much.' Mae rested a hand on Willow's shoulder before turning to Hannah. 'Why don't you go and put your new toy away and wash your hands before we eat?'

Mae quickly set the table while Willow finished serving the stir-fry and carried the plates across to the table. She'd been hoping Melody would be around to eat with them and had made extra, but she still wasn't back at the house by the time Hannah returned and sat herself at the table.

'This smells delicious,' Mae said as she picked up her knife and fork. 'It's a treat to have someone cook for me for a change.'

'It's a treat to be able to cook again. I can't wait until my kitchen's installed. I've got it all planned out: we're going to have white tiles with a white, high-gloss countertop to give it a clean, fresh feel, but the room will be warmed up with soft pewter cabinets and oak flooring. I found a gorgeous Belfast sink at a salvage yard that's cleaned up beautifully.' She sighed and twirled some noodles onto her fork. 'I can see it so clearly in my head, but I'm not sure it'll happen now. A fancy kitchen probably won't be in the budget.' There probably wouldn't *be* a budget for much longer.

The kitchen plans didn't stop there. There was going to be a sweet window seat overlooking the garden, upholstered with some gorgeous vintage fabric Willow had put aside especially, and bifold doors would open out onto the beautifully paved patio area (the patio area didn't exist yet, but it would, one day). A huge oak table would take centre stage, ready for them to sit down to eat with their rosy-cheeked children. Again, the children didn't exist yet, but Willow couldn't help looking to the future.

Unfortunately, Willow's plans for the future weren't guaranteed.

'Have you heard anything more about the house?' Mae asked, so Willow pushed the images of her beautiful babies aside and filled her in on the latest development.

'So, more waiting,' she concluded. 'I think we're going to have to look at a short-term let when Ethan gets back, which isn't ideal, budget-wise, but if the house isn't safe, we don't have much choice.' She shrugged. 'Who knows, we may end up losing the house and end up renting long term.'

'Will it come to that?' Mae asked.

'Maybe,' Willow said, quite able to envisage her hopes and dreams slipping away. They'd been slipping away for some time already. Losing the house would only add to it.

'Do you mind if I have another bath?' Willow asked once the dishwasher was stacked after their meal. She rubbed at her lower back and winced. 'I think I overdid it moving a dresser this morning. My back's been niggling since this afternoon.'

'Of course, go ahead,' Mae said. 'There's some paracetamol in the cabinet if you need it.'

'Thanks, but I think the bath and an early night should be enough.' She yawned, suddenly realising how tired she was. Either she was working too hard or her body was trying to coax her back into the sumptuous bed upstairs. She felt her muscles relax at the mere thought of sinking beneath the sheets.

'There are fresh towels in the cupboard,' Mae said. 'Help yourself.'

Willow was about to drag her weary body up the stairs when she heard scratching at the back door. As Mae was on the other side of the kitchen, Willow headed to the door, shuffling back as the cat bolted inside.

'Oh, no, no, no.' Mae scuttled across the kitchen, plucking the cat from the lino and carrying it back towards the door with her arms outstretched so the cat made little contact with her body. 'Whatever you do, don't let this cheeky little bugger into the house. I'm sure he's trying to adopt us, but it's not happening.' Plonking the cat outside, Mae quickly hopped back into the kitchen and closed the door behind her.

'That's not your cat?' Willow slid her eyes round to Hannah, who was still sitting at the table. She *knew* the Frosties thing was unorthodox. The little girl flashed a grin before dropping her gaze down to the tabletop.

'Absolutely not,' Mae said, dusting off her hands. 'The last thing I need is more responsibility.'

'He is pretty cute, though,' Willow said. 'In a Grumpy Cat sort of way. I'd adopt him myself but Ethan doesn't fare too well around cats. It sets his asthma off.' She looked back at the door, worrying about the poor fur ball. 'Do we have an animal sanctuary around here?'

Mae laughed. 'Oh, I wouldn't worry yourself too much over that one. You haven't felt how podgy he is! It wouldn't surprise me if he had a perfectly good home but was just trying his luck with all the neighbours.'

'You think?' It wasn't beyond the realms of possibility, and he did seem to be in decent enough condition, apart from the jagged ears, and he probably couldn't help the perma-pissed-off expression on his little feline face. Resting bitch face wasn't just for humans, after all.

'I really do,' Mae said. 'He's a chancer, like most of the male species of this world.'

Willow didn't necessarily agree with the last part of that statement, but she was convinced enough that the cat wasn't in any danger and took herself upstairs to sink into a heavenly warm bubble bath.

Chapter Twenty-One

Melody

Working in the ice-cream van turned out to be a lot of fun. So much so, it wasn't like working at all. Melody and Hugo had a laugh, joking and teasing in between customers (of which there were a lot. If the proposed ice-cream parlour in the park proved as popular, Hugo and his brother didn't have a lot to worry about). And the very best part was the sampling of the products.

'Oh my God,' Melody moaned as she tasted the strawberry cheesecake ice cream. The ice cream was soft and creamy, yet there was added texture from the crunchy biscuit base and real strawberries swirled throughout. 'This is amazing. I need a cone. A big one.'

Melody had sampled each of the ice creams on offer, but this was by far her favourite.

'It's the least I can do after your afternoon's work.' Hugo selected a large waffle cone from one of the shelves. It was a bit of a squeeze in the van and they'd spent most of the day switching between serving the customers and sitting at the front, as it was near impossible to function with two bodies in the main part of the van. But, as the customers had waned, Hugo had lured Melody from her resting place with a plastic sampling spoon. Now, as he reached for the cone, his body pressed against hers and there was little room to manoeuvre out of the way.

'Sorry,' Hugo said as they stood chest to chest. 'It's a bit tricky with two. This is why James and I work separate shifts. There were one too many compromising situations and people were starting to talk.'

Melody covered her mouth as she started to giggle. 'Is that a cone in your pocket, or are you just pleased to see me?'

'That's what James said. Talk about creating an atmosphere.' Hugo shuffled towards the tubs of ice cream and scooped out two generous portions of the strawberry cheesecake, balancing them one on top of the other in the cone. Melody watched as he added strawberry sauce, wondering why she felt so deflated that he'd moved away. For the briefest of moments, she'd suspected Hugo was going to lean in for a kiss, but it wasn't as though she *wanted* him to kiss her. She might have felt a bit daring earlier in the day, her mind muddled after the Ferris wheel incident, but she couldn't actually kiss Hugo. It would feel as though she was betraying Ollie.

'So, it's your last evening in Clifton-on-Sea,' Hugo said as he handed over the giant ice cream. 'What would you like to do? More photos of the harbour? A last walk along the beach?'

'I haven't actually had a proper walk on the beach yet,' Melody admitted and Hugo's eyes widened.

'You're kidding me? You can't visit a seaside town and not have a paddle.'

Melody shrugged. 'I've been distracted.' She gave Hugo a pointed look. 'And working my ass off all afternoon.'

'Hey, it was a good photo opportunity.' Hugo pointed at the camera, back in its rightful place around her neck.

She'd been snapping away as they worked, capturing the fun. It was an interesting angle on the photo festival's theme and she couldn't wait to have a proper look at the images, even if they didn't end up as part of her collection. 'Any chance I could take a look at those?' Hugo did a good impression of a cartoon puppy, all wide eyes and fluttering eyelashes.

'I'm not sure.' The fingers on her free hand found the camera's strap. 'Maybe.' She was leaving tomorrow. She wouldn't see Hugo again. What harm would it do letting him have a peek? If he judged her, thought her work was utter crap, what would it matter? She wouldn't be sticking around long enough to hear it.

'Really?' Hugo asked. 'You'd seriously let me have a look?'

Melody shrugged. 'We'll see.'

'Man, I wish I'd asked to see your—'

Melody whipped round (as best as she could in the limited space) and pointed her ice cream at Hugo. 'Do not finish that sentence unless you want to go home wearing an ice-cream hat.'

Hugo held his hands up, palms out. 'Easy. I wasn't going to say anything untoward.'

Melody narrowed her eyes, but she lowered her ice-cream weapon. 'Why don't I believe you?'

'Maybe because you're not very trusting of people? Because something – or someone – has hurt you and you've built this wall up around you in the hope it'll protect you from being hurt again?' Hugo shrugged. 'Or maybe it's because I'm a pig with filthy thoughts.' He reached over to close the van's hatch. 'Come on. We've got some paddling to do before you leave.'

Grabbing Melody's non-ice-cream-wielding hand, Hugo led her out of the van, locking up before drawing her down to the beach. Her feet sank into the dry sand as they reached the bottom of the steps, and she was sure she could already feel the grains working their way into her socks and between her toes.

'I'll hold that while you take your shoes and socks off,' Hugo offered, pointing at the ice cream. They'd wandered down from the steps to the shoreline, the water lapping rhythmically just ahead. The sand was wetter here, sturdier, and Melody looked back at the footsteps they'd left behind. The beach was quieter now, with only a handful of people visible along the stretch of sand. The holidaymakers had packed up their picnics and blankets and headed back to their lodgings as afternoon merged into evening, the sun still bright but less fierce now. The pier was still alive, the sounds – both natural and manufactured – still audible over the sloshing waves.

'We're seriously going for a paddle?' Melody asked as the ice cream was plucked from her fingers. She'd already eaten one of the scoops, but the other was starting to melt, the pink ice cream dripping down to her fingers.

'Hell, yes.' Hugo pulled a face at Melody. 'It's in the Clifton-on-Sea rule book. Thou shalt not leave town without first having a paddle. Didn't you read it?'

Melody rolled her eyes, but bent to untie her shoes. 'I didn't. Are there any other rules I should know about?'

'Let's see...' Hugo drummed his fingers on his chin. 'Thou shalt build at least one mighty sandcastle, complete with a moat, seashell decorations and a Union Jack flag.'

Melody removed one of her trainers, balancing on one foot to remove her sock. 'I haven't done that either. And I don't have a bucket and spade to build one with.'

Hugo gave a slow nod of his head. 'You're a rebel. I like it.'

Melody removed the other shoe and sock and grabbed the ice cream, licking a dollop that was melting and trickling down the cone. 'Any more rules I'm breaking?'

With his hands now free, Hugo began his footwear removal. 'Please tell me you've played bingo. That's a *major* Clifton-on-Sea rule. Plus, you could win yourself a keyring that will fall apart as soon as you leave town, if not before.'

Melody shook her head. 'Nope, sorry. No bingo.'

Hugo shook his head at her and sighed. 'I do hope you know the most important rule when it comes to the seaside.' He placed his shoes and socks together neatly on the sand while Melody waited for the answer. 'Last one in's a rotten egg.' And with that, he pelted towards the water, whooping and leaping in the air as the freezing cold water washed over his bare feet. Melody hesitated for just a second or two before she sprinted after him.

Melody's feet were damp and gritty as they made their way along the promenade, her cut-off shorts wet and sticking uncomfortably. The paddle had started off well; it was actually fun as she and Hugo kicked at the water, splashing and laughing and generally acting like overgrown children. But why should the young get to have all the fun? Why shouldn't two adults, firmly in their mid twenties, enjoy the simple pleasure of attempting to drench their pal?

'I hope that's waterproof,' Hugo had said when they'd taken a breather, pointing at the camera still looped around her neck.

'It is.' Melody lifted the camera and took aim at Hugo, who pulled a cheesy, superhero-style pose with his hands planted on his hips while he looked out across the water, chin slightly raised. Melody had stepped backwards to get a better shot, but her foot had become tangled in a strand of seaweed and she'd ended up on her arse, the freezing water seeping through her shorts.

Hugo had laughed.

A lot.

The bastard.

'You could at least help me up,' Melody had grumbled. Luckily, her ice cream had long gone, otherwise it would have been ruined.

'Sorry,' Hugo said as he waded over. He held a hand out for Melody, which she grasped tightly. But instead of hauling herself up, she had tugged hard, sending Hugo onto his knees in the water so they were both equally as soggy.

'Here we go,' Hugo said now, pointing across the road. 'Bingo.'

Melody looked at him with disbelief. 'We are not playing bingo.'

'Yup, we are.' Taking her hand, he led Melody across the road, dipping into the arcade. Melody was assaulted by lights and sounds as Hugo led her towards the back of the vast room. A couple of steps led up to the bingo area, where low stools were arranged in front of lit-up grids of numbers. A game was already in session, and although there were currently only three people taking part, it didn't dampen the caller's enthusiasm.

'Sit there.' Hugo placed his hands on Melody's shoulders, pushing down gently until she yielded and sank onto the stool. 'We need tokens. I'll be back in a sec.'

Melody turned to the grid in front of her as Hugo headed for the token machine. There were little sliding windows to cover each number when it was called instead of the bingo dabbers her nan used, and it was all done electronically, but still… It was *bingo*. It was naff and cheesy but, as Hugo had pointed out, it *was* a seaside tradition. Taking her camera in hand, she took a couple of shots of the multicoloured boards, making sure she caught the grubby, horribly patterned carpet in the background. She probably wouldn't use any of these photos at the festival, but she had nothing better to do while she waited.

'Right, ladies,' the bingo caller roared into his microphone. 'Are we ready for a new game?'

Melody glanced around the room and noted the participants were indeed all of the female variety as Hugo had yet to return.

'Just in time!' Hugo threw himself onto the neighbouring stool, placing a couple of drinks down next to the grids before slotting a token into his machine and handing another to Melody. 'Come on, hurry or you'll miss out.'

'Believe me, I'm not afraid of that,' Melody said, but she inserted her token anyway. Her grid was brought to life and she copied Hugo by making sure all the windows were open. She rolled her eyes as the game began, but Hugo simply grinned back at her.

Half an hour later, Melody was begrudgingly admitting she'd had fun, mostly due to laughing at Hugo's supercompetitiveness. He'd sat hunched over his grid, ready to pounce whenever one of his numbers was called, rubbing his hands in anticipation as he awaited the next. He'd made a fist, pulling it in towards his body with a hissed 'yes!' every time he won, which was frequent enough to reward them thirty-five coupon points by the time they'd finished.

'You choose,' Hugo said once they'd made their way over to the prize counter. Melody had failed to win a single game (and claimed it was a fix).

'They're your points.' She peered at the prizes on offer and scrunched up her nose. 'And it's all crap.'

Arrayed in front of them, and with various point values, was a selection of tat: dinosaur erasers, flimsy but brightly coloured combs, plastic whistles, sticky aliens encased in plastic eggs, rubbery spiders, and individually wrapped pieces of bubble gum. In the end, Hugo chose a rainbow of plastic beads threaded onto an elastic chord, and an orange-flavoured lollipop, both of which he gave to Melody.

'A memento from your trip,' he said as he placed the bracelet on her wrist. It was designed for a child, so it was dangerously stretched, but it was a sweet gesture.

'I'll never take it off,' Melody said with a faux-gushing tone.

Hugo took her hand and led her through the maze of arcade machines towards the exit. He kept doing that. Holding her hand. And Melody kept letting him. She quite liked it, though she tried not to.

The sun was starting to dip, the evening turning chilly, as they stepped out onto the pavement. The pier was illuminated now, the noise still carrying across, vibrant and full of life.

'I need to get the van back,' Hugo said as they crossed the road and started to make their way back along the promenade. 'And Scoop will be wondering where I am.'

'I should be getting back to the bed and breakfast.' Melody wrapped her free arm around her body, suddenly feeling the chill. 'I've still got a soggy bottom, and I've got an early start tomorrow.'

'You're going straight away?' Hugo asked and she nodded.

'That's the plan.'

They walked along in silence, the only noise coming from the sloshing waves and decreasing sounds from the pier, still hand-in-hand. The ice-cream van was just ahead, the bed and breakfast not much further. Soon this – whatever it was – would be over.

'It's been great meeting you,' Hugo said once they'd reached the van. 'It's a shame I didn't get to see the photos.'

'Come here.' Melody huddled in close to Hugo outside the van and, holding her camera at arm's length, took a photo of them both. She brought the image up on the screen, laughing at the face Hugo had pulled, his tongue lolling and eyes crossed. 'I think this is the best photo I've ever taken.' She handed the camera to Hugo, who nodded in agreement.

'You've certainly caught my best angle.'

'This is definitely going in my collection for the photo festival. I wouldn't be surprised if I won.'

'You never said what the prize was,' Hugo said. 'If you win with my photo, will I be entitled to half?'

'There are two – one judged by professionals, the other by the public. Each is a thousand pounds, but it's about more than that. For me, anyway.'

Hugo leaned against the van, tilting his head as he waited for further information. Melody squirmed, not sure she was ready to reveal more, to open up the wound she was trying her best to squeeze shut.

'Someone believed in me and my photos.' She frowned, trying to say the words that had been trapped inside for the past year. She found she couldn't, no matter how much she pushed, so she gave the simplified version she could manage. 'They thought it was something I should pursue. Professionally. This is my way of putting it out there, testing the water. If I'm laughed out of the festival, I'll know I'm not good enough.'

'And if you win?' Hugo asked.

Melody grinned. 'Then it's a huge fluke, obviously. Or a mistake.'

Hugo reached out and rested a hand on her arm. 'You need to have more faith in yourself.'

'That's what Ollie used to say.' Melody dropped her gaze to her camera, switching it off. 'Anyway, I'd better get going. It's been fun, these last couple of days. I wasn't expecting that.'

'You weren't expecting to have fun at the seaside?'

Melody shook her head and raised her camera. 'I thought I'd be too busy concentrating on this. Thanks for distracting me.'

Hugo smiled, but it was tinged with sadness or regret and he couldn't quite pull it off. 'Any time. Good luck with the festival.'

'Thanks,' Melody said, already backing away. 'Good luck with the ice-cream parlour. You should definitely go for it.'

She turned then, and made her way back to the bed and breakfast.

Chapter Twenty-Two

Mae

Why was she *always* in a rush in the mornings? She was always up early to arrange breakfast for her guests, and it wasn't as though mornings and the tasks they required were a new thing, yet here she was, hurrying Hannah along while multitasking the brushing of teeth, selecting an outfit and hunting for the cat. He'd slipped in when she'd foolishly opened the back door that morning and, other than the flash of fur as he propelled himself into the kitchen, hadn't been seen since. She'd checked all the rooms downstairs, had searched every nook and cranny, but the little bugger must have sneaked upstairs. She was up there now, toothbrush in mouth, a pair of three-quarter-length jeans trailing over an arm, making silly come-here-kitty sounds as she moved from room to room.

'Hannah,' she said, her voice distorted by the toothbrush. 'Can you put that toy away and look for the cat?'

Hannah gasped and dropped the remote control for her new Minion toy on her bedroom floor. 'Chilly's here?' Obviously, when Mae asked Hannah to 'put that toy away' her daughter had heard 'leave it dumped on the floor', but Mae didn't have time to argue.

'Yesh. But he neesh to go outshide.' Mae's voice was becoming more and more distorted by the teeth-brushing, so she moved through to the bathroom to spit. She turned around to check the bath, the cabinet, even shoving her hands in between the towels in the airing cupboard, just in case. 'Hannah? Did you find him?' She'd rinsed her brush and plopped it into the holder before returning to Hannah's room. Hannah was lying on the edge of her bed, her hair trailing down to the carpet as she hung over to peer underneath. 'Is he there?' Sidestepping the Minion, she crouched to have a look herself.

'Nope.' Hannah righted herself and shook her head. 'Shall I go and get him some Frosties?'

'No. Absolutely not.' Mae crossed the room, calling over her shoulder, 'Keep checking, please.'

Mae had already searched her own bedroom, plus the bathroom twice, and as the guests' rooms were closed and presumably locked, Hannah's bedroom was the only other option. She'd have searched the room herself but she was already running late and not even dressed yet.

'Any luck?' she asked once she'd dressed and applied her trademark make-up: striking red lipstick, an expert-standard eyeliner flick, and a well-defined eyebrow.

'He's not here.' Hannah's bottom lip started to protrude ever so slightly as she thumped her arms across her chest. 'I wanted to play with him.'

'He's not our cat, darling,' Mae said as she started a search of her own. She knew her daughter well enough to know her efforts would have been less than thorough. In fact, the under-the-bed search was probably the limit. 'Once we find him, he has to go back outside.' If they ever found him. This cat had taken hide-and-seek to a whole new level.

'That's not fair,' Hannah grumbled. 'I want him to be mine.'

'Life doesn't work that way, I'm afraid.' Mae checked the time. Damn! 'Right, little lady, time to get you dressed. What do you want to wear…?' Mae was cut off as Hannah shot in front of her, arms stretched out wide as she pushed herself against the wardrobe.

'No, Mummy! I don't want to get dressed.'

'You have to. Mummy has to work, so you're going to spend the day with Nanny.'

'But I *always* spend the day with Nanny.'

Parental guilt gnawed at Mae's gut, but she pushed it away. She had no other choice. 'You love spending the day with Nanny. Maybe she'll take you down to the beach for a bit? Shall we put your new sandals on, just in case?'

Hannah shook her head, eyes wide as Mae neared. 'I want to stay in my pyjamas.'

'Nope.' Mae shook her head. 'Not happening. That's a slippery slope we're not starting on. You need clothes and shoes and your hair brushing.'

'My brush is over there.' Hannah pointed across the room, to her chest of drawers. 'I want you to brush my hair first.'

Mae followed the direction of Hannah's finger, her eyes narrowing as they returned to her daughter. 'What's going on? You hate me brushing your hair.'

Hannah's eyes were stretched wide, her lips pressed together, arms still outstretched.

'Hannah?' Mae raised an eyebrow. 'What's going on?'

Hannah shook her head, eyes still stretched wide, lips still pressed together, arms still outstretched.

'You don't want me to go in the wardrobe, do you?'

Mae stepped forward. Hannah whimpered.

'No,' she cried as Mae prised her away from the wardrobe. The door had opened just a crack before the cat pelted out, feet scrabbling on the carpet before it lunged for the open bedroom door. Mae followed it down the stairs, hobbling down the steps in her platform heels. The cat made straight for the kitchen, mewling as it waited for Mae to open the back door. Once she did, the cat scuttled out into the garden and leapt up onto the wall before disappearing onto the shed roof in the neighbouring property. Mae closed the door firmly before heading back up the stairs. She was still running late, but at least she now had a chance of getting back on track.

Mae helped Hannah change into a pair of shorts, a flowery T-shirt and her new sandals without any further mishaps. She even managed to brush Hannah's tangled hair without too much fuss.

'There,' Mae said as she secured Hannah's hair into a ponytail. 'You're done. Now we can get going.' But Mae's progress was halted when the doorbell rang. Suppressing a sigh, she hurried down the stairs, her heart sinking when she caught sight of the familiar shape of Mrs Hornchurch through the frosted glass. She'd heard what her mum had said about her neighbour's loneliness, and Mae felt for the woman, she really did, but she was running late, yet again. If she was lucky, she could get away with a ten-minute chat. If she was unlucky...

'Good morning, Mrs Hornchurch.' Mae had plastered a smile on her face milliseconds before she swung the door open and now she filled her voice with an enthusiasm she didn't actually feel.

'Good morning, dear.' Mrs Hornchurch smiled up at Mae, her already creased features crinkling further with the movement. 'I know you're busy so I won't keep you.' If Mae had a pound for every time she'd heard her neighbour utter those words, she wouldn't have to pull pints at the Fisherman to make ends meet. 'I was just wondering if...' Mae didn't get to hear Mrs Hornchurch's musing as a crash behind her interrupted her neighbour's train of thought. 'Oh my goodness, what was that?'

Mae didn't hang around long enough to discuss the possibilities. The crash sounded like it had come from up above, so she turned and scurried up the stairs, calling out her daughter's name as she went. Hannah was standing at the top of the stairs, eyes even wider than they'd been earlier while hiding the cat in the wardrobe, the remote control for her Minion toy in her hands, thumbs still hovering over the controls. As soon as she saw her mother, she burst into tears, the remote control tumbling to the ground.

'What happened?' Mae asked, torn between comforting her daughter and rushing to Melody, who was slumped on the carpet. Killing two birds with one stone, she held out a hand for Hannah to take and crouched in front of Melody. 'Are you okay?'

'I'm fine. Ow!' Melody had attempted to stand, but she dropped back down onto carpet, wincing and hissing through her teeth.

'I'm sorry, Mummy,' Hannah wailed, pushing her face into Mae's shoulder. 'It was an accident.'

'What happened?' Mae asked again, and Melody pointed at the Minion toy, upturned on the hallway carpet.

'I tripped over it as I came down the stairs from my room,' she explained, attempting to stand again. Mae jumped up, offering a supporting hand. 'I think I twisted my ankle as I landed.' Melody attempted to put her foot down and hissed again.

'You should get that seen to,' Mrs Hornchurch said, suddenly behind them. Mae hadn't realised the woman had followed her up the stairs.

Mae looked down at the injured ankle, which was already starting to look a bit red and puffy. 'I'll take you to the walk-in centre – excuse the pun – and get you seen to.' She placed an arm around Melody's waist. 'Do you think you can make it down the stairs and to the car?'

'Maybe.' Melody winced as her foot made contact with the ground again, but she persevered with a half-hop, half-hobble mash-up, pressing her lips together against the pain.

'I can look after Hannah,' Mrs Hornchurch said as Mae helped Melody into the passenger seat of her car. 'It'd be no trouble.'

Mae smiled gratefully at her neighbour. Mrs Hornchurch could be a pain in the arse sometimes, but she had a heart of gold. 'Could you sit in with her until my mum gets here? I was supposed to drop her off, but I'll ask her to pick her up instead.' Mae would also need to get in touch with Frank and Corinne to let them know she'd be late for her shift. Again.

'Of course, dear.' Mrs Hornchurch popped her head into the car. 'I do hope it isn't broken. I have a walking stick gathering dust if you need it. It belonged to my husband but, well, it's no use to him now.'

'Thank you.' Melody pushed a smile through the grimace of pain she'd adopted. 'I'll let you know.'

Mae scooped Hannah into a hug, promising her that Melody would be okay, before climbing into the car. The walk-in centre was only a short drive away, so Mae made sure Melody was booked in and settled as well as she could be in one of the plastic chairs before she nipped outside to make her phone calls. It was Frank who answered when she called the Fisherman, and he told Mae not to worry about her shift as Corinne was there and they'd manage between them.

'Thanks, Frank. I'll be there as soon as I can and I'll make it up to you,' she said before saying goodbye and moving on to the next call. Mae hadn't spoken to her mum since her outburst outside the café, but both were happy enough to brush it under the carpet.

'Mrs Hornchurch said she's happy to sit with Hannah until you get there,' Mae said after explaining the situation.

'I'll pop over now,' Eloise said. 'I haven't seen Mrs Hornchurch for a while so I'll stop and have a natter before we head off.'

'I think she'd like that,' Mae said, feeling guilty she'd felt a flash of annoyance towards her kind-hearted neighbour earlier.

She returned to the waiting room, stopping at the water dispenser and filling a couple of plastic cups. She sat down and handed one to Melody.

'How are you feeling?'

'Not too bad now I'm sitting.' She lifted her foot. The ankle was definitely swollen now. 'It's throbbing, but I'm pretty sure it isn't broken or anything.'

'I'm so sorry,' Mae said. 'Hannah shouldn't have been playing out in the hallway.'

Melody shrugged. 'It was an accident, and I wasn't paying attention. I was messing with my camera so didn't see it in front of me.' Her camera, as ever, was looped around her neck. 'It looks like my hobby is out to get me.'

'I still feel so incredibly guilty.'

Melody reached out and gave Mae's hand a squeeze. 'Don't. Like I said, it was an accident. If anything, I should have been looking where I was going.'

Mae nodded, though she couldn't shift the niggling feeling that she was responsible for whatever injury Melody had sustained. What if her ankle *was* broken and she couldn't continue with her project? Mae couldn't stand the thought she'd trampled over somebody's dream. Whatever happened, Mae would have to make it up to Melody, somehow.

Chapter Twenty-Three

Melody

The waiting room at the walk-in centre was pretty busy, with patients ranging from the very young (a baby, only a few months old, with a disgruntled disposition, which may or may not have had something to do with the rash blooming across her left cheek) to the elderly, hunched over in their not-very-comfortable seats (Melody had only been waiting for around twenty minutes and she could no longer feel her arse cheeks, though she was sure they were still attached). In between, there were toddlers, happily scattering the contents of a plastic toy box across the floor while their parents looked on in dismay, most likely thinking *they* were *poorly before we got here. They'd better bloody show signs of illness when we finally get in to the see the doctor*, school-aged children, bored of looking at the same torn and drawn-on books from the small pile on a table, and adults with varying degrees of illness or injury.

Despite the number of patients waiting their turn, the seat next to Melody was empty so she was able to rest her foot on it, the ankle elevated slightly as it lay on top of Mae's handbag. It was a gorgeous vintage handbag, black leather with rounded handles and gold clasps, and epitomised Mae's glamour. She hadn't been particularly keen on using the beautiful bag as a cushion for her foot, but her ankle was throbbing painfully and Mae had insisted.

'Are you sure I'm not going to ruin it?' Melody asked, again. The handbag was an actual vintage piece from the fifties, rather than a retro-style, mass-produced product that could be easily replaced, and Melody felt terrible that her foot was plonked on top of it.

'It's survived this long.' Mae shrugged. 'And it's only a handbag. Not all that important in the grand scheme of things.'

'But it's important to you. It's part of your identity.'

Melody had never met anybody with such a strong sense of style as Mae in real life. Even now, on an ordinary Wednesday morning and wearing a pair of three-quarter-length jeans and a checked, sleeveless blouse, Mae looked as though she'd stepped out of a vintage copy of *Vogue*. Her make-up was flawless and striking, her hair pinned and secured with a cerise rose to one side, while soft waves rested on her shoulders, not one strand out of place. Melody, in contrast, had simply pulled her hair, still damp from the shower, into a ponytail and slicked on a layer of strawberry lip balm that morning.

'You always look so immaculate,' Melody said, her voice full of admiration. She couldn't remember the last time she'd bothered with make-up, but she suspected it was before Ollie, back when she cared about her appearance. She only wore the lip balm now because it had added SPF.

'My appearance doesn't match the inside,' Mae said. 'Believe me. I find I'm winging it more and more with every passing day. I only wish my life was as organised as my wardrobe.'

'Have you always dressed like this?' Melody asked and Mae shook her head.

'Only for the past three years. It's the image I like to present to the world. The image of having my shit together.' She caught Melody's eye and grinned. 'But that's our little secret, okay?'

Melody nodded. 'I won't tell a soul.' She took a sip of her water. 'How did it happen, though? How did you go from normal Mae to Ms 1950s Glamour? What made you decide *this is the person I want to be*, at least on the surface?'

'It was my granny, really. We used to play around when I went to her house when I was little, rolling our hair and trying on her make-up. She showed me all kinds of hairstyles she wore as a young woman, so on the day of her funeral, I decided to pay tribute to that, to remember the fun times we'd had. I did my hair and make-up and, when I looked in the mirror, I didn't see me. I saw this other woman. This strong, independent woman who hadn't been abandoned by the father of her child – and her own father, if we're digging a little deeper. She didn't need a man to prop her up. She was made of stern stuff, this woman in the mirror. She was capable. I wanted to be her more than anything, so I've kept the mask on ever since.'

'I wish I could do that,' Melody said. She thought about the photo in the back pocket of her shorts, the photo she slipped onto the bedside table at the B&B each night and returned to her pocket in the morning so it was always with her. 'I wish I could be somebody else.'

Mae tilted her head. 'What's wrong with the person you are?'

'I could ask that about you,' Melody pointed out.

'That's true,' Mae said. 'Shall we not go there?'

Melody laughed. 'It's starting to feel like we're sitting on a psych's couch rather than these awful plastic chairs.'

Mae shifted on her seat. 'Not terribly comfortable, are they? Hopefully we won't have to wait too much longer.'

The wait was another hour. Mae helped Melody to hobble across the waiting room and into the designated room, where the doctor examined the ankle before proclaiming it was nothing more serious than a sprain.

'You'll need to rest it for a few days – definitely no running or walking long distances for the next week or two. I'll give you a leaflet with some gentle exercises you can do at home to keep the joint moving without making the injury worse.'

A week or two? Melody thought as the doctor wheeled herself across the room on her chair. What about her project? She was due back at work in a few days!

'I can also give you a tubular bandage to help with support and swelling.' The doctor, having wheeled herself back to her desk, handed a leaflet to Melody. 'You can take paracetamol for the pain if necessary, and if the swelling increases, you can wrap some ice in a damp towel and apply it to the ankle for fifteen to twenty minutes every two to three hours.'

Melody listened to the advice, allowed her ankle to be wrapped in the bandage, and hobbled out of the walk-in centre without saying a word.

'What am I going to do?' she finally asked once they were at the car. She leaned against the bonnet, catching her breath after the painful shuffle across the waiting room and car park. 'I'm supposed to be on a train, in a new town. I'm going to have to go home and forget all about my project.' Melody reached for the camera, still looped around her neck, feeling its familiar, comforting weight in her hands. 'I don't want to go home. Not yet. I'm not ready.'

'You're going to come home with me.' Mae opened the passenger door and eased Melody into the seat. 'And you're going to rest for a few days, like the doctor said. The room you're in isn't booked for nearly two weeks, so we don't need to worry about that. And I'm obviously not going to charge you, since it's my fault you're in this position in the first place.'

'It was an accident,' Melody said.

'An accident that could have been prevented.' Mae closed the door and moved round to the driver's side, sliding onto the seat next to Melody. 'I'm not sure what we'll do about your project, but let's concentrate on letting that ankle heal first.'

Melody had little choice in the matter. She could hardly walk across to the car, even with Mae's support, so there was no chance she could go off on her travels at the moment. The only other alternative was returning home early, and the idea alone made her feel queasy.

Mae went into full-on mum mode when they arrived back at the bed and breakfast, settling Melody on the sofa, leg propped up on cushions, blanket draped over her despite the heat, generally fussing over her.

'Shouldn't you be getting to work?' Melody asked as Mae brought in a tray filled with sandwiches, cake and tea. 'I'll be fine here now, I promise.'

Mae chewed on her bottom lip, weighing up the possibility. 'Are you sure?'

'I've only sprained my ankle,' Melody said. 'It's slowing me down, but I'll be fine.'

'I could give you Mrs Hornchurch's number, just in case. And my number, obviously, but it'll take me a while to get here. Mrs Hornchurch is just next door.'

'Seriously, Mae, I'll be okay.' Melody lifted the remote, which Mae had pressed into her hand earlier. 'I'll have daytime TV to keep me company.'

Mae hesitated, still weighing up her options, before she nodded. 'I will leave you those numbers, though, just to be on the safe side.'

The house was silent once Mae left, so Melody switched the TV on, turning the volume up to fill the room with noise. She didn't like the quiet. The quiet gave you space to think, to remember. It brought your fears and weaknesses to the surface.

Melody turned the TV up a little bit more.

Chapter Twenty-Four

Willow

Willow was enjoying working on the dresser. It was hard work and the sanding had been particularly arduous, but she loved seeing items like this given a new lease of life, watching as they were transformed from something stuck in the corner of a room, largely forgotten, to a beautiful, useful piece that would take centre stage again. So far, she'd stripped the dresser, sanded it down, and primed the wood before Gary applied the first coat of duck-egg-blue paint. Once it was dry, she'd apply another coat or two, attach new hinges to the little cupboard doors and apply the vintage paper to the wall behind the shelves. The finishing touch would be the salvaged handles, which she'd paint the same shade as the dresser before screwing them onto the cupboard doors.

Gary had been busy keeping her topped up with coffee, nipping out to buy sandwiches for lunch, answering the phone, and serving the customers in the shop. Willow loved her shop, loved chatting with the customers, but it was the creative side of her business she truly adored, and taking on Gary had allowed her to lose herself in her projects while safe in the knowledge that the shop was in capable hands.

'Good news,' Gary said as she stepped into the shop, wiping her hands on an old towel. 'We've sold the last of the planters. I said we'd deliver them when we close up this evening. I hope that's okay? I checked the diary and there was nothing in there.'

'Nope, that's fabulous.' Willow hopped up onto one of the stools behind the counter. She'd have a little break while she waited for the paint to dry on the dresser. 'It'll be nice not having to lug them in and out of the shop each morning. Speaking of which, would you be able to help out with the delivery? I don't think I'd manage them on my own.'

The backache Willow had experienced the day before had eased off, but she didn't want to push it too much, just in case.

'Sure,' Gary said. 'It isn't as though I haven't had enough practice. You should start charging a gym subscription for this place.' He grinned at Willow and she stuck her tongue out at him.

'Go and stick the kettle on before I give you more heavy lifting to do.'

Gary saluted as, still grinning, he made his way to the little kitchen. 'Yes, ma'am.'

'You're learning,' she called after him. 'Now if we could just practise the bowing as I enter the room, that'd be grand.' She chuckled to herself as Gary disappeared, but the joyful smile slipped from her face as the shop door opened and a practised, professional smile took its place.

'Hello. Can I help you with anything, or are you just browsing?' She was already sliding off the stool as the customer – a woman in her early thirties and clearly pregnant – made her way to the counter, leaning against it gratefully, almost gasping for breath. Full-on summer clearly wasn't a good time to be heavily pregnant.

'Would you like a glass of water?' Willow asked, concerned about her laboured breathing. 'Or a seat?' She grabbed the stool, but the customer shook her head.

'Oh, no. Thanks,' she said between breaths. 'I'll be all right in a second. It's these steep streets. And this, obviously.' She shifted and rested a hand on her protruding bump. 'I've got another three months to go and I already feel like a small elephant.' She giggled and rolled her eyes. 'I dread to think what I'm going to be like at the end. A blimp, probably.'

'I think you look lovely,' Willow said. 'Blooming.'

'Blooming fat and sweaty,' the customer said with a grin. 'Anyway, the reason I'm here...' She reached into her bag and pulled out her phone, tapping away before turning it to face Willow. 'We've been given this furniture for when the baby's born. It's from my partner's grandparents' attic, and while it's lovely...' She swiped through the collection of donated furniture: a wardrobe, a chest of drawers, a rocking chair and a cot. 'It's all a bit mish-mashed and not what I had in mind for the nursery.'

Willow could see the problem. The furniture looked sturdy enough with minimal damage over the years and would clean up quite easily, but each piece was made from a different type of wood.

'My friend bought a sideboard from you a while ago and I loved it, so I was wondering if you could do something with all this?' The customer pressed her lips together, her eyes wide and hopeful.

'Of course.' Willow handed the phone back. 'Do you have time to go through some ideas now, or shall we set up an appointment for you to come back?'

The customer checked the time on her phone. 'I was on my way to a pregnancy yoga class, so it's probably best if I come back.'

'No problem.' Willow grabbed her diary from the drawer. 'When are you free?'

'I could come over tomorrow lunchtime, if that's okay with you?'

'Perfect.' Willow grabbed a pen to jot down the appointment. *Lunchtime – nursery furniture consultation.* 'I'll see you tomorrow.'

With a wave, the customer waddled out of the shop. Willow waited until the door had closed behind her before she slumped onto her stool, suddenly weary. She emitted a long sigh as she slouched against the counter.

'You look like you need this.' Gary appeared with two cups of coffee, carrying them carefully across the shop and placing them on the counter.

'I need something stronger, kid,' Willow said.

'It's two for one between six and seven at the Fisherman tonight,' Gary said and Willow laughed.

'I'll bear that in mind. For now, this coffee will have to do.'

Willow really was exhausted by the time she made it back to the bed and breakfast that evening, the planters safely delivered to their new owner. She'd dropped Gary off at home afterwards before driving on to the B&B. Driving to and from work was becoming a bit of a habit. She'd have to break it and get back to walking before it was too ingrained. The walk was good, gentle exercise and the fresh air didn't hurt either.

Her phone was ringing as she stepped inside the house, so she headed straight up to her room to answer it. She hadn't spoken to Ethan that day, so she was glad to see his name on her screen. Being apart from her husband wasn't something she was used to and she couldn't wait until he was home again.

'Hey, you.' She felt her throat tighten as she spoke, the threat of tears imminent. Ethan being away was clearly getting to her more than she'd realised. She needed to get a grip – it had only been a few days!

'Have you heard anything more from Liam?' Ethan asked.

'Nope, we're still waiting on the surveyor.' Willow sat on the bed, stretching her legs out full-length as she chatted to her husband. She was starting to feel a bit better now she was hearing his voice. If she closed her eyes, it was almost like they were in the same room together. 'I can't wait for it to be sorted. Why do we seem to have all the bad luck?'

'Will,' Ethan said, and she heard him sigh softly. 'This is just a blip. It'll get sorted.'

'I'm not just talking about the house.'

'I know.'

Neither of them spoke for a moment. Willow lay down on the bed, tucking herself into the foetal position as she listened to the soft breathing of her husband. She wanted him to come home – or to the bed and breakfast, at least. She wanted to forget all about their recent quarrels and enjoy being together again, like it had been in the beginning.

'Sorry,' Willow said, breaking the silence. She sat up, running a hand over her eyes. 'I'm just tired and stressed. Ignore me.'

'Willow...' She sat up straighter as she heard Ethan sigh again. 'We need to have a serious think about what we do now. Where we go from here.'

'You sound like you have something in mind.'

'I do,' Ethan said, and her stomach twisted painfully. She had a feeling she wouldn't like what she was about to hear.

Willow was reeling after the phone call. She should have seen it coming, really, after all the trouble they were in, but it simply wasn't a possibility for her. She'd have thought Ethan would have fought more, for her sake at least, but it obviously meant more to Willow and she wasn't as willing to throw years of love, passion and hard work away, just like that.

The urge to curl back up on the bed and weep was strong, but Willow wasn't one for giving in to her emotions, so she made her way downstairs, finding Melody on the sofa in the living room. She hadn't expected to see her fellow guest in the house as she was supposed to have moved on that morning, but she spotted Melody's bandaged ankle propped up on cushions before she could voice her surprise.

'Oh my God, what happened?' she asked, striding over to the sofa and crouching in front of Melody. Melody pushed herself into a sitting position, wincing slightly.

'I tripped this morning. Wasn't looking where I was going.' She rolled her eyes. 'Mae took me to the walk-in centre and it's just a sprain. The painkillers are helping and the swelling's stopped, but I'm not going anywhere for at least a day or two.'

'So you're putting your project on hold?' Willow knew how much it meant to Melody by the way her eyes lit up when she spoke about it, and she knew how gutting it was to face the possibility of losing something precious to you.

'It looks like it,' Melody said with a shrug.

Willow reached out to rub Melody's arm. 'You're okay, though. That's the main thing, right?'

Willow couldn't believe she was delivering platitudes. She *hated* being on the receiving end of platitudes, but she wasn't sure what else to say, so out it popped.

'You're right.' Melody nodded, a sad sort of smile on her face. 'There are people far worse off. A sprained ankle is nothing in the grand scheme of things.'

Willow was well versed in looking at the grand scheme of things, though she hadn't been very good at counting her blessings lately. And after speaking to her husband, it seemed she was about to have one less.

'Can I get you anything?' she asked Melody. 'A cup of tea? More cushions?'

'A cup of tea would be lovely, thank you.'

Willow popped the kettle on and grabbed a couple of mugs, plopping a teabag in one and spooning coffee into the other. She heard a scratching at the door and, when she peered out of the window, saw the cat pacing up and down in front of the door. It stopped pacing for a moment, reaching out a black paw to scratch at the door before resuming the march.

Willow felt sorry for the poor thing. What if it wasn't a chancer? What if it was desperate for food and shelter, for a loving home? But she couldn't let it in. This wasn't her home and Mae didn't want the cat in her house, no matter how much it persisted.

The kettle clicked off, so she moved away from the window and turned her attention back to the drinks, pouring water into the cups and reaching for the milk. She froze, her fingers not quite grasping the fridge door handle, a short gasp muffled as she pressed her lips together.

This certificate is awarded to Hannah Wright for her fantastic effort and enthusiasm with shapes. Well done!

Willow's gaze moved from the certificate, proudly displayed on the fridge, to the painting next to it. Willow wasn't sure what the blobs of red, green and blue paint represented, but she knew how proud Mae must have been when her daughter produced it. No amount of looking at the grand scheme of things or counting her blessings could dull the ache as Willow stared at the fridge door, imagining her own fridge – when she eventually had one in her own kitchen – devoid of artwork and certificates or any signs of family life. She'd had such high hopes for her and Ethan, but it looked as though all her daydreaming and planning would be for nothing. There would be no babies with Ethan. No family to squeeze around the kitchen table. In fact, if things didn't improve, there'd be no kitchen for a table to sit in at all.

Tearing her eyes away, Willow opened the fridge, grabbed the milk and finished making the drinks. She avoided looking directly at the displays as she returned the milk, and by the time she carried the drinks into the living room, any visible signs of a wobble had vanished. She'd become almost an expert at hiding the cracks lately.

Chapter Twenty-Five

Mae

The Fisherman had been enjoying a quiet period after the lunchtime madness. The only customers remaining were Tom, perched on his usual stool at the bar, and a couple decked out in walking gear who didn't seem to be in any hurry to do any actual walking. Mae and Frank had set out the dominoes and were in the middle of a fierce battle; whoever lost the game had to hang the bunting and blow up the two dozen balloons for a party taking place that evening. It wasn't a job either of them wanted to do.

'Ooh, bad move,' Frank said as Mae placed a tile down on the table. He rubbed his hands together while Mae rolled her eyes.

'You've said that every time. Stop trying to psyche me out – it isn't working.'

'You should save all that hot air for blowing up those balloons,' Tom piped up, chuckling to himself.

'How long have you been sitting on that one?' Frank asked and Tom shrugged his shoulders.

'About twenty minutes.'

'He's right, though,' Mae said. 'Stop wasting your breath because you *will* need it later.'

'Only for karaoke.' Frank cracked his knuckles and placed his tile.

Mae groaned. 'There's going to be karaoke?'

'Doreen insisted, apparently.'

Doreen, a local pensioner and loyal customer at the Fisherman, was the birthday girl.

'I thought it was a surprise party? How can she insist on having karaoke at a party she doesn't know is happening?'

Frank shrugged. 'Who knows? I only do what I'm told.'

There was a hoot behind them and Corinne wandered over with cups of tea for Mae and Frank. 'Since when?'

'Since our wedding day. You're a tyrant and you know it.' Frank winked at his wife as he took the proffered cup.

'If I'm such a tyrant, why haven't you blown those balloons up yet? I asked you to do them two hours ago.'

'Because the party doesn't start until seven.' Frank checked the time on the clock hanging on the beam above the bar. 'And that's nearly three hours away.'

'It's nearly two, actually.' Corinne handed Mae her tea and plonked herself down on a stool. 'I told you the clock was knackered.' She tutted and shook her head. 'That bloody Gary King.'

'What did he do this time?' Mae asked.

'Got himself roaring drunk – a*gain* – and somehow ended up knocking the clock down. He says it wasn't him, but I know it was, the little arsehole. He could hardly walk straight when he left last night, but at least he didn't spew on my floor this time.'

'He's on his very last warning,' Frank said. 'Any more monkey business and he's barred.'

'Any more monkey business and he'll have my boot up his arse.' Corinne patted Mae on the arm and stood again. 'Don't forget those balloons, Frank, otherwise my other boot will have your name on it.'

'See what I mean?' Frank whispered once his wife was out of view. 'Tyrant.'

Mae ended up winning the game of dominoes, though she took pity on Frank and helped blow up the balloons after a momentary gloat. They hung the bunting across the bar and stuck the balloons up in small clusters around the pub.

'Can I get you another?' Mae asked Tom Byrne as she collected his empty glass from the bar. He'd been perched on that stool when she'd started her shift after taking Melody to the walk-in centre, and had probably been there since opening, but Tom wasn't quite the drinker you'd expect from someone who spent every hour possible in the Fisherman.

'Yes, please,' Tom said with a quick nod of his head. He looked at his watch and raised his bushy eyebrows. 'It's been a long day. And quiet.' He glanced around the pub, which only had three customers at the moment.

Mae grabbed a clean glass and started to fill it with Tom's preferred bitter. 'It'll pick up soon. It'll be two for one in a bit. That always brings people in.'

'Young uns.' Tom tutted. 'Rowdy and legless.'

'They're not all that bad.' Mae placed the pint on the bar. Although Tom had been in the pub for hours, this was only the first pint Mae had served him. He rarely drank much – the Fisherman was more about socialising for Tom, especially since he'd retired a few months ago. He'd been divorced for a number of years and now lived alone, and as he didn't have any children, Mae suspected he was lonely with only his cat for company. So he spent a lot of time in the Fisherman, chatting with the staff and customers, stretching out his drinks for as long as possible, though Frank and Corinne wouldn't have minded if he didn't bother with the pretence at all. He was always welcome at the Fisherman, drink or no drink.

'I think I'll have this pint and be off, just to be on the safe side,' Tom said. 'Our Tiddles will need feeding anyway.'

'Aren't you staying for Doreen's party?' Mae asked. 'It might be fun, especially if Doreen's got any single friends.' She winked at Tom, who grumbled something inaudible before taking a sip of his pint.

'Speaking of fun,' Tom said, placing his pint back down on the bar, 'have you been on a date with that vet of yours yet?'

Mae groaned. Was *everyone* discussing her love life now?

'He's a decent bloke, you know,' Tom said. 'You could do worse.'

'He's lovely,' Mae agreed. 'But I'm not interested. Not in Alfie, or any man in general.'

'So I don't stand a chance then?' Tom winked at her and took another sip of his pint. 'Oh, speak of the devil. Look who's here.'

Mae turned and there was Alfie, stepping into the pub. Although he'd more than likely come straight over from the surgery, he'd removed his scrubs and was instead clad in a pair of jeans and a rather tight T-shirt that hinted the local vet wasn't a stranger to the gym.

'All right, vet?' Tom called out, raising a hand. 'We were just talking about you.'

Oh, for—

'Were you?' A smile flickered at the corners of Alfie's mouth as he made his way over. 'All good, I hope?'

'Nobody has a bad word to say about you,' Tom said. 'Least of all this one.' He nodded his head towards Mae, the corners of his lips twitching.

Mae shot secret daggers at the interfering old git before turning to Alfie. 'He's been drinking all day. Ignore him.' She inched away from Tom, hoping Alfie would follow, putting them both at a safe distance from further interference. 'What can I get you?'

'Just an orange juice, please. I'm pacing myself.'

Mae reached for a glass from the shelf beneath the bar. 'How come?'

Alfie pointed upwards, at the bunting she and Frank had hung rather haphazardly earlier. 'Doreen's invited me to her birthday party, so I'm here for a few hours. I've got a couple of surgeries scheduled for tomorrow and having a hangover won't mix well with that.'

'Doreen invited you? Herself?'

Alfie nodded, a grin creeping onto his face and giving him a boyish look. 'It's the worst surprise party known to man.'

Mae grabbed a bottle of orange juice from the fridge. 'I didn't know you and Doreen were friends.' She flipped the bottle-top off and placed the juice on the bar.

'I treated her toy poodle a couple of months ago and ever since we've been like that.' Alfie lifted his hand, his index and middle fingers entwined. 'She pops by the surgery at least once a week with a box of surplus veggies from her husband's allotment. I'm getting pretty good at cooking a veggie madras.'

'Sounds delicious,' Mae said.

Alfie rubbed the back of his neck and looked down at the bar, sneaking a glance up at Mae as he spoke. 'You could come over and try it some time?'

'A madras is far too spicy for me. I start to sweat eating a tikka masala.'

'I could make something else. It doesn't even have to be made from Doreen's veggies...' Alfie's eyes were wide, hope beaming from each of them. They were beautiful eyes; dark and intense while having the ability to soften whenever Alfie smiled or laughed.

'Alfie…' Mae tore her eyes away from his gaze, afraid they would mesmerise her into agreeing to almost anything. Secretly, she sometimes wondered what it would be like if she lowered her defences and allowed herself to fall in love again. She got on well with Alfie, and she couldn't help being attracted to him, but there was just so much at stake.

Alfie lifted his hands. 'It's okay. I know the drill. No dinner.'

'You know it'd be a lot less awkward if you accepted that we're just going to be friends, don't you?' She heard Tom mumble something from his corner of the bar. It sounded very much like 'you're a bloody fool, girl', but she chose to ignore it.

'And give up?' Alfie shook his head. 'Nah, I'm made of sterner stuff than that.'

Luckily, Tom didn't say anything further and Alfie moved away from the bar to secure a seat as the pub began to fill up for Happy Hour.

'Are you still here?' Corinne asked as she joined Mae behind the bar. 'I sent Frank down ages ago to send you home.'

'He's over there.' Mae pointed across the pub, where Frank was setting up the karaoke machine in a corner. 'He did try to send me home, but I insisted on staying on a bit longer to make up for this morning.'

Corinne tsked. 'You don't have to make anything up. It isn't like we're mad busy in the morning.'

And yet they kept giving Mae shifts. She wasn't daft, and she also wasn't comfortable taking money without earning it.

'I'll help you through Happy Hour and then I'll get going,' Mae said as a compromise. 'Mum's giving Hannah her dinner, so it's fine.'

Corinne observed Mae for a moment before sighing. 'If you must.' She gave Mae one last reproving look before moving towards a waiting customer. 'Remember, you're on a warning, Gary. I'm not mopping your puke up again. If I think you're even close to spewing, I'll throw you out myself and you'll be barred. Got it? Good. Now, what can I get you?'

Happy Hour on a Wednesday was always the liveliest midweek shift, so Mae was kept busy for the next hour, serving the customers their two-for-one drinks and collecting empty glasses whenever there was a lull at the bar.

'Are you going to have a go at the karaoke?' she asked Tom as she collected glasses from the bar.

Tom scoffed. 'I don't bloody think so, unless Frank and Corinne want the place cleared quickly at closing.'

'I bet you've got a lovely singing voice,' Mae said, and Tom scoffed again. 'I'm glad I won't be here for the karaoke, to be honest. Do you remember Edith's rendition of "Killing Me Softly"?'

'Remember it?' Tom asked, his eyebrows lifting. 'My ears are still bleeding from it. She has a good sense of irony, that one, though. She killed us, all right, but there was nothing soft about it.'

Mae pressed her lips together to stop herself from giggling. Poor Edith. She'd been blessed with a good set of lungs, but unfortunately she didn't have the voice to go with it. Frank had secretly nicknamed her Foghorn Leghorn since.

'Do you think your vet will have a go?' Tom asked, which was met with an exasperated sigh from Mae.

'He's not *my* vet.'

Tom shrugged and lifted his pint. 'That's not what Corinne says.' He winked at Mae before bringing the glass to his lips and taking the tiniest sip.

'Corinne's wrong,' Mae said before wandering along the bar to serve the new set of customers.

'Corinne's never wrong,' Tom called out before chuckling to himself.

'Time's up, missus,' Corinne said, tapping her watch as she passed Mae behind the bar. 'Home time.'

'I'll just go and collect some glasses before I go,' Mae said. She heard a tsk as she slipped from behind the bar and headed for the tables. She'd amassed a tall stack by the time she reached Alfie's table, carefully adding his glass to the top of the pile, but she put them down on the table when she saw his companion.

'Hello, you.' She crouched so she could stroke the dog sitting under the table. He moved his head to give her better access to his neck, which was covered by a green bandana, and she gave it as good a scratch as she could. 'Aren't you a cutie?'

'Don't tell him that,' the dog's owner, who was sitting next to Alfie, said. 'His ego's big enough already. He's becoming the Kanye of the dog world.'

'This is the perfect example of when pets take on the traits of their owners,' Alfie said with a grin.

'Don't listen to him,' the friend said. Mae had seen him in the pub a few times – mostly because she was drawn to the dog he sometimes brought with him.

'Don't worry, I never listen to Alfie,' she joked.

Alfie nodded and sighed. 'It's true.'

The friend – Mae couldn't recall his name – leaned in towards Alfie. 'You should try being a bit more interesting, mate. It helps.'

'Thanks for the advice.' Alfie stood and shuffled out from his position behind the table. 'Another?' He indicated the empty glass on the table, which Mae grabbed, along with the stack she'd accumulated.

'Go on then, you've twisted my arm.'

Mae turned back towards the bar, but Alfie reached out and placed a hand on her arm. 'Why don't you join us for a drink?'

Mae looked at the bar, which had emptied now Happy Hour was over. 'I can't. My shift's just finished and I need to get back to the bed and breakfast. Hannah's maimed one of the guests so I need to get back and make sure she's okay.'

'What happened?' Alfie asked, so Mae explained about the wayward Minion and the morning's trip to the walk-in centre.

'I feel terrible. She was supposed to check out this morning, but I've insisted she stay on a few days, at least until travelling will be more comfortable. The problem is, she's in the middle of a photography project, but she can hardly carry on with a busted ankle.'

'Wait a minute,' Alfie's friend said. 'Is this Melody you're talking about?'

'You know her?'

The friend nodded. 'We met a couple of days ago. I had no idea she was still here.'

Mae cringed. 'That's because she's stuck on my sofa with her ankle all bandaged up.'

'Is it bad?' the friend asked.

'The doctor didn't seem too concerned. She said Melody had to rest it for a few days and then take it easy for the next week or two.'

'I'll pop over and see her in the morning, if that's okay?'

Mae nodded. 'I'm sure she'd appreciate the company.'

She finished her shift just as Doreen arrived, shrieking with surprise at the party that had been organised on her behalf. Corinne, Frank and part-time barman Tobias had taken over bar duties, so Mae slipped out, heading to her mum's to pick Hannah up. The sun was still bright as they headed for the car, and the afternoon at the beach had brought out the freckles across her daughter's nose. She reminded Mae of Hannah's father with the sun-kissed tinge to her skin, but Mae pushed the thought away as it only made her ache to think of the potential relationship her daughter was missing out on.

Hannah chatted all the way home, filling Mae in on her day with Nanny. They'd taken a picnic lunch down to the beach, paddling and playing Frisbee and building sandcastles in the sunshine.

'It sounds like you've had lots of fun,' Mae said as she pulled up as near to the bed and breakfast as she could manage. 'I used to like going to the beach with my grandpa and building the *biggest* sandcastles.'

'Why don't I have a grandpa?' Hannah asked and when Mae peeked at her daughter in the rear-view mirror, her little brow was furrowed with curiosity.

Hannah did have a grandfather. She had two, in fact, but neither were in her life. Her own father had buggered off without a trace and, although Mae had been close to them, all contact from her ex's family had stopped as soon as Shane dumped her. She'd reached out to them regularly until shortly after Hannah's first birthday, but none of them had been interested in meeting the little girl.

'Not everybody has a grandpa,' Mae said as she unbuckled her seatbelt. She climbed out of the car and helped Hannah out of her seat. 'But you're lucky, because you have a wonderful nanny, plus Uncle Frank and Aunt Corinne. They all love you *so much*.'

'They all love you too,' Hannah said as she took hold of Mae's hand. 'And so does Alfie, so you're *extra* lucky.'

It's official, Mae thought as they made their way along the pavement towards the house. Everyone was shipping Mae and Alfie, apart from Mae herself.

Chapter Twenty-Six

Willow

Willow's face was aching. She'd plastered on her best and well-practised happy-go-lucky face a couple of hours ago and she couldn't let it slip. Not yet. Not while she was with Mae and Melody. The pair were settled on the sofa with glasses of wine, Melody's injured ankle propped up between them, while Willow was curled up on one of the chairs by the window. They'd opened a bottle of wine after Mae had put Hannah to bed, but Willow had declined. Under the circumstances, it had taken a Herculean effort.

'Do you know what?' Willow said now, unfurling from her position in the chair, the bitterness she felt inside almost spilling over and nudging her fake cheer aside. 'I'd love to join you in a glass of wine, if that's okay?'

'Of course,' Mae said, pushing herself up from the sofa. 'I'll go and grab you a glass.'

Willow couldn't recall the last time she'd had a drink, but it must have been well over a year ago, so the wine soon took effect. She felt looser by the second glass, freer, less bogged down with worry and fear. Her head was fuzzy, but at least it wasn't buzzing with questions about the future, with their corresponding negative replies.

Separating herself from her worries and fears was a rare treat, and she found herself relaxing into her seat, allowing herself to let go more than she had for years.

'I can't believe you're both still single,' she said as Mae refilled their glasses from a fresh bottle. 'You're both so gorgeous.'

'I think you're a little bit tipsy,' Mae said and Willow shrugged.

'Perhaps, but it's true either way.' She took a sip of her wine, closing her eyes to savour the long-forgotten flavours.

'It's a bit difficult dating when you have a little one in tow,' Mae said.

'Not impossible, though.' Willow lifted her eyebrows in an *am-I-right?* fashion. 'So, what's stopping you? I bet you have loads of opportunity to meet men, working behind that bar.'

Mae placed the bottle of wine on the table and returned to the sofa, curling her feet up underneath her. 'Not as much as you'd think.'

'But there is *some*.' Willow leaned forward, poised for gossip. 'Come on, share.'

Mae squirmed in her seat and Willow felt bad for prying and making her feel uncomfortable. Willow had been on the receiving end of probing questions too many times herself to put anyone else through it, and she was about to apologise and engineer a swift change of topic when Mae spoke.

'There is someone, I guess.' Her words were quiet, hesitant, but she continued. 'He's liked me for a while, but I've always turned him down when he's asked me out. I do like him, but I can't take that risk.'

'What would you be risking?' Melody asked and Mae sighed.

'Everything.'

'You've been hurt pretty badly,' Willow said. She could see it clear as day, now she was looking for it. Mae's smile was as fake as her own.

'Haven't we all?' Mae laughed to make light of it, but Willow wasn't fooled.

'You've built up a wall to protect yourself,' Melody said. 'That's why you won't let yourself date this bloke.'

Mae shrugged. 'I guess.' She took a sip of wine. A rather large one.

'What's he like?' Melody asked. 'This guy who's chasing you?'

Mae laughed again, but it was genuine this time. 'I wouldn't say he's chasing me. Mildly interested, more like.'

'Is he mildly interested in anyone else, though?' Melody asked, and Mae considered the question for a moment.

'Not that I've noticed.'

'You'd notice,' Melody said, matter-of-factly. 'If you were interested in him it'd jump right out at you and make you insanely jealous.'

Mae took a sip of her wine before turning to Melody. 'I'm not sure that's a good thing, is it? Being insanely jealous?'

Melody shrugged. 'It'd show you care, deep down.'

'Or maybe it'd be a case of wanting what you can't have.' Mae gave her own version of the *am-I-right?* eyebrow quirk. 'Anyway, enough probing of me and the men in my life. What about you?'

'What about me?' Melody asked, her face a perfect picture of innocence.

'I was talking to some guy in the pub earlier who says you've been hanging out over the past couple of days.'

Melody's brow creased. 'Hugo?'

Mae shrugged. 'I don't know who he was, but he was extremely pleased to hear you're still here. So, come on. Spill, lady.'

Melody lifted her free hand up, palm out. 'There's nothing to spill. Hugo's been showing me around town, that's all. To help with my project.'

'So there's no romance on the cards?' Mae's eyes narrowed, her tone teasing.

'Absolutely not. Like you, I've sworn off men. Willow's the only one romantically involved around here. She's the only one madly in *lurve*.'

'See, this is what I want.' Mae threw her hand in Willow's direction. 'True, uncomplicated love. I don't want the risks. I don't want the possibility of being hurt and let down. I just want love. Easy, pure and simple love.'

Which seemed like an appropriate time for Willow to burst into tears.

The tears seemed to sober her up instantly, washing away the false cheer the wine had provided her with at the same time. She apologised profusely, covering her face to hide the tears and her shame. It seemed she wasn't quite as adept at keeping her emotions to herself as she'd thought.

'I'm sorry,' she said as she felt a hand on her shoulder. She peeked: it was Mae, worry etched on her face.

'Don't be.' Mae, keeping one comforting hand on Willow's shoulder, reached for a box of tissues. 'Let it out, whatever it is.'

Willow pulled a tissue out of the box and began to mop the tears. She paused, horrified, as she spotted Melody across the room, struggling and wincing as she manoeuvred herself off the sofa.

'Don't get up, please.' Willow grabbed another tissue and blew her nose. 'You'll hurt yourself even more.'

'She's right. Stay where you are.' Mae had such an air of authority as she spoke, so firm yet caring, so *mum*-like, that it brought a fresh wave of tears. The hand on Willow's shoulder pulled her in closer, Mae's other arm wrapping around the opposite shoulder so Willow was completely encircled. 'Oh, sweetheart. What is it?'

Mae rocked her gently as she wept. She felt foolish for crying in front of virtual strangers, but now she'd started, she couldn't seem to stop. After months of keeping it burrowed deep inside, it all came pouring out, writing itself on Willow's cheeks, erased by the sweeping tissues, but not forgotten.

'Oh God, I'm so sorry,' Willow said, voice rasping, once all the tears had pushed their way through.

'Stop apologising.' Mae was still holding Willow, one hand making soothing circles between her shoulder blades. 'You have nothing to be sorry about. People get upset. I know I do, more often than I let anyone else know. It isn't a crime. It isn't a weakness.'

Willow smiled, but it was a sad smile, a forlorn shadow of the beaming smiles she usually presented to the world. 'Then why do we hide it so well?' She huffed out a laugh. 'Today being the exception, of course.'

'I don't know, really.' Mae drew a tissue out of the box and dabbed at the residual moisture on Willow's cheeks. 'But we shouldn't. It doesn't do anybody any good to bottle it all up.'

'I've made such an idiot of myself,' Willow said.

'You really haven't. Yesterday, I yelled at my mum about having a vibrator to keep me happy. *That's* making an idiot of yourself.'

'A few weeks ago, I started crying in the cereal aisle at the supermarket,' Melody said. 'A song came on the radio that reminded me of somebody I love, and I just started howling. There was snot and everything and they made me go and sit in the manager's office until my mum came to collect me.'

'And you think that beats the vibrator story?' Mae asked. 'It was out in public and loud enough for anyone nearby to hear.'

Melody grinned. 'Okay, you win.'

Willow sniffed beside Mae. She'd thought she was spent, but their kindness was encouraging more tears.

'What is it?' Mae asked, hand still gently circling on Willow's back. 'You can tell us. Maybe we can help.'

Willow shook her head. 'You can't.' She dabbed at her eyes. 'Things with Ethan and I... It isn't as easy and uncomplicated as it seems.'

'Is he... not really working away?' Melody asked gently. 'Have you two split up?'

Willow shook her head. 'No, we're still very much together, and he's definitely working away. It's just... well, it's just the two of us and it looks like it's always going to be that way.'

Melody's brow furrowed, not quite getting it, though Mae's grip tightened. 'You want to start a family.'

'Yes.' Willow paused momentarily, pressing her lips together to stop the anguished cry from escaping. 'We both do. Desperately. But it isn't happening.'

'Do you know why?' Mae asked.

Willow shook her head. 'We've been trying for just over two years now. We've tried everything: more sex, less sex, legs in the air, every position you can think of. We've changed our diet and started exercising more, we've quit drinking, and still nothing. Ethan thinks we should go and see our GP, but I'm too scared. What if they tell us we can't have babies? What if we're busy creating a beautiful family home for nothing? At least now there's hope.'

'Oh, sweetheart.' Mae pulled Willow into a bone-crushing hug. 'There's always hope.'

Willow smiled sadly. 'But sometimes that hope comes to nothing.'

'There are other ways,' Melody said. 'Have you thought about IVF?'

Willow nodded as she dabbed at her eyes. 'It's one of the things we've been disagreeing about. I want to keep trying for a little while longer, but Ethan's keen to start looking into the alternatives. He thinks we should have used the money we're spending on the house for IVF.' Willow felt her chest start to heave again as a fresh wave of tears built. 'But now it looks like we could lose the house – and the money too. Ethan thinks the only solution to save the house is for me to give up my shop and go back to my marketing job. I know he's right; the shop doesn't bring in a massive amount once you've taken the overheads into account, but I adore my work and that shop means the world to me, but then so does the house. I don't know what to do.'

The only thing she was able to do, it seemed, was to drop her face into her hands and weep some more.

Chapter Twenty-Seven

Melody

The sun was already bright, fighting through the curtains and filling the room with warmth and light as Melody woke. Mind still groggy with sleep, she stretched her legs, groaning as she felt her ankle twinge with the movement. Ah, yes. The sprain. She was still in Clifton-on-Sea – and would be for at least another day or two until she could hobble to the train station unaided. She doubted she'd have the chance to move on to another town at this rate, which meant she'd have to use the photos she'd already taken for the festival. Hopefully she'd already captured a gem or two, but she wasn't convinced. The last few weeks had probably been a massive waste of time. Why had she agreed to take part in the festival in the first place? If it wasn't for Ollie and her promise, she'd have given up by now.

But she had made that promise, and she was determined to keep it, even if she humiliated herself in the process.

Pulling back the covers, she winced as she sat up, but it was her head rather than her ankle this time. How much had they drunk last night? She remembered shaking the last dregs of the second bottle into her glass after poor Willow had gone up to bed – had they opened a third?

With a gargantuan effort, Melody made it into an upright position, taking the weight on her non-injured foot. Limping across to the shower room was painful, but a vast improvement from the previous day, and she managed to shower and change into her last pair of clean shorts and a vest top. The two sets of stairs were a battle, but she made it down to the kitchen and rewarded herself with a couple of painkillers.

'Is it any better this morning?' Mae asked as Melody helped herself to a mini Danish pastry from the breakfast bar and limped to the table where Hannah was ploughing through a bowl of cereal at an alarming rate.

'A little.' Melody stretched out her foot, which was encased in a fresh bandage. 'I don't think I could manage a trek up the cliffs, though.'

'Definitely not.' Mae placed a hand on Melody's shoulder and gave it a squeeze before dropping onto the seat next to her. 'You need to take it easy. I'm working again today, but I'll make you some sandwiches for lunch before I go.'

'You don't have to do that,' Melody said.

Mae gave her a pointed look. 'And you're going to venture out in search of food, are you? I said you need to rest and I mean it.'

Mae's tone was so firm, Melody was half tempted to salute. 'Speaking of venturing out, is there a laundrette round here? I haven't seen one on my travels, but I could do with some clean clothes.'

'Use the washing machine here.' Mae thrust a thumb behind them, to where the machine was sitting.

'Are you sure?' Melody didn't want to take advantage, but she had to admit the thought of hobbling across town in search of a laundrette wasn't appealing.

'Offering you the use of the washing machine is the least I can do,' Mae said.

Hannah's spoon clattering into her bowl made them both jump. 'Done! Now can I watch telly?'

'Don't you want to play outside while it's nice?' Mae asked, but Hannah shook her head.

'Nanny said we're going splashing at the beach again today. That's enough outside. *Please* can I watch my cartoons?'

Mae threw her hands up in the air. 'Fine. But we're leaving in ten minutes, okay?'

She took Hannah's rapid retreat as agreement.

'Is Willow still around?' Melody asked as Mae grabbed Hannah's bowl and carried it over to the sink.

'I heard her leave really early this morning. I wanted to see how she was – you know, after last night – but she'd gone before I made it downstairs. Hopefully I'll catch up with her later.'

'Life is so unfair sometimes,' Melody said with a sigh.

'It really is,' Mae agreed. She washed the breakfast things while Melody nibbled at her pastry. She had a whole day stretching ahead of her with little to do other than laundry, so she'd bring her laptop down and use the free time to search through her photos for possible festival-worthy shots.

'Do you need a hand with your washing before I head out?' Mae asked once she'd dried the dishes and put them away.

'No, thanks. I'm sure I'll manage.' Using the table for support, Melody stood and hobbled out of the kitchen, heading up to her room. While she was up there, she grabbed her laptop as well as her washing to save another painful trip later.

'I've made you some sandwiches,' Mae said when she returned to the kitchen. She tapped the fridge as she passed. 'Feel free to help yourself to anything else you want. I'll be back early evening, so don't worry about cooking.'

'You don't have to...' Melody began to say, but Mae held up her hand.

'I insist.' She headed out into the hallway as the doorbell rang, returning a moment later with Mrs Hornchurch.

'I just wanted to see how the patient's getting on,' the neighbour said, smiling at Melody. 'You're looking perkier this morning. There's a bit of colour in your cheeks.' She held up a clingfilm-wrapped plate. 'I also brought you some leftover pie – it's pork and apple, my mum's old recipe – which I thought you might like for lunch. It'll save you having to make anything yourself.'

'How thoughtful,' Mae said, taking the plate and adding it to the fridge alongside the sandwiches.

'Thank you, Mrs Hornchurch,' Melody said. 'You're all being so kind to me.'

Mrs Hornchurch gave a wave of her hand. 'Just being neighbourly. You give me a shout if you need anything, dear.'

'I will, thank you.'

'I was just on my way out, Mrs Hornchurch,' Mae said, attempting to shepherd her neighbour back out into the hallway, but Mrs Hornchurch was having none of it.

'No worries, dear. I'll stay and keep Melody company for a few minutes.'

'I think Melody might like to rest,' Mae said and Mrs Hornchurch nodded.

'Absolutely.' Mrs Hornchurch turned to Melody. 'You sit down, dear, and I'll pop the kettle on.'

'That isn't really what I meant.' Mae flashed Melody a panicked look, but Melody wasn't put out by Mrs Hornchurch's company.

'Actually, that would be great,' she said. 'I'd love a cup of tea.'

Mae raised her eyebrows. 'Are you sure? Wouldn't you rather have a lie-down?' She was giving Melody a get-out clause, but Melody thought the neighbour was sweet and probably more in need of company herself than the other way around. And it wasn't as though she was busy. She could spare a few minutes for a chat and a cup of tea.

'It's fine, really. You get off and we'll have a nice natter, won't we, Mrs Hornchurch?'

Mrs Hornchurch beamed. 'I like this one, Mae. She can come back any time.'

Mrs Hornchurch ended up bustling Melody out of the way as she attempted to put her clothes into the washing machine, insisting on taking over the job. Melody wasn't entirely comfortable with the near-stranger handling her smalls, but Mrs Hornchurch turned out to be a formidable character and Melody felt she had little choice in the matter. The neighbour insisted on sticking around long enough to peg the washing out on the line, so it was late morning by the time Melody finally opened her laptop.

She was starting to feel peckish and was considering diving into her pre-prepared lunch when the doorbell rang. The painkillers from earlier had kicked in, so the journey from kitchen to front door wasn't too unpleasant and more than worth it when she saw Hugo standing on the doorstep. She felt her mouth stretching into a smile and didn't think she could have halted its progress even if she'd wanted to.

'Hugo! Hi!' Her voice was too high. Too keen. She needed to tone it down. She leaned casually against the doorframe. 'Are you here to see Mae or…'

Hugo clutched his chest. 'I'm here to see you, obviously. I find you too irresistible to stay away.' Melody rolled her eyes, but she was secretly pleased. 'Mae mentioned you were still here – and injured.' He looked down at her bandaged ankle. 'And said you might appreciate some company.' He held his arms out wide. 'So, here I am.'

'You'd better come in then.' Melody limped out of the way, leading the way to the kitchen. Too late, she realised her laptop was still on the table, open and displaying a shot of the evening coastline at Fleetwood.

'Wow.' Hugo looked from the laptop to Melody, his brow lifting and mouth agape. 'Is this one of yours?'

'Yes.' Melody lunged at the laptop as best she could with her injury and snapped the laptop shut. 'Can I get you a cup of tea? Coffee?'

'You're amazing,' Hugo said, ignoring the offer of a drink. 'As a photographer, obviously. As a person, you're all right. Not too bad.' He grinned at Melody and she nudged him in the ribs with her elbow. 'Seriously, though, you should show off your work more. Can I?' He indicated the laptop and Melody relented with a small shrug. What the hell? He'd already seen one – and it wasn't even one of her better shots.

'Wow,' Hugo said, over and over again, as he clicked through the photos. Melody hovered nearby, cringing, spotting all the flaws immediately. It was all too much, so she limped away, sitting at the opposite side of the table so she couldn't see the screen.

There was a sudden whoop of delight and Hugo rubbed his hands together. 'Ooh, what is *this*?' Melody leapt from her seat, wincing as her foot made contact with the floor. She hobbled back round to Hugo's side, cringing again when she saw the photo. 'Have you been stalking me? I *knew* you fancied me. Are there any more?'

The photo Hugo had spotted was the one from the beach, the one she'd taken of him and Scoop down by the shallows. She'd totally forgotten it was in there.

'Is that you?' She made a pretence of leaning in close and squinting at the image that was unquestionably Hugo Marsland and his dog. 'Oh my God, it *is*. How weird.'

Hugo turned to Melody, an equal mix of bemusement and smugness on his face. 'Come off it, Melody. We both know you zoomed in to take a snap of the Adonis on the beach. And it's no coincidence that Adonis is me.'

'Oh, piss off.' Melody sank back into her seat, taking the pressure off her foot. 'I was taking a photo of Scoop. You just happened to be there too.'

'Yeah.' Hugo nodded slowly before turning back to the laptop and clicking through the rest of the photos. 'Sure. I believe you.' He sneaked a sideways look at her and she stuck her tongue out at him.

'You really never show these to people?' he asked once he'd finished. Melody shook her head.

'Only those closest to me,' Melody said. She reached over to close the laptop, feeling her shoulders relax now her photos were out of sight.

'You're going to ace the festival,' Hugo said. 'There are two prizes, right? You'll win them both, hands down.'

'Steady on.' Melody moved the laptop safely out of Hugo's reach. 'You'll be giving me a seriously inflated ego. Almost a match for yours.'

Hugo gave a slow, sad shake of his head. 'Nah. You'll never reach the levels I've cultivated over the years.'

'Good point. What was I thinking?' Melody sat down at the table. Her ankle was starting to throb again but it was too soon for more painkillers. She thought she'd hidden her discomfort well until Hugo placed a hand on her arm, his brows pulled down.

'Are you okay?'

She nodded. 'Just a bit sore.'

'How long are you going to be out of action?'

'A few days.' Melody shrugged. 'Maybe more. Who knows?'

'Well, there's one good thing to come out of this,' Hugo said. 'At least we get to hang out for a bit longer.'

'Yes, but what's the *good* thing?' Melody teased and Hugo laughed.

'Ouch. My ego won't stand for that.'

'Speaking of standing,' Melody said. 'Do you think you could pop the kettle on? I would, but...' She lifted her foot and adopted a 'poor me' face.

Hugo filled the kettle, following Melody's instructions to locate cups, teabags and coffee. They divided the sandwiches and pie from the fridge, which they ate at the table while Hugo entertained her with funny tales from the ice-cream business.

'Are you any closer to making a decision about taking on the premises in the park?' Melody asked and Hugo shook his head.

'James is still dragging his feet. Understandably, given what a huge gamble it'd be, but I'm itching to get going with it. I really do think we could make a success of it.'

Melody pinched off a piece of pie crust and popped it into her mouth. It was delicious; buttery yet light. 'What would you do with Maisy once you're up and running?'

'Keep her going,' Hugo said. 'We'd have the best of both worlds then: the parlour in the park and the van out on the seafront. We could still use her for events too. We don't necessarily have to give her up.'

'You'd be doubling your workload,' Melody pointed out.

'And hopefully doubling our income.' Hugo shrugged. 'It'll be hard work, but I love a challenge. That's why I've befriended you.'

'And who said we're friends?' Melody said. 'I'm merely tolerating you.'

Hugo sighed. 'Story of my life.' Melody almost felt sorry for him until his face cracked, displaying a huge, toothy grin.

'Are you ever serious?'

'Not if I can help it. Life's too short to be serious.'

Melody nodded. 'You're right about that.'

'You should have fun at every single opportunity.' Hugo raised his eyebrows. 'So, are you ready?'

Melody wiped the crumbs from her fingers on a sheet of kitchen roll. 'For what?'

Hugo stood, holding a hand out towards her. 'To have some fun. It's too nice a day to be stuck inside.'

'I don't know if you've noticed.' She stuck her foot out again. 'But I'm not fit for outdoorsy stuff.'

'You won't have to walk,' Hugo said, hand still reaching out. 'Trust me.'

Chapter Twenty-Eight

Willow

She'd left the house early, her feet placed carefully on each step as she moved slowly down the stairs, the door easing shut behind her to create as little noise as possible. She'd waived breakfast, choosing instead to remove herself quickly before the others woke. The grumpy-looking cat was sitting on the wall outside the house, watching as she scurried along the garden path. It meowed – once, quietly – but she didn't stop to stroke him, or even offer a hello.

The sun was still weak as she climbed into her van, eyes shooting back towards the bed and breakfast to make sure she hadn't been spotted. She appreciated Mae and Melody's empathy the previous evening, appreciated more than anything that they hadn't uttered the flippant 'well, there's always adoption' she'd come to expect whenever she confided her worries to people, but she couldn't help feeling ashamed. She'd revealed far too much, far too soon, and her stomach roiled whenever she pictured herself bursting into tears in Mae's living room. She couldn't imagine Mae mopped up the tears of many of her guests, and she felt foolish for giving in to her emotions so publicly.

Coupled with the shame was the guilt Willow often felt. She had a good life, a life better than most. She had a job she loved (though that was now in jeopardy too), a husband she *adored*, and the beginnings of a beautiful home. She knew she was privileged to have these things, so was she greedy for wanting more? There were people out there with *nothing* and yet she was crying over the one thing she couldn't have.

She drove to the shop, slipping inside before locking the door behind her and heading straight to the workroom. It was too early to open the shop but she was determined to complete the dresser today, to concentrate on the finishing touches so she wouldn't have the headspace to think about how she was going to face Mae and Melody later, or how she would cope with losing the shop, or the ever-present fear that she would never give Ethan the child they both so desperately wanted.

Her phone rang shortly before eight o'clock and while she normally pounced on the phone when she saw her husband's name on the screen, she was reluctant that morning because she knew Ethan would be able to detect her distress. He'd know it had nothing at all to do with the house or the shop, would know Willow had failed yet again.

Her period had turned up the previous evening, shortly before Mae opened the first bottle of wine, shortly before Willow burst into tears and poured out her worst fears. Though uninvited and certainly unwelcome, the arrival of her period was not surprising since it was bang on time, as it always was. Still, the sight had been shocking. Devastating. Though she tried so very hard not to, Willow had still clung to the hope that this time it would happen. This month, finally, she wouldn't be greeted by the regular visitor, wouldn't feel those warning cramps shortly before that ate away at her dreams, slowly and determinedly, until a trip to the loo confirmed all hope had vanished, for that month at least.

Willow had become an expert at hiding her desires outwardly: she no longer turned to mush as she passed tiny baby clothes in the shops (in fact, she marched straight ahead as though she hadn't noticed them at all), she no longer stared at pregnant women, the world around her disappearing as her eyes bore into their bumps, and she'd stopped stockpiling pregnancy tests, just to double-check her body wasn't deceiving her.

But inside she was in constant turmoil. She *did* notice those tiny baby clothes, even if she fixed her gaze straight ahead, and those baby bumps were like a knife slicing through her abdomen. She'd unsubscribed from all the baby-related newsletters she'd signed up for as it was too upsetting every time one dropped into her inbox and she still wasn't pregnant, but then she'd subscribe again pretty much straight away as she didn't want to miss out on any information in case she *did* manage to get that positive result. And she signed up for and then deleted her account on pregnancy and baby forums in a rotation even more regular than her menstrual cycle.

Her real-life friendships had suffered too. She'd started to distance herself from the friends with babies and children when it first became clear she and Ethan were going to struggle to have a family of their own, spending her time with childless couples and, even better, her single friends. But even they started to procreate, dropping off one by one, so even those without long-term partners announced the imminent arrival of their offspring. Outwardly, Willow had been thrilled at the news. Inwardly, she was plotting her escape so she could grieve for the babies she would never have.

She still kept in contact with her old friends, but it wasn't the same. Willow kept herself at a safe distance as she couldn't bear to see the constant reminders of what she couldn't have, and she always had an excuse at the ready to miss all but the most important occasions to get together. And even now, when she and Ethan were in dire need of emergency accommodation, she couldn't bear to ask for a sofa to sleep on, as being in the middle of her friends' family life would have sent her over the edge. The constant *why them and not us* would have been toxic for the friendship, however flimsy it now was.

Willow had devised these coping mechanisms, but she knew Ethan could see right through them. He'd know, just by speaking to her, and she'd have to relive it all again: her period signalling another failed month, crying in front of Mae and Melody, her general feeling of being a failure. Of being a useless wife and human being.

'You are *not* a failure,' Ethan told her, as she knew he would. She also knew before she heard the words that she wouldn't believe him. He didn't mention the shop during their conversation, knowing Willow could only cope with one loss at a time. But it was still there, murmuring in the background, and she knew she'd have to face up to the possibility of giving up on another dream soon.

She returned to the dresser once she'd hung up, determined to forge ahead with the project and not think about the other things clashing around in her head, and was tightening the screws on the new cupboard door handles when Gary arrived. It was the final job for the dresser so it was almost ready to meet its new owner. It was her favourite part of her job, presenting a new piece to a client, watching their reaction and hoping they would be as in love with the item as she was. She'd miss making people's faces light up more than anything if she lost her shop.

'You look rough.' Concern was etched on Willow's face as she placed the screwdriver on the floor and stood up. 'Are you okay? Do you still have that bug?' She crossed the workroom and placed a hand on Gary's forehead. It wasn't particularly warm, but he had a greyish tinge to his face, his eyes ringed and watery.

'Not sure,' Gary mumbled. He swayed slightly and Willow reached out to steady him.

'You should go home and get back in bed.'

Gary shook his head. 'Nah, I'll be all right in a bit.' As the words left his mouth, he screwed up his face, his hand moving up to his mouth. He hesitated for just a split second before he bolted towards the loo. Willow headed for the kitchen, filling a glass with water and waiting outside for Gary to emerge. When he did, he looked even worse than before.

'You're going home,' Willow said as she handed the glass over. 'I'll drop you off.'

'But the shop…' Gary's voice was weak, his free hand clutching at his stomach.

'The shop will be fine. You, on the other hand, are not.' She grabbed the keys and jiggled them. 'Come on. You need to rest.'

Willow made sure all the van's windows were wound down before she set off. Gary didn't live too far away, but the last thing she wanted was a vomit van. Her own stomach was feeling a little delicate after last night's wine. It had been quite a while since she'd given up the booze in a bid to lead a healthier lifestyle and her body was unused to it. Cleaning up vom would push her over the edge, she was sure.

'Will there be someone in to look after you?' she asked as they pulled up outside Gary's house. She knew Gary lived with his mum and an older brother.

'Mum and Kev will be at work, but I'll be all right. I'll just get my head down for a bit.' Gary unbuckled his seatbelt and pulled on the door handle. 'Sorry about this. I've let you down.'

Willow tutted. 'Don't be daft. You haven't let anybody down. You can't help being ill. Go and get some rest and I'll see you when you're better, okay?'

Gary nodded and clambered out onto the pavement. He closed the door before lifting a hand in a farewell gesture and sloping off towards his front door. Willow waited until he was safely inside before she set off back to the shop.

With the dresser practically finished and no Gary to distract her, she had a long day ahead of her.

She kept herself busy with a smaller project she could carry out in the shop rather than out in the workroom, creating heart-shaped keyrings out of fabric scraps and embroidering simple messages onto them. She'd made similar ones in the run-up to Mother's Day, selling a good number both in the shop and online. This time, instead of limiting herself to 'Mum', she branched out with a wider range of messages. Hand-stitching required concentration, so her mind wasn't free to wander towards Mae, Melody and the baby-that-might-never-be.

She was engrossed in stitching intricate letters to form 'Love You' on the latest keyring when the shop's door opened and the pregnant woman from the day before huffed her way inside. Inwardly, Willow groaned. She'd forgotten all about the appointment they'd arranged, hadn't even looked in her diary, and she wasn't looking forward to discussing the furniture for this fortunate woman's unborn child. Outwardly, however, Willow rose from her stool, smile fixed in place as she greeted the woman, offering tea, coffee and a seat at the counter.

'I'm sorry, I didn't catch your name,' Willow said as she placed cups of coffee down on the counter.

'It's Yasmina.'

'What a beautiful name,' Willow said as she hopped onto a stool beside her new client. She'd become a bit obsessed with names since she and Ethan had started trying for a baby, storing away her favourites in case she ever got the chance to use them.

'Thank you.' Yasmina beamed, a dimple appearing in her left cheek. 'It was my mum's choice. Dad wanted to name me after his grandmother, but Mum put her foot down. She said there was no way a child of hers was being named Agnes, though those old-fashioned names are coming back, aren't they? I quite like Ida for a girl, but my husband isn't keen.'

Does she realise how lucky she is? Willow wondered as she pulled a notepad and pen towards her.

'Are you having a girl?' she asked, pen poised.

'We don't know.' Yasmina placed a hand on her bump. 'We wanted a surprise. Bump is just called Poppet at the moment.'

Willow nodded, smile pushed into place. 'So, will you be going for something quite neutral, colour-wise?'

Yasmina nodded and pulled her phone out of her pocket. 'The room's already painted. I thought it might help if I showed it to you.' She showed Willow a series of photos of a reasonable-sized room painted a soft grey. One wall, made up of large square panels, was painted in a pale slate-grey, creating a feature and focal point.

'I want to put the cot against the darker wall,' Yasmina said, swiping across the collection of photos to show the pieces of furniture again. 'With the wardrobe and drawers on the opposite wall and the rocking chair in front of the window.'

Willow tapped her pen against her chin as ideas mulled around her head. 'I could paint the cot a soft grey to match the three walls. It'll look striking against the darker grey, and of course I'll use baby-safe paint. The other pieces could be painted in the darker shade, with some vintage papers on the drawer fronts to lift the piece and make it more stylish and unique. I have some soft grey paper in at the moment, with a white floral design I think would suit the room perfectly. I can show you if you'd like?'

'That'd be great, thanks.' Yasmina took a sip of her coffee while Willow slipped off her stool. She made her way into the workroom, taking a moment to take a few deep breaths before she hunted out the paper she had in mind. She sometimes didn't know how she held it together so seamlessly and it was only now she was on her own that she could allow the mask to slip.

'Here we are.' She returned to the shop with the papers, along with a bundle of fabric. 'I also found this, which I could use to reupholster the rocking chair.'

Yasmina ran a hand over the fabric. 'I love it!' It was a cream fabric with a pattern of little grey elephants. 'It's so much better than the moth-eaten fabric on there at the moment.'

Willow perched on her stool and started making notes. She managed to get through the remainder of the consultation, arranging a convenient time to pick up the furniture, a timescale, and the cost.

'Thank you so much,' Yasmina said as Willow showed her to the door once all the details had been covered. 'I was a bit dubious when I saw the furniture, but I can't wait until they're in there now.'

'I'm looking forward to working on them,' Willow said, which was true. Yes, she wished she could work on a nursery in her own home, but she loved bringing furniture to life again, and this was a big project she could really sink her teeth into.

She closed the door behind Yasmina and gathered the cups to wash in the little kitchen. It was a good project. Fun. And she'd be bringing an expectant mum so much joy.

Her shoulders started to shake as she washed the cups and she was suddenly grateful Gary wasn't in the shop as a fat tear plopped into the sink. She allowed herself to have a little weep, then she dried her eyes and returned to the shop and the little fabric keyrings.

Chapter Twenty-Nine

Melody

Hugo had carried her from the bed and breakfast to his car, like the reverse of a new bride being carried over the threshold. Melody hadn't been convinced the trip was a good idea; Hugo could hardly carry her around all day, and she wasn't sure she'd want him to. She felt vulnerable in his arms, which wasn't a comfortable feeling in the slightest. But she had to admit the few minutes of discomfort were worth it as the car pulled up on a sandy track beside a handful of ramshackle buildings. There was a thin strip between the buildings, revealing a tiny glimpse of sea, shimmering in the bright sunshine. It was breathtaking, even from the limited view on offer.

Melody allowed Hugo to guide her out of the car and didn't so much as murmur her disapproval as he lifted her into his arms again. She was too busy gazing ahead, down the sloping sandy track to a tiny strip of fine sand, which in turn met the gentle lapping of the sea. The sound was spectacular, the pull and push of the water the only noise she could hear. There was no raucous pier doing its best to drown out the sounds of nature, no families creating a combined cacophony, no seagulls crying out as they searched for scraps of food. There were no other people around, no animals or birds from what she could make out, just Melody, Hugo, and the beautiful scene set out before them.

'Welcome to Chapel Cove,' Hugo said as they took in the view. Melody was already reaching for her camera, even as she was still perching upon Hugo's outstretched arms. She clicked away, trying to capture the beauty and tranquillity of the cove. It wasn't your typical British seaside scene – there wasn't a bucket or spade in sight, there were no shops selling rock and tacky souvenirs, and there was a severe lack of the smell of fish and chips – but it was simply stunning and Melody wanted to commit the image not only to memory, but to her photographic collection.

'You can put me down now,' Melody said as she realised poor Hugo was still acting as a human chair. 'Your arms must be aching.'

'Not at all.' Hugo placed Melody down gently on the pale sand and flexed his arms in a cheesy bodybuilder pose as she sat down. 'I'm made of strong stuff.'

Melody shook her head, though she was fighting a smile. 'Sit down, you doofus.' She patted the sand beside her and her gaze returned to the gently lapping sea. 'It's so peaceful, isn't it?'

Hugo sat down, crossed-legged, and nodded. 'I bring Scoop here sometimes so he can have a good run along the shallows without having to worry about other dogs. He even ventures in for a full-on paddle some days.'

Melody grabbed a handful of sand in her fist and allowed it to slowly cascade back down to the beach. 'We should have brought him.'

'Next time,' Hugo said, and Melody didn't point out how unlikely it was there would be a next time. Once her ankle was healed – or at least healed enough for her to walk on without wincing too much – she'd have to go home and face the life she'd avoided for the past few weeks. She wasn't looking forward to her return, and not just because the simple act of living had become so hard. She'd felt real moments of pure joy here in Clifton-on-Sea, a sensation she hadn't thought she was capable of producing any more, and she'd miss those moments, however fleeting they'd been. She remained tight-lipped as she gazed out towards the horizon, the familiar guilt jabbing her in the gut as she realised she'd been happy in those moments.

'I keep forgetting you're not going to be here for much longer,' Hugo eventually said. They'd both remained silent for the past few minutes, enjoying the view before them, lost in their own thoughts.

'I'll be gone in a few days. Maybe even sooner.' She looked down at her bandaged ankle. 'It depends how I get on.'

Hugo nudged her playfully with his shoulder. 'We should keep in contact.'

'What's the point?' she asked.

Hugo uncrossed his legs and drew his knees in towards his body, resting his chin on them. 'You can be quite harsh when you want to be.'

'I'm sorry.' Melody's question had come out much more abrupt than she'd intended, but that didn't mean it wasn't a valid point. 'It's just…' She grasped another fistful of sand as her brain scrabbled to find the right words.

'You have a boyfriend.'

The idea was so ridiculous, Melody almost laughed. She frowned instead, great big furrows appearing in her forehead. 'No, I don't have a boyfriend.'

'A girlfriend?'

Melody unclenched her fist, releasing the sand she'd collected in one go. 'No girlfriend. No significant other.

No other at all, significant or otherwise. It's just me, and that's the way I want it to stay.'

'Oh.' Hugo frowned this time. 'I thought…' He shrugged. 'I thought you'd been keeping me at a distance and were resisting my obvious charms because you were involved.' He tried to flash his cheeky grin at Melody, but it didn't quite make it onto his face.

'I'm not involved. I'm… going through some stuff.'

Melody clenched her fist again, but there was no sand in there this time. It sounded so flippant. So unimportant. 'Going through some stuff'? It didn't even begin to explain the devastation she'd gone through, the pain and the tears and the fight to keep going each day. She'd wanted to give up, to just lay down and stop fighting, because what was the point without Ollie?

'What kind of stuff?' Hugo asked. His voice was gentle, almost lost in the slight, salty breeze. Melody rarely spoke about her past, but she felt she owed it to Ollie to explain. To take back that flippant remark and let Hugo know what Ollie had meant to her. And so, sitting on the secluded beach, Melody told Hugo about the best friend she'd known most of her life. The friend who'd helped shape the woman Melody had become. They'd laughed together, cried together, fallen in love with boys (and later men), fallen out of love, grown from gangly children to curious teenagers to young women ready to take on the world, sharing these pivotal moments so wholeheartedly that they'd become part of the fabric of each other's lives. Memories and experiences melded together so seamlessly, Melody wasn't always sure where she ended and Ollie began.

'She was everything to me,' Melody said, though her words couldn't convey just how special their friendship had been. 'She believed in me, even when I didn't believe in myself. She didn't speak to me for a week when I applied for a secretarial course at college instead of the photography course she'd talked me into picking. Being a photographer was my dream – being a secretary wasn't. She knew that and was so disappointed when I chickened out.' Melody smiled. 'It was the longest week ever, for both of us. Her protest was supposed to last until I came to my senses and withdrew my application and reapplied for the *right* course, but she caved before I did. My fear was too overwhelming, even though I missed Ollie so much.' Melody closed her eyes and lifted her face to the hot sun. 'I miss her now. Every day. I still can't believe she isn't here and I'll never get to speak to her again.'

Melody felt a hand on hers, grains of sand scratching lightly against her skin. She opened her mouth to continue, but found her words were lost. What else was there to say? Ollie was gone and Melody missed her so much it took her breath away. Instead of speaking, she reached into the back pocket of her shorts and pulled out the photograph, running a finger over the young, grinning face of Olivia Greyson, eyes crinkled, dimples at their maximum adorability.

'Is that you and Ollie?' It was the first time Hugo had spoken since Melody started to delve into her past. She nodded, still not ready to speak. 'How old were you?'

Melody flipped over the photo, though she knew the answer already. Inscribed on the back, in Ollie's mum's neat handwriting, was *Ollie and Melody, Blackpool, 1998*. She flipped the photo over again, to the image of the best friends sitting astride a couple of donkeys, grins filling their faces and displaying the joy the day at the seaside had brought.

'We were seven.' Melody handed the photo to Hugo so he could take a closer look. 'I'd gone to Blackpool with

Ollie's mum and dad and her baby brother. I'd forgotten about it until Ollie's mum gave me the photo. She'd been going through some of their old photos for...' Melody closed her eyes again. *For Ollie's funeral.* She couldn't say it. 'And she thought I might like this one. She said we looked so happy and that's how she remembered us as little girls. Always smiling.'

'It's a lovely photo,' Hugo said. 'Special.'

Melody nodded. 'It's what brought me here. On this trip. Ollie finally convinced me to give photography a go. She made me promise, you see, before...' *Before she died. Before she left me, for ever.* 'She said life was too fucking short to settle for second best. I should grab life with both hands while I could and reach for my dreams, otherwise I was wasting the life I'd been given.' Melody took the photo back from Hugo and touched the very tip of her finger to Ollie's face. 'So when I read about the local photography festival, I signed up. I didn't give myself chance to think about it. I just did it, so I couldn't chicken out. I'd made that promise to Ollie. I couldn't let her down.'

Her face was wet, she realised. She'd been crying. Why hadn't Hugo said anything? Made her stop? She reached up to wipe the tears from her cheeks with the back of her hand, not realising she was leaving behind patches of sand.

'The theme of the festival is childhood memories. I had this photo propped up on my bedside table, the very essence of a happy childhood before life turns shit. So I decided on the British seaside theme and here I am. Taking photos. Like it matters.' Melody shoved the photo roughly into her pocket. Her hands formed fists beside her and she started to take slow, deep breaths before she lost control.

'It matters to you,' Hugo said. 'And it mattered to Ollie. You're doing it for *her*, remember?'

Melody shook her head, over and over again. 'No. I'm doing it for *me*. Because it's something *I've* dreamed of. Ollie wasn't interested in photography! She was a counsellor. She helped people, every single day. She made a difference, yet here I am, squandering life. I don't help people. I'm selfish and undeserving. Why should I be here, enjoying life, when Ollie isn't?'

Melody's hands became angry fists again. She was shaking, jaw clenched. It wasn't *fair*.

It wasn't *fucking fair*.

She struggled to her feet, her ankle crying out, the pain slicing through her lower leg as her foot slipped on the sand. She hissed a breath in through her teeth, but she continued to move anyway, hobbling across the sand towards the sandy track.

'Hey! Wait!' Hugo was up off the sand before she'd made it a couple of agonising steps. 'You can't walk on that ankle. Not here.' Before Melody could respond that she could walk anywhere she pleased, she was being scooped up into Hugo's arms.

'Put me down!' she roared, hitting at his arms, his chest. Her jaw clenched harder each time she made contact.

'It's okay. I'll take you home.'

Melody shook her head. She was still hitting out, but there was no longer any force behind it. 'I don't want to go home. I can't go home.' Her voice cracked and hot tears started to stream down her cheeks, making tracks in the patches of sand she'd left earlier. 'I can't go home, Hugo. Not without Ollie. It's too hard.'

'The bed and breakfast,' Hugo said gently. 'I'll take you back to the bed and breakfast.'

Again, Melody shook her head. She couldn't go back like this. A mess. Broken. She needed a bit of time to compose herself. To wash her face, at least.

'Come back to mine for a bit,' Hugo said. He'd already started to move up towards the car. 'See Scoop. He always manages to cheer me up. If he can't bring that beautiful smile back to your face, nothing will.'

'What about James?' The last thing Melody wanted when she was looking – and feeling – so ghastly was an awkward chat with Hugo's brother.

'Don't worry, he won't be there.' Hugo smiled at her. 'I promise.'

They made it back to the car and Hugo helped her into the passenger seat, making sure her ankle wasn't bashed in the process.

'I'm sorry,' she said as they pulled away from the cove, the beautiful scene fading from view. 'For being a snappy cow at times, for being a mess. For making your T-shirt all soggy.'

Hugo looked down at his T-shirt and gave Melody a knowing, sideways glance. 'You just wanted me to have to take my wet T-shirt off, didn't you? Hey, if you want a peek at my hot bod, all you have to do is ask.'

Melody smiled, despite the tears still dampening her cheeks. 'I'd appreciate it if you kept it on, thanks.'

Hugo shrugged. 'Your loss.'

'I'm sure I'll live,' Melody said, though she often wondered how she managed to with such a damaged heart.

Chapter Thirty

Mae

Mae's shift at the pub had started early as she'd been recruited to help with the clean-up operation after Doreen's party the night before. Mae didn't mind the earlier start as it meant she could finish mid afternoon and spend a bit of time with Hannah before the activities revolving around dinner and bedtime began. Hannah was having a wonderful time during the school holidays, going to the cinema and building sandcastles on the beach, but it was a pity none of it had involved Mae so far. They wouldn't have time to venture far that afternoon, but they could certainly squeeze in an ice cream and paddle before dinner time.

She'd dropped Hannah off at her mum's before heading towards the harbour. The sun was already bright, the holidaymakers strolling around in their shorts and T-shirts, the smell of sun cream wafting in through the open car window. The radio had been playing a summery tune from the early nineties and Mae couldn't help singing along, feeling freer than she had in a long time. She turned onto the road that ran along the harbour, following it round to the Fisherman. The cries as the seagulls swooped through the air drowned out the radio as she parked beside the pub, their white bodies dipping and rising and looping back round towards the harbour wall before bobbing back out to sea again, repeating their dance over and over until a passer-by tossed something onto the ground and all seagull-hell broke loose. The passer-by yelped and staggered out of the way as a dozen or more seagulls descended.

'Can't be from round here,' Frank said, nodding towards the littering bloke, 'if that came as a surprise.'

Frank was leaning against the pub's wall, smoking a crafty cigarette. He'd been promising to give up for decades. Corinne had been promising to cut off his fingers if she caught a cigarette between them for just as long. Neither had kept their promise.

'Must be a tourist,' Frank surmised before taking a final drag.

'You're not getting snobbish in your old age, are you?' Mae asked. 'You'll be complaining next that they take over the place every summer.'

'Hardly.' Frank disposed of his cigarette in the metal wall-mounted bin beside him. 'Tourists keep us going. We'd go under in a heartbeat if we had to rely on the likes of Tom Byrne and his everlasting pints.' A grin spread across Frank's face as he ushered Mae inside. 'And speaking of Tom Byrne...' He rubbed his hands together and opened his mouth to speak.

'I hope you're not spreading gossip about our customers, Frank Navasky,' Corinne's stern voice carried out across the pub. She was standing beside the buffet table, an open bin liner in hand as she plonked last night's party debris inside it. 'Because that's my job.' Dropping the bin liner, she scurried over, grasping Mae by the arm. Her grin was even larger than Frank's, giving her an almost manic expression as she practically vibrated with the force of holding the gossip in.

'Well?' Mae looked from Corinne, to Frank, and back again. 'What is it?'

'Not a word!' Corinne barked at her husband before turning to Mae again, her grip tightening in her excitement. 'It's Tom. Last night...' She pressed her lips together and an excited yelp escaped. 'He made himself a lady friend.'

'A lady friend?' Mae asked and Corinne nodded. 'Who is she?'

Corinne shrugged. 'We don't know. A friend of Doreen's, we presume. I don't think she's ever been in here before, but old Tom took a liking to her. They chatted for *hours* and even did a duet on the karaoke. Elton and Kiki.'

'Tom?' Mae raised her eyebrows as she looked between Corinne and Frank. They were pulling her leg, surely. 'On the karaoke?'

'He was actually pretty good,' Corinne said.

'There's a rumour going around that they were necking out the back,' Frank said. 'But Gary King started it, so I'm not entirely convinced it's true.'

'It's the first time he's shown an interest in a woman since the divorce, though,' Corinne said. 'So it's a step forward at least.'

'He's getting back on the horse.' Frank winked at Mae. 'So to speak.'

A rather unsavoury image popped into her head, but she pushed it away.

'If old Tom can try again,' Corinne said, giving Mae a pointed look. 'What's stopping a young lass like you?'

Mae patted the hand still lightly gripping her arm. 'Do you want a list?'

The question remained in her head for the duration of her shift, stubbornly bashing against the lining of her brain, over and over again. If Tom, who'd been almost spitting venom in his bitterness after the divorce, could put himself back out there and have another shot at romance, why couldn't she? Tom's wife had taken everything: their home, their friends, Tom's dignity (according to the man himself), and had left him nothing but a couple of bin bags of clothes and his beloved cat. She'd have taken the cat too, Tom said, except the cat and his ex hated each other to the point of violence.

But still, after all that, he'd found a woman who made him forget his hatred of karaoke and actually get up and sing.

But Tom and Mae weren't the same. Tom didn't have a young child to consider. He could afford to take a risk. He could take as many of the damn things as he wanted. Mae, on the other hand, had to be more guarded.

Unusually – or perhaps not, considering the gossip flying around – Tom didn't make it into the pub during her shift.

'You off already?' Frank asked as Mae started to gather her things. He looked up at the clock, which still claimed it was ten past one. He checked his watch and tutted. 'That bloody Gary King. I've a good mind to bill the little toerag for a new one.'

'Maybe you'll get a new one for your birthday next month?' Mae suggested and Frank frowned.

'Gary and I don't usually exchange birthday gifts. We're not that close.'

Mae tutted. 'Not from Gary.' She reached up on tiptoe to kiss Frank on his stubbly cheek. 'I'll see you tomorrow.'

'See you tomorrow, love. I'll try and wheedle all the details from Tom – if he shows up.'

'Maybe he wants to keep his private life *private*,' Mae said. She'd been on the receiving end of the Navaskys' meddling, and although they meant well, it certainly hadn't been welcome.

'Then he shouldn't be up there singing lovey-dovey songs for all to see.' Frank thrust his thumb at the corner where the karaoke machine had been sitting. 'Nope, it's public knowledge now.'

'Leave the poor man alone,' Mae said, though she knew her words would fall on deaf ears. With a final wave, she left the pub and headed for her mum's to pick Hannah up for their afternoon of fun.

They managed to catch the Punch and Judy show on the promenade, Hannah sitting cross-legged on the sun-warmed ground with an ice cream from the nearby van. Once the show ended, they headed down to the beach, taking off their shoes and socks so they could feel the squishy sand between their toes as they padded along to the shallows. The water was freezing cold and made Mae shriek as the gentle waves lapped over her toes, but the shock soon turned to joy as she and Hannah giggled, holding hands as they waded a little further out. The sloshing water creeping up her calves brought such precious memories and, if she closed her eyes, she could almost feel her grandpa beside her. Could almost imagine heading back to the bed and breakfast and finding her granny baking an apple pie, her hair dusted with flour, the whole house smelling divine.

What would they think of her now, she wondered, as the water splashed against her calves. Would they be proud of the life she was creating for herself and Hannah? Proud she was reaching for her dreams, running the little bed and breakfast she'd always fantasised about? Or would they be disappointed she'd taken the wrong paths in life, even if she had finally managed to find a place where she was pretty much content? Would it be enough for them, she thought, for her to be content? She thought of Hannah, clinging to her hand so tightly, giggling with every wave that rolled towards them. Did she want her daughter to feel simply *content* in life? Was it enough? Didn't she want Hannah to be so happy her heart might burst, for her to grab life and squeeze every last drop from it? And if being content wasn't enough for Hannah, why was it enough for Mae?

After their paddle, they headed back to the bed and breakfast, their feet still damp and sandy inside their socks and shoes. Both were smiling, despite the not-very-comfortable shoe situation, and Mae vowed they would do this more often, that she wouldn't let the boring, everyday stuff get in the way of having fun. Being content wasn't nearly good enough for either of them.

'Hello, Mrs Hornchurch,' she called out when she saw her neighbour out on the pavement outside her house. 'You look lovely. Very sparkly.'

'Thank you, dear.' Mrs Hornchurch beamed as she smoothed down her cardigan. It was a deep plum colour with tiny flecks of silver glinting in the light. Underneath the cardigan was a black V-neck top, also glittery with silver specks, which she'd teamed with a pair of wide-legged trousers. It was a vast change from her neighbour's usual attire of pleated skirts, cosy jumpers and fluffy slippers. Mae noticed now that her hair had been curled to create soft waves and she was wearing just a hint of peach gloss on her lips.

'Off anywhere nice?' Mae asked, and she was sure Mrs Hornchurch's cheeks took on a tinge of pink.

'I'm going out for dinner.' Mrs Hornchurch tucked a curl behind her ear. 'With a friend. They should be picking me up any minute now.'

'Sounds lovely. I hope you have a nice evening.'

'Thank you, dear.' Mrs Hornchurch looked past Mae, her face lighting up as a car approached. She gave a little wave to the driver as the car pulled up at the kerb.

'Oh my God,' Mae whispered as Mrs Hornchurch slipped into the passenger seat of the car. Her neighbour blew a glossy kiss through the window as she sailed past, the driver of the car staring fixedly ahead, avoiding Mae's eye. It didn't look as though Mrs Hornchurch was simply having dinner with a friend to Mae. It looked as though her neighbour had jumped back into the dating game.

With Tom Byrne.

Mae decided on a quick dinner of turkey wraps. She hoped her guests would join her, but Willow declined through her closed bedroom door, claiming she wasn't very hungry, and Melody wasn't in the house. Mae hadn't expected Melody to venture out on her busted ankle, but perhaps she'd felt better and needed a bit of fresh air. She couldn't have gone far, anyway.

'Mummy...' Hannah appeared in the kitchen doorway, her eyes wide as she clung to the frame. 'Chilly's scratching at the front door.'

Mae grabbed the cheese grater from a cupboard and unwrapped a block of medium cheddar. 'Who?' She cut a slab of cheese off the block and started to grate it.

'Chilly. The cat.' Hannah peered out into the hallway for a moment before turning back. 'He wants to come in. He's hungry.'

'No.' Mae, still grating, shook her head. 'He isn't our cat. We can't feed him, otherwise he'll keep coming back.'

'But he loves turkey wraps,' Hannah said, her confidence at the statement unwavering. 'They're his favourite.'

'I thought Frosties were his favourite.' Mae paused her grating momentarily to raise her eyebrows at her daughter.

Hannah clapped a hand to her forehead. '*Mummy!* They're his favourite *breakfast*. Turkey wraps are his best for *dinner*.'

'Is that so?'

Hannah gave a solemn nod. 'Yup. He'll eat it all up, I promise. Even the yucky tomatoes.'

'No.' Mae sighed wearily and shook her head. 'He isn't our cat. He can't have any turkey wraps.'

'But…' Hannah's brow creased as she scrabbled around her brain for a more substantial argument. '*Please*, Mummy.'

'No. I'm sorry.' Grating the last chunk of cheese, she removed the grater and gave the bowl a little jiggle to flatten out the peaked mountain of cheese strands before placing it on the table. Hannah watched her, her eyes growing wider and her bottom lip protruding.

'It's not *fair!* Jack's daddy let him have a puppy for his birthday.' Hannah thumped her little arms across her chest. 'And he's already got a rabbit and three goldfish. If I had a daddy, he'd let me keep Chilly, I know it! You're just *mean*.'

'Darling…' Mae reached for her daughter, but Hannah had already turned and was fleeing along the hallway before Mae had even managed to take a step towards her. She ran as fast as her little legs could take her, racing up the stairs while Mae looked on, torn between chasing her and having a chat, and letting her cool off for a few minutes first. She was still standing in the hallway undecided when she heard scratching at the front door. Decision made, Mae marched to the door and flung it wide, glaring down at the cheeky little bugger who was busy gouging lengths into the doorframe, his paws moving up and down in a steady rhythm.

254

'You!' She pointed a finger at the cat, her voice stern. 'Stop. That. Now!'

The cat froze, green eyes staring intently up at Mae, paws – and claws – still up against the doorframe. And then it was gone, just like that, zipping off towards the garden wall and leaping up onto it before scuttling along to the gatepost and vaulting across to the opposite post, where it continued to Mrs Hornchurch's wall. Mae couldn't help feeling ever so slightly bad that she'd scared the cat, but she couldn't put up with it chiselling at her doorframe. Or working its way through another box of Frosties. And worse, giving Hannah false hope that they could take it in and welcome it as part of the family.

Mae sank down on the doorstop, dropping her face in her hands. Life had seemed so much easier only half an hour ago as she and Hannah jumped over waves, but now it was back to the hard slog she'd grown accustomed to. So much for having more fun!

Hannah was sitting at the table again, a suspicious strand of cheese resting on the corner of her mouth, as Mae stepped back into the kitchen. She moved slowly towards the table, her mind racing to find the right words to explain not only the cat situation, but the lack of a daddy situation too.

'I'm sorry, Mummy,' Hannah said, and Mae thought she was referring to the cheese she'd whipped. 'It's just I love Chilly so much.'

'I know, darling.' Mae rested a hand on Hannah's shoulder and dropped a kiss onto her soft, fruit-scented hair. 'But Chilly isn't our cat. He may belong to somebody else. We can't just claim him. Imagine how upset his owners would be if we took him from them.'

Hannah thought about it for a moment before nodding. 'I'd be sad if somebody took my pet.'

'Exactly.' Mae sat down at the table and passed a tortilla wrap to Hannah. 'I'm not being mean, sweetheart. It just wouldn't be fair.' She took a wrap for herself and spread a thin layer of the cream-cheese mix she'd prepared earlier onto it. 'And about not having a daddy around...' She placed the knife on the edge of her wrap and pressed her hands together, prayer-like, resting her chin on her fingers as though she were seeking guidance from a higher power.

'It's okay, Mummy.' Hannah shrugged and plopped a handful of cucumber pieces onto her wrap. 'Daddies *are* mean as well as nice. Jack's daddy won't let him play on the iPad when he's been naughty.'

The front door opened then, and Mae half expected the cat to come strolling into the kitchen, throwing himself into a vacant seat before helping himself to a slice of turkey.

'I can walk from here, honestly,' she heard Melody's muffled voice say out in the hallway. 'Thank you for today. It's been... interesting. Sorry again about your T-shirt.'

'It's fine, honestly,' a male voice said. 'And if you ever need to talk – about anything – you know where I am.'

Intrigued – and with the scent of more gossip potent – Mae jumped out of her seat and slipped out into the hallway before the mystery guest disappeared.

'Hello!' she trilled, hating herself immediately for the tone and accompanying wave. She whipped her hand away and tucked it safely behind her back. 'I was wondering where you'd got to. I see you've brought a friend.' Mae looked at the mystery guest, recognising him as the bloke with the dog from the pub.

'Sorry,' Melody said. 'Hugo was helping me home.'

'*Carrying* her home, to be precise,' Hugo said. He gave an overdramatic nod of his head. 'I know what you're thinking. Gentlemen like me are a dying breed.'

256

'I bet she wasn't thinking that at all, you pleb.' Melody turned to Mae and rolled her eyes. 'Ignore him. He thinks he's charming. It's best to play along. Until his ego starts to reach dangerous proportions.'

Hugo placed a hand on his chest. 'I'm wounded.'

'Me too.' Melody stuck out her foot. 'I need to sit down.'

'I'll give you a hand,' Hugo offered. 'Where to?'

Mae indicated the kitchen behind her. 'We were just about to eat dinner. Why don't you join us, Hugo? There's plenty.'

Yes, there was definitely gossip here to sniff out. These two were into each other, Mae had no doubt about it. First Mrs Hornchurch and Tom Byrne, and now these two lovebirds.

'I wouldn't want to intrude,' Hugo said as he helped Melody hobble into the kitchen. 'Actually, this looks delicious. Scrap what I just said.'

'You wouldn't be intruding, anyway.' Mae indicated the seats opposite hers and Hannah's. 'Sit. Eat. Enjoy.'

'If you're really sure…'

'Absolutely.' Mae sat in her own seat and resumed her cream-cheese spreading before adding turkey slices and salad. She helped Hannah to fold and roll her wrap, slicing it in half to make it easier on her little hands.

'So, how did you two meet?' she asked as she rolled her own wrap. She noticed Melody's cheeks start to pinken, but couldn't resist. When her own love life was non-existent, she had little choice but to live vicariously through others.

'It was up on the cliff,' Melody said. 'He was incredibly annoying, but he showed me the harbour so I forgave him.'

'Actually,' Hugo said, shaking his head. 'We met outside the fish and chip shop. Melody was admiring my dog.

257

Not that I can blame her. He's a handsome chap.' Hugo winked. 'Just like his owner.'

Melody gave Mae a pointed look. 'See what I mean?'

'You have a dog?' Hannah asked. 'What's it called? Is it friendly? Does it play ball? Can I take it for a walk?'

Hugo smiled across at Hannah, not fazed by her barrage of questions. 'His name's Scoop Dog, though he's just Scoop to his friends. He's very friendly, but he can get a bit shy sometimes around new people. He *loves* to play ball. And Frisbee. And he has a little stuffed monkey with squeaky ears.'

Hannah giggled. 'Can I take him for a walk?' She turned to Mae. 'Mummy, can I take Scoop for a walk?'

The cat, it seemed, had been taken down from his pedestal. At least for now.

'Scoop is lovely,' Melody told Hannah. 'And brave. He was very poorly, but Hugo's been looking after him, so he's all better now.' She turned to Hugo and grinned. 'He's quite the hero.'

'Me or the dog?' Hugo asked and Melody rolled her eyes.

'You know I was talking about you. Stop fishing for more compliments.'

Mae wasn't sure if Melody was aware of the chemistry flying between her and Hugo, but Mae certainly picked up on it. She'd assumed she was so out of the game herself that she wouldn't recognise the signs, but they were there, plain as day. Melody had developed a bit of a thing for her new pal – and the feeling was mutual.

Surprisingly, Mae felt a tiny pang of jealousy as she watched the pair across the table, teasing and sparring while flashing not-so-subtle smiles at one another. Mae swore at one point she caught Melody biting her bottom lip as she gazed at Hugo biting into his turkey wrap, love hearts practically popping out of her eyes, cartoon-style.

She could have this, she thought as she reached for a slice of tomato and popped it into her mouth. The fun, the flirting, the companionship. Mrs Hornchurch had lost a husband and best friend rolled into one, the man she'd made a life with, a family with, and if she could be brave and put herself out there again after years of being alone, what the hell was stopping Mae from taking a chance on love again? All she had to do was say yes the next time Alfie asked her out, which he surely would.

Chapter Thirty-One

Willow

Willow's exit from the bed and breakfast wasn't quite the pre-dawn flit she'd carried out the previous morning, but she still managed to leave the house without bumping into any of the others. She skipped breakfast again, but this time it was because she couldn't quite face the thought of food. She was hungry as she hadn't eaten dinner last night, but her stomach was swirling with apprehension due to the importance of the day ahead. Today, the surveyor would be making a visit to the house to assess the damage to the foundations, and Willow was a bag of nerves about the outcome. It was too early for the assessment, but Willow couldn't help constantly checking her phone, desperate to find a message from Liam.

Despite her best intentions, Willow had driven back to the B&B in the van after work, so she slipped into the driver's seat now, checking her phone one last time before shoving it into her handbag and out of temptation's way. She'd get back on track with the walking once Ethan was back to keep her company during the journey, but for now she took the familiar route from the seafront to the shop in the van, parking in her usual spot beside the shop before heading inside. She had so much to do today; besides worrying about the house foundations and inevitable call, she also had to go out to buy paint for Yasmina's nursery furniture, send out any orders that had come through online, make a start on a couple of small commissions due next week, and deliver the completed dresser. She hoped Gary was better as she'd really struggle on her own with the workload. Still, she appreciated the work, while she was lucky enough to have it. Once the report came in from the surveyor, it would be time to face the reality of losing her shop.

Willow had just started on the first commission – a clock made from a vintage china plate, the only remaining piece from a wedding set from the early seventies – when there was a tap at the shop's door. Putting down her drill and perching her protective goggles on top of her head, Willow made her way out into the shop and was pleased to see Gary standing on the other side of the glass panel in the door.

'Feeling better?' she asked once she'd swung the door open and stepped aside to allow Gary into the shop.

'Much better. Thank you.' Gary stepped into the shop and closed the door behind him.

'Good. Hopefully the bug's completely gone now, but do say if you start to feel unwell again, okay?'

Gary scratched the back of his neck. 'I'm sure I'll be okay from now on. Coffee?'

'That'd be lovely. I'll be in the workroom.' Willow hurried back inside, grabbing her phone and checking for any missed calls or messages. She'd only left the phone for thirty seconds or so, but she couldn't miss Liam's call.

Nothing. She placed the phone on the table, within easy reach, and slipped the goggles back down over her eyes. The call hadn't come by the time she finished the clock, and her phone remained silent as she and Gary trundled a bench upcycled from old pallets out onto the pavement.

'Willow!'

With the bench in place, she'd been about to head into the shop when she heard her name being called. She turned around and peered down the street, where Melody was ambling slowly towards her, supported on one side by a man with a dog.

'Good morning!' Melody was out of breath but cheery by the time she reached Willow and the shop.

'Are you supposed to be up and about yet?' Willow asked, looking down at Melody's foot. She was still wearing the bandage, though the swelling seemed to have eased.

'Probably not,' Melody said. 'But it's too nice to be cooped up inside and I haven't walked the whole way. We're parked just over there.' Melody pointed in the direction she'd just walked from. 'I've been meaning to pop over to pick up some souvenirs. I'll be going home soon so Hugo's helped me over.'

'It's starting to feel better then?' Willow indicated to Melody's ankle as they filed into the shop. Hugo fell behind, tying the dog to a drainpipe before joining them.

'I no longer see bright lights in front of my eyes when I stand on it,' Melody said. 'Or feel the need to scream the F word, so I'm taking that as a good sign.'

'Come and sit down.' Willow pulled a stool out from behind the counter and patted the seat. 'What kind of thing were you looking for?'

Melody, with Hugo's assistance, hopped up onto the stool. 'I liked those seashell candles you had in the window. I was thinking about getting some of those for my mum.'

Willow headed for the window display, picking out the small seashells filled with scented wax. She placed them on the counter for Melody to have a closer look at. Melody picked them up, lifting each of the different coloured candles to her nose and inhaling deeply.

'They smell gorgeous.' Melody put eight shells aside: two of each scent. 'Mum will love them.'

It was the first time Willow had seen Melody since her confession the other night, and while she'd assumed it would be incredibly awkward, Melody was acting as though no revelations had taken place at all, which was a relief and Willow decided it was best to play along.

'Ooh, I *love* this.' Melody slipped down from the stool, making sure to land on her good foot. She limped across to a jewellery display made from an old cake stand and picked up a little bird brooch. It was made from silver wire and tiny, jewel-coloured buttons that shimmered as she twisted it in the light. 'I have to have him.'

'Let me buy you this,' Hugo said, gently plucking the little bird from Melody's fingers. 'It'll be a memento of not only Clifton-on-Sea, but me. Something to remember me by.'

'As if I could ever forget you.' Melody limped back to the stool and slipped onto its seat again. 'And you can take that smug look off your face, mister. That wasn't a compliment.'

Hugo tapped the side of his head. 'It was in here.'

Melody smirked. 'I'm not sure I want to know what goes on in there, pal.'

Willow watched the pair as they played verbal tennis and suddenly missed Ethan more than ever before. Chatting on the phone wasn't the same as actually being together, and she hoped he'd be home soon. Whatever state that home turned out to be in.

The phone call from Liam still hadn't come by the time Melody and Hugo left the shop, the candles and the bird brooch packed in paper bags. It hadn't come as she left the shop in Gary's capable hands to head over to the DIY store to pick up the paint for the nursery furniture. She'd just

264

pulled up outside the shop again when her phone finally did ring, and she pounced on it, jabbing at the answer button before she missed the call. Liam's name hadn't been on the screen, but perhaps the surveyor was phoning her directly.

'Hello?' She unclicked her seatbelt, but remained seated in the van.

'Is that Willow St Clair?' the voice on the other end asked.

'It is.' Willow wiped a sweaty hand down the thigh of her dungarees.

This is it, she thought, panic rising and making her feel queasy. *My future rests completely on what I'm about to hear.*

'Hello, Willow. I'm calling from RTA OMG. We've received information you were involved in a minor car incident within the last two years. Is this correct?'

Willow squeezed her eyes shut. She fought the urge to swear at this time-wasting idiot, but refrained. It wasn't in her nature to scream and swear at strangers, even when provoked.

'No. It isn't true.' She opened the van door and jumped down onto the pavement.

'Are you sure, Willow?'

She slammed the van door shut, and she may or may not have imagined it was making contact with this joker's head.

'I'm sure. I think I'd remember.'

'Perhaps it was a very minor incident, Willow.'

'So minor I instantly forgot all about it?' Willow held back a sigh. 'I don't think so.'

'But Willow…' he said. 'I have information about this incident.'

Willow pushed open the shop door and stepped inside, raising a hand in greeting to Gary. 'If you have the information, why don't you tell me what happened?'

'I don't have all the details, Willow.' Why did he keep saying her name? It sounded creepy. 'That's why I need you to tell me what happened.'

'*Nothing* happened. I was *not* in an accident, minor or otherwise.' Gary gave her a questioning look and she rolled her eyes up to the ceiling.

'Perhaps it was a friend's car, Willow. You were a passenger.'

'No.'

'But Willow. My information says you were in a minor incident in the last two years. You could be entitled to up to two thousand pounds compensation.'

Jeez, what did she have to do to convince this muppet? Why couldn't she hang up on him like a normal person? Why did she have to be so bloody polite?

'Willow?'

She hadn't responded, simply walked across the shop with the phone up to her ear.

'Want me to deal with it?' Gary whispered, but Willow shook her head.

'Are you there, Willow?'

'Yes, I'm here. I'm going to tell you one more time and then I'm going to hang up, okay? Because I'm waiting for an important phone call.' She paused, allowing her words to sink in before continuing. 'I've *never* been in a car accident, as a passenger or the driver. No big accidents, no small ones. *Nothing*. Okay? I'm going to hang up now.'

'But Willow…' she heard before she pressed the end call button.

Typically, she had a message when she hung up. It was from Liam, asking her to call him back as soon as possible.

Chapter Thirty-Two

Melody

Hugo had been showing off his 'skills', playing the part of (a taller) Tom Cruise in *Cocktail*, with bottles of strawberry, toffee and blueberry sauce flying in the air (as much as they *could* fly in the ice-cream van). The queue outside the hatch had taken a keen interest in the juggling act – particularly the mums, Melody noticed – and Hugo was loving the attention. Unfortunately, his ego got the better of him and he turned to wink at his small but adoring crowd. And that's when it all went a bit wrong.

Hugo missed the strawberry sauce.

It clattered to the floor, the noise disturbing his concentration.

His arms flailed.

He ended up with the nozzle of the blueberry sauce stabbing him in the corner of his eye.

With one hand covering his eye and a loud swear, he stumbled.

Onto the strawberry sauce.

He slipped on the bottle and ended up sprawled on the floor.

Well, as close to sprawled as he could get in the confined space of an ice-cream van.

Melody probably should have hobbled over to see if he was okay, but she couldn't move – unless her shoulders shaking uncontrollably counted. She pushed a hand over her mouth, but there was no stopping the laughter. It erupted, long and hard, her head thrown back as tears started to stream down her face.

There was a groan from the floor of the ice-cream van. 'It's not funny.'

Melody pressed her lips together. He was right. He could be hurt.

So why was a muffled giggle still escaping?

'Sorry.' Melody cleared her throat and wiped her cheeks. 'You're right. It isn't funny.' She shuffled round from the seat at the front of the van and squeezed herself onto the floor, holding out a hand. Hugo took it and she helped him sit up. He rubbed at the eye that had been attacked by the blueberry sauce nozzle.

'Are they still watching?' he asked, turning his uncovered eye to the hatch.

Melody tried not to laugh in his face. It was a struggle. 'Yes, I think they are.'

'Shit.' Hugo hung his head and Melody reached out to rub his back soothingly. His shoulders started to shake and for a horrifying moment she thought he was crying. But she smiled when she heard the rumblings of his laugh, joining in as he laughed in earnest. He covered his face with his hands and shook his head.

'I've made myself look like a right plank, haven't I?'

'I'm afraid so.' Melody ruffled Hugo's hair and grinned. 'The plankiest plank.'

'My eye hurts.' Hugo rubbed it again and grimaced.

Melody batted his hand away and peered at it. It was a little bit pink and watering. 'I don't think you're going to lose it.'

'Do you think I'll need a patch? Like a pirate?' He brightened at this idea, but Melody shook her head.

'I think it'll be fine if you stop messing with it.'

'You could kiss it better,' Hugo suggested. 'Just to make sure.'

Melody rolled her eyes, but she leaned forward and planted a gentle kiss on the injured eye.

'There. Better?'

Hugo nodded. 'But I also hurt my lips.' He puckered up, but Melody gave a tut and rose to her feet, coming face to face with one of the mums peering through the hatch.

'Is he okay?' She pointed down at Hugo, who was still sitting on the floor, gently prodding at his eye.

'He's fine, apart from his dented ego. What can I get you?'

Melody took over ice-cream duties for the rest of the afternoon. Luckily the space was small, meaning she could keep her weight on her good foot most of the time. Her ankle was definitely healing, meaning she could hobble around quite comfortably now, but she wasn't sure it could manage a full shift without any support.

Melody had one more full day ahead before she had to return home and she'd briefly considered a quick visit to another seaside town for a few more shots, but in the end she'd decided to stay on in Clifton-on-Sea for the remainder of her trip. And it wasn't just because of her dodgy ankle.

'Thank you for your help this afternoon,' Hugo said as he closed the hatch after their final customer of the day. 'And for not laughing *too* much.'

'I did laugh quite a bit,' Melody said, and the mere remembrance of Hugo splatting to the floor was enough to set off another fit of giggles.

'All right, all right, you've had your fun.' Hugo attempted a stern look, but it crumpled almost immediately and he was grinning. His eye, thankfully, had lost its pink tinge and was no longer watering.

'I have had fun today,' Melody said, sounding surprised. She felt a fluttering in her stomach, a lightness against the familiar weighty dread.

'Do you still feel guilty about it?' Hugo asked.

'Of course.' Melody shrugged. 'But I think I always will, to some extent. But you were right yesterday.'

After taking Melody back to his place and deploying Scoop as a soothing tactic, Hugo had listened more to Melody's story, learning more about Ollie and their friendship.

'Ollie sounds like a wonderful person,' he'd said as he brought out cups of tea and a plate of biscuits. 'Kind, caring, and she obviously loved you to pieces and wanted the best for you.'

Melody had picked up a biscuit, but couldn't bring herself to place it to her lips. 'She did.'

'Wouldn't she still want the best for you?'

Melody placed the biscuit back on the plate. There was no way she could eat it.

'Of course.'

'And wouldn't she want you to be happy?'

'Well, yes. Obviously.'

'And live the best life you possibly could?'

Melody had sighed. She'd heard all this before, from her parents, from Ollie's mum and brother, even through their own grief and despair. But that didn't make it any easier.

'It's tragic that Ollie died so young,' Hugo said. 'But that doesn't mean you should waste your life. You should live it to the full, for both of you. Enjoy it. Experience it, the good and the bad. Because not everybody is lucky enough to do so.'

'Haven't you learned by now that I'm always right?' Hugo asked now. He sat down in the van's driver's seat and pulled on his seatbelt.

'I've learned that you've got a big head,' Melody said, following suit in the passenger seat. 'And that you can't juggle.' She giggled as Hugo flashed her a reproachful look. 'But yes, you are *sometimes* wise, despite appearances.'

'Hey!' Hugo's mouth gaped. He pulled down the sun visor and checked his reflection in the little mirror. 'Oh. Yes. I see what you mean.' He started the engine and pulled away from the promenade, heading towards the bed and breakfast. 'It will get easier, you know, with time. Hearts don't heal as quickly as ankles.'

'Or eyes.' Melody giggled again at the memory, pressing a hand to her mouth to stifle it before it took hold.

'I'm never going to live that down, am I?'

Melody shook her head. 'Nope.'

'Then I'm almost glad you're leaving in a couple of days.'

'Perhaps I'll return, just to taunt you about it,' Melody said with another giggle.

Hugo shrugged. 'Then it'll be worth the pain and humiliation.'

Melody felt her cheeks warm and a small smile played on her lips. The usual guilt spiked, but she fought it back. Ollie would have liked Hugo. She'd have seen through his overinflated ego and seen the Hugo Melody could. The kind Hugo. The sweet Hugo. The Hugo she would quite like to return to Clifton-on-Sea to hang out with again.

'Perhaps I'll do that then.'

'Really?' Hugo pulled over, as close to the bed and breakfast as he could.

'We'll see.' Melody unclicked her seatbelt and opened the van's door. 'Are we still on for tomorrow?'

'Absolutely. You, me, Scoop and Chapel Cove.'

'I promise not to cry this time,' Melody said before hopping out of the van and landing on her good foot. She closed the door and gave a wave before heading to the house.

Chapter Thirty-Three

Willow

'Are you serious?'

Willow couldn't quite believe what she was hearing. She placed a hand over her mouth, as though she could block all her emotions, squash them back deep down inside where they were safe from spilling out, and sank onto the stool behind the counter. Her hand moved to her stomach, which was suddenly swirling up a storm and leaving her feeling queasy. She saw Gary hovering in the background, his eyebrows pulled down low as he listened to Willow's side of the phone call.

'I am,' Liam said on the other end of the line. 'I absolutely am.'

'Gosh.' Willow shook her head while letting out a long, slow breath. Her hand moved from her stomach to the counter, clutching the edge for dear life. For the second time that week, she could have cried in public.

'Willow,' Liam said, his voice measured. 'This is a good thing. It means we don't have to underpin.'

Willow nodded, though Liam couldn't see her. 'I know, and I'm so happy about it. I'm just...' Willow shrugged and blew out a short, sharp breath. 'Shocked, I guess.

I was expecting – and preparing – for the worst: the cost, the time…' Losing the shop. Perhaps losing the house too. 'But now you're saying it isn't as bad as you thought and this other thing you need to do…' Willow couldn't recall the exact terminology – she'd been too focused on the fact that her dream home could be back on track within days rather than weeks. 'You're saying it's quicker and cheaper and we could be back in the house soon.'

'You could move back in straight away,' Liam said. 'There's really no need for you stay away. I'm sorry I overestimated the damage, but I really did think it was too dangerous for you to remain in the house.'

'It's okay. It's better to be safe than sorry.' And she really had enjoyed the luxury of a comfy bed and the bubble baths, as well as the company of Mae and Melody while Ethan was away.

'I'll make it up to you,' Liam said. 'I'll work extra hard to get us back on track. Starting now.'

Willow's face relaxed into a smile, as though her body was finally catching up with the good news. 'Are you saying you were slacking before all this?'

Liam laughed. 'I'd never admit to that.'

'I'll pop over this evening for a proper catch-up,' Willow said. 'And you can explain that… non-underpinning thing to me again.' There was no way she could explain it to Ethan at the moment, but she attempted to anyway, phoning him as soon as she ended the call with Liam.

'Everything okay?' Gary asked, stepping closer as Willow tapped on Ethan's name in her contacts.

Willow grinned. 'Everything's perfect.' She held up a hand as her husband answered. She got the gist of her conversation with Liam across: the house wasn't quite as banjaxed as they'd suspected, meaning they could push ahead with the refurbishment without going too much over budget. The extra cost certainly wouldn't mean giving up the shop, which was a massive relief. Willow wanted to hop off the stool and hug each and every item she'd created, knowing she was free to continue her passion, free to unleash her love and creativity and make her customers happy.

'This is fantastic news!' Unlike Willow, the update sank in faster for Ethan and she could tell from his voice he was relieved. She could picture him punching the air. 'Phone me later, once you know for definite what's going on. Or put Liam on the phone and he can explain.'

'Are you saying my explanation wasn't sufficient?' Willow teased.

'Not at all,' Ethan said. 'I'm totally up to speed with the "stuff" they're going to "sort of inject" into the ground.'

'Those are technical terms. You won't get any better from Liam.'

'Hmm. Perhaps we should give it a go, just in case.'

'If you insist.' Willow sighed, but she was grinning. Even she hadn't had a clue what she'd been wittering on about. 'I'll speak to you soon.'

'I'll *see you* tomorrow,' Ethan said, and Willow felt as tingly as a teenage girl chatting to her first crush.

'Tomorrow?'

'Yep. We've managed to sort everything out at this end, so I'm coming home.'

There was really no stopping it now, but at least when Willow burst into tears this time, they were the happiest of tears.

She headed over to the house as soon as she closed up the shop, stopping for a cup of coffee, a Jammie Dodger and a chat with Liam and the other builders. Willow wasn't sure what brand of coffee they were drinking, but it wasn't her usual and it wasn't very pleasant at all, but she forced it down out of politeness.

'You can move back over when you're ready,' Liam said as Willow took another Jammie Dodger from the packet. She nibbled the biscuit, hoping it would take away the taste of the vile coffee. 'And we'll get cracking on the foundations as soon as we have the materials. In the meantime, we'll get through some other jobs. Will you be staying in the same room as usual? Just so we can work around it, or maybe temporarily move you to another room if we need to.'

'I was thinking about staying on at the bed and breakfast for the rest of this week and next,' Willow said. 'I'm booked in anyway, and I don't really want to cancel on Mae.' Plus, it was so damn cosy over at the bed and breakfast! Why not make the most of it while she could? There'd be plenty of time to slum it over at the work site/ house in the weeks to come. Plus, she wanted to introduce Ethan to Mae and Melody as she felt they'd become quite friendly over the past few days and she didn't want to feel as though she'd lived a separate life from Ethan over that time.

'I'll keep popping over, though,' she told Liam. 'Just to keep you on your toes.'

She'd also bring a decent jar of coffee over.

Before she left, she had a little tour of the house, refamiliarising herself with the rooms. She'd only been away for a matter of days, but it felt as though so much more time had passed. She stood in her kitchen, imagining the table, filled with the sweet faces of her children while she, heavily pregnant with yet another addition, cooked them a nutritious meal. Ethan was there too, helping the older ones with their homework, and a cat lounged on the window seat, soaking up the sun (because in Willow's fantasies, Ethan was no longer asthmatic and the sun was always shining).

She moved upstairs, slipping into the room that would one day become the nursery. She pictured the furniture she would lovingly restore, shelves stuffed with books and toys, the sunshine streaming through the window, curtains fluttering in the breeze. This would be a happy room, full of the love that already made Willow ache.

Climbing back into her van after her tour, she drove along the seafront towards the bed and breakfast. She wound down the windows, taking in a lungful of salty breeze. The tension of the past week seemed to lift with each deep breath, her shoulders feeling less tense, her head lighter. She hadn't realised quite how much the house blip had taken a toll on her until the pressure was lifted, and she didn't know whether to laugh or weep again with relief now she knew everything really was going to be okay. Instead, she let out a loud whoop, startling a woman walking along the pavement. She pulled the child she was with closer to her body while glaring at the passing van.

'Sorry!' Willow called, but it was too late. The van had trundled past and the woman and child had resumed their journey. Willow giggled. She couldn't help it. She didn't find scaring the poor woman funny at all, but out it had popped anyway. And she found it such a stress reliever that she didn't attempt to stop. She laughed and laughed – and must have looked quite manic to anybody passing by – until the bed and breakfast came into view. The street, as usual, was packed with cars, so she continued on, eyes roaming for a free spot. There was a space ahead, but it wasn't quite big enough to slip the van between the two cars. But maybe just—

Thud!

Willow slammed on the brake as she felt the impact from the front of the van. She wasn't quite sure what had happened but her heart raced uncomfortably and a feeling of dread sat heavy in her stomach. A tingling sensation spread across her fingers as she unbuckled her seatbelt and tugged on the van's door handle. She jumped down onto the road and dashed to the front of van, a hand muffling the gasp leaving her mouth as she saw the small body slumped on the tarmac.

Chapter Thirty-Four

Mae

'You and Hugo seem close.'

With Hannah watching CBeebies in the family room, Mae had joined Melody in the living room with a cup of tea while Hannah's fishfingers and mini potato waffles were cooking under the grill. *Pointless* was on the television, though neither of them was really paying attention.

'He's been a great friend,' Melody said.

Mae wrapped her hands around her cup and tucked her bare feet underneath herself as she sat on the sofa. 'Just a friend?'

Melody nodded. Then shrugged. And then shook her head. 'I don't know what's going on with us, to be honest. When I got here, there was no way I was looking for a relationship. Or a holiday fling. I just wasn't interested in men.'

Mae smiled. She knew the feeling.

'But I like Hugo. He comes across as a bit big-headed sometimes, but he's not really. He can be quite sweet.'

'And he's pretty cute,' Mae said. 'There's a definite twinkle in his eye.'

Melody giggled. 'There was more than a twinkle in his eye today.' She giggled again before pressing her lips together to stop it in its tracks. 'I shouldn't laugh – no matter how funny it was at the time.'

'What happened?' Mae blew on her tea and settled down to listen to the story of Hugo and his ill-fated juggling act. Melody couldn't help giggling again as she relived the tale.

'It sounds like he was trying to impress you,' Mae said once she'd finished. 'Showing off. Displaying his skills. Sort of.' She caught Melody's eye and they both had a giggle.

'I do like him,' Melody said. 'But I'm going home in a couple of days.'

'That is tough,' Mae said. 'But there's nothing stopping you making the most of those couple of days.'

'Apart from me,' Melody said, but she didn't elaborate and, from the dejected expression on her face, Mae thought it best not to push. Besides, she was hardly one to be doling out relationship advice.

'I'll miss having you around when you go,' she said instead. 'And Willow, when she leaves next week. It's been nice having some female company.' Some company at all, if she was honest. She'd enjoyed being able to unwind during the evening, chatting over a glass of wine rather than staring at the television until it was time to curl up in bed, alone.

'Willow's only up the road,' Melody pointed out. 'You should get together. Let your hair down. You never know, you might just meet the man of your dreams.'

Mae nudged her playfully. 'Like you met Hugo.'

Melody groaned. 'Never *ever* let him hear you refer to him as that. His head will never fit through a regular-sized doorframe again. He struggles as it is.'

'So he *is* the man of your dreams,' Mae teased. She grinned when Melody kept her mouth firmly closed. 'Don't worry, your secret's safe with me. I won't tell a soul you're head over heels in love.'

Melody picked up a cushion and thwacked a giggling Mae with it. 'I am not in *love* with him.'

'Lust then,' Mae said, and Melody blushed. 'Ha! I knew it! You fancy the pants off him!' Mae leaned in and lowered her voice. 'Have you kissed him?'

Melody shook her head. 'Not properly. He kissed me on the night we met, but it was just a peck. And uninvited, I might add.'

'But you want to kiss him.' Mae took a sip of her tea. 'You should go for it, while you have the chance.'

'And so should you.' Melody gave Mae a pointed look that made her squirm.

'What are you talking about?'

Melody gave Mae another light thwack with the cushion. 'I'm talking about Alfie. He likes you, you like him. Why not give it a go?'

Usually, Mae would have been ready with her speech about being happy on her own, but today the words were reluctant to emerge. She'd been asking herself the same question ever since she'd spotted Mrs Hornchurch and Tom Byrne heading out for their date. And last night, after she'd removed her mask – the red lipstick and eyeliner flick, the pins from her hair, the outfit – and slipped beneath the cool sheets of her bed, she'd wondered for perhaps the first time since Shane left her whether she could really endure being on her own for ever. Whether she could face this empty bed night after night, whether she could watch Hannah grow up knowing that, one day, her daughter would embark on her own path in life and Mae would be left with nothing but fleeting visits and the memories of a happy home. And for the first time, she admitted – to herself, at least – that she wasn't happy being on her own, that she *was* lonely, even now, and afraid of the future she'd mapped out for herself.

'Mae?' Melody gently probed when she failed to answer.

Mae shrugged, her brow creasing. 'I'm not really sure what's stopping me any more.'

She placed her cup down on the table and headed into the kitchen to turn the fishfingers and waffles, but paused on the threshold when she spotted Hannah, crouched on the floor. She'd dragged one of the chairs over to the cupboard, climbing up so she could take down the box of Frosties, which she was now feeding to the cat.

'How many times, Hannah?' Mae sighed as she stomped over, plucking the cat, mid chew, from the floor and carrying him to the back door.

'But *Mummy*,' Hannah wailed, little legs scuttling across the kitchen. 'He's hungry.'

Mae tucked the cat under one arm so she could unlock the door, but Hannah used the opportunity to fling herself in front of it, blocking the cat's exit.

'He isn't our responsibility,' Mae said as she attempted to manoeuvre Hannah out of the way one-handed. 'He isn't our cat. He'll never be our cat. So *please* stop feeding him, *especially* Frosties.' She sighed as her attempts to move her daughter failed. 'Come on, Hannah. He can't stay.'

'No.' Hannah's face was scrunched in anger, her eyes dark and challenging. 'I love him.'

Not in the mood for another argument, and with the cat starting to fidget, Mae crossed the kitchen and headed out into the hallway, hurrying as a wailing Hannah chased after her. She reached the front door first and plonked the cat down on the path before returning to the kitchen to wash her hands; she couldn't bear to even think what that cat was riddled with.

'I'll just go outside and get him,' Hannah said. Her face had softened, her cheeks now wet with tears. 'I'll bring him inside. You can't stop me.'

'Hannah,' Mae said, adopting her most stern voice. 'Don't you dare.'

Hannah's mouth twisted as words fought to emerge. Finally, with her little hands clenched into fists, she settled on three words that made Mae flinch.

'I hate you!' the little girl roared before stomping out of the room, but instead of storming out of the house in search of the cat, she thumped her way up the stairs, slamming her bedroom door behind her.

'Trouble with Chilly again?' Melody asked when she returned to the living room.

Mae groaned. 'She's told you the name she's given him?'

Melody nodded. 'Yep. They've got quite a backstory, the two of them. Apparently Chilly is a talking cat, but only Hannah can hear him. He sneaks into the house when you're asleep and snuggles up with Hannah.'

Mae flopped down on the sofa. 'It wouldn't surprise me if that was true. I swear the furry little fleabag has a set of keys. I don't know how he gets in here sometimes, apart from a certain little lady letting him in. I don't know why she even likes him so much. He's hardly the cutest cat, is he?'

Melody's eyebrows lowered. 'I don't know. He has a certain... charm.'

'If "charm" is a codeword for scruffy-looking and grumpy, then yes.' Mae picked up her cup and took a sip. 'I always feel the need to fumigate the place when he's been around.'

Melody's eyebrows were low again. 'Aww, bless him. I want to take him home myself.'

Mae's eyes lit up. 'Ooh, good idea!'

Melody lifted her hands up. 'It's not happening. Can you imagine taking him on a train?'

'I can imagine waving him off while he trundles off into the sunset,' Mae said. 'I often daydream about it.'

There was a sudden screech outside the house, the sound of tyres against tarmac. Jumping up, Mae plonked her cup down on the table, not noticing the tea sloshing onto the wood in her haste. She flew to the window and pulled the blind aside, craning her neck to see what the commotion was. Outside, just ahead of the house, she saw a white van, its door flung wide open and a form that looked very much like Willow flying out onto the road.

'What is it?' Melody, with her ankle still strapped up, wasn't as speedy at getting to the window.

'It's Willow.' Mae made a dash for her shoes, which she'd slipped off earlier, shoving her feet into them before careening out into the street.

'Willow!' she called as she clattered along the pavement. 'What is it?'

'Oh God.' Willow turned to her, eyes wide. A hand went to her mouth, her eyes seeming to bulge from their sockets as she turned towards the road. Mae followed her gaze.

'Shit!' She flung herself down, a hand reaching out to the familiar shape of the cat that had been making a nuisance of itself for weeks. His eyes, usually glowing green and full of scorn, were closed.

'Is he…?' Willow shuffled closer. 'Have I…?'

'I'm not sure.' Mae placed a cautious hand on the cat's side, increasing the pressure slightly when he didn't stir. 'He isn't moving, but I think he's still breathing.'

She pulled her hand away. It was smeared with black cat hair and blood. There was a keening noise, and when Mae looked up, Willow was kneeling on the road, her head in her hands.

'It's okay.' With trembling fingers, Mae unfastened the tiny buttons on her peach cardigan. 'He'll be okay.'

'I didn't see him,' Willow said. 'I didn't see him.'

'I know, darling.' Mae shrugged off her cardigan and wrapped it around the cat's body, lifting him gently off the road. There was more blood underneath.

'Oh God. What's happened?' Melody asked, limping towards them. She gasped when she saw the bloodied cat.

'Can you ask Mrs Hornchurch to sit with Hannah?' Mae asked, pulling the cardigan-wrapped cat closer to her body and cradling him.

'Of course.' Melody placed a hand on Willow's shoulder and guided her to the pavement.

'There's food under the grill,' Mae said. 'Hannah's dinner.'

'I'll sort it, don't worry.'

'Where are you taking him?' Willow asked as Mae moved away from the van.

'To Alfie. He's a vet. Can you hold Chilly while I grab my keys?' Without waiting for an answer, she pressed the cat into Willow's arms and ran to the house, hoping Hannah wouldn't venture out of her bedroom and spot her beloved cat's blood on her hands. She grabbed her keys and bolted back out into the street as quickly and stealthily as she could.

Willow insisted on accompanying Mae to the vet, cradling the broken cat while Mae drove. Luckily, Alfie was still at his surgery when they arrived, bursting through the doors and babbling at the receptionist.

'Mae?' Alfie popped his head out of his door, eyebrows knotted. 'What's happened?'

285

'The cat.' She nudged Willow, who was still clutching Chilly, towards the vet. 'He's been hit by a van.'

Alfie opened his door wide. 'Come through.'

They scurried into Alfie's surgery, placing the cat down gently on the table as instructed. Willow explained what had happened, her face growing more ashen by the second.

'I'm sorry,' she said, backing away towards the door. 'I'm going to be sick.' Throwing a hand to her mouth, she bolted from the room. Mae looked from the poor cat to the door, torn about where she should be.

'It's probably best if you wait out in reception,' Alfie said as the veterinary nurse joined them. 'I'll come out and see you once I've assessed the little fella.'

Mae backed out of the room, her gaze never leaving the poor cat. What had she done? If she hadn't been so quick to eject him, he wouldn't have been in the road. He wouldn't have been hit and possibly about to die.

How was she going to break the news to Hannah?

'Will he be all right?' she asked, her voice barely above a whisper, as she paused on the threshold.

Alfie flashed a smile full of sympathy, but not promise. 'I'll do my best for him.'

'His name's Chilly, by the way,' she said before she slipped from the room and went in search of Willow.

'Alfie will look after him,' Mae said, not for the first time, as she and Willow sat out in the waiting room. She wasn't sure how long they'd been sitting there but the sun had started to dip outside and there were no other people – or animals – waiting to be seen. The only other person was the receptionist, who was busy behind her desk.

'I can't believe I did this to him,' Willow said, not for the first time. When Mae had found her, she'd been kneeling on the floor in front of the loo, her face grey and clammy. Mae had gathered her in her arms and Willow had promptly burst into tears.

'It was an accident.'

'I still hit him.' Willow rose from her seat and wandered over to the noticeboard full of posters for flea and worming treatment, thank-you cards from the owners of past patients, and notices about payment methods.

'He'll be okay.' Mae nodded, over and over again, hoping her words were true, otherwise she'd have to break her little girl's heart. Hannah didn't know about the cat yet; Mae had phoned to update Melody and Mrs Hornchurch a while ago, and they'd told Hannah that Mae had popped out to Nanny's. Mrs Hornchurch had allowed Hannah to eat her dinner in the family room in front of the television, so Hannah was more than happy with the situation.

'Willow, sweetheart, come and sit down.' Mae held out a hand, but Willow didn't take it and instead wandered towards the door, peering through the glass panel. She turned abruptly when the door to Alfie's surgery opened.

'Is he okay? What's happening? Is he going to be all right?' Willow pounced, both verbally and physically as she bounded towards Alfie.

'He's awake now,' Alfie said, and both Mae and Willow breathed huge sighs of relief. 'He's had quite a few stitches, but I've X-rayed him and there don't appear to be any broken bones. He is, however, feeling rather sorry for himself.'

'If he looks miserable, that's just his everyday face,' Mae said, smiling weakly.

'So he's going to be all right?' Willow asked again.

'I can't promise anything,' Alfie said. 'But I think he's a lucky kitty. I'm going to keep him in, at least overnight. Carrie's just making him comfortable in his bed now.

Tomorrow we'll see if we can trace the owner. He isn't chipped and he doesn't have a collar, so we're going to have to do an old-fashioned poster-on-lamppost job.'

'What if you can't trace his owner?' Willow asked.

'We'll cross that bridge when we come to it,' Alfie said. 'Now, I don't know about you two, but I could do with a stiff drink. Fisherman?'

Normally, Mae would have declined, but these were not normal circumstances and she actually felt she could do with a drink to steady her nerves. She could leave her car outside and pick it up tomorrow before her shift at the pub.

'Do you want to go and see him before we go?' If Alfie was surprised by Mae's acceptance of a drink with him, he didn't show it. He led the two women to a wall of cages, where Chilly was curled up in one of them. He had bandages around his middle and one of his paws, and a little cone of shame.

'He's dosed up on painkillers,' the veterinary nurse said as they peered in the cage at the cat. 'So don't be alarmed if he isn't responsive.'

'I'd like to pay for his treatment,' Willow said as she placed a finger on the grate. 'It's my fault he's in here.'

'There's no need,' Alfie said. 'He isn't your responsibility.'

Mae's gaze dropped to the floor. Hadn't she said something similar to Hannah earlier?

'He isn't your responsibility either.' Willow lifted her chin. 'And you weren't the one who hit him with their van.'

'I'm a vet.' Alfie shrugged. 'I'll care for all animals, whether they have owners or not. If you're feeling flush, there are some local animal charities I could recommend that would love a donation, though.'

288

They said goodbye to Chilly and headed across to the Fisherman. Alfie invited the veterinary nurse and receptionist along, but the receptionist declined as she had to pick her children up from the childminder's. Carrie, however, was free to join them.

'Will he really be all right?' Mae asked. They'd grabbed a table while Willow, who had insisted on buying a round of drinks, queued at the bar.

'I'll be keeping my eye on him, and I think he's probably used up one of his nine lives, but I think he'll get through it. He seems like a tough cookie.'

Mae leaned against Alfie, suddenly exhausted by the evening. 'Thank you. For looking after him. He means a lot to Hannah, even if he isn't ours.'

'It's my pleasure,' Alfie said. 'I'll look after him as though he was my own pet.'

'Like you do with all the animals?' Carrie piped up beside them. 'I know I've only been working with you for a couple of days, but I've already noticed what a big softie you are.'

'Ssh. Don't tell everyone,' Alfie said. 'I have a macho image to uphold.'

Carrie cocked an eyebrow. 'Really?'

Alfie shrugged. 'Okay, maybe macho is too strong a word…'

Carrie snorted. 'You think?' She grinned then, leaning in to nudge Alfie. 'I'm kidding. You are very manly, especially in your scrubs.'

Mae, who had been sitting shoulder to shoulder with Alfie, straightened in her seat. What was going on here? Was Carrie simply teasing Alfie – or was she flirting?

'I bet you say that to all the boys,' Alfie said and Carrie looked down at the table before peeking up at him through her lashes.

'I really don't.'

Oh God. She *was* flirting and Mae was sitting in the middle of it like a gooseberry.

'I'll go and give Willow a hand with the drinks,' she said, standing and backing away from the table. She joined Willow at the bar, one eye still on the table. She watched as Carrie placed a hand on Alfie's arm, throwing her head back as she laughed at whatever joke he'd told. Mae mentally rolled her eyes at the display. Alfie could be amusing, but Carrie was laying it on a bit thick.

'Are you okay?' she asked, tearing her eyes away and placing a hand on Willow's back.

Willow shook her head. 'Not really.' She lifted a glass of brown liquid. 'But this will help.'

Mae looked across at the table where Carrie was listening intently to whatever Alfie was saying, leaning in close and pushing an impressive cleavage under his nose. She lifted her own glass, tipping the brandy into her mouth and grimacing as the alcohol burned her throat.

It didn't help at all.

Chapter Thirty-Five

Willow

The first thought that entered Willow's head when she woke on Saturday morning was Ethan and his imminent arrival. He was booked on a flight that morning and should arrive back in Clifton-on-Sea by lunchtime. Willow would leave the shop in Gary's capable hands so she could pick Ethan up at the station and take him back to the bed and breakfast to drop off his things before they went out for lunch and a catch-up. Willow felt a giggle bubble up from her tummy. It would be like dating again, when the relationship was fresh and the anticipation of what lay ahead for them was unknown yet alluring, the stresses and strains yet to make an appearance.

But the giggles ceased when she remembered the previous evening. The van, hitting Chilly, the blood, the stillness. Alfie was hopeful he'd pull through, but what if he didn't? She pulled her knees in towards her body, pressing her face into the duvet. What had she done? Instead of the butterflies of a few moments ago, she now felt a shiver of dread in her stomach, the tang of bile in her throat. She lurched from the bed, stumbling to the bathroom where she fell to her knees in front of the toilet bowl, dry heaving until her throat felt raw. She pulled herself up onto her feet, her legs shaking beneath her, and stumbled to the sink, where she splashed her face with cold water and rinsed her mouth. Looking up into the mirror, she was aghast at the face staring back at her. Her eyes were dull and ringed with grey, her skin the colour of raw dough, and her cheeks had lost their rosy glow.

I guess this is what a cat killer looks like, she thought as she drew her eyes away from her reflection. She returned to her room to grab her washbag. She tried not to gag as she gave her mouth a thorough brush, attempting to rid herself of the reminder of her session at the toilet bowl. She dressed in a navy-blue belted sundress, which she wouldn't usually wear for work as it was impractical when she was getting messy in the workroom; but she wanted to look nice when she saw Ethan, and her usual short dungarees and ancient T-shirt just wouldn't cut it. The dress fell just above the knee and swished as she walked, making her feel girlish as she headed into the kitchen. The pastries, cereal and fruit were set out on the breakfast bar, but Willow couldn't face food as her stomach was still feeling delicate.

'Morning,' Mae said when she saw Willow. She was sitting at the table, attempting to coax Hannah into eating a bowl of cereal. 'You look nice.'

Willow lifted her mouth into what she hoped was a smile. She'd piled on the make-up, which was obviously having the desired effect. 'Ethan's coming home today, so I thought I'd make the effort.' She glanced over at Hannah, then back to Mae. 'Do you think I could have a word? In the living room?'

'Of course.' Mae turned to her daughter. 'Eat that and then you can watch telly for *ten minutes* before we leave for Nanny's.' She pushed back her chair and followed

Willow through to the living room, where Willow closed the door behind them.

'I didn't want to mention the accident in front of Hannah,' she said, her voice low. 'But I was wondering if you'd heard from Alfie.'

Mae shook her head. 'Not yet, but I'll let you know as soon as I do.' She reached out and gave Willow's arm a comforting squeeze. 'I'm sure he'll be fine, though.'

Willow nodded. 'I hope so.' She placed a hand on her stomach as it churned again, and prepared to sprint if the need arose. Luckily, it settled down and she headed outside, hesitating for a moment before climbing into the van. She briefly considered walking to the shop, preferring the fresh air to being cooped up, but she'd need the van soon as she was due to pick up the nursery furniture from Yasmina's house mid morning.

At the shop, she made a cup of coffee and took it through to the workroom where she switched on her computer and printed out the labels and invoices for orders that had come through overnight. She packed the items and put them aside to take over to the post office later. Sitting down at the counter, she took a tentative sip of her coffee. It tasted awful, but then she had started her morning with her head down the toilet bowl, so it wasn't a surprise. She tipped the coffee down the sink and returned to the shop to get on with her morning duties. She was in the middle of dusting the window display when her phone started to ring. She picked it up, her stomach performing a non-nauseating flip when she saw her husband's name on the display.

'Hey, you.' She picked up the duster with her free hand and continued with the job. 'Are you at the airport?'

'I am,' Ethan said. 'But I won't be boarding any time soon. The flight's been delayed.'

Willow stopped dusting and stood up straight. 'For how long?'

'A few hours, at least. The time changed three times while we were on our way to the airport. At the minute, we're looking at two o'clock.'

'Two o'clock?' Willow tried to keep the whine from her voice, but failed. There would be no lunch date, it seemed.

'Sorry,' Ethan said. 'I'll let you know when I know for sure, okay?'

'Okay.' Willow forced a smile, hoping it would be conveyed in her voice. 'I can't wait to see you.'

'Me neither. I've missed you.'

The door opened and Gary stepped inside, raising a hand in an awkward wave. Willow waved back with her duster. 'I've missed you too. Maybe we can go out for dinner instead of lunch?' Willow wasn't particularly looking forward to the food – she was still feeling queasy – but she was disappointed about the lunch date.

'Do you know what I'd love?' Ethan said. 'Fish and chips on the beach.'

Willow smiled, genuinely this time. 'Just like our wedding day.'

'Except it'll be just the two of us this time.'

Willow's smile grew wider. 'Sounds perfect. That's what we'll do.'

'Great. Can't wait,' Ethan said. 'I'll let you get back to work and I'll call you with the details later. Love you.'

'Love you too.' Willow pressed her lips together so she wouldn't giggle when she noticed Gary looking uneasy in the corner, his cheeks turning pink as he tried to look busy. She'd already embarrassed him the day before by bursting into tears (they were happy tears, but tears all the same, and Gary hadn't been at all sure how to deal with them). She hung up and gave Gary the post-office task. She'd never seen him looking so grateful as he bustled out of the shop with a bag full of parcels.

With Gary's help, she loaded the nursery furniture. Yasmina was in no fit state to be lugging furniture, but she did a good job of guiding the pair onto the van so they didn't have to recreate any of the Chuckle Brothers' 'to me, to you'-style fumbling. She said goodbye to the outdated furniture, saying she couldn't wait until it returned looking fresh and modern.

'I'll do my very best,' Willow promised before she and Gary made their way back to the shop. They placed plastic sheeting down on the floor before unloading the pieces into the workroom. The first job would be to strip the varnish from the wood, so Willow removed all the drawers and unscrewed the doorknobs in preparation. She wouldn't be using the mismatched doorknobs and had instead chosen some simple round knobs to keep the pieces cohesive, but she put the old knobs aside as they would more than likely come in useful for another project in the future.

With the furniture prepped, she grabbed the varnish stripper and a paintbrush, but when she opened the tub, she almost heaved over the plastic sheet protecting the flooring.

That job, she decided, would have to wait until her stomach wasn't feeling quite so weak.

'I'm going to leave the nursery furniture until Monday,' she said as she joined Gary out in the shop. 'New week, new project.' She sat down on her stool at the counter, pushing away the coffee Gary had made while she was in the workroom. She couldn't face another attempt at coffee yet.

'Gary,' she said as she pulled her diary out of her drawer and marked off the nursery furniture pick-up. 'Are you still feeling unwell?'

Gary shook his head as he scratched the back of his neck. 'Nope. Completely better. Why?'

'Just checking,' Willow said with a shrug. She picked up her phone and gave Liam a ring to check on the progress at the house. It felt good to be proactive with the development again after a few days of the house sitting idle.

'We're cracking on with the roof,' Liam said, and the sound of activity clearly going on in the background confirmed this. 'It's a simple enough job as it looks in pretty good nick. We just need to replace the felt and a few tiles. We'll check the guttering while the scaffolding's up, which shouldn't take long, and we'll be able to get started on the foundation repairs on Monday.'

New week, new project.

'That's great,' Willow said. 'Ethan won't be back until this evening, so we'll pop by on Monday for a proper catch-up. I might even bring over a new packet of Jammie Dodgers if you're lucky.'

'The jam and custard ones are my favourite,' Liam said.

'I'll see what I can do.' Willow looked up as the shop door opened. It was Mae. She tried to assess whether she'd arrived bearing good or bad news by her facial expression alone, but couldn't say with confidence either way. 'I have to go now, but give me a call if you need anything.' She said goodbye and hung up before leaping from her stool and pouncing on Mae, firing off a million questions in quick succession.

'It's good news,' Mae said, though the beaming smile now on her face said it all. 'Alfie said Chilly woke up in a pretty good mood considering what he's been through – though how he could tell with that face is a mystery.' She laughed, but Willow didn't join in. She was in no mood for a joke – not until she knew for sure that Chilly was going to pull through relatively unscathed.

'So he's going to be okay?' she asked and Mae nodded.

'I went to see him myself when I picked my car up from the surgery. He's on pain medication, but he seems happy enough, despite the face, and he's eaten, which Alfie says is a good sign.'

'He's going to be okay,' Willow said, shortly before she turned, ran to the loo, and promptly threw up.

Chapter Thirty-Six

Mae

'Come and sit down. We'll get you a glass of water.' Mae guided Willow to the stool behind the counter once she emerged from the loo. She pushed down gently on Willow's shoulders until she sank onto the seat. She had to admit, she was surprised by the reaction to the news of Chilly's recovery. Last night, after the distress of the evening's events, it hadn't been such a shock when Willow had been overcome, but now, after delivering the good news, Mae was concerned.

Willow's assistant brought a glass of water over, which he pressed into Willow's quivering hands.

'Here you go,' Mae said, rubbing Willow's back. 'Small sips.'

Willow took a couple of sips before placing the glass down on the counter and rubbing at her eyes. It didn't matter about her carefully applied make-up – it was already ruined.

'Sorry about that. I think I've caught Gary's bug.'

Mae turned to the assistant, who was scratching at the back of his neck while glancing around the shop. Glancing everywhere but at the two women.

'I thought I recognised you,' Mae said, nodding her head. 'You're Gary King. From the Fisherman.' Mae crossed her arms, her eyes narrowing slightly. 'You broke Frank's clock.'

'That wasn't me,' Gary said, the neck-scratching intensifying.

'What's going on?' Willow asked, looking from Mae to Gary. 'What clock?'

'The clock behind the bar at the Fisherman.' Mae pointed at Gary. 'This one broke it while tanked up. I don't think it's a bug Gary's had.' Mae raised her eyebrows at Gary, waiting for a confession. It didn't come. Gary simply dropped his gaze to his shoes, as though pleading with them to rescue him from the sticky situation. 'I think Gary here has been suffering from a hangover, judging by the amount he's been putting away at the pub.'

'Gary?' Willow's eyes slid slowly from Mae to her assistant. He was still staring down at his shoes. Still waiting to be rescued. 'Is it true?'

'I'm sorry,' Gary told his shoes. 'But I never actually said I had a bug.'

'You never said you were hungover either.' Willow's tone was filled with disappointment rather than anger. Gary looked up, briefly, before giving his shoes his full attention again.

'I'm sorry, Willow. It won't happen again.'

'I hope not.' Willow took another sip of water and placed a hand on her stomach.

'I need to go and start my shift at the pub,' Mae said, resting a hand on Willow's back. 'Are you going to be okay? Perhaps you should go home and rest.'

'I don't feel too bad now,' Willow said. 'But I will go home if I start to feel unwell again.'

Mae hesitated a moment, but she was already late for her shift after the detour. As accommodating as Frank and Corinne were, she didn't want to take the piss.

'Look after her,' she told Gary in her best stern-mum voice before she left. She drove across town to the harbour, apologising profusely as she clattered into the pub.

She popped over to the vet's surgery during her lunch break, hoping to catch Alfie during a quiet period so she could have another peek at Chilly. She couldn't believe the transformation she'd seen that morning. When they'd left the cat last night, he'd been barely conscious, and yet that morning he'd been up and walking, albeit in a lopsided fashion due to the bandage on his paw. He'd mewed at Mae and it had been one of the best sounds she'd ever heard. She'd been so relieved and knew Willow would be too, but when she'd tried to phone her to pass on the news, she'd been sent straight to voicemail. Mae had been too impatient to wait to spread the good news, so she'd driven over to Willow's shop.

'We were just heading out for some lunch,' Alfie said when she arrived at the surgery for the second time that day. 'Why don't you join us and then we can check on Chilly when we get back.'

Mae looked from Alfie to Carrie, who was slipping a jacket on beside him.

'I'm not really hungry,' she said, which wasn't technically true. She was rather peckish, but lunch with Alfie and Carrie wasn't even a tiny bit appealing. She'd felt enough of a gooseberry the night before in the pub, and the feeling would only intensify if she crashed their lunch date.

'Just a coffee then?' Alfie offered a small smile, his eyebrows shifting upwards almost imperceptibly. He turned to Carrie, placing a hand on her arm. 'You don't mind if I skip lunch, do you?'

'Of course not.' Carrie beamed at Alfie, the very image of the perfect, accommodating girlfriend. 'Would you like me to pick something up for you? A sandwich? Ham salad, tiny bit of mayo, no onion?'

'My favourite,' Alfie said. 'You remembered.'

Of course she did, Mae thought. *Because that's what perfect girlfriends do.*

Maybe it was the wanting-what-you-can't-have factor, but Mae was suddenly feeling territorial over Alfie. He was *her* friend. She should know what his favourite sandwich filling was (she didn't), she should have lunch plans with him instead of tagging along as a third wheel. He'd been interested in her long before Carrie rocked up with her swishy blonde hair and supermemory skills.

'So...' Alfie leaned in towards her as Carrie left the surgery. 'Coffee?'

Mae lifted her wrist, looking down at her watch while fiddling with its strap. She'd already been late for her shift, and she really wanted to see Chilly before she returned to the pub, but she also wanted to spend some time with Alfie. Perhaps gauge how he felt about Carrie. Gauge whether he was interested in her in anything other than a professional capacity. Maybe her mum had been right. Maybe she'd rejected him one too many times and he'd moved on. Not that Mae could blame him; his co-worker was incredibly pretty and she didn't come with years' worth of emotional baggage.

'A quick coffee,' Alfie said, guessing – wrongly – that she was about to decline.

'How quick?'

Alfie offered a smile, displaying a row of neat teeth. 'I'll drink it scalding hot if you want me to.'

Mae rolled her eyes. 'That won't be necessary. A trip to A&E with a burned mouth will only slow us down.'

'So?' Alfie tilted his head to one side. 'Is that a yes?'

Mae shrugged, but she was already heading towards the door. 'I suppose it is.'

They ended up at a small café a couple of streets back from the harbour. They ordered their coffees to go, strolling down to the harbour to take in the view. Mae placed her coffee on the wall, resting her elbows on the stones.

'Carrie seems nice,' she said, her tone as neutral as she could manage.

'She's great.' Alfie joined Mae in the wall-leaning. 'We'd be lost without her. Or still stuck with Anna.' Alfie shuddered and Mae laughed.

'She couldn't have been that bad.'

Alfie looked at Mae, his features deadly serious. 'She really, really was. I could have wept with joy when Carrie turned up.'

All right, mate. No need to go overboard.

'She's very pretty.'

Subtle, Mae thought, mentally kicking herself.

Alfie nodded. 'She is. And she's a laugh. She even made Tom laugh in the pub the other day.'

Mae pushed herself away from the wall and picked up her coffee. 'I think his good mood is more to do with his new lady friend.'

'Ah, yes.' Alfie's face lit up. 'Tom and Edna, sitting in a tree.'

'You know Mrs Hornchurch?'

Alfie nodded and took a sip of his drink. 'She comes to the surgery regularly for flea and worming treatment. For her dog, obviously.'

Mae grinned. 'I'm glad you clarified that.' She took a sip of her drink and leaned against the harbour wall again. 'You know everybody round here, don't you?'

Alfie shrugged. 'Mostly the people with pets. It's a smallish town and I'm the only vet. People either have to bring their pets to me or trek out of town.' He winked. 'It's almost like an evil genius masterplan, setting up here.'

'No offence, but you're hardly evil genius material.'

Alfie placed a hand on his chest. 'Ouch.'

'You know what I mean. You're way too nice. I've seen the way you care for animals.'

When he'd handled Chilly earlier, he'd been so gentle, so aware of his injuries and the possible emotional issues the accident might have caused. He'd made a subtle fuss of the cat – a tickle of Chilly's chin, a head scratch, even a little kiss to the top of his head before he returned him to his temporary home.

'I'm going to take it as a compliment then,' Alfie said.

'You should.' Mae hoisted herself up onto the wall, her legs dangling over the edge. 'Have you had any luck tracing Chilly's owner?' she asked before she was tempted to dole out any more compliments.

'Not yet. If I'm honest, I wouldn't be surprised if it turns out he doesn't have a home. He looks like he's been in quite a few serious scrapes without being treated. But I'll do my best. I'm going to put up some posters around your area. If he's been hanging around there frequently, he's more than likely from round that way.'

'Do you need any help?'

Alfie had lifted his coffee cup to his lips, but Mae could still see the smile behind it. 'That'd be great, thanks. If you're not busy.'

Mae shook her head. 'Not busy at all. Besides, it's the least I can do after I practically threw the poor bugger under the van.'

Alfie reached a hand out, placing it on Mae's arm. She didn't move away immediately as she normally would.

'This wasn't your fault. Anybody else would have shooed him out of their kitchen.'

Mae shrugged. 'I suppose. Anyway, what time do you want me?'

'Around six? I'll call round with the posters.'

'Perfect.' Mae looked up at the sky. It had suddenly turned grey and brooding with the threat of rain. 'I should be getting back to the pub.'

'I should be getting back to the surgery too. Carrie might be waiting with my sandwich.' Alfie patted his stomach. 'As much as I appreciate a good cup of coffee, it's no substitute for lunch.' He helped Mae hop down from the wall. 'I'll walk you back.'

'No, it's okay.' Mae managed a small smile. 'You get back to your sandwich.'

And Carrie.

'Do I have to go to Mrs Hornchurch's?' Hannah whined, her eyes glued to the television. 'She makes me play snakes and ladders and it's *so boring.*'

'Snakes and ladders is fun.' Mae slipped her arms into a cardigan, fastening it over her jade-green tea dress. The day had started to turn chilly and the short sleeves of her dress wouldn't cut it.

'You play it then.' Hannah curled her feet underneath herself on the sofa. 'And I'll stay here.'

Mae grabbed the remote and switched the television off, causing a squeak of protest from the sofa. 'I need to go out. We're trying to find Chilly's owner.'

Hannah narrowed her eyes to slits. 'I don't want you to find Chilly's owner. They'll take him away.'

Mae had told Hannah about the accident, though she hadn't gone into too much detail and had downplayed his injuries as she didn't want Hannah to blame her for

Chilly's near-death experience. She felt guilty enough already.

'Come on.' Mae held out a hand and Hannah reluctantly took hold of it. Together, they headed next door, ringing Mrs Hornchurch's bell. Mae hadn't yet asked her neighbour if she would watch Hannah while she helped Alfie with the posters as she hadn't been in when she'd tried earlier, but Mrs Hornchurch was always happy to help out and enjoyed the company – and the games of snakes and ladders, apparently.

'Oh...' Mae said when Mrs Hornchurch opened the door. 'Are you on your way out?'

Mrs Hornchurch wasn't dressed for a night in with a hot cocoa. She was wearing a coral-belted dress with a matching jacket, heeled court shoes and was clutching a rather fancy leather handbag.

'I am, dear.' Mrs Hornchurch smoothed down her dress. 'I'm off out to meet a friend for dinner.'

A friend, Mae mused. *Or Tom Byrne?*

'But I can spare you a few minutes.' Mrs Hornchurch opened the door wider, wafting the floral perfume she was wearing towards them.

'It's okay,' Mae said, backing away. 'Enjoy your dinner. And say hello to Tom for me.' She winked at Mrs Hornchurch, giggling as the older woman's mouth gaped.

'You can't have any secrets around here, can you?'

'I'm afraid not,' Mae said. 'But take no notice. Go out and have fun. Just don't do anything I wouldn't do.'

Mrs Hornchurch laughed and it was such a girlish sound, it surprised them both. 'Get away, you cheeky monkey. It's dinner, nothing more.'

Saying goodbye, Mae waved at her neighbour before turning and leading Hannah out of Mrs Hornchurch's garden and back to their own house next door.

'Does this mean I don't have to hang out with Mrs Hornchurch?' Hannah asked as Mae opened the door.

Mae ruffled her hair. 'Not unless you want to play gooseberry.'

Hannah scrunched up her nose. 'Is that like snakes and ladders.'

Mae laughed and shook her head. 'It's nothing like snakes and ladders. Not nearly as much fun.' The doorbell rang behind her, making her jump. It was Alfie, slightly earlier than planned. She'd half expected to see Carrie with him, forcing her into another gooseberry situation, but he was alone and Mae was more relieved than she would ever admit to being.

'I'm afraid we have a problem,' she told Alfie. 'I was going to ask Mrs Hornchurch to watch Hannah, but she's going out for dinner with Tom.'

Hannah tugged on Mae's skirt until she looked down at her. 'I thought she was playing gooseberry.'

Mae pressed her lips together to smother the giggle brewing. She turned to Alfie with a shrug. 'It looks like I can't offer my services after all.'

'I don't know,' Alfie said. 'Three hands are better than two.'

'You mean bring Hannah with us?'

Either that or Carrie *was* here, lurking and ready to ruin Mae's evening.

'Why not?' Alfie crouched down so he was at eyelevel with the little girl. 'Would you like to help us find Chilly's owner?'

Hannah pulled a face and shook her head. 'No.' She folded her arms across her chest. 'I would *not* like that at all.'

'Hannah doesn't want us to find the owner,' Mae explained. 'She wants us to keep Chilly ourselves.' She shifted her gaze to Hannah. 'Which isn't happening.'

'Mummy doesn't like Chilly,' Hannah said. 'She probably wishes he was dead.'

Mae's eyes widened and her cheeks grew hot. She was mortified. Of all the things to say to the vet who had worked hard to make sure that didn't happen!

'That isn't true,' she told Alfie before turning to her daughter. 'Hannah, I don't wish he was dead, or even hurt. I just don't think we should be feeding him when he has a home already.' Making a quick decision, she grabbed Hannah's hand and guided her back outside. 'Come on, let's help Alfie. Chilly will be missing his owners. Let's make sure he finds them.'

She had to prove to Alfie that she wasn't the callous cat-hater Hannah was making her out to be. Actions spoke louder than words, so she would find the poor cat's owner one way or another.

Chapter Thirty-Seven

Melody

Hugo had picked her up early that morning, with Scoop and a picnic waiting in the car. He hadn't had to carry her down to the beach at Chapel Cove this time, though he'd gallantly offered his services. They'd made a slow journey down the sandy track, Scoop already bounding ahead, intent on having a paddle in the sea. There were two other people on the beach, an elderly couple strolling hand-in-hand by the shallows, but other than that the cove was as peaceful as before.

'I wonder why more people don't come here,' Melody mused as she sank down onto the sand, stretching out her bad leg. 'It's so beautiful.' She'd brought her camera along, and picked it up now, focusing on Scoop as he bounced and yapped at the gentle waves.

'It's the lure of the bright lights.' Hugo dropped down next to Melody, holding a hand above his eyes to offer a bit of shade so he could keep an eye on Scoop. 'People prefer the pier and the arcade. It's too remote here – you can't even get a pint. The nearest pub is back towards town. I think there used to be a café or something at the top of the track, but everything's boarded up now.'

'I like it,' Melody said, lowering her camera. Scoop was bounding towards them now, the sand sticking to his wet paws.

'Me too.' Hugo reached out for Scoop, giving his ears a good scratch when he leapt into his lap. 'And so does this little dude.' The 'little dude' jumped at Hugo's chest and attacked his face with his tongue, licking him fast and furiously, despite Hugo's protestations. Melody giggled as she watched, grabbing her camera to capture the moment Hugo fell back onto the sand, the determined dog still lapping at his face.

'You could have helped me,' Hugo said once he'd managed to wrestle the dog from his face.

'I'm here to bear witness.' Melody waggled her camera. 'Not interfere.'

'Are you going to enter my photo in the festival?' Hugo asked. He pulled a small ball from the pocket of his shorts and tossed it towards the water. Scoop tore after it.

'Hardly,' Melody said, fighting the smile pulling at the corners of her mouth. 'I'd quite like to win.'

Hugo's mouth gaped and he placed a hand on his chest. 'You're a cruel woman sometimes.'

'I'm the perfect antidote to that alarmingly large ego of yours. It goes some way to keep it in check.'

'So your cruelty is actually kindness?' Hugo thought about it for a moment before shaking his head. 'Nah, I don't buy it. You're just mean.'

Melody laughed. 'You're probably right.' She nudged Hugo. 'For once.'

'Ouch.' Hugo clutched his chest again. 'You're not holding back today, are you?' He reached down for the ball Scoop had returned and deposited at his feet. He threw the ball again, watching as the dog raced after it.

'You know I think you're pretty awesome really, don't you?' Melody was asking Hugo the question, though she, too, was watching the dog intently.

'I think you're pretty awesome as well,' Hugo said, his eyes no longer on the dog. 'So we're a good match.'

'Apart from geography-wise.' Melody dug her hand into the sand. Despite the sun warming the sand, it was cool beneath the surface. 'I'll be going home tomorrow.'

Home. The place that should contain Ollie but didn't. She wasn't sure she was ready to go back to that, but she didn't have much choice. Besides, she couldn't run away for ever. Ollie was gone, but her family were waiting for her return, not to mention her job and flat. If there was one thing she'd learned from meeting Hugo, it was that life moved on, whether you were prepared for it or not.

'It isn't tomorrow yet.' Hugo pushed himself up onto his feet and held a hand out to Melody. She took it, not even wincing any more as she put weight on her bad ankle. She wouldn't be running any marathons any time soon, but it was definitely on the mend. Their hands remained entwined as they wandered along the beach, sticking to the wetter, sturdier sand, Scoop trotting alongside them with the ball still wedged between his jaws. They passed the elderly couple, who smiled in greeting, and continued along until they reached the rocks that cut off the beach and rose up to the surrounding cliffs.

'I'm starving,' Hugo said as Scoop attempted to clamber up onto the rocks, the ball abandoned on the sand. 'Fancy a run back for the picnic?'

Melody stuck her foot out. 'With this ankle?'

'Who said you'd be the one doing the running?' Hugo stood in front of Melody, bending slightly at the knees, his hands held out behind him. 'Hop on.'

Melody laughed. 'You want to give me a piggyback?'

Hugo straightened and turned to Melody with a shrug. 'How else am I supposed to show off my strength and fitness? Besides, I really am hungry, so up you get.' He reassumed the pose and with only the slightest hesitation – was he actually serious? – Melody leapt onto his back. It had been quite some time since she'd had a piggyback – it had more than likely been back at primary school – but it was fun, for her at least. Hugo trotted off, speedier than Melody had imagined a person would be with her perched on their back, with Scoop pounding the sand just ahead of them. The salty breeze whipped at her loose hair and she laughed, feeling free and full of joy. With a whoop, she threw her hands up in the air, giggling as she was thrown off balance, her hands quickly finding Hugo's shoulders again.

What would Ollie say if she could see Melody now? Would she be cross Melody was enjoying life without her? Or would she laugh along at the spectacle and encourage Melody to whoop again?

Melody leaned down towards Hugo's ear. 'Is this really as fast as you can go?'

Hugo responded by picking up the speed and Melody whooped again, though she clung on tight this time as she did so.

In typical British summer style, it started to drizzle, the grey clouds seeming to appear from nowhere, as they reached the sandy track. They sheltered in the car, spreading the picnic food out along the dashboard and on their laps as best they could.

'This isn't exactly what I imagined when I packed the picnic this morning,' Hugo said, still panting slightly from the piggyback jog along the beach. 'Sorry.'

'Don't be daft,' Melody said as she unwrapped a foil-wrapped stack of cheese and pickle sandwiches. 'A picnic is fun wherever you eat it.'

Hugo tore a small chunk off his pork pie and passed it behind him, to where Scoop was sitting on three legs, the fourth paw held aloft in a pleading manner. 'You're right. The beach isn't going to be much fun now, though.'

'It might clear up.' Melody peered through the window, which was quickly filling with blobs and rivulets. Rather than slowing down, the drizzle was turning into a full-on downpour. 'Or maybe not.' She shrugged at Hugo before biting into her sandwich.

The rain hadn't stopped by the time they'd finished eating, so they said goodbye to Chapel Cove and headed back into town, dropping a full and sleepy Scoop off at Hugo's place before heading for the arcade. They skipped bingo this time and instead slotted two-pence pieces into machines, watching as they fell onto the sliding shelves, hoping they would push more coins off the end and into the tray below so they could scoop them up triumphantly and add them to their paper tubs of coins. They played the fruit machines, battled against one another at air hockey, and attempted to win stuffed toys in the grabber machines.

'It's a bloody fix,' Melody grumbled as the monkey in purple dungarees slipped from the claws she was controlling and fell back down into the pile of cuddly zoo animals.

'Let's have one more go.' Hugo pushed a coin into the machine and set the claw going in the direction of the monkey. The claw lowered, grabbed the monkey around its middle, and lifted it into the air. Melody expected the monkey to drop as the claw moved towards the end of the machine, but it remained in the metal claw, sitting comfortably until they opened and released the monkey into the tray for collection.

'Yes!' Hugo performed a little dance with his fists before bending to retrieve the prize. 'Scoop is going to love ripping this to shreds.' He grinned at Melody before winking. 'Only kidding. For you, m'lady. A souvenir of your trip to Clifton-on-Sea.'

'I already have a souvenir.' She lifted her wrist, displaying the plastic beaded bracelet Hugo had earned from his bingo winnings. 'And I have my gorgeous brooch back at the B&B, but thank you. I shall name him Cliff, in honour of his origins.'

'His origins are probably China,' Hugo said, checking the label. Melody swatted him on the arm and prised the monkey from his hands, cuddling him to her chest. 'What do you fancy doing now?'

'Don't you have to get to work?' Melody asked. It was mid afternoon and she'd already taken up most of Hugo's day.

He shook his head. 'James has taken over for the day. I'm all yours.' He took hold of Melody's hand and guided her out of the arcade. It had been dark inside the arcade, but the clouds had cleared outside, the sun shining again, and they both held a hand up to shield their eyes from the sudden glare.

'How about an ice cream?' Melody asked, pointing down the promenade, where the van could be seen in the distance.

'To rub it in James's face that he's working and we're not?' Hugo asked. A grin spread slowly across his face. 'Let's do it.'

Melody swatted him again. 'And you say I'm mean? I actually meant because it'll be my last chance and I haven't had one of your bubble gum cones yet.'

'I think that's called killing two birds with one stone,' Hugo said before leading the way. The beach wasn't nearly

314

as full after the earlier downpour, despite the sun beating down once again. They bought ice creams and ate them while wandering along the sand.

'How's your ankle holding up?' Hugo asked as they passed an abandoned sandcastle. It was huge, three castles high, built up pyramid-style, with a wide moat. Shells and pretty pebbles decorated the structure while little paper Union Jack flags fluttered in the breeze.

'It's fine, unless you're offering to give me another piggyback.'

'Maybe later.' Hugo held up his raspberry ripple ice cream. 'Bit busy at the minute.'

Melody paused. She couldn't pass the sandcastle. She handed Hugo her ice cream and tucked Cliff-the-monkey under his arm before grabbing her camera and crouching on the sand. She took several shots, hoping to capture both the hard work and the joy that must have gone into creating it.

'Thank you.' She retrieved her ice cream and monkey and continued along the beach. They climbed the wide steps back up to the promenade when they reached the pier.

'Do you fancy it?' Hugo looked up at the Ferris wheel, which was already lit up in anticipation of nightfall.

'Why not?' Melody asked. She popped the last of the waffle cone into her mouth and followed Hugo to the ticket booth. This time she didn't freak out. She climbed into the carriage, sliding along the seat to make room for Hugo, and felt her stomach flutter as they rose up towards the sky. She took a couple of photos of the seaside town while they were up there, but mostly she enjoyed the view, the sensation of being lifted and gently brought back down before starting all over again, and she enjoyed the feel of Hugo's hand in hers as they experienced it together.

As they reached the top, just before they started their final descent, Melody spotted a couple of donkeys in the distance, plodding along the beach, side by side. Two young girls sat on the donkeys' backs, one hand clinging to the reins, the other outstretched and meeting the other girl's hand in the space between them. Melody's heart ached at the sight, imagining herself and Ollie on another set of donkeys, on another beach, a lifetime ago. But she pushed a smile through the pain and squeezed Hugo's hand a little bit tighter as they started to glide back down to the ground again.

Chapter Thirty-Eight

Willow

The rain was pouring, big fat droplets splatting against the shop's windows before they stretched and wriggled their way down the pane. The sun had disappeared behind the purply-grey clouds, throwing a blanket of doom over the town.

'So much for summer,' Willow said with a sigh as she dropped her chin onto her hands, her elbows resting on the counter.

'Don't forget this is a British summer,' Gary said, his voice low and hesitant. Things had been a bit awkward since Mae's visit that morning, with the two of them tiptoeing around each other, their conversations strained. Gary had apologised for taking the piss and Willow had accepted, on the condition it didn't happen again. Going out and having fun with your mates was good, but allowing it to impact on your work was not.

But there was still an atmosphere in the shop. Despite the apology, Willow remained disappointed. She'd trusted Gary, had felt they were a good team, but now it seemed it was one-sided. Plus, her mind was elsewhere, wandering from the shop to an imagined airport; so, while she would normally try to clear the air and make things more bearable, she was distracted. Ethan's flight had been delayed again, meaning it would be at least four-thirty before he landed in Manchester. By the time he made it back to Clifton-on-Sea, evening would have well and truly set in. It seemed unlikely they'd be eating fish and chips on the beach, especially with the rain.

And there was something else niggling at Willow. Something she wouldn't allow herself to think about, to hope for. It was a silly idea and one best left alone before it could cause any damage to her already fragile state.

'I've been thinking,' Gary said, and while Willow would usually have smiled and said 'careful there, Gary, you don't want to hurt yourself' or something equally playful, that day she simply tore her gaze from the streaming window and raised her eyebrows as she awaited elaboration. 'That clock, the one Mae said I'd broken.'

'The one at the pub?'

Gary nodded and, feeling brave, took a couple of steps towards Willow. 'I don't remember doing it, but I don't always remember the stuff that happens on our nights out.'

'Oh, Gary.' Willow's eyebrows knitted together. 'You shouldn't get yourself into such a state. Anything could happen.'

Gary scratched the back of his neck. 'I know. My mum says the same thing.'

Willow smiled, but it wasn't anywhere close to a full-watt beam. 'Mums are wise. You should listen to her more.'

Gary nodded and braved another step, reaching the counter, though he was still a few steps away from Willow. 'I think I probably did break the clock. I can be a bit of a knob when I'm drunk.'

Willow laughed. She couldn't help it. 'At least you're honest. *Sometimes*.' She winked at Gary, to show she was

318

kidding and, emboldened, he covered the last few steps so he was facing Willow, only the counter now between them.

'I was thinking of replacing Frank and Corinne's clock.'

Willow gave an encouraging smile. 'That's a good idea. I'm sure they'd appreciate it.'

'Maybe I could make them one?' Gary scratched the back of his neck again, and Willow noticed his cheeks taking on a pinkish tinge. 'With your help?'

Willow sat up straighter, the full-watt smile firmly in place now. 'That's a wonderful idea, Gary. Of course I'll help you. Have you got any idea what kind of clock you'd like to make?'

Gary nodded, the pink deepening on his cheeks. 'Frank likes to play dominoes. There's a pub team and stuff.' Willow nodded, encouraging him to continue. 'I know there are some dominoes in that box the Monopoly and Scrabble sets came from, so I thought I could make a clock with those, using the dots on the dominoes instead of numbers.'

'That's a really good idea.' Willow slipped off her stool. 'I've obviously taught you well.'

The rest of the afternoon was spent in the workroom, the door open so they could listen for any customers should they brave the foul weather. They found a piece of scrap wood that would make a perfect base, sanded it down and applied a walnut stain. Under Willow's instruction, Gary drilled a hole in the centre for the clock mechanism before marking out and then hot-gluing the domino pieces in place, making sure the dots added up to the numbers on a clock face. With wire added to the back for hanging, the clock was complete.

'Thanks for your help,' Gary said, holding out the clock so he could marvel at his creation.

'It was a pleasure.' Willow was grateful to Gary too, as the project had kept her mind away from Ethan's delayed arrival and the other thing, the thing she was desperately pushing from her mind. 'Would you like me to wrap it for you?'

'Yes, please.' Gary handed his masterpiece over with a shy smile. 'I'll take it over to the pub once I've finished here.'

Willow took the clock out to the shop, placing it down carefully on the counter. She noticed the window was clear again, all traces of rain gone and the sky bright, as though the sun had been shining down on them all day. She grabbed sheets of bubble wrap and pale-blue tissue paper, wrapping the clock carefully before adding white satin ribbon, tying it into a neat, practised bow.

Her phone beeped with a new message as she was admiring her handiwork. Ethan was about to board his flight. He'd be home in a few hours.

The rain hadn't made a comeback, which was lucky as Willow was standing on the platform at the station, her eyes constantly travelling between the track, the station's clock and her phone, in case she'd missed a message from Ethan. There were half a dozen others on the platform, mostly with wheeled suitcases and rucksacks, waiting for a train to take them away rather than waiting for a loved one's return.

Finally, just before seven, a train rattled into the station. Willow craned her neck as the doors opened, her stomach a riot of butterflies as she searched for her husband. She was beginning to suspect she'd made a mistake and this wasn't his train at all when he appeared in the doorway of one of the carriages. Willow waved before making a dash along the platform, reaching Ethan as he stepped down, lugging his suitcase behind him. He dropped it on the floor and held his arms wide, wrapping them tightly around Willow as she threw herself against his chest.

'I've missed you,' he said into her hair.

'I've missed you too.' Willow realised she was crying – again – and giggled. She released herself so she could wipe the tears from her eyes. 'I didn't think you'd ever make it back.'

Ethan rolled his eyes. 'Tell me about it. Nightmare!'

'You're here now.' Willow slipped her hand into Ethan's. 'Let's go back to the bed and breakfast and drop this suitcase off. We've got a date, remember?' The sun had shone brightly for the rest of the afternoon, drying up the beach enough for their planned fish and chip supper.

Wheeling the suitcase behind him, Ethan followed Willow's lead to the van. They stowed the case in the back but Ethan stopped Willow before she could climb into the driver's seat.

'I've really, *really* missed you,' he said before kissing her, his hands cupping her face as though she might shatter without the gentlest of touches. They didn't break apart until they'd earned a round of wolf whistles and jeering from a group of passing teens.

'Get in there, mate.'

'Give her one from me.'

'Get a fucking room.'

'Are you dogging?'

Willow pressed her face into Ethan's chest, his crumpled T-shirt muffling her giggle.

'The youth of today. No bloody respect,' Ethan said, but he was grinning. 'Come on, let's go before they come back with a bigger audience.'

The bed and breakfast was empty when they arrived. Willow gave Ethan a quick tour of the communal areas before leading him to their room. She unpacked his case while Ethan had a quick shower to rid himself of the fug of his day at the airport and the flight home. He changed into fresh jeans and a T-shirt before they headed down to the beach, picking up bags of fish and chips on the way. The sunshine hadn't encouraged too many people back to the beach after the rainfall, so they easily found a quiet spot near the cliffs.

'Does it taste as good as our wedding reception meal?' Willow asked as they sat with their supper on their laps.

Ethan blew on a chip. 'Even better.' He popped the chip into his mouth and groaned.

'We'll be able to do this all the time when we're in the new house,' Willow said. 'We'll only be across the road. I can't wait to lie in bed with the window open so I can listen to the waves.'

'Don't forget your bath,' Ethan said. 'Isn't that top of your list of the things you want finished?'

'It was.' Willow dropped the chip she was holding back into the bag and turned to Ethan. 'But there's something else we need to finish first.'

Ethan nodded. 'Ah, yes. The kitchen.'

Willow shook her head. Her lips were itching to spread into the biggest grin of her life, but she fought it. For now, at least. 'No, not the kitchen.'

'Then what?' Ethan popped another chip into his mouth.

'The nursery.'

Ethan nodded, still chewing. He swallowed and grabbed another chip. 'Yep, that is important. I'd quite like to be able to cook too, though.'

'You don't understand,' Willow said as the chip went into Ethan's mouth. 'The nursery is *really* important. We'll need it sorted. Within the next nine months.'

Ethan chewed his chip slowly, his eyebrows lowering further with each chomp. Willow reached into her bag and pulled out a white stick, laying it flat on the palm of her hand. Ethan swallowed. Hard.

'Is that…?'

Willow nodded, the smile finally breaking free. 'It's a pregnancy test. A positive pregnancy test.'

'But you said…' It seemed Ethan had lost the ability to finish his sentences.

'I know, I thought it wasn't going to happen this month. My period started, but it was really light and then it just stopped. I thought it was because of the stress with the house. I didn't think…' She looked down at the test she'd bought at the chemist's after closing the shop, feeling foolish as she handed over the money. Foolish for daring to hope, again. She'd taken so many tests over the past couple of years, each time becoming more and more desperate, taking them before her period was due, taking them again once it had started, just in case her body was wrong, just in case her period wasn't a period at all but spotting. She'd stocked up on tests, storing them in the bathroom cabinet, but it was too tempting to use one with every suspected 'symptom'. She hadn't dared buy a test for months, until now.

'I would have waited,' she told Ethan, 'and taken the test once you were back. But I thought I was kidding myself.' *Again*, they both added silently. 'I thought I'd take the test, get it out of my system, and carry on as normal.' She pushed the test towards Ethan. 'But it was positive.'

'It's positive,' Ethan said, his eyebrows still low. He wasn't smiling. He wasn't whooping for joy. But Willow couldn't blame him. She'd been numb with shock at first too. She'd sat on Mae's loo, taken the test and carried it through to the bedroom, not even bothering to look at the little windows. She'd freshened her make-up, checked her phone for messages, her emails – anything to prolong time before she had to read the results. She'd known it was going to be negative, but she wanted to cling to that tiny shard of hope for as long as possible.

She'd been floored when she saw two lines instead of one.

Shock, and not joy, had been the overriding emotion as she stared down at the stick, at those lines that meant she'd finally achieved what she'd dreamed of for so long.

Now, though, she was ecstatic. It had taken every single drop of restraint not to yell the news across the station platform when she'd spotted her husband. She'd itched to share the glorious news all the way back to the bed and breakfast, had wanted to rip the shower curtain aside and declare her pregnant state as Ethan showered, had wanted to forget about the food and the beach and tell him there and then in the guest room, but she'd waited until now. The fish and chips on the beach had formed an unexpected but special memory of their wedding, and she wanted to recreate that moment now, on this important day.

'We're going to have a baby?' Ethan lifted his gaze from the test to his wife's face.

Willow nodded, her eyes shining with joyous, unshed tears. 'We're going to have a baby.'

If you'd been close to the cliffs that day, you'd have heard a cry of delight and wonder as a man leapt to his feet and picked up his wife, spinning her round and round on the sand as they laughed and cried and dreamed of a rosy future.

If you'd been a seagull close to the cliffs, you'd have swooped down on the chips as they flew from the couple's laps, falling down on the sand like greasy confetti.

And if you were Willow St Clair, you'd have been the happiest woman on earth. And also a little dizzy.

Chapter Thirty-Nine

Mae

Alfie had printed out posters with Chilly's photo on them, along with details of where he was being taken care of and how to get in contact. They taped the posters to lampposts along the seafront near Mae's home, as well as in a few of the neighbouring streets. Hopefully, being close to the beach, they'd be spotted by the owner, or someone who recognised the cat. It was getting late by the time the trio taped their final poster, so Alfie suggested popping into one of the cafés that were still open towards the pier for a hot chocolate. Normally, Mae would have declined, citing bedtimes and busy evenings, but Hannah had heard the magic, chocolatey word and accepted on their behalf.

'Nanny makes the best hot chocolates,' Hannah said as they made their way along the promenade. 'She lets me have cream you squirt like this…' She held up a little fist, sticking out her index finger and bending it in and out. 'And sometimes she lets me squirt it right into my mouth.'

'Does she really?' This was news to Mae.

'Yup.' Hannah nodded. 'She lets me have marshmallows too. The little pink and white ones. They're the yummiest.' Spotting a seagull ahead, she zoomed off, arms outstretched like the wings of an aeroplane. The bird, working on an abandoned cheeseburger, waited until the very last moment before it took flight.

'I hope it was okay to suggest hot chocolates,' Alfie said as they strolled after Hannah, who was now swinging round and round a lamppost just up ahead.

'Are you kidding? You've made her day.'

'Mummy...' Hannah said, coming to a wobbly stop. 'My feet are tired. They don't want to walk any more.'

'Maybe you should stop chasing poor seagulls and spinning round lampposts,' Mae suggested. She reached Hannah and held out a hand, but the little girl refused to take it, clasping her hands behind her back. 'It isn't much further, and then you get to have a yummy hot chocolate, remember?'

'My feet are sleepy. Can't I have it here?'

Mae shook her head. 'I'm afraid not, little lady.'

'You could ride the rest of the way on my shoulders,' Alfie suggested.

Hannah, suddenly energised, bounced up and down on the spot. 'Yes, yes, yes! Shoulders!'

'You don't have to...' Mae started to say, but Alfie was already hoisting Hannah into the air and dipping his head so that she could rest on his shoulders, her little legs dangling on his chest.

'You did that way too easily,' Mae said as they set off again.

'Nieces and nephews,' Alfie said. 'Five of them. I've had plenty of practice over the years.'

'I bet you're a fun uncle,' Mae said, looking up at Hannah, who was clinging to Alfie's head with her little hands.

Alfie laughed. 'I'm a pushover. They've got me wrapped around their little fingers, every last one of them.'

'They're lucky to have you,' Mae said, wrapping her arms across her body. The sun had dipped and the evening was cooling off. 'Hannah doesn't have any uncles, fun or otherwise. Or aunts, actually. I'm an only child and you know the deal with the other side of her family. Mum has a couple of brothers, but they don't really keep in touch.'

'She has Frank and Corinne, though,' Alfie said. 'I've seen the way they are with Hannah. They adore her.'

Mae nodded. 'That's true. They're the best godparents Hannah could wish for.'

'Family doesn't always have to be blood-related,' Alfie said. They crossed the road, where the café was lit up and looking warm and cosy. Alfie lowered Hannah to the ground and they filed inside, sitting by the window so they could see the bright lights of the pier. They ordered hot chocolates from a surly-looking waitress: a mint-flavoured one for Alfie, salted caramel for Mae, and a whipped-cream-and-marshmallow-loaded hot chocolate for Hannah.

'Do you think you'll hear from Chilly's owner?' Mae asked as Hannah attacked the whipped cream with a tall spoon.

Alfie shrugged and blew on his own drink. 'Maybe, maybe not. Like I said earlier, he may not have owners at all.'

Mae leaned in towards him, keeping her voice low. 'What'll happen to him? If nobody comes forward?'

'I'll try and rehome him, once he's healed.'

'You won't...' Mae's eyes slid towards her daughter, who was more interested in hunting for gooey marshmallows than the boring grown-up conversation taking place. Still, Mae couldn't say the words out loud, just in case.

Alfie's eyes widened and he shook his head. 'No way. Absolutely not. I'd take him home myself if I had to, though I don't think Winston would approve, at least not to begin with.'

Winston was Alfie's dog, who sometimes accompanied him to the Fisherman for a bowl of water and a sneaky pork scratching.

'He's a spoiled bundle of fur who gets jealous if I so much as look at another dog while we're out walking. You should see him when I get home, smelling of dozens of different animals. The betrayal in his eyes!' Alfie chuckled and took a sip of his drink. 'I took another dog in a few months ago. He was in a bad way, so I took him home with me to keep an eye on him, but Winston wasn't impressed. We couldn't find any owners, but I managed to rehouse him, so Winston was happy again.'

'You really love animals, don't you?' Mae said and Alfie shrugged.

'I'd be lousy at my job if I didn't.'

Mae took a sip of her drink. She was desperate to ask about the surgery – or more specifically about Carrie – but she didn't dare. It was quite possible she'd built the Carrie situation up in her mind, seen flirtation where there was none, felt the stirrings of jealousy when there was no need, found an easy and convenient excuse to remain dateless and safe. Maybe Alfie was interested in Carrie, maybe not. Either way, Mae was afraid of hearing the answer.

Hannah pushed her luck as they left the café, using her sweetest voice to ask if she could have one tiny go on the Ferris wheel. True to his word, Alfie demonstrated his pushover personality and agreed instantaneously, leading the little party across to the pier. Mae insisted on buying the tickets, and though Alfie attempted to overrule her, it turned out he wasn't just a pushover when it came to youngsters.

'I want to go in first,' Hannah said when it was their turn to embark. 'And I want to sit next to Alfie.'

'It looks like you've got yourself a new fan,' Mae whispered once they were sitting in the carriage, Hannah at one end, looking out over the beach, with Alfie in the middle and Mae sitting at the other end.

'She's a great kid,' Alfie said. 'Just like her mum.'

Mae rolled her eyes, though she felt her lips tugging themselves upwards into a totally involuntary smile. 'Smooth, Alfie. Real smooth.'

Alfie shrugged. 'It's one of my many talents.'

Mae held her hands up, palms out. 'I won't ask what the others are.'

'That's probably wise.' Alfie pulled a face. 'Most of them involve animals.'

It was with a splutter of unexpected laughter that Mae began her ascent on the Ferris wheel. They started off with small, jerky movements as the wheel picked up more passengers, and it was when they reached the top that Alfie admitted one of his biggest fears.

'Heights?' Mae asked, her mouth drooping. 'Why did you agree to come on this thing if you're afraid of heights?'

Alfie swallowed, keeping his gaze firmly on his feet rather than out of the carriage to take in the view of the town. 'Hannah was so excited and I wanted to make her happy.'

'By giving yourself a heart attack?' Mae shook her head. She didn't know whether to laugh at the predicament or give Alfie a good ticking off. In the end, she grabbed his hand, squeezing tight as the wheel swooped down to the ground and rose back up again. It occurred to her that Alfie could be making the whole thing up. A scam designed to make her feel sorry for him and hold his hand. But the bone-crushing hand-holding she received in return told her this probably wasn't the case.

'That wasn't so bad, was it?' she asked as they climbed out of the carriage at the end of the ride.

Alfie, still clinging to Mae's hand, took slow, carefully placed steps, as though he didn't quite trust they were on solid ground again.

'I'm never going on that again,' he said. He caught Mae's eye and they both laughed. 'You must think I'm such a wuss.'

'Are you kidding? I think you're incredibly sweet for facing your fears just to make my little girl happy.' Reaching up on her tiptoes, she kissed Alfie's cheek.

'I died, didn't I?' Alfie turned to the Ferris wheel, which was on the move again. 'That thing plummeted to the ground, and I died and went to heaven.'

Mae tutted and gave him a playful dig in the ribs with her elbow. 'Are you always this cheesy?'

Alfie tilted his head to one side as he considered the question. 'Yes, I'm afraid I am.'

'Luckily for you, I quite like cheese.' Mae threaded her arm through Alfie's, taking Hannah's little hand with her free one as they started to wander towards the bed and breakfast. It felt quite nice to be walking so close to Alfie, so she couldn't help feeling a tinge of regret when Hannah complained about her feet and ended up being hoisted onto his shoulders again, riding the rest of the way home in style.

'Thanks for your help with the posters tonight – and the near-death experience,' Alfie said once they'd reached the bed and breakfast and Hannah was back on the ground again.

'You're welcome.' Mae dug into her handbag for her keys. 'It's been fun.'

'Putting up the posters or watching me nearly wet myself on the Ferris wheel?'

Mae pulled her keys from the bag, slotting one into the front door before turning to Alfie. 'What do you think?' She giggled and pushed open the door. 'Say goodnight to Alfie, Hannah.'

'Goodnight, Alfie,' Hannah said before hopping up the steps and making a dash into the house, heading, Mae guessed, straight for the television in the family room.

'Seriously, though…' Mae said. 'It's been fun.'

'Fun enough to finally accept if I asked you out to dinner? I mean you might as well – we've been on two dates already today.'

Mae frowned. 'We have?'

'Yep. Coffee at the harbour this afternoon, and a hot chocolate and death-defying Ferris wheel ride this evening. They totally count as dates. So, what do you say?'

Mae thought of her ex and the monumental way he'd let her down, the way he let their daughter down every single day with his absence. But then she thought of Mrs Hornchurch, dressed up tonight, ready to start a new adventure, and the sinking feeling she'd felt in the pit of her stomach when she thought she'd missed her chance with Alfie.

'What about Carrie?' she asked, still trying her best to scupper her chances. Still doing her best to protect herself.

Alfie frowned. 'What about Carrie?'

'There seemed to be… something between you. Chemistry, if you like. I thought that maybe…' Mae shrugged. She sounded silly. Feeble. Not the strong, independent woman she liked to project to the world.

'Mae…' Alfie took a step closer, the frown still on his face but not quite so deep-set. 'I've known you for six months. I've asked you out at least once a week since then. What makes you think I'd have the slightest interest in anybody else?'

Mae had a list of reasons, not least because Carrie was beautiful and confident and had more in common with Alfie than she did. Besides, Alfie had known Mae for six months and had asked her out at least once a week since then – and she'd declined every single time. There was only so much rejection a person could take.

'I'll keep on asking,' Alfie said, as though he could read her mind. 'I'm very determined.'

'Stubborn,' Mae said, smiling even though she begged herself not to. 'I think that's the word you're looking for.'

Alfie shrugged. 'Same thing. Either way, I'm not giving up. On you. On us.'

'You're that sure we're meant to be?'

'Absolutely. I wouldn't risk rejection and humiliation on a weekly – sometimes daily – basis if I didn't.'

'Maybe you should try again, one last time?'

Alfie placed a hand on his chest and adopted an earnest look. 'Mae Wright, I think you're gorgeous and fascinating and you pull the most amazing pint…'

'Easy,' Mae interrupted. 'You're laying it on with a trowel there, mate.'

Alfie shrugged. 'It's all true.'

Mae grinned. 'I never said it wasn't true, but still.'

'Do you think I could get on with this?'

'Go on then.' Mae fought a grin. 'It isn't as though you haven't had enough practice.'

'Mae Wright.' Alfie adopted his earnest look once more. 'I won't tell you how gorgeous and fascinating you are again, or praise your pint-pulling skills, because it turns out you know all this already. Instead, I'll simply ask if you would give me one little chance to wine and dine you at a time, date and venue of your choosing.'

'I get to choose where we go?' Mae asked. 'Why didn't you say that in the first place?'

Alfie narrowed his eyes ever so slightly. 'Is that a yes?'

Mae gave one curt nod. 'It's a yes.'

Chapter Forty

Melody

It was her final morning in the little attic room at the Seafront Bed and Breakfast. The sun was already shining, fighting its way through the curtains as she drew back the covers and placed her foot tentatively on the carpet. Her ankle was holding up well and she hadn't taken any painkillers for a couple of days, so she was pleased with its progress. She still wouldn't be cartwheeling upon her return home, but she could at least make the journey comfortably.

She showered, using the fragrant raspberry-and-lime products Mae had left in the welcome basket, before dressing in a pair of three-quarter-length leggings and a long, roomy T-shirt, which would be perfect for the train journey home. She packed her belongings into her rucksack and slung it over her shoulder before heading down to the kitchen for her last breakfast in Clifton-on-Sea.

'Ah, here she is,' Mae said as Melody stepped into the kitchen. 'Good morning. I hope you slept well?'

It seemed there was a little bon voyage gathering in the kitchen, with Mae, Hannah, Willow and her husband,

Ethan, who Melody had met briefly the evening before. Even Hugo was there, sandwiched between Mae and her daughter.

'Mummy says you're leaving today,' Hannah said. 'You won't live here with us any more.'

'No, but I'm sure somebody else will take my place soon,' Melody said, smiling at the little girl. 'Somebody far more interesting than me.'

'Impossible,' Hugo said, flashing a grin.

Melody rolled her eyes and grabbed a slice of toast from the rack in the centre of the table. 'You'll have forgotten me by tomorrow.'

Hugo frowned. 'Rubbish! I'll always remember you…' He narrowed his eyes. 'What was your name again?'

'Charming.' Melody stuck her tongue out at Hugo as she reached for the butter.

'What time's your train?' Mae asked. She got up and crossed the kitchen to put the kettle on.

'Quarter past ten, so I'll have to get going soon.'

'I can give you a lift up to the station,' Willow offered. 'I'll be heading over to the shop soon. I'm supposed to be there already, but we fancied a lie-in.' Her eyes flitted towards her husband and she blushed.

'I was going to offer my taxi services too,' Hugo said.

Melody picked up a knife and loaded it with butter. 'Even though you can't remember my name?'

Hugo shrugged. 'What can I say? I'm a gentleman.'

'A gentleman?' Melody scraped the butter onto her triangle of toast. 'As if.'

Hugo opened his mouth in mock indignation. 'Who carried you around when you busted your ankle? And I made a picnic. *And* I won that stuffed monkey for you.'

Cliff-the-Monkey was currently in Melody's rucksack, sitting on top of her washbag.

'It sounds like someone's in *lurve*,' Willow said in a sing-song voice. She winked at Hugo before her face seemed to droop, the smile diminishing and her eyebrows pulling down. 'Will you excuse me for a minute?' She scraped back her chair and scurried from the room, with the sound of her feet pounding up the stairs a moment later.

'Is she okay?' Hugo asked.

'I'm sure she is,' Ethan said. 'But I'll go up and check anyway.' He grabbed the glass of water sitting in front of Willow's vacated place at the table and headed upstairs.

Mae returned to the table with a pot of tea. 'Would you like me to make you some sandwiches for the journey?' She placed the pot next to the toast rack and crossed the kitchen to grab some cups from the cupboard.

'Thanks, but I'll be fine,' Melody said.

'Are you sure?' Mae placed the cups on the table and sat down in her seat. 'It'd be no trouble at all.'

'Does that offer extend to all of us?' Hugo asked with a cheeky grin.

'You're already getting a free breakfast,' Mae said with a mock-stern look. 'Don't push it.'

'At least with me gone, you won't have to put up with this idiot,' Melody said. She grinned at Hugo before biting into her toast.

Hugo folded his arms across his chest and leaned back in his chair. 'You'll miss me. You all will.'

'I'm sure we will.' Melody tilted her head to one side and narrowed her eyes. 'But what was your name again?'

After breakfast, the bon voyage party gathered in the hallway. Melody said goodbye to Mae and Hannah, thanking them for their hospitality and, despite Mae's protestations, insisting on paying the board for the extra days she'd stayed in Clifton-on-Sea.

'But it was our fault you ended up stuck here,' Mae said.

'I didn't feel stuck at all, in the end.' In fact, the past few days had been Melody's favourites of her entire mission over the past month.

'You'll keep in touch, won't you?' Mae said when it became clear she couldn't persuade Melody. 'Let us know how the photography festival goes?'

'I will.' Melody reached out and hugged Mae and Hannah in turn before turning to Willow.

'It's been lovely to meet you. I hope the house refurb goes smoothly from now on.'

Willow glanced at her husband, a smile creeping across her lips. 'We do too.'

'It was lovely to meet you too,' Melody told Ethan. 'Even if it was only briefly.' She bent down to pick up her rucksack and her laptop bag. 'I guess this is it. Take care everybody.'

'Remember what I said about keeping in touch,' Mae said as she walked with Melody to the front door. 'And good luck with the festival.'

Melody stepped outside, Hugo close behind her. They made their way along the path, the warmth of the sun already beating down on them. Even though she'd been in the town for less than a week, Melody was going to miss Clifton-on-Sea. She'd been in a bit of a bubble since arriving, meeting Hugo and trying to face up to a life without Ollie, but now it was time to emerge from the safety of an anonymous town and confront reality, no matter how impossible a task it seemed.

She paused after stepping through the gate, turning and taking aim with her camera, capturing the bed and breakfast that had provided a base over the past few days. Things had changed since she'd stepped inside – *Melody* had changed – and as scary as the future seemed, she was glad she'd ended up there.

'Ready?' Hugo asked gently as she switched off the camera.

Melody nodded. 'I'm ready.'

Hugo's car was parked a little up the road. They loaded Melody's rucksack and laptop bag into the boot before climbing inside and making the short journey to the station. Melody's eyes darted left and right as she attempted to capture every last detail of the town before she left. All too soon, the long, single-storey brick building of the station appeared before them, its green doors thrown wide as people wandered in and out, some wheeling suitcases behind them, others with nothing more than a handbag or briefcase.

'You don't have to come to the platform with me,' Melody said once the car was parked and she had her rucksack slung on her back and her laptop bag looped over one shoulder.

'I'd like to,' Hugo said. 'If that's okay?'

Melody smiled, glad they'd get to spend a few more minutes together. 'Of course. That'd be nice.'

'Good.' Hugo took the laptop bag from Melody and flung it onto his shoulder. 'Let's go then.'

They passed through the cool station, grabbing takeaway drinks from the little tearoom before heading out to the single platform. It was crammed, but a train, heading to Preston, pulled into the station and gobbled up the majority of the waiting passengers.

'You'll keep in touch, won't you?' Hugo asked once the train pulled away. Rather than looking at Melody as he asked the question, he was staring ahead, across the tracks at the cluster of trees beyond the metal fence.

'I have your number.' Melody reached into her pocket and pulled out her phone, giving it a little jiggle before she returned it. 'And I want to know how you get on with the ice-cream parlour. I think I deserve some freebies after the shifts I put in at the van.'

'So you'll come back?'

Melody blew on her tea. 'I'll go anywhere for free ice cream.'

'Plus, you'll never be able to stay away from this.' Hugo indicated himself and Melody pretended to gag.

'Get over yourself. I'm after your frozen treats, not your body.'

'Are you sure about that?'

Melody could hear the distant rumble of an approaching train, but she couldn't seem to shift her body to look for it.

'I'm sure,' she said, but it came out feeble and not at all convincing.

'Hmm...' Hugo narrowed his eyes. 'You don't sound sure at all.'

Melody shrugged and took a sip of tea. It was far too hot and burned her tongue, though she managed not to wince. 'Believe me, I am.'

Hugo leaned in towards Melody. 'I don't believe it at all.' He'd lowered his voice and it was swallowed by the thunder of the oncoming train. Melody finally dragged her gaze to the track.

'This is my train,' she said, and again her voice whimpered out feebly. The doors opened and passengers spilled out onto the platform, moving quickly towards the station, nudging past Melody and Hugo and squashing them together.

'Look at you, pressing yourself up to me,' Hugo said. 'I knew you were into me.'

'Keep dreaming, pal,' Melody said, but it wasn't full of her usual conviction. Where was the girl from the cliffs? The girl who'd had little time for the so-called charms of the local dog-walker?

She cast her eyes towards the train. The departing passengers had all drifted away and the new passengers were taking their place onboard.

'I'd better go now.' She felt her stomach tangle itself into knots as she turned to Hugo. She could admit it to herself now she was about to leave, now it was safe: she thought Hugo was utterly gorgeous, inside and out. She didn't know if she would ever see him again, but she knew she hoped she would.

'Take care, Melody.' Hugo unhooked her laptop bag and handed it over. She flung it onto her shoulder and turned towards the train, but a hand pulled her back. She didn't have time to think, to talk herself out of it. Hugo was kissing her, and she found she was rather glad and her only regret was that they hadn't done this sooner, that they hadn't spent their whole time together like this. If she'd really thought about it, the guilt would have crept in. It would have placed her hands on Hugo's chest and gently pushed him away, would have shaken her head and said she couldn't do this. But in that moment, there was no guilt. There was just Melody, Hugo and a train that was in danger of leaving without her.

Epilogue

October

She'd spent weeks studying her photos, agonising over the decision about which three she would exhibit – and ultimately enter into the competitions – at the photo festival. But Melody was happy with her choice as she stood before them now, proud these three photos were the results of her hard work. The first showcased the Ferris wheel on the pier at Clifton-on-Sea, its lights shining bright against the inky blues and purples as night began to fall, the top of the carousel just visible in the bottom-right-hand corner. The second photo she'd chosen was one of the last she'd taken on the beach: the giant, seashell-decorated sandcastle with the foamy waves captured in the background. And the final image was a close-up of one of Hugo and James's ice creams. The ice cream was the focus, but in the background you could see a couple of donkeys plodding along the beach, with the pier and its funfair rides beyond. It was Melody's favourite photo as it encapsulated every childhood seaside holiday she'd ever had and provided a summary of her entire trip that summer.

'Ollie would be so proud of you, you know.'

Melody closed her eyes briefly before turning to Ollie's mum. Lisa, along with Melody's parents and younger brother, had joined her at the festival's final exhibition evening, where the winners of the competitions would be presented with their prizes.

'Do you think so?'

Lisa placed a hand on Melody's shoulder and gave it a gentle squeeze. 'I know so.' She leaned in to kiss Melody on the cheek before moving to the side to make way for a fresh wave of supporters.

'You're late,' Melody said, adopting a mock-stern voice, her hands on her hips and her eyebrows knitted.

'I'm sorry. The train was delayed. Can you forgive me?'

Melody tilted her head to one side as she observed Hugo. He'd dressed up for the occasion and he certainly scrubbed up well in his black tailored suit and crisp white shirt. Looking like that, she'd forgive him anything.

'You're forgiven.' She reached up on her tiptoes to kiss him briefly on the lips. It wasn't the kind of kiss she really wanted, but they were in public, with her parents just yards away. They'd met Hugo a couple of times already and liked him, but they didn't need to see quite how happy Melody was to see him. She released him and stepped towards her other guests, who were already sipping champagne, apart from Willow, who was sporting a tiny baby bump underneath her dress.

'Thank you for coming.' Melody hugged Willow, Mae and their partners in turn.

'We wouldn't have missed it,' Mae said. 'Your photos are beautiful.'

'Thank you.' Melody couldn't help the beam from taking up the lower portion of her face. 'I've somehow managed to sell some prints already – and not just to Mum and Dad.'

Although the ice-cream photo was her personal favourite, the public seemed more enamoured with the Ferris wheel composition.

'Do you realise all your photos are from Clifton-on-Sea?' Mae said. She tapped a finger on her chin. 'I wonder why that might be.'

'Could it be she fell in love with the place?' Willow teased.

'Or she fell in love *in* the place.' Mae winked, giggling at Melody's panicked, wide-eyed look. Luckily, Hugo had wandered over to her parents and was busy chatting away and hadn't heard.

'Aww, stop it,' Willow said, though she was giggling too. 'You're making her blush.'

Melody fought hard to compose her features. 'I didn't *fall in love* in Clifton-on-Sea.' At least, not during her first visit. She'd visited numerous times over the past couple of months – and Hugo had made the trip to stay with her too – and saying goodbye had become increasingly difficult.

'Somebody else did, though,' Willow said, nudging Mae. 'You can't keep these two apart.' She nodded at Mae and Alfie. Although Alfie was slightly angled away from Mae as he chatted with Ethan, he had his arm around Mae's waist. 'You should have seen them on the train, snogging like a couple of teenagers.'

Mae's mouth dropped open. 'We were not!'

Melody grinned. 'Now who's blushing?'

Mae took a sip of champagne and gave a shrug. 'What can I say? I have a gorgeous boyfriend and I can't keep my hands off him. I'm making up for lost time.'

'Ooh...' Willow grabbed Melody's arm. 'Did you hear that? She used the word *boyfriend*. Last time I asked, she said they were "getting to know each other", which I took to mean they were having lots of sex but weren't an actual item.'

Mae tutted. 'I meant we were taking things slowly.'

'Sorry.' Willow patted her bump. 'It's my hormones: everything's about sex at the moment. Gary told me he'd brought the wood in the other day, and I assumed he was propositioning me. Turns out he'd brought the scrap pieces of wood in from the van and stored them in the workroom. Talk about awkward. We haven't looked each other in the eye since.'

Melody placed a hand over her mouth to muffle a giggle. 'Poor Gary.'

'Poor me,' Willow said. 'I'm turning into a sex pest.'

'How's the pregnancy going otherwise?' Melody asked. The last time she'd seen Willow, she was still constantly on the verge of throwing up.

'Really well. I haven't been sick for six days, which is a relief. It's an odd combination, feeling super-turned-on and vomitty at the same time.'

Melody pulled a face. 'That doesn't sound pleasant at all.'

Willow shook her head. 'It really isn't.'

'It'll all be worth it, though,' Mae said and Willow's features softened.

'Absolutely. I can't wait until we bring our gorgeous new baby home. Speaking of which, the house is finally finished and we're having a housewarming party next weekend. You're both invited – with your *boyfriends*, of course.' She nudged Mae again, who rolled her eyes. 'Speaking of which...'

A champagne flute appeared in front of Melody, shortly followed by a peck on the cheek.

'I thought you might need a refill,' Hugo said. 'The presentation is about to start.'

'Thank you.' Melody took the glass in one hand and Hugo's hand in the other. With their little group, they made their way to the gathering in front of the podium, where the organiser of the event was standing.

'Teasing aside,' she said to Mae as they waited for the presentation to begin. 'How's it going with Alfie?'

Mae's lips spread into a smile as she sneaked a glance at her boyfriend. 'It's amazing. *He's* amazing, and so good with Hannah. She adores him, especially as he lets her look after the animals at the surgery. She wants to be a vet when she's older and work with him full time.'

'And how's it going with Chilly?'

Mae rolled her eyes. 'The little bugger hid under the bed in the attic guest room. Scared the life out of the occupant when he jumped up onto the pillow in the middle of the night.' Mae shook her head as Melody laughed at the image. 'Remind me again why I adopted him?'

'Because he was desperate for a new home? Because you're a kind and caring woman? Because you thought it might help you get into Alfie's pants?'

Mae sniggered. 'I didn't need any help with *that*. Willow isn't the only one with sex constantly on their mind.'

'You don't seem too put out about that,' Melody said.

'Are you kidding?' Mae gave a little shiver. 'It's amazing. I can't believe I went so long without. Besides...' She leaned in towards Melody and lowered her voice. 'It saves on the batteries.'

Melody pushed a hand over her mouth to muffle a giggle.

'What's so funny?' Hugo asked.

Melody cleared her throat and put her serious face back on. 'Nothing.'

Hugo narrowed his eyes, but didn't probe any further. Instead he reached into his pocket and pulled out a set of keys. 'I totally forgot in all the excitement of your exhibition, but look what we picked up today.'

Melody gasped and took the keys, resting them on the palm of her hand. 'It's yours?'

'Yup.' Hugo pulled his shoulders back and lifted his chin. 'You are now looking at the co-owner of Alessandra's, Clifton-on-Sea's soon-to-be-opened ice-cream parlour in the park.'

After lots of discussions and number-crunching, Hugo and James had decided to go ahead with the purchase of the former café, naming the new ice-cream parlour after the grandmother who'd inspired their careers.

'I'm so proud of you.' Melody reached up on tiptoe to kiss Hugo, forgetting for a moment where they were. A gentle cough behind her broke the moment.

'It's starting,' Melody's mum said. She gave Melody's shoulders a little squeeze. 'Good luck, love.'

The presentation began with a rather long-winded speech from the organisers of the event before they moved on to the prizes. First up was the professionally judged award, with the top three photos from the festival winning cash prizes. Melody felt Hugo's grip on her hand tighten as the third-prize winner was announced. It tightened further as the second was announced, and became bone-crushing as the organiser prepared to announce the overall winner.

None of the prizes was awarded to Melody.

'Never mind, love,' Melody's mum said.

'You're an amazing photographer,' Hugo said. 'Don't ever forget that.'

'What a load of bullshit,' Mae muttered, and received glares from some of the other guests.

'And now we're going to announce the people's choice award,' the organiser announced as the winners returned to their places, cheques in hand. 'For the past few days, members of the public have viewed the exhibition and been given the opportunity to vote for their favourite photos. There's just one overall winner for the people's choice award, with a prize of one thousand pounds.'

The bone-crushing hand squeeze returned.

'Competition was stiff this year,' the organiser said. 'And I'd like to take this opportunity to thank all the exhibitors again. It has been a truly magnificent event and the talent here is tremendous.'

'Just bloody get on with it,' Mae muttered, earning herself a few more glares.

'But without further ado, the winner of the people's choice award is…' The organiser left a dramatic pause while he opened the envelope. '"Ferris Wheel at Nightfall" by Melody Rosewood.'

There was a roar of applause. She was squeezed, kissed, patted on the back, but she didn't feel any of it.

'That's me,' she whispered, her voice inaudible over the congratulatory noise around her.

'I knew you could do it,' Hugo said, and then she was being propelled forward – whether by her own steam, or someone else's, she wasn't sure. She shook the organiser's hand and received the cheque in a daze, her eyes roaming the crowd for her friends and family. They were there, but they'd been swallowed by the crowd and she couldn't pick them out.

She pressed the cheque to her chest and closed her eyes.

She'd done it.

For herself, and for Ollie, who had *always* believed in her.

She spotted her then, in the middle of the crowd, applauding as though her life depended on it. She caught Lisa's eye and found she was mirroring the smile on her face: happy, proud, but with a tinge of regret. Earlier, Lisa had said Ollie would be proud of Melody's bid to reach her dreams, and now, finally, Melody believed her. And, with the award under her belt, she could start to believe in herself too.

If you enjoyed *The Little Bed & Breakfast by the Sea*, then turn over for an exclusive extract from Jennifer Joyce's *The Little Teashop of Broken Hearts*!

Chapter One

There are lots of different kinds of kisses, from friendly pecks on the cheek to passionate, tongue-swirling embraces and detached air kisses (the latter of which aren't even kisses at all, in my opinion). Currently, I'm being subjected to a rather enthusiastic (and rather wet) hello kiss, my entire face on the receiving end of a thorough licking.

'Hello to you too, Franklin.' I pull the podgy French bulldog's wriggling body away so that his doggy kisses lap at the air instead of my face, and place him down on the pavement outside my little teashop, winding his lead around the drainpipe and securing it. Franklin – or rather his owner, Birdie – is a regular at the teashop. They arrive each Friday morning, after Birdie's shampoo and set at the salon two doors down. I adore Franklin. He's utterly gorgeous with his smooth, tan fur with a darker muzzle and a small patch of cream on his chest. His pink-lined ears are always alert and his chocolatey eyes are always on the hunt for a treat.

'You spoil him,' Birdie says with a good-humoured tut as I reach into the pocket of my pink-and-white polka-dotted apron and pull out a homemade, bone-shaped doggy biscuit. I don't have a dog of my own – I don't have any pets as the tiny flat above the teashop is barely big enough for me – so I make the treats especially for Franklin. I don't mind. I love baking, whether it's for my human customers or their four-legged companions.

'I can't help it.' I hold out the treat and Franklin takes it gently between his teeth, drawing it from my fingers. 'He's so adorable.' I pat Franklin on the head before Birdie and I step into the teashop. It's quiet inside, with only one other customer sitting at the table closest to the counter. Robbie works for his mum at the florist's three doors away, but I suspect he spends more time sipping banana milkshakes in my teashop than he does arranging flowers.

'What can I get you today?' I ask Birdie as she sits at the table by the window so she can keep an eye on Franklin.

Birdie doesn't even bother to glance at the menu or specials boards. 'Is the apple crumble on today?'

'Of course.' Apple crumble is Birdie's favourite dessert, so I always make sure there's a dish ready on Friday mornings. 'Warm custard?'

Birdie grins up at me, her eyes sparkling. 'Perfect.'

I've always loved baking. It's my passion and has been ever since my grandmother tied a floral apron around my waist (wrapping the belt around my middle three times before tying it in a bow as I was only a tiny three-year-old at the time) and helped me to whip up my first batch of fairy cakes. I remember the warmth of the oven as Gran opened the door, the delicious smell of the hot buns, the anticipation of waiting for them to cool. I remember the gloopy icing sugar and the rattle of the tub of hundreds and thousands, the rainbow of bright colours as they tumbled onto the still-wet icing sugar.

Most of all I remember the sweet, sugary taste as I finally bit into the very first cake I'd ever made. The wonder that I, Madeleine Lamington, had mixed up a bunch of ingredients and produced an actual, edible and delicious treat. It was magic, pure and simple.

I've been making magic ever since.

Gran taught me everything she knew about baking – all the recipes passed down from her own grandmother, all the little tricks she'd honed over the years, and I'd always dreamed of opening my own teashop serving delicious treats, but it didn't happen straight away. There was a long road ahead after I left school clutching an A* GCSE in food tech. A road that involved college, A Levels and waitressing.

Later came greasy kitchens and grumpy bakers, more waitressing and admin jobs to pay the bills (plus a soul-destroying stint as a cold caller trying to flog double glazing to people who had no desire to buy it. The only saving grace with that job was meeting Penny, who would become my best friend and ultimately help me to achieve my dream).

Through it all, I baked and I dreamed and now I'm the proud owner of number 5 Kingsbury Road, aka Sweet Street Teashop. It's hard work, but I love every single minute of it. There is little else I enjoy more than seeing the pleasure my cakes, puddings and biscuits bring to my customers.

'Cup of tea?' I ask Birdie.

'Yes please. I'm gasping. I had one at the salon, but the sheer volume of hairspray clogging up the air has undone all its good work. I'm spitting feathers.'

I make Birdie's much-needed tea, placing it on her table before heading into the kitchen to warm the custard and spoon a generous serving of apple crumble into a red-and-white polka-dot bowl. I like polka dots. I like patterns in general, mixing and matching them throughout the teashop, from the bright, patterned tabletops (each of my five tables has a different pattern, ranging from a simple but cheery polka-dot design to a yellow rubber duck print) to the crockery I use to serve my desserts.

'Lovely, thank you,' Birdie says as I carry her order through to the teashop and place it before her on the table. 'I don't know how I'd get through the week without my Friday treat.' She pats her slightly rounded tummy. 'My body would thank me if I gave it a miss though.'

'Nonsense. We all deserve a treat. Speaking of which …' I pull the little bag of doggy treats out of my apron pocket and hand them over to Birdie. 'For Franklin.'

'Thank you, dear.' Birdie takes the bag and pops it into the handbag hooked onto the back of her chair. 'You really shouldn't go to so much trouble.'

'It's no trouble at all.' I place my hand on Birdie's shoulder briefly before I move through to the little room adjoining the kitchen. Part storeroom, part office, the room is filled with boxes and sacks and the roll-top bureau that once belonged to Gran and now acts as my desk.

'Is it busy out there? Do you need a hand?' Mags, one of my wonderful assistants at the teashop, looks hopeful as she glances up from the desk. Mags has been working with me for almost a year, taking on the role of baker, waitress and bookkeeper (she really is Wonder Woman without the metallic knickers) when Sweet Street Teashop opened. I'm pretty poor at facts and figures (any numbers that don't involve pounds, kilograms or other such measurements sail way over my head) but Mags is brilliant. Give her a pencil and a calculator and she's perfectly happy to sit in this windowless room and take care of the business side of the teashop. Equally, give her a bowl, wooden spoon and access to ingredients and she's just as happy and capable. I'd be lost without Mags.

'We're not busy at all,' I say as I step into the room. If only. 'There's only Robbie and Birdie out there.' I close the door and lower my voice. 'How are the books?'

The corners of Mags's bright red lips turn down. 'Not so good.' She shakes her head. 'We need more customers. And fast.'

I'm already scarily aware of this fact. Have been since I opened the teashop doors almost a year ago and welcomed three customers that day. When, by the end of the week, I'd served a grand total of twenty-six customers – including my dad and my mum and her partner – I knew we were in trouble. The problem was, knowing this fact didn't provide me with a solution for how to fix it.

'Do you think another round of flyers would help?'

Mags shrugs her shoulders. 'Perhaps. It didn't have much of an impact last time, but we have to get the word out there somehow. Shall I get on to the printers?'

I press my lips together, unsure of the answer. Mags is right – we do have to spread the word – but printing flyers is a cost I could do without, especially when the outcome isn't looking particularly promising. We've tried dropping flyers through letterboxes or handing them out to shoppers in the town centre a few times, and we've targeted specific groups, such as the local NCT group and the over fifties leisure classes, but it's had little impact so far and we're still pretty much welcoming the same core group of regulars that we started with. We need a proper push, something to attract a wider customer base.

'Hold off for now,' I say, opening the door and stepping over the threshold. 'We'll put our heads together later and have a proper think. I'm sure we'll come up with a solution.'

We have to, otherwise the dream will be over and we'll both be out of a job.

Chapter Two

Kingsbury Road is a gorgeous little oasis away from the hustle and bustle of Woodgate town centre. With its quaint cobbled road and short terrace of double bay-fronted shops facing a community garden, you can almost imagine you're in a picturesque village rather than within spitting distance of a shopping mall and busy high street. We're a twenty-minute drive away from Manchester City Centre, but there's nothing urban about Kingsbury Road.

Unfortunately, as beautiful as our little road is, it's a largely forgotten-about side street with little footfall despite its close proximity to the town centre. Attempts to entice hungry shoppers over in this direction haven't been working out too well for Sweet Street Teashop.

There are five shops in the terrace, starting at one end with Paper Roses, a craft supplies shop, and ending with Sweet Street Teashop. Sandwiched between us is a florist – where banana milkshake addict Robbie claims to work – a hair and beauty salon and a letting agency. I can see Rehana and George from the letting agency right now, sneaking past the window with their cardboard cups and greasy paper bags from one of the coffee shops on the high street. Despite sitting next door to Sweet Street, they never pop in for their morning coffee, preferring instead to sip their caffeine from branded cups.

We have everything they could possibly want first thing on a Saturday morning – freshly baked croissants and bagels, pancakes and waffles with whipped cream and fresh fruit or gooey maple syrup, Danish pastries and cinnamon buns and all the coffee they could wish for – but we've never been able to tempt them away from the lure of the high street.

'What are you doing here?' Mags asks when she emerges from the kitchen with a batch of chocolate chip muffins and sees me hovering by the window. I'm tempted to wave at Rehana and George as they scurry past but I chicken out. 'You shouldn't be here. It's your day off.'

Mags thinks I work too hard. She's probably right but I don't feel I have a choice right now. Not when my business is sinking faster than a mafia target tossed into a canal wearing concrete boots.

'I'm not here.' I step away from the window as Rehana and George disappear from view. 'Not really. I'm just picking up the leftover apple crumble from yesterday.' I head into the kitchen, leaving Mags and our sole customer (Robbie, again) in the teashop. Victoria, the final cog that makes up the Sweet Street machine, is blitzing bananas in the blender for Robbie's daily milkshake. Making milkshakes and washing up is as far as Victoria's expertise stretches when it comes to the teashop's kitchen. I tried to teach her the basics when she first started working with us, but it was a bad idea. Very bad indeed. Sometimes, if you inhale deeply enough, you can still smell the charred fairy cakes.

But Victoria is great out front, serving the customers and chatting with them. I'm a bit awkward when it comes to the face-to-face stuff, feeling much more at ease with my mixing bowl than my fellow human beings, but Victoria's a natural. She's the youngest of the Sweet Street team at twenty-two (I'm six years older and Mags is thirty-something. Mags won't tell you what the 'something' is and I won't risk my safety by passing it on) and though she has a tough exterior, she's as soft and squishy as a melted marshmallow inside. The lead singer of a band, Victoria is waitressing at Sweet Street until they're offered a record deal.

'How did the gig go last night?' I ask as I open the fridge and pull the apple crumble out.

Victoria turns the blender off. 'Good. He didn't turn up though.'

'He' is a manager that Victoria's band are hoping to impress so he'll sign them and rocket them to stardom. She's talked of little else over the past few weeks so I'm gutted for her.

'Why not?' It seems pretty shady to me to arrange to watch a band's gig and then not bother to show up. Especially when Victoria's been so excited about the gig and what it would mean for the band's future.

Victoria shrugs. 'He didn't promise anything. We've got another gig next week so Nathan's going to see if he'll come to that.'

I want to tell Victoria not to get her hopes up but I know she will. She and the band (including her boyfriend, Nathan) formed when they were still at school and they've been working hard to achieve their dream ever since, performing insignificant little gigs for little to no money just for exposure. I know how it feels to have a dream, to want to turn your passion into a career so much it's actually painful and the thought of not reaching your goal is enough to make you cry. I've been there. I *am* there, because although I have the teashop, it's quickly slipping from my grasp and I don't know what I'll do if I have to say goodbye to it so soon.

'I'll cross my fingers for you,' I say instead.

'Thanks.' Victoria smiles at me and she looks so young, despite her heavily lined eyes and piercings. Victoria has ten piercings – one each in her lip, nose, right eyebrow and bellybutton, plus three studs in each ear. She also has three tattoos but her leggings and oversized hoodie combo currently cover them up.

Victoria finishes the banana milkshake and takes it out to Robbie while I transfer the leftover apple crumble from its heavy dish into a plastic container. When I return to the teashop, I'm pleased to see a couple more customers enjoying coffee and pastries by one of the windows.

'Don't forget Paper Roses' order this afternoon,' I say to Mags as I pop the tub of apple crumble into a canvas bag and hook it onto my shoulder. The girls at the neighbouring craft shop run weekly classes and usually order a small selection of cakes for their tea break. I'm so grateful for their custom, I often buy sequins, spools of ribbon and other supplies from the shop even though I don't have a crafty bone in my body.

'I won't,' Mags says. 'Now get out of here and enjoy your day off before I have to physically eject you.' Mags places her hands on her wide hips and cocks an eyebrow in challenge. I hold my hands up in surrender.

'Okay, okay, I'm going.' I say goodbye to Mags and Victoria before I head out, praying custom magically picks up during my absence.

Dad lives on his own, in the house I grew up in on the outskirts of Manchester City Centre. The three-bedroomed house is too big for him to potter about in on his own but he likes to cling on to the memories of our family before it fractured. Mum and Dad divorced seven years ago but while Mum is happy with a new partner, Dad can't seem to move on. I worry about him and it breaks my heart that he's alone, which is why I visit every weekend – without fail – with his favourite dessert. We'll sit in the kitchen with a bowl of warm apple crumble and custard and a cup of tea while we catch up.

'Will tinned custard do?' Dad asks, as he does every single week. I play along, releasing a long sigh.

'I suppose it'll have to.' Gran taught me to make my own custard, which I use in the teashop, but it's a bit of a faff at the weekend when I just want to relax.

Dad heats the apple crumble and custard in the microwave while I make cups of tea and then we sit at the table and Dad asks, 'How's your mum?'

Like the tinned custard, this question is routine and, as always, I feel awful when I answer. I want to tell him she's not so good. That she and Ivor have split up, that she's regretting ever leaving Dad after twenty-three years of marriage. That she wishes she'd worked harder, that she hadn't given up, that she was mistaken when she'd said that she cared about Dad but didn't love him any more.

But I can't.

Mum's happy.

And she still cares about Dad but doesn't love him any more. She loves Ivor.

I'm happy for Mum, really I am, but I feel for Dad. I've been the dumped party, the one left behind. Left devastated.

'She's okay,' I tell Dad, though I know it won't be enough. Mum is a wound Dad likes to prod, even if it hurts like hell. When I split up with my last boyfriend, I couldn't bear to think about him, let alone talk about him. I've shut the door on my relationship with Joel and locked, bolted and welded it shut. But Dad likes to know every little detail of Mum's life because if he's out of the loop, he's truly lost her.

'Did she have a nice holiday?' I nod, a mouthful of hot apple crumble and custard rendering me unable to speak. 'I bet she's tanned, isn't she? She only has to think about the sun and she's golden. Not like me, eh?' Dad lifts up an arm, flashing his pale, freckly skin. 'Luckily you got your mum's colouring.'

While I've inherited Dad's auburn hair, I don't have his perma-pale skin tone. All our family holiday snaps show Mum and I beaming at the camera, our teeth a flash of white against golden flesh while Dad grimaces, his skin painfully raw with sunburn. It doesn't matter how frequently he applies his Factor Fifty, Dad will always, *always* burn to a crisp. It was one of the reasons he refused to holiday abroad and why Mum makes up for it now with Ivor, jetting off at least twice a year. I have a postcard from their latest trip to Hawaii on my fridge.

'I haven't seen her since they got back,' I tell Dad. I hope that this will offer some comfort to Dad. To know that while I visit him often, I'm not off playing happy families with Mum and Ivor the rest of the time.

'You should see your mum more often. I bet she misses you.'

'I saw her just before they went away,' I say, though this isn't technically true. It was a month before they left but we've both been busy – Mum with planning her trip and me with trying to keep the teashop afloat – and we don't have the same easy relationship I have with Dad. Not any more.

'This is good apple crumble,' Dad says as he scoops a giant spoonful towards his mouth. 'Just like Gran used to make.' He wedges the spoon into his mouth and closes his eyes. This is the best compliment I could ever receive. Gran baked the most delicious desserts and if my own creations taste nearly as good as hers, I'll be very proud of myself.

'How's the teashop going?' Dad asks once we've finished eating. He usually pops in at least once a week but I haven't seen him since my visit home last weekend.

'Great.' I force a smile on my face and nod my head like Churchill the dog. 'Really great.'

There are some things I can't lie about. I'm truthful while telling Dad week after week how happy Mum is without him or while telling my friend Nicky that the guy she's been bombarding with unanswered texts probably isn't interested in her. I don't lie about these things, no matter how difficult it is to tell the truth, but I do lie to Dad about the teashop. I can't tell him that it's failing. That I'm failing. That the money Gran left me in her will may have been wasted on a dream that has not come true.

'It's no wonder it's doing so well if you keep making desserts like these.' Dad gathers our empty cups and dishes and carries them over to the sink to wash up. When the doorbell rings, he holds up his wet, soapy hands. 'Would you get that? If it's those energy people, tell them to bugger off. I'm happy with the service I've got.'

'Will do,' I say, though I know I won't. I'll stand there while they blather on about the better deals they can offer and then I'll politely decline, apologising as I gently close the door. I don't do confrontation. Ever. Luckily it isn't a door-to-door 'I'm not trying to sell you anything' salesman. It's a woman (without a clipboard, ID badge or charity tabard), who takes a startled step back when I open the door.

'Oh.' Her eyes flick to the door, checking the number, checking she has, in fact, got the right house. 'Is Clive in? I'm Jane? From next door?' She poses the last two statements as questions, as though I may have an inkling who she is.

'Jane?' Dad booms from the kitchen. 'Come in!'

I open the door wider and Jane-from-next-door takes a tentative step over the threshold, the corners of her lips twitching into an awkward smile. She follows me through to the kitchen, where Dad is drying his hands on a tea towel.

'I've brought your screwdriver back.' Jane reaches into the handbag looped over her arm and pulls the tool out, holding it out to Dad between finger and thumb, as though it could burst into life and attack at any given moment.

'Did it do the trick?' Dad asks as he takes the screwdriver and places it on the table.

Jane nods, the awkward smile flicking at her lips again. 'Yes. Thank you.'

'Thought it would.' Dad moves towards the kettle, plucking it from its stand. 'Would you like to stay for a cup of tea?'

Jane's eyes brush over me, the smile flickering on her lips again. She looks like she's got a tic. 'You've got company.'

'That's just Maddie.' Dad fills the kettle and flicks it on. 'My daughter.'

'Oh!' The smile is wider now, more genuine. I try not to feel offended by the 'just' in Dad's introduction. 'I see! Of course. Hello, Maddie.'

I raise my hand and give a little wave, the awkward bug having been passed on.

'So,' Dad says. 'Tea?'

Jane eyes me briefly before she turns to Dad. 'I have to dash, actually. Maybe another time? Tomorrow?'

Dad nods, already striding across the kitchen so he can see Jane-the-neighbour to the door. 'Sure.'

Jane beams at Dad, placing a hand on his arm now he's reached her. 'Thank you again for the screwdriver.'

'Any time.'

I watch as Dad and Jane disappear into the hall, hear their muffled voices as they chat at the door. The kettle's boiled by the time Dad returns to the kitchen.

'What was that all about?' I ask Dad, indicating the screwdriver still on the table.

'Jane asked to borrow it yesterday. Asked me if I knew anything about plugs. She needed to replace one of hers so I wrote down some instructions and let her borrow the screwdriver.'

I want to drop my face into my hands. '*Da-ad.* She didn't want to borrow a screwdriver! She wanted you to go over.'

Dad shakes his head. 'Nah. Jane's not like that. She's very independent. Capable, like.'

Facepalm, round two. 'She didn't want you to go round to replace the plug.' If there was ever a plug in need of replacing in the first place.

Dad grabs the tea caddy and pulls a couple of bags out. 'What are you talking about?'

'She fancies you.' I am almost giddy. With relief. With hope. A woman fancies my dad. He doesn't have to be alone any more! 'Jane-from-next-door fancies you and she was trying to lure you round to her house.'

Dad shakes his head as he plops teabags into two cups. 'Oh, no. It's nothing like that. Jane's friendly, that's all. A good neighbour.'

I'm not convinced. I fling myself at Dad, wrapping my arms around his middle and planting a noisy kiss on his stubbly cheek.

'Jane-from-next-door has a crush on you. I'm sure of it.'

'Don't be daft,' Dad scoffs. 'People our age don't have "crushes". And I'm not interested anyway. I'm too old for all that nonsense.'

By nonsense, I assume Dad means having fun and being happy with somebody other than Mum.

'You're never too old for love. Besides, you're sixty-two and sixty is the new fifty, which is the new forty, so you're practically a spring chicken.'

Dad grabs the kettle and pours boiling water into the cups. 'I don't think your logic pans out quite right there.'

'Oh yes it does.' I open the fridge and take out the milk, passing it to Dad. 'I want you to be happy.'

'And you can't be happy and single?' Dad raises his eyebrows at me and I feel myself squirm.

'You can. Of course you can.' I'm an example of that. I've been single for a year now and I've never been happier. I push the thought of waking up wrapped in Joel's arms away, of feeling safe and loved. 'But aren't you ready to move on? To find someone new?'

Dad places the fresh cups of tea on the table and looks pointedly at me. 'Are you?'

ACKNOWLEDGEMENTS

Thank you to the amazing book-blogging community, especially Kaisha (The Writing Garnet), Laura (Laura Patricia Rose), Shaz (Shaz's Book Blog, plus guest reviewer Emma), Rachel (Rachel's Random Reads), Laura (Laura Bambrey Books), Simona (Simona's Corner of Dreams), Sophie (Book Drunk), Kelly and Lucy (The Blossom Twins), Becca (Hummingbird Reviews), Laura (Lozza's Book Corner) and Alba (Alba In Bookland). Definitely go and check out their wonderful blogs!

Thank you to the SCWG for the advice, book talk, encouragement. This writing lark wouldn't be half as much fun without you! Also thanks to Beth Cahill and Ann Coggan for talking books with me.

Thank you to the HQ Digital team, especially my editor Charlotte Mursell.

A special thanks to Andrew Cahill for the songs. When I was putting together a playlist of summery songs to write the book to, I asked for suggestions on Twitter and Facebook. Andrew provided me with a million songs to add – this is only a slight exaggeration. Special thanks must also go to Louise Wykes – the Minion is for you!

Finally, thank you to my family, who continue to support me and my books, with extra special thanks to my husband, Chris, and our daughters, Rianne and Isobel.

ONE PLACE. MANY STORIES

Bold, innovative and
empowering publishing.

FOLLOW US ON:

@HQStories